Transformation

Cielo tapped on my shoulder to let me know the magic was done. I turned and found her in girlish form, wearing nothing but a white shirt that whispered against her legs. I couldn't help noticing they were as long and smooth and perfectly molded as a pair of taper candles. . . . My breath went ragged at the edges.

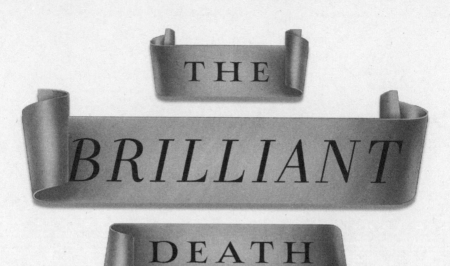

THE BRILLIANT DEATH

AMY ROSE CAPETTA

PENGUIN BOOKS

PENGUIN BOOKS
An imprint of Penguin Random House LLC, New York

First published in the United States of America by Viking,
an imprint of Penguin Random House LLC, 2018
Published by Penguin Books, an imprint of Penguin Random House LLC, 2019

Visit us online at penguinrandomhouse.com

LIBRARY OF CONGRESS CATALOGING-IN-PUBLICATION DATA IS AVAILABLE
Penguin Books ISBN 9780451478467

Printed in the United States of America

10 9 8 7 6 5 4 3 2 1

Set in Manticore   Book design by Kate Renner

For my dad
who gave me books from his shelf
and stories from the past,
who has three daughters
and has always believed in our magic

The Beginning

When I was a little girl, I thought my father was the king of Vinalia.

Our family lived in a round-walled castle that seemed to grow from the mountainside. Father's favorite chair had been carved out of a black walnut tree. When I squinted long enough, it became a throne.

The first time I saw him kill someone, it made perfect sense. A king had to protect his family and his mountains.

I shouldn't have been out of bed that winter night, but I traveled down to the kitchens, feet soft brushstrokes on cold stone, and stole a glass of milk. When I turned to leave by the back stairs, two men blocked my path. Father stood on the lowest step with his arm fastened around a stranger's neck. Snow clumped wetly on the man's shoulders.

I didn't dare move closer. If I'd been in a white nightgown, Father would have seen me by now, but the di Sangro family wore red, so everything I owned was a deep shade that turned black in the moonlight.

I watched as cold beads slicked the outside of my glass, a pretty thing that had been handblown in the city of Amalia.

Father's grip tightened on the man's neck while my grip weakened. Father grabbed a knife from his sleeve and stabbed the man's side.

I dropped the glass.

The moment became a small eternity, giving me time to fear what came next. Father's anger. My punishment. I closed my eyes tight, twisting the story in a new direction. *The glass will dissolve into a pile of sugar. The milk will turn into a white, white moth and fly away.*

When I opened my eyes, the snow light coming through the window caught on a pair of wings. Pale wings. A moth fluttered, gone before I could be sure of what I'd seen. I pushed one toe past the hem of my nightgown; it found no shards of glass. I knelt, licked my fingertip, and touched it to the stone. It came back gritty with crystals. I brought them to my tongue. Sweet.

I gasped.

Father turned toward me, finished with his business. His brown eyes held only torchlight. "Wait here, Teodora," he said, shifting the dead man's weight against his shoulder. Father opened the heavy door and disappeared into the kitchen gardens for a long mire of a minute.

I burned to ask about magic, but I knew what he would say. *A strega is an old woman who has listened to too many stories.* When he came back to the doorway, his shirt blotched with damp, I lit on a new question. I had to speak quickly, before my boldness faded into the shadows. "Was it your fate to kill that man?"

I was only Niccolò di Sangro's second daughter and had no right to ask. I thought he would wave his hand vaguely, sending me back to bed. Father sat down at the coarse wooden table and patted the chair next to his.

"That's Beniamo's seat," I whispered. As if my older brother, asleep in the North hall, might be able to hear us from inside his dreams.

"We won't tell anyone, will we?" he asked.

I shook my head. Sat down. My feet swung lightly, inches from the floor.

Father reached into his sleeve and withdrew the knife. As he placed it on the table, I drank every detail: a spiral handle; a swerving crossbar; a long, thin blade that looked harmless until my eyes reached the point. I couldn't find a single drop of blood. Father must have stabbed the snow outside to clean it.

The knife was sharp. The knife was lovely. I could see both of those truths, twisted together.

Father marked my reaction. "You don't reach for it, but you don't shy away." He sounded pleased, but then his eyes pinched. "Why are you downstairs?"

So he had not seen the glass, the milk, the magic. "I was thirsty."

I wondered how far the white moth had flown.

Father nudged the knife toward me. It lifted easily, much lighter than I had expected.

"You truly aren't afraid, are you?" he asked.

"What is there to be afraid of?"

He chuckled, the sound as heavy as wet snow. "Well, I was younger than you when I learned what it means to be a di Sangro." Father cupped his hands around mine like he was teaching me to pray. "You asked me if it was my fate to kill that man." His eyes went dim. "Family is fate."

One

The Least of Many Wrongs

Seven Years Later

One perfectly ripe summer day, I left the castle wearing a clean red dress and carrying a basket. I told a man from the village that I wanted to have supper in my favorite field, and he should join me. I'd been working to copy my older sister's smile, the one she used to make men say yes without thinking. And that was what Pietro did.

We set off up the mountain, talking of small things. His trip to the Violetta Coast, the new grapes he would harvest this year. He had no reason to suspect that the basket swinging from my arm was empty.

The hike from the village started out hot and stayed hot. By the time we reached the crossroads, Pietro and I were shedding drops of sweat as fast as the earth could drink. We crested a ridge and I came to a stop. "*This* is your favorite field?" Pietro asked.

"Yes," I said, clutching at a breath. "Isn't it perfect?"

The flowers were wilted and as white as old bone. The grass had given up and matted itself in defeat. Pietro gave me a look, one I had seen on dozens of different faces in Chieza. People thought I was odd.

Not a liar, a strega, or a thief of men's lives.

I spent my days with my half brother, Luca, or I wandered the mountain alone. *Odd.* I hadn't made friends with the girls in the village. *Odd.* If I wanted to live among the people on this mountain, I would have to keep earning that title. I couldn't have anyone scratching to see what was underneath it.

"Where would you like to eat?" Pietro asked.

I led him to a spot with fewer spiking weeds. The gentians and poppies that warred brightly on other slopes were missing here. I loved this field, not for its beauty but for where it sat on the mountain, tucked out of sight.

Pietro shaded his eyes against the sun and gave me the wobbly smile of someone who thinks he might have made a mistake but still hopes to gain from it. I put down the picnic basket and wiped the sweat from my palms. It was time to work.

First, I took Pietro's measure. He was older than me by half a lifetime, and I could see years of sun and wind trapped in his warm brown skin. He worked grape fields that had been owned by his father—now his. He had a number of lovers besides his wife. She probably kept her own, but she didn't get to boast of them in town, lilting their praises over cheap wine. And then there were Pietro's children, two little boys with hazelnut eyes. I had seen them hanging off him like a coatrack.

I wanted to dislike him. It would make the rest of this easier.

I'd been staring for a while—one benefit of being the odd di Sangro girl—when Pietro stepped in to tuck a bit of wayward hair behind my ear. He pitched his voice low, a bit rough, a bit gentle. "You look hungry, Teodora."

This wasn't the first time a man had brought his own ideas up the mountain. Having a father in the castle meant all I had to do was say no to make this attention dissolve like snow at high summer.

This time, though, I hesitated. I had always thought Pietro was beautiful. Whenever I saw him across the square in the village, my eyes danced after him. Now I let myself imagine what it would be like to take him as a lover. There would be kisses like moonlight, soft and brilliant. I would let him touch me with his practiced hands. I would keep the one rule of the village girls—I wouldn't let him inside. But everything else would be allowed. Everything else would be encouraged.

A flare from the white sun slapped me awake. I was not some silly girl who wanted silly things. I was a di Sangro.

"I think we should talk," I said.

"Yes," Pietro agreed, not moving away. His voice was warm, spreading.

I backed up, and a little distance broke the spell. "Now," I said, "would you like to tell me the story of how you are cheating my father?"

Pietro went a shade lighter than the dead grass.

"No? Then I will have to tell it myself." I knew by then that Father was not the king of Vinalia, but he was an important man. We might have a new Capo, a son of the famously decadent Malfara family who loved to brag about bringing the country together under one flag, but the true power in Vinalia still sat with the five families.

I circled Pietro, the dry ground knocking like hollowed wood beneath my boots. "Your grape arbors have been under the protection of the di Sangro family since your great-great-grandfather's time, but in the two years since you inherited them, money has gone missing. Not ragged chunks of the profit. A quiet sum. We trusted you to stop, but it has gone on and on. Maybe you have fallen in love with the gambling tables in Prai. Maybe you have a girl who aches for the newest fashions from the north. Maybe you thought we wouldn't notice, and you love the idea of fooling us. Do you see the dangers of letting someone else tell your story?" I twirled my fingers lazily. "I can twist it in any direction I like."

Pietro fell to his knees, wrapping his sweaty arms around my middle. I should have hated his weakness. I should have pushed him away. Instead I sank my hands into his loose, dark curls.

His voice doubled in thickness, becoming a sob. "I love my wife, Teodora."

"Really?" I asked. "Because you seemed ready to—"

"That money is for our children," he said, shaking me off the subject of his lust. "The five families have no right to it."

"We are not the Palazza," I said, as hard as unfinished stone. "We don't claim a right. We earn that money." Father worked to keep the Uccelli—the poorest region in Vinalia—from falling into complete ruin. I had seen how difficult that task was, how it had turned him old before his time.

I touched Pietro's chin and tilted his face up—not to me, but to the blank white eye of the sun. "Don't we make sure that your fields aren't set on by vandals?" Pietro nodded hastily. "And aren't there fair prices and people lined up to buy your wine?" He nodded again, a swallow held captive in his throat. "And when there is a siege, where does your family take shelter?"

All the people of the Uccelli could fit inside our castle walls, which was a good thing considering how often Vinalia was invaded. That was part of the false logic of unification— if we stood tall together, we wouldn't fall prey to the stronger powers of Eterra. But we had already weakened ourselves in long battles, including the ones the Capo waged against his own people.

"The new taxes from Amalia are too much," Pietro said. "We can't pay both."

I twisted my lips as if I'd been sucking on lemon rinds. The Capo had claimed a man's loyalty in less than a year, when we had worked countless generations for it. Either Pietro trusted the new government in Amalia more than the di Sangro family, or his fear of the Capo was greater. Neither of these messages would delight my father.

I knelt down in the dead grass. "Niccolò di Sangro is not here today. You are in the hands of his odd little daughter. Thank God for small mercies." I shoved Pietro's curls out of his eyes and asked, "Would you like to be a bookend?"

He squinted at me like I was a word in an impossible language. "What?"

I sighed. "I'm trying to give you a say in your future." Some of the men I came for were murderers. Others had taken women without their permission, and I had little problem plucking such men from the world. Pietro was nowhere near the worst. I wondered if there was any way we could let him pay the family back, quietly. But Father had said it so many times, I heard the words in his voice, like dark jagged stone. *The moment we let people think we can be swindled, we will be always swindled.*

I touched Pietro's forehead and thought about how soon

he would be different. How quickly things changed. "The di Sangro family will look after your wife and children," I promised. "And your grape arbors."

The magic came when I called for it. I closed my eyes, breathing in air laden with heat. *Turn him into something pleasant*, I thought.

I opened my eyes and walked to the place where Pietro had stood. A glass and metal box sat at my feet, with a barrel at the center covered in raised dots, and a small hand crank on one side. I wound it tight and nestled the box in one hand. Notes came fast and clear. It was a complicated weaving. The song of a man who kept a wife and lovers, who worked hard, stole often, and had two boys with hazelnut eyes.

I picked up my new trinket and placed it in the empty basket.

꧁✦꧂

HALFWAY DOWN THE MOUNTAIN, COOL AIR PRESSED ON MY skin, lifting fine hairs. I looked to the peaks behind me to see if bad weather was moving in. A solemn gray cloud perched over the mountaintop—and then a wind chased it away, leaving the day vivid and blue. Where the cloud had been a moment ago, someone walked toward me down the slope.

Odd.

The Uccelli only boasted a few passable roads, and the nearest ran five miles to the south. This traveler must have been skirting rocks and ravines for hours, yet his steps were light. Or *her* steps. From a distance, I couldn't tell if I was looking at a man or a woman. The stranger had skin so pale,

I thought of the wine casks in our cellar, hidden away from the sun. A sheet of black hair shimmered to the beat of each step.

I studied the person's clothes for a clue about which part of Vinalia they came from. Black trousers, brown boots laced above the knee, and a white shirt, all of basic stock. The cloak demanded more interest. Its fabric gripped both light and shadow. From some angles the fabric seemed rich green, and from others I could have sworn it was purple.

I told the magic to be ready, though I hoped I wouldn't need it. I had never transformed two people in the same day.

"That's a lonely walk," I called out. "Have you seen anything interesting?" Another one of Father's tactics. *Get a man talking, and he will hand you a weapon. Keep him talking, and he will show you where to point it.*

"I'm glad you asked," the stranger said, walking fast, speaking in a half-shouted voice as the distance between us closed. "I have seen three and a half interesting things today. The first was a tree that had swallowed another tree whole. Have you ever seen that? I had to wonder what the little tree had done to offend the big one." When I answered with a swath of silence, the stranger said, "Moving on. The second interesting thing was my foot, the left one, which turned a shade of purple I have never seen before."

With one more stride, the stranger and I were on the same patch of the mountain, close enough that I could make a full inventory. Here was a long nose, a set of greenish eyes, cheekbones like two dangerous ridges.

The stranger circled me slowly. I countered the circle, as if we were caught up in a dance, or a duel. "The half of an interesting thing was a rabbit I nearly ate. But then it told me a funny story, and I had to let it go. I guess you could say the *story* was interesting, but only to a rabbit. When I let him run off, my stomach informed me I had better find something to eat. So you can imagine my excitement when I caught sight of one final interesting thing. Supper."

He—for I had started to think of this person as a young man, though his voice had the songlike quality often found in women—nodded down at the basket I was holding. I clutched the handle tight enough that the rough weave marked my fingers.

The stranger held out a long, flat palm. "May I?"

I let a moment sit between us, unraveling, before I held out the basket. There could be no real harm in it, I told myself.

The stranger accepted the handle with great care, knelt on the grass, and plucked out the music box. For a hungry person, he didn't seem disappointed to find a metal contraption instead of a hearty supper. I felt the slight shadow of a touch as he stroked the side of the glass box. He applied his long, pale fingers to the little crank.

"What's your name?" I asked at last. If this was a dance, I had fallen three steps behind.

The stranger ignored the question, taking in the tinny sounds of the music box as a person savors a fine meal. He even closed his eyes, and I found myself staring at marble eyelids that looked cool to the touch. The stranger's mouth stretched into a dreamer's smile, private and satisfied.

It made me feel as though I had trespassed, even though this person stood on di Sangro lands.

I reached to snatch the music box away just as the

stranger's eyes snapped open. He angled his face up, and in the full light of the sky, his eyes were blue and brown as well as green. The swirl of colors felt impossible to name.

"It's a fugue." He handed the music box back to me with a deepening smirk. "Aren't we all."

The magic spiked inside me. Did it want me to stop this stranger before he could bring trouble to the Uccelli? I wasn't doing my di Sangro duty. I was allowing a pale, perfectly molded stranger to dance circles around me.

"What do you want here?" I asked.

He stood and picked up my basket, lingering over its emptiness. "I thought you might have something for me. Perhaps those briny olives, the green ones that have been well soaked so the salt stays on your lips?" I was suddenly aware of my *own* lips. I glared at the stranger, certain he'd done that on purpose.

He took a step closer, tighter than any of the dances I knew. I found a new color in his eyes. Yellow. "You can tell me," he said. "It's safe." His breath was soft on my skin. His words slipped past my mind, straight to my magic.

It didn't wish to change him into a red ribbon or a bone knife or a stamp for sealing letters. It didn't wish to change anything.

A cloud of disappointment slid through the young man's eyes, turning them almost gray. "There's nothing you wish to tell me?" He seemed to be waiting for a specific answer, though I couldn't imagine what words he thought I would hand over.

I gave my head a tiny shake.

With a hard sigh and a long stride, the stranger headed

down the mountain. At the crossroads, he turned toward Chieza.

The magic said *follow*.

But I would already be getting home late, and I had failed spectacularly to find out this person's name and purpose. The least I could do was attend the rest of my afternoon lessons. I'd promised Luca I would be there. And I wouldn't feel better until I had Pietro settled. My di Sangro duties stretched out, as long and treacherous as a mountain range.

The stranger turned into a speck in the distance. Above him, clouds gathered and trotted like dogs at his heels.

I turned and headed back toward the castle.

2

I found my father and brothers in the torture chamber.

It was buried under the castle, deep in the muscle of the mountain. I had to walk through near-endless wine cellars to get there, and my candle had dripped down to a fat waxen thumb by the time I arrived.

"Ah, Teo," Father said. Torchlight picked out the first silver hairs that had crept in among the brown.

Beniamo turned to me, his eyes shining like the moon on dead water. "Go back up and help Fiorenza with dinner. You won't like what we're talking about."

I crossed my arms over my body and held tight. "When have I ever skipped a lesson?"

"When you forgot because you were out on the mountain," Luca muttered without looking up from the notes he was inking.

My little brother was my greatest ally in the castle, and I had let him down. The failure sat like a stone in my shoe, rubbing against the larger discomfort of meeting that stranger on the mountain. "When have I ever skipped a lesson because I was too delicate to stomach it?"

"You have nothing to fear, Teo," Father said, patting my shoulder. "I won't get into the worst of the details today."

"Don't water the wine because I'm drinking it," I said, frowning up at him. Father gave the boys lessons in politics, history, land ownership, anything he thought would profit a di Sangro son. I had started paying attention when I was ten because the magic loved the sound of Father's voice. Soon I had learned all of the best ways to intimidate a person, to turn his own ideas against him. Everything I'd done to Pietro—besides one brief moment of magic—I had learned at Father's knee.

I sat down, wedging myself between the chair and the desk, and grabbed at paper, an inkwell, and a pen. "Well, then," Father said roughly. "If we're all settled. We'll begin where we left off. At the Well of Blades." He pointed to a deep pit at the farthest corner of the room.

"Does it work?" Beniamo asked, sitting forward.

"Are you asking if it can still send someone to a slow and miserable death? No. The glass was removed years ago. This dungeon hasn't held prisoners for generations." Father stared down Beniamo. "This is a history, not a practical guide."

Father moved on to other tortures. A pole that could be tied to women's hair, to tear the scalp free. A pot for boiling. As the list grew, my stomach rioted. The di Sangro family didn't rely on torture anymore, but that didn't mean we had turned our backs on violence. We treated it like an old friend, one we visited whenever things grew difficult.

I couldn't help thinking that magic was the best solution to our problems. I didn't have to kill anyone. I could simply stopper them as though I were putting them in a collection of small bottles.

But you can't turn them back, the magic whispered. *How is a music box better than a hole in the ground?*

It was true that I didn't know how to change people into human form again. But I could always learn.

When? the magic asked. *How?*

I shifted under the unfair weight of the question. I had no idea if I would ever learn more about the power that lived inside me. It wasn't as if my di Sangro duties included daily magic lessons.

"What was the first instance of torture used against heretics within the five families?" Father asked.

Luca answered Father's question, and the next one. His intelligence rushed ahead of mine, which was stuck in muddy thoughts of my day on the mountain, and Beniamo's, which had never been able to keep pace. Beniamo's body shifted into hard ropes of anger as Luca proved, over and over, that he was the smarter of the two brothers.

When no one was looking, I kicked Luca in the ankle and mouthed, *Slow down.*

Luca tilted his chin away, ignoring my good advice.

My eyes went to every little scar and burn on his skin. I didn't want a new one to tend to. Since we were young, Beniamo had punished us when he thought life had treated him unfairly. That included any moment when Father favored Luca, heaped praise on Mirella, or showed me affection. It began in the nursery, when Beniamo would corner us and tell us our crimes. The runners of rocking horses crushed our forearms. Wooden swords bruised our stomachs. Metal pieces from the Game of the Goose were heated in fireplace ashes and set to our skin.

"What is the swiftest method of bloodletting?" Father asked.

"Arteries," I said, leaping in before Luca could. "Preferably in the neck."

"That sounds simple enough," Beniamo said, looking me over as if seeking a good place to cut.

My voice prickled in my throat, but I knew that if I told Father about what Beniamo was doing, my older brother would deny it now and double the punishment later. And he had moved beyond nursery games.

I took Beniamo's measure quickly, the same way I had with Pietro. The magic whispered, *He would make a nice pair of boots*. I clamped my teeth, grinding the idea to dust. It was one thing to change our enemies. It was another to use magic against family.

Father asked a new question, but I barely heard it before Luca's voice rang out with the answer.

Beniamo's eyes cut a rough line to our little brother.

❧✦❧

AFTER A LONG DAY OF MAGIC AND DUNGEONS, MY BEDROOM promised relief. I knew every pockmark in the stone, every trinket on the shelves. It would have been a perfect sanctuary if Luca hadn't plunked down on the edge of my bed, punishing me with his saddest stare.

"You left me there for an *hour* while Father stuffed my head full of bloody history. He's nicer when you're in the room. Less like a commander in some invisible war and more like . . . well . . . a father."

I was so often jealous of the way Father treated the boys that it rarely occurred to me there might be jealousy flowing in the opposite direction. I let out a small "Hmm," but I was distracted.

I needed to find a spot for Pietro.

I'd already covered nearly every surface in the room with ornaments. I tried setting Pietro next to porcelain dishes, a decorative fan, a set of red prayer beads, a compass with a cover of dull gold. I kept picking him up again. Pietro didn't sit near the top of the ranks of terrible men. He deserved a special place.

My brother paced, his body a cup spilling discontent everywhere. "Did you hear what I said?" He tossed a pillow at my stomach to get my attention, not knowing that the pillow had once been the baker's son.

"How are your experiments coming along?" I asked in a naked attempt to change the subject.

Luca's expression opened like a book. His fascination with the natural world encompassed every leaf and star and vein of crystal he could find in our mountain's dull rock. Now it seemed he had fallen in love with something called electricity. "Even you will be impressed, Teo. Light without flame! It's magic."

My own magic perked at the use of that word. But if I told my brother the truth—that I'd been able to transform people and objects since I was nine—he wouldn't understand. Luca believed he was a modern Vinalian. How could I explain magic to a boy who worshipped science and reason?

If I had learned one thing in seven years, it was this: magic is *not* reasonable.

"I told Father about electricity too," Luca mumbled.

"Ah," I said, finally digging up the roots of Luca's foul mood. "And what did he say?"

"He growled something about torchlight being good enough for our fathers," Luca said, tossing his hands in the air. "I told him that other family heads are heeding the future. Altimari and Moschella sent their sons to university."

"Fourth and fifth sons," I reminded, not liking how easily Father's side of the argument flew out of me.

"I looked at universities in Eterra," Luca said, scowling down at his hands, which he did whenever he didn't wish to face the truth. "Of course Vinalia has the best work in the sciences, a long tradition of advancements, even if the rest of Eterra thinks we're backward. I told Father I want to go to Gravina. Soon. And that's when he told me he needed me to stay here while he travels across the mountains for Mirella's wedding, as if that makes any sense." My little brother was writhing against his fate like a fish in a net. He would never go off to the famous universities at Gravina to learn about science, any more than I would leave the mountains and study magic.

I passed the music box from hand to hand and observed Luca, his skin touched with red at the neck, the first place where his anger showed. His complexion was a touch lighter than my own summer-browned and beauty-mark-dappled shade of olive, but we had the same dark brown eyes. All around his, Luca's face had started to change. Round cheeks gave way to sharp bones underneath. He had recently grown one blasphemous inch taller than me. When I looked at him,

I saw the boy he had been a few years ago, and the man everyone wanted him to be now. Time blurred, the past and the future sliding against each other unpleasantly.

He caught me staring. "What are you doing, Teo?"

"Didn't you pay attention this afternoon?" I asked. "I'm torturing you. It's an ancient technique." I thought I would win a laugh, but Luca winced. The di Sangro lessons troubled him deeply. Each step down this path carried my brother further away from himself. "I'll talk to Father."

"You will?" Luca asked, flinging his arms around my neck.

I finally set the music box on my bedside table beside a potted rose that never stopped blooming. "Anything for you," I said. My eyes skimmed over Pietro, all the men I had changed. "Anything."

AT DINNER, I ATE AS IF I WERE INVENTING THE CONCEPT. I started with three pieces of bread and then moved on to white beans with rosemary, rabbit stew, a course of cheese and olives. When the brine hit my tongue, I recalled the stranger on the mountain. His hands all over my basket. Or *her* hands. Either way, they hadn't found what they were searching for.

I pushed the olive dish away.

"You have an appetite," my stepmother said approvingly, noting the ruins on my plate.

I took another bite of stew, sopping it with more bread. "I missed supper."

Fiorenza took in my words, and then the rest of me with a single glance. "Where were you?"

"I went to the village to see if I had a letter from Rosina." She was a girl from the far side of the Uccelli. A girl who hadn't caught word that I was odd, whose father or cousin I hadn't changed into a clock. We met in Chieza on a market day. She walked at my side, sifting her fingers through snowfalls of linen, stirring barrels of dried beans, so gentle with everything she touched. She never took her eyes off me.

At the end of the day, at the fringes of the woods, she asked me to come with her to a barn at the edge of the town where young women brought their lovers. The idea startled me so much that it pried open my lips.

I didn't say a thing. I only kissed her once, as hot and swift as a fireplace poker, and ran off.

Rosina and I had never exchanged letters. Even if I'd known where to send one, I had too much to say, and no words that would change anything. It was no great secret that a man might choose to kiss another man, and certain women took women to their beds, yet these things were rarely spoken of, and never seen. I could kiss Rosina at the frayed edges of the woods, but when the time came, I would have to marry a man.

I could not pretend Rosina and her dark eyes out of the world, though, so I had invented a friendship with her to explain the baubles in my room. "She sent me a music box," I said. "It plays a lovely tune."

Fiorenza gave me the sort of look that always followed such an announcement, as if she'd taken a bite of her frangipane and found the almond gritty. But I couldn't let Fiorenza think the trinkets in my room were gifts from men. And I couldn't tell her the truth.

"I heard a bit of news when I was in Chieza," I said over

the sound of my little sisters arguing, Father and Luca arguing, Fiorenza and Mirella arguing, all of them adding layers to the din. "It was about Pietro, that farmer with all of the grape arbors."

Father and Beniamo swung toward me, and I savored the moment when I knew I had their attention.

"Well? What has become of our good friend Pietro?" Father asked in an unmistakable tone. Everyone at the table knew that when he spoke the word *friend* with such a lingering bite, he didn't mean someone close to his heart.

"Pietro didn't watch his step, it seems," I said. "He fell into the Storyteller's Grave." The ravine to the west of the village had earned that name because men from Chieza drank and stumbled to its edge, shouting stories into the darkness. The least fortunate fell in. With so many missing men to explain, the ravine had become useful to me.

Father hung his head and said in a half-chanting voice, "God's will be done."

Echoes ringed the table, but I didn't dare let those words touch my lips. What had happened to Pietro on the mountainside wasn't God's will. It was mine.

Beniamo shifted in his chair. "This keeps happening. It can't be chance. Someone is doing away with our enemies." His forehead shone, his breath sour with wine and disappointment. My brother wanted to be the one doing the killing.

"If a person is ridding the world of our troubles, shouldn't we thank them?" I asked.

Father pointed his fork at me, the tines catching a glint of light. "Teo is right."

For that, I received a pinch on the leg that would have made a less prepared girl scream. Above the wooden surface of the table, Beniamo gave no sign he was hurting me. I tried not to imagine what he would do if he found out I was the one stealing his excuse to hurt those men. I twisted and breathed slowly, willing time to pick up like a river and rush me to the end of this.

Talk moved away from Pietro, landing where it always did, on the subject of Mirella's wedding. She went silent at the attention, slowing the prim dance of her fork. My own food writhed in my stomach. Father talked about the alliance with the Otto family as Beniamo dug at my leg. His ragged, bitten nails pressed through the sturdy cloth of my dress.

"May I take the little girls to bed?" I asked hoarsely.

"Yes, yes," Father said, turning his fingers into a broom and sweeping his young daughters away from the table. "This is not a matter for wildflowers." That was what he called Carina and Adela, though I could remember a time when I had been the wildflower. Mirella had always been a rose, trimmed and perfect.

I rushed away from the table, limping slightly. When we reached the nursery, I had to shake my little sisters from my limbs as they asked for a story.

"The Pear Girl," Carina said.

"The Castle without a Soul," Adela countered. She was only eight, but that commanding tone had already earned her the name "Little Tyrant." Carina had a wilder nature, and a smile as pink as strawberries.

I settled them both onto Carina's bed. "In that time," I said, starting neither of the stories they had asked for but an old favorite of mine, "there was a strega who could change into a scrap of wind, or a drop of water, or the sunlight that kisses a pretty girl's cheek."

Carina giggled and held her hands up to her own face. Adela nodded sagely.

The stories were an escape from the bruise ripening on my leg, but they brought their own pain. The same one, every night. What if I was the only strega in Vinalia? These tales were as old as starlight—I had never heard of a *new* strega story. I had taken over the telling from Fiorenza when I'd turned twelve. Father had always disliked this particular chore, although he wouldn't say why. Maybe he thought strega tales were too common, too whimsical for a di Sangro child. Maybe his life was so gray that their bright colors seemed a lie. I had always loved them. But as the years went by, their words seemed less like a promise and more like an ache.

"Another," Adela demanded as soon as I finished.

"I have to go see Father." I had given Luca my word.

"Another *short* one," Adela said, squinting shrewdly. She had already learned to bargain, and her di Sangro lessons hadn't even begun.

"Once there was a strega," I said, and Carina and Adela looked off into the distance, as if a strega were the most far-flung, impossible thing. As if they didn't have one sitting right in front of them.

❦

I STOOD IN FRONT OF THE OPEN DOOR TO FATHER'S STUDY, shifting on restless legs. Something about lingering in his doorway turned me nine years old, as easily as flipping the pages to an earlier chapter in a book.

"Come in, Teo," Father said.

I crossed the stone floor of the room Father called his study. This castle had been built centuries ago, not as a palazzo for a fine family but as a stronghold to protect the mountain. A black walnut chair and a desk laden with papers didn't change the nature of it, any more than a pair of pants would change a wolf into a prince.

Still, Father had covered the walls with books. He had the most thorough library in the Uccelli, shelves bricked from top to bottom with tomes, and not one held the words *magic* or *strega*. It was like staring at the world's largest collection of mirrors and not seeing your own face.

Father finally looked up from his letters. News came to us in a slow pour of honey, from other family heads and from Father's brothers and cousins who conducted di Sangro business throughout Vinalia. Then there were letters asking for help and favors, written by anyone in the Uccelli who could scrape together a sentence. Father entered everything of importance into an endless series of ledgers. Births, deaths, matters raised and settled, visitors from across the mountains.

"Look at this," he said, slapping a piece of paper down on the wood. "A man who thinks I should kill his cousin over a goat. As if I should sharpen my knives because the cheese is a little chalky. He's been loyal to the family, so I will have to scare off the cousin. But no killings. I don't trade in men's lives for so little."

I nodded.

I wanted to ask: *How little is too little? Did Pietro really have to be done away with? How do you know? Is there a feeling that pairs with such a truth? A moment when the world tips and can't be righted any other way?*

But I had built a neat cage for questions like those long ago. When I didn't speak, or leave, Father asked, "What do you want?" in the same flat tone I had heard him use on squabbling villagers and desperate merchants.

"It's about Luca. He wants—"

"Things he can't have," Father said, cutting me off. "Like any young man. Is this about the wedding? I told him I need him here." When Father made up his mind, the result was a current in a fast-moving river. People crossed at their own peril. "It will be good for Luca to see how it feels to be in charge, don't you think?"

I thought Luca would rather tumble down the mountain headfirst.

"Well, Teo?" Father asked, his forehead crimping with concern. He could do this in a single moment, change from a family head who declared things to a man who begged opinions from his daughter. I longed to tell him he was right, because it would make us both happy. But tonight I gave him something that, over the years, had become rarer than any spice or metal traded in the ports along the Violetta Coast. I gave him the truth. "I wanted to go with you over the mountains. To Mirella's wedding."

"And why shouldn't you?" he asked, everything about him sharp again, down to the scratch of his ink on the ledger.

"Luca needs me." I couldn't leave my little brother alone in the Uccelli. What if trouble stirred while Father was gone? Luca had no idea how to run things. His mind, though keen, was a compass needle pointed firmly in another direction.

Father flicked through a few more letters. "That's all?"

I thought about Pietro, the music box, the collection upstairs that grew and grew.

"That's all," I said.

Father picked up a letter, not from the top of the pile. He'd set one aside. "We received a summons with the Malfara family crest." He showed me the icon of the running wolf, stamped into a blister of red wax. Father shook one hand in a rude gesture he rarely used. His disdain for the Capo in Amalia was as rich as the rabbit stew we'd eaten for dinner. All I knew about the youngest son of the Malfara family was that he'd raised his own army to unite Vinalia, often by force, and then declared himself our glorious new leader. Father didn't like to speak of the man. The Capo was a sickness he was ignoring, hoping it wouldn't fester or grow worse.

Father tapped one finger against the envelope. "Will you read this for me?"

I could sense he wanted to give me some little task, to make me feel important. Apparently, Father felt like I was nine years old tonight too. I almost grabbed the letter, but the magic rushed to stop me. It wanted to hear Father speak. After all of the ways I had displeased it, I couldn't deny it such a small thing. It craved his voice, the way I craved the sight of green after the white plague of winter.

"You read it," I said. "I'll advise you."

Father smiled and reached for a knife as thin as a feather, working it along the top of the envelope. My thoughts slid to the other knife, the stiletto with the twisted handle and the killing point. The one undoubtedly hidden in his sleeve.

The seal broke, dead flakes of wax falling away. Father pulled the letter from the envelope. The paper was as thick and creamy white as besciamella, a gold edge spun all the way around.

Father scowled. "Men who waste money on beautiful things . . ."

"End up decorating the gutters," I finished.

Sometimes Father felt more like a collection of favorite sayings than a person, but anyone who looked around the castle would see that we lived by his words. Whatever the di Sangro family had was put to use, including children. Luca would travel, like Father's brothers, doing the family's work in other towns, other cities. Mirella's marriage to Ambrogio Otto, a family head in the making, would forge a strong alliance between the Otto and di Sangro lines. Beniamo was being groomed to take over from Father.

I had made myself useful too.

Father held up the letter, and I snapped to attention. "'The great and noble di Sangro family,'" he said, reading in the pompous voice the villagers used when they put on puppet shows. "'The head of your family is now dead.'" His voice tripped, fell flat. "'A representative must . . .'"

He lost his grip on the paper as a tremor worked its way through his muscles. One hand reached for me, tossed by an invisible wind. It dropped, and he followed, sliding to the floor as I ran around Father's desk.

I knelt, afraid to touch him as he writhed. I reached for the magic, begging it to do something. But changing Father into a decorative box or a brush to sweep ashes wouldn't help.

I needed help.

"Please," I cried, but the word didn't go far. My voice was a bird with broken wings. "Mother!"

Father curled on his side, breath scraping the air.

I capped my mouth with both hands, afraid more useless words would fly out, battering my heart as they went.

Mother was dead. She could do nothing to save him. I could do nothing to save him.

I held Father up by the shoulders. His weight sagged against me like wet sand, his face slack. "Don't go," I begged simply, as if it were still a matter of him traveling across the mountains and leaving me behind.

I stood to run for Fiorenza, but the white paper with glittering edges claimed my view. It had fallen to the floor beside Father. I spent one precious second hating it. The letter wasn't beautiful at all. It was the color of death, Father's skin a pale match. The words stared up at me—a few scant lines of ink. I knew what they meant.

The Capo had declared war on the di Sangro family.

3

Fiorenza had the portrait hall turned into a sickroom. Father lay across a cushioned table. The faces of long-dead di Sangro family heads stared down at me, the grit of blame in their dark brown eyes.

"I don't want him moved upstairs until the doctor can be fetched from Arresti," Fiorenza said.

"There are nearer doctors," I argued, my mind in ragged threads from what had happened in the study. I couldn't seem to tie the simplest knots of logic. All I knew was that Father had to be cured.

"We must have someone absolutely loyal," Fiorenza said, and I could see what a fool I'd been. The Capo meant to kill Father. We couldn't hand the knowledge that he still drew breath to someone who might have ties to the Palazza.

Father stayed perfectly still on his makeshift bed, but his heartbeat darted and hid like a frightened child. Luca put his scientific knowledge to use, drawing small amounts of blood and disappearing to test them in his vials. Mirella knelt at his side for hours, her voice moving in hills and valleys over the well-worn paths of prayer. Carina and Adela climbed right into Father's sickbed and told him the story of Pearina.

Beniamo sat in the far corner and stared at everyone with mounting irritation. When Father's breath caught and struggled in his throat, my brother leaned forward.

Mirella prayed for Father to improve.

I hoped he would start back to life.

Beniamo waited for him to die.

Night bled into a new day, and as the sun rose, visitors from Chieza ringed Father's body. Fiorenza sifted through the crowd, murmuring, "Thank you for your prayers. Your discretion is appreciated."

The villagers knew that if they spoke of what they saw, someone would come when they least expected it and deliver a punishment. That someone would probably be me.

"Your father will heal, I am sure of it," the priest's cousin told me in a rickety tone. I knew she meant well—they all did—but by the tenth time I heard those words, it felt like the villagers were passing around a dull knife, each one stabbing me in turn.

What was more, I heard the name of Melae slipped into their prayers. The goddess of death had never quite disappeared from Vinalia, no matter how hard the Order of Prai tried to scrub away every trace of the old religion they called heresy, and men like Luca called history, and everyone else kept in a drawer in case they needed it. According to ancient belief, Melae helped a dying person take on two new forms, spirit and flesh, each one bound for a new fate as soon as they parted.

I knelt at Father's side and closed my eyes, pretending I wanted to be nearer to God and not simply farther away from the sight of Father's gray skin. Whispers churned behind me.

"Melae protect him."

"Melae greet him."

"Melae walk with him."

"Go!" I shouted, startling the villagers into flight. They left in a great drove, eyeing me as they pulled their prayer shawls tight. In less than a minute, Father and I were alone. I tried to take his hand but snatched back from skin as dull as stone.

People only invoked Melae's name when the end was in sight.

🙵

I MADE IT MY BUSINESS TO DEAL WITH THE LETTER.

I found my thickest pair of leather gloves—which had once been a man with a penchant for selling di Sangro secrets—and scooped the paper up from the hearth in Father's study with the shovel meant for fireplace ashes.

I expected my heart to clench and my breath to come in starts. I didn't expect the magic to speak up, and tell me in a cold voice: *dead.*

Father isn't dead, I snapped, still angry at the magic for not doing anything when I needed it most.

No, it said. *The letter.*

How could a letter be dead? The magic insisted that whatever had hurt Father was gone. Still, I wasn't about to touch the page that had brought on so much pain. There had to be poison lurking in it somewhere.

I left it perched on the shovel and read from a safe distance.

The great and noble di Sangro family. My stomach seized at the flattery and ridicule. *The head of your family is now dead.* My eyes stuck on that last word. Anger fought its way up, past my throat, burning at the back of my eyes. *A representative must report to the Palazza in one week's time.*

I folded the letter into neat squares and shoved it in my pocket, slipping off the gloves. So this was what the Capo wanted. To treat with a new family head, one who wasn't Father.

༽❖༼

I WENT DOWN TO THE KITCHENS, WHERE I KNEW I WOULD FIND Fiorenza. She reigned over the wooden table, her hands covered in flour. Around her, piles of dough were stretched into long rectangles for cornetti. Turning flour and lard and a handful of sugar into pastry took hours, and a person could empty an entire body's worth of feelings into the work. Fiorenza had taught me long ago that stillness helped no one. Of course, Beniamo had been given a different lesson. He had been taught to wait, and to let what he wanted come to him.

Our single kitchen servant turned on a sharp heel at the sight of me, either out of respect at my state of near-mourning, or out of fear at how I looked after a night with only a passing nod at sleep. She left me alone with Fiorenza in the whitewashed room, pinked by morning light. The rose tint should have softened my stepmother's face, but worry lines plucked at her mouth and the creases of her eyes.

Fiorenza handed me a small tin of lard. It was my job to pinch off pieces and add them to the dough. I took great care with the dollops, placing them just the right distance away from each other. I worked up the courage to ask an unbearable question. "What happens if Father doesn't wake up?"

Fiorenza kept her eyes on her kneading. "Watch your tongue."

My stepmother loved Father. I saw it in the way they argued, her voice as lively as water at a boil. But I loved him too, and he would not want us to wait for him to come back from the gray land between the living and the dead. Not when there was a war on the table and the family to protect.

I folded my apron to protect my fingers, and I set the letter on the table in front of Fiorenza. "Don't touch it."

As she took in the words, I let myself dream of the best way to change the Capo. I could turn him into a pretty piece of paper and tear it to bits. A bottle of ink that I could dash to the floor. A flake of ash, bitter on my tongue, but not bitter enough to stop me from swallowing it.

Fiorenza looked up from the lovely white paper. "So the Capo thinks he will kill my husband and claim my children."

"They'll come for all of us if we don't send someone," I said.

Fiorenza, who could argue any point until it had the polished glow of truth, only said, "Yes."

I folded over the dough. Its slack weight reminded me of Father's skin, the way it had seemed to melt at my touch.

"Which one of us will go?" I asked.

I already knew it would be Beniamo, and that I would argue until I was allowed to go with him. Not as the representative, of course—that was impossible. They would laugh a girl out of Amalia if she claimed to be the head of the di Sangro family. But that letter had some magic in its weave, and I knew magic.

Not well, my magic reminded me.

Fiorenza nodded at the letter. "Take that back to your father's study and burn it in the grate."

"And then what?" I asked. "Should I fetch Beniamo?"

Fiorenza only blinked down at the table and went back to working the dough.

❦

I SET THE LETTER DOWN IN THE STUDY FIREPLACE AND SET A candle to it. Strange flames washed over the page, yellow and green, the color of a bruise as it struggles to heal.

A *flick* came from behind me, the sound of a great wind snapping. I turned from the hearth to face the rest of the study. The room lacked windows, and the air at the heart of the castle usually felt as still as a word unspoken.

I heard light, airy footsteps in the hall.

Follow, the magic said.

When I reached the door, the back of a slender young man moved away from me, leaving the castle at a clip. He had a fall of black hair. A green-purple cloak.

The boy on the mountain.

What was he doing here? Had he been in Father's study?

I ran to overtake his steps, grabbing him by the elbow. He whirled around, tears studding his greenish eyes. A surprised blink chased them away.

"I'm sorry," I said. I had made a mistake. These eyes were familiar but set in a slightly rounder face than I'd expected. And while the person I'd grabbed ahold of stood tall and slender, she had curves that could not be denied.

"How long do you think you'll need my arm?" she asked

in a low voice, looking down at my fingers as if they were welcome visitors.

I darted my hand away. "What are you doing here?"

"What are *you* doing here?" she asked, her voice pitched a step higher than the boy's had been, but otherwise a perfect mirror. I remembered the stranger so clearly. He had strolled into my head as easily as he strolled across the mountain.

"This is my home," I said.

"You're a di Sangro," she said. "Of course. That answers so many questions all at once."

"I met your brother on his way over the mountain. He wouldn't tell me his name," I said.

Or *his purpose*, I thought.

My mind tied a tricky knot, one that had been out of reach all day. The boy on the mountain hadn't wanted to say what he was doing here. So few visitors came over the Uccelli, let alone ones dressed nobly enough to hail from the Capo's court in Amalia.

He had carried the letter.

I gripped the girl's arm.

"That's a bit tight," she said with a nervous smile. "You either like me much less or much more than you did a minute ago."

Her words summoned heat to my face. "I need to find your brother," I said.

"I'm afraid I can't help you there."

"Why? Because you're part of his scheme?" I asked, with none of the care I had used to lay out a snare for Pietro. The patience I'd had only yesterday scattered, gone. "Did you come here to see my father dead?"

The girl's face set in the hard lines of truth. "I came to

ask Niccolò di Sangro a simple question. I had no idea your father would be . . . well . . ."

"Dying?" My voice snapped in half over the spine of the word.

She didn't deny it like the people at Father's vigil. She didn't lie to me one moment and whisper to Melae the next. "I'm sorry he's been taken from you," she said, looking down at her hands. They were long-fingered, empty.

Sadness turned my grip to water, and the girl slipped away. As she rushed toward the front door, she turned back and gave me a pained smile.

Don't let her go, the magic said.

It had told me the same thing when the stranger on the mountain walked away and I'd chosen not to follow. The girl in the door vanished, her green-purple cloak snapping out of sight. It was the same length, the same richness, etched with the same faint pattern. It was the exact same cloak, and of course her brother could have lent it to her. But she had never admitted she *had* a brother. His existence wasn't the only way to explain this—it was simply the one I'd seen at first glance.

The boy on the mountain, the girl in the hall.

"They're the same," I said.

Yes, the magic hissed, disappointed in me for taking so long.

Which meant the person who had just strolled out the front door had delivered the poisoned letter to Father.

I picked up my skirts. I had felt powerless all day, but as I ran out of the castle, giving chase, I returned to what I was best at, what I'd bent my life and magic toward: punishing enemies of the di Sangro family.

THE PATH FROM THE CASTLE LED DOWN TO CHIEZA, THE TOPS of pink-red tile roofs as bright as a batch of flowers beneath us. The stranger rushed down the dusty road toward the village, disappearing around a sharp turn. I staggered downhill, setting my boots sideways against the steep grade, pebbles flying off the side of the mountain into open air. Running like this reminded me of a game Mirella and I had invented when we were little, pretending that we were avalanches, that if we gathered enough speed and strength, we could change the face of the mountain.

The path spat me out near the edge of Chieza. I passed white homes rivered with dust, bougainvillea bursting its way up the walls. Villagers walked slowly in the midday heat, simmering and shouting. They usually stayed inside until the passeggiata, when the air was cooler and gossip had built to a head. But with Father on his deathbed, they had far too much to talk about.

Then they caught sight of me, the second di Sangro daughter, tearing through the village when she should have been keeping a vigil at her father's side.

In the crowds, I spotted a figure, taller than the rest, with hair like a bottle of ink poured straight down his back.

Her back.

I was running again, chasing the stranger down, until I almost caught up to her on the far side of Chieza.

"Stop!" I cried.

The stranger looked back at me. The twist of the shoulders, the span of the chest, told me this was the boy I'd met on the mountain. The dress I'd seen in the castle had been shucked and traded in for plain traveler's clothes.

He took one look at my face and ran twice as fast.

My feet knew these woods, had memorized every place where rocks spiked upward in small fists and where roots broke the path. As soon as I had the boy's back in sight, I called up my magic. It sang through me like a second bloodstream, beating like a second heart.

Give him the ugliest form you can, I said, keeping the boy squarely in sight. He ran like a rabbit, flitting back and forth, and the magic hit the tree next to him. It turned into a giant fish balanced on its tail, mouth pursed at the sky. I tried again—*uglier, please*—and hit another tree. It became a dung heap, complete with flies.

The boy looked over his shoulder and laughed.

If I hadn't hated him before, I did now. He wasn't properly afraid of me.

Knowing how proud and precise the magic was, both the giant fish and the dung heap would smell soon. I could only imagine what the villagers would say when they came across such things.

I stopped bothering with magic and took off at a blinding run, hacking my steps off when the woods broke open. The ravine gaped before me, a wide dark mouth. The Storyteller's Grave laid claim to my breath no matter how many times I saw it. There was no easy way across—only long, ragged paths around in both directions.

I looked to see which the stranger had chosen.

Neither, it would seem. He stood a few steps away, facing the ravine, completely naked. My eyes went to the matching dents at the lowest curve of his back. At first I thought this was the world's strangest distraction. Then I thought he'd chosen to give up and pitch himself into the darkness— although I couldn't imagine why he needed to be unclothed.

Now, I told the magic.

It murmured inside of me, rushed and frantic. I couldn't understand what it wanted to say.

The boy knelt to the pile of clothes at his feet, his spine standing out like a ladder. He reached for the little leather book.

Then he changed.

It was like the world itself had turned a page. Again, a *flick* sounded, echoing in the empty ravine. The boy was replaced by a bird with stunning black feathers, a high gloss, and red patches that showed when he flapped his wings. He grabbed the book in his talons and swept the string of the cloak up in his beak.

He flapped away, across the ravine.

This stranger was a strega. That was why the magic hadn't wanted me to change him. I had finally met someone else with magic—not in a story, but right in front of me, flapping and cawing. It felt like I had spent my entire life speaking a secret language and then stumbled on someone else who was perfectly fluent.

But that didn't change the fact that this strega had brought the letter from Amalia. It didn't bring Father back from the edge of his own dark ravine.

When the bird reached the far side, I expected him to fly in hard strokes, over the scrub meadows, past the tree line. Away from me. Instead he dropped the book only a few feet from the edge, landing beside it on delicate bird feet. He nudged the pages with his beak, and the book fell open.

Pale skin flashed, and, with a quick whirl, the cloak covered the better part of the boy's nakedness. He stood up and faced me across the ravine. The strega tilted his head, a bit birdlike even now, waiting to see what I would do.

The magic leapt at the challenge. I told it to calm itself. I was here to punish this strega, not impress him. I turned around and grabbed the longest stick I could find, closed my eyes, and thought, *A bridge. I need a bridge, strong enough to hold me.*

I swore I could hear the magic grumble.

I dropped the branch and it shot across the ravine, smooth as a plank. Not a showy change, but it worked. Then I tried to take a step and my stomach pitched. I could barely place one foot on the thin beam.

I filled my lungs before starting across, afraid a troubled breath would set me off-balance. I anchored my eyes to the strega's on the far side. Blue, gray, green. Halfway across, I hit a knot in the wood. My toe scuffed, stuck.

And I was falling.

Sky above, darkness beneath. Then the colors vanished, and everything turned grainy and gray. My heart went blank with fear. I would hit a rock, or my mind would give way, and a merciful darkness would claim me.

I fell.

And fell.

A wind curled itself around my body. Warm, whipping, strong enough to lift me. The plummeting in my guts dissolved, and a new feeling swam in. I sailed skyward, through gray, toward impossible shades of blue.

The wind dumped me on the grass.

This was the wrong side of the ravine, the one I had

started on. The wind rushed away, and a few moments later a great breath rustled the pages of the book on the far side.

Flick. The boy was back again. He gathered the green-purple fabric around him before standing up.

The strega had become a wind to save me. *Why?* Before I guessed at an answer, another thought struck hard. He had lifted my body, carried me. Was that the same as brushing his hands all over me?

"Are you spent?" he called. I couldn't help but notice his hard breathing, the rush of color in his cheeks. "I could keep going, if you like."

I stared at the strega, unable to speak.

"Good," he said. "Now, let me tell you I had no idea that letter would harm your father. Why would I poison him and then go pay him a visit?"

"You wanted to steal something," I said, trying to sound certain, but only half-convinced, of my own logic.

"You think I'm a thief?" the strega asked. "Interesting. You know, the first thing a person accuses someone of is often their own preferred sin. But you can search me, if you like." He finished with a broad smile that might as well have been a bow.

I forced myself to think of Father shaking on the floor, in the grips of the letter's poison. I had been confused and charmed by this strega once. It wouldn't happen again. I steadied my voice against the tremble that came when I slipped back to that moment in the study. "You deserve to die."

"Is that how you thank someone who lifted you bodily from a ravine?" the strega asked. "I would think a card, or maybe some nice pears."

"I didn't ask you to save me!" I shouted.

"It was a gift, freely given!" he shouted back.

"The five families don't believe in such a thing," I muttered. As far as I could tell, it was less common than magic. "Every man, woman, and child in the Uccelli is loyal to the di Sangro family," I added, dangerously aware that those words might not be true anymore. "One of our people will catch you."

"Really?" he asked, smiling as if we were playing a game and he had just taken all the points. The strega thumbed to a new page in his book, and the change came with another great *flick*. Where he had been standing a moment ago, there was the girl I'd seen in the castle. The cloak clung to her body, the fabric pulled tight by her breasts, flaps open slightly and showing a sliver of her skin, as pale and glowing as a moonlit path. "Who, exactly, will you tell them to look for?"

The strega turned, cloak swishing over her bare legs, and started the long, lonely walk up the mountain.

4

When I got back to the castle, I hurried past the portrait gallery. I couldn't pay respect to Father with my dress torn, my magic muttering curses, and my heart half-drowned in failure.

I climbed the stairs to find Fiorenza and Luca waiting in my room. My brother sat on the bed, his hands pressed together between his knees. My stepmother hovered, touching her fingertips to the music box as it pricked its way through Pietro's song. "This is pretty," Fiorenza said. She didn't ask about where I'd been, the dust on my dress, the hitch in my breath.

Something was wrong.

When my stepmother stared at me, I was hit by a double slap of sadness and beauty. One of my first memories was Fiorenza's misery. It spun me back to her first year with us, when she missed her home, her family, the bright splash of flowers and deep indigo waves of the Violetta Coast. She had been a celebrated young woman from a noble family, with amber eyes and skin that seemed to match in shade and a slight glowing property, rich brown hair that fell almost to her knees. Father was—well, Father. And yet Fiorenza chose him, and came to live with us, a mother that I longed for more than I dared to admit. Every night when I went to bed I feared she would leave, fleeing our grim mountains before I could wake. But she stayed and taught me about *the brilliant life*. It was a truth that many Vinalians lived by, she said, choosing to battle the harshness of this world with as many forms of beauty as possible. Fiorenza made cornetti instead of wading in thoughts of Father's death. Now she played music to keep herself from crying. "I need you to help ready Luca for his trip," she said. "And accompany him over the mountains."

"What?" I asked.

"Luca's *trip*," she said, repeating the words carefully. Fiorenza had always been good at telling a story, and I could see a truth hidden within this one, like a secret room that opened up when I looked at the right angle.

She had chosen Luca to respond to the Palazza's summons.

Luca's knees stuttered up and down. He knew how dangerous it was to go behind Beniamo's back and act as if Luca were head of the family. And yet Fiorenza had decided it was the best course. She was the acting head of the di Sangro line until Father regained his health, or until he died and one of his sons took his place. My stepmother had the space of a few breaths to make such a move. It would look, to the rest of the world, like a play for power. For herself. For her son.

"Are you sure you don't want to send Beniamo?" I whispered, thinking of my brother's dead eyes, how they only came alive when he thought he was being robbed of something that was rightfully his.

Fiorenza shook her head. "Your father had doubts about how Beniamo would fare on such a journey."

In a great crash of understanding, I saw why Father had insisted on Luca staying behind for Mirella's wedding. It was a way for Luca to gain some experience, to give him confidence. Father had decided, well before the letter arrived, that Luca would someday be the head of the di Sangro family.

Jealousy swelled at the back of my throat, but I forced words around it. "If that's what Father wants."

Fiorenza took a deep breath, a storm mustering all of her winds. "You leave tonight."

"Tonight?" I cried. After chasing that strega all over the mountain, I needed a wheelbarrow full of dinner, a hot bath, and several nights' worth of sleep. But Fiorenza was right. It would take three days to cross the Uccelli, and another to reach Amalia. And the longer we stayed here under Beniamo's nose, the more likely he would sniff out our true purpose. "Fine," I said.

Fiorenza clutched me to her. She wore the same sweet powder as always, smelling of oranges and anise, but it couldn't cover the sweat that came from replacing sleep with fear. She pressed me tighter, and I felt a hard lump below her neck. Fiorenza usually wore a string of Violetta pearls, but this was the wrong size and shape. I pulled away to see a ring of dull iron in the smooth spot at the center of her collarbone. It stood out against her red silk dress and hard-won grace.

"Where did you get this?" I asked, drawn to the dark ring. Touching iron was supposed to keep away hardship, a belief that lingered from the days of the old gods. It had been worn down to a superstition, just as the old temples scattered through Vinalia had been worn down to beautiful ruins.

"This was your mother's," Fiorenza said.

"But you two never met," I said, my voice as raw as the dough Fiorenza had been working earlier. Even now, thinking of Mother did that to me.

Fiorenza lifted the charm away from her skin and worried the cord between two fingers. "Your father gave it to me when he asked me to marry him. Not the sort of gift most young women received, but I could see that it meant a great deal to him." The forceful bottling of tears made her eyes gleam. "He made me promise that in times of trouble, I would wear it for protection."

Yours, the magic whispered.

"Can I bring it to Amalia?" I asked. "For luck?" I couldn't stop staring at the dark, careworn metal. My hands wanted to grab for it, instinct scrubbing away both reason and manners.

Fiorenza took a steadying breath. She slipped the ancient-looking leather cord from around her neck and put it over my head. "It was meant to protect me. And I was meant to protect you." The iron fell into place at the neckline of my dress.

Fiorenza turned to Luca, hugging and kissing him so many times that I thought we would never be able to leave the Uccelli. When she was gone, I immediately wished her back. Luca broke out in a sweat, sick with fear, and I had no balm for it.

The red of late afternoon snuck in through the narrow windows. The day was slipping away from us. "Meet me in your rooms an hour from now," I said. "And don't just pack your microscope and slides."

"This is wrong, Teo," Luca muttered lowly. "You know it's wrong."

"Fine," I said. "Bring the microscope, but leave room for at least one fresh pair of clothes. You're going to ripen fast on the road to Amalia."

Luca glared at me as if the attempt at humor was as bad as a stab in the heart. I didn't want him to answer the summons, but I couldn't see any other way. "In some situations, there is no right thing," I said. "Only the least of many wrongs."

"You sound like Father," Luca said, each word carved out of pain.

"It's one of his favorite sayings."

Luca rubbed his forehead with one hand, frustration peeling away years until he was a little boy again. "You see? I should know that."

My brother wouldn't look at me, and all I could do was stare at him. The new head of the di Sangro family.

The choice made sense from where Father sat. Luca was smarter, more evenhanded than Beniamo. Most families followed the rule of the eldest son, but for men fate could be nudged in a new direction. Niccolò di Sangro was a third son. He had worked the hardest, proved himself the cleverest, sacrificed for the di Sangro family without question. Father must have seen the same qualities when he looked at Luca.

I wanted to know what he saw when he looked at me. I wanted to be the one to answer the summons. "I would do this for you, if I could."

Luca tried to smile, but it wouldn't take hold. "It's a shame you aren't a boy, Teo."

The family nickname I had always loved seemed to mock me. Teo was a boy's name—one I'd insisted on when I was barely old enough to stand. Father had been charmed, and Fiorenza had taken it on with her usual grace. Luca hardly called me anything else. But having a boyish name at home didn't change how people would see me when I went out into the world.

I thought of the strega at the ravine, and the different forms that all seemed to belong to one person. A boyish body and a girlish one, swapped with ease. In both cases, the strega was tall, with dark hair and pale skin, but there was no mistaking a change had occurred.

I tried not to let hope push me straight into the arms of idiocy. "Maybe it's something I *can* do," I said, laying the words like stones, one by one, with great care. I wanted this—wanted it more than anything I'd ever imagined.

Luca looked at me, a frown gracing his lips. "You mean dress up as a boy?" he asked. "That works in stories. There's no way it would trick everyone at the Palazza."

"It wouldn't be a trick." There was nothing false about strega magic. If I became a boy, it would be real. Another version of me, as true as this one.

I almost told Luca about my magic then and there. But I didn't have a way to change—not yet. Only a picture in my mind, of a strega who could flick back and forth as easily as the wind played over the trees.

The last bar of sunlight painted a red line across the floor. We would be leaving soon.

"We'll get on the road first," I said. "And then we'll see what can be done."

LUCA LEFT TO PACK, AND I THREW MY OWN THINGS INTO A CANVAS bag. A spare traveling dress, stockings, underthings, rags for my bleeding, and as many coins as I could scrape from the dresser drawers. I looked around the room at the collection I had built up. I picked out the music box, the prayer beads, the gilded mirror, and the potted rose that bloomed all year. They might be useful as bribes. Anyone who believed in *the brilliant life* would see their worth.

With my pack weighing down one shoulder, I took the stairs to Mirella's tower.

The year my older sister started to bleed between her legs, she was whisked away from the castle. I was only eight and cried every day, believing she was lost to me forever, like Mother. It didn't matter how many stories Fiorenza told me, how many promises Father made that Mirella would return. When she did, it wasn't for long. She came and went like a fickle season, spending much of the year with the other four families, slowly and carefully choosing a husband. When Mirella came home, she lived in a tower all by herself. Each window slit that belonged to her, each perfectly shaped white stone, toppled me with jealousy.

I stood now at the border of Mirella's round tower room. Leaded windows from Prai had been put in, and through them our mountain wavered blue in the twilight. Mirella sat at her desk, writing with such fierce strokes that it looked like they would rip through the paper and scar the wood.

She didn't even notice my arrival. She must have been trapped in thoughts of Ambrogio, the man she had finally chosen for her husband. If the Capo had tried to kill Father, it was likely he had moved against the rest of the families. Ambrogio might be the new head of the Otto line, or he might be dead. While I went over the mountains to Amalia, Mirella had to sit and wait and worry. This was the fate of the first daughter, and I could see clearly enough to know I wanted none of it.

I wanted to be a di Sangro son. Now that I had named it, there was no question in my mind.

I cleared my throat. "Luca and I are—"

"Fetching the doctor," Mirella said. "Yes, Fiorenza told me. Go swiftly and come back safe." She shook powder over her freshly inked paper, folded it, and held it out to me. She didn't even bother with a seal. There was no time to melt the wax. "If you see Ambrogio, give him this."

"No," I said, unable to bear the weight of a third failure. Father had collapsed as I'd watched. The strega had escaped because I couldn't stop him. "I can't promise—"

She pressed the letter into my hands, clenching our fists together in a sort of seal. A bittersweet smile did nothing to change the grim look in her green-glazed brown eyes. "You are stubborn, little sister." Mirella's voice was hoarse, worn to a nub from too much praying. "Be stubborn enough to see Ambrogio gets this." I nodded, hugged her, and left on quick feet.

They carried me to the nursery, where Adela waited with her demands. "*Three* stories tonight. You promised."

Carina clapped in a quick, delighted flurry.

"I only have time for one," I said, speaking as quickly as I dared, not wanting to draw attention to my hurry. Adela opened her mouth to argue, so I began. "The day the princess met the strega, she thought it was only an old woman hobbling down the road." I let my voice travel the curve of that road, while my mind forked onto a new path. A strega boy— who was also a girl and a bird and a great wind—had handed my father a letter and taken away the person I loved most.

But the strega had also given me a gift, something more than lifting me from the ravine. A gift that would come with me over the mountains, packed in my heart like a secret.

I wasn't alone.

☙✦❧

Last, I visited Father.

I wanted to kiss his cheek, but I knew it would upset me when Father didn't rub the spot where I'd set my lips, saying it would bring him luck. Everything Father and I did together was like a passage from one of the strega stories, comforting because it stayed the same, even if little differences crept into the telling. But things had already changed without my permission. If I found some way to turn myself into a boy, everything would.

I slid my hand inside Father's sleeve, caught between his arm and roughspun fabric. I knew, from memory, where he hid the stiletto. It came away in one satisfying sweep.

It was the same knife from seven years ago. I had not gilded the memory. The handle twisted in a way that called up the sight of wind-blasted trees. I longed to run a finger over the S-shaped curve of the crossbar. The narrow blade drew my eyes to the killing point.

I tucked it in the hidden loop inside my sleeve. Father had them put into all of my dresses, against Fiorenza's wishes.

"I promise I'll bring it back," I whispered.

If I was right about what sort of trouble awaited us at the Palazza, I would need this more than Father did.

☙✦❧

WHEN I CLIMBED THE STAIRS TO LUCA'S ROOM, HIS PACK SAT silently, abandoned on the bed. A pale night shouldered in through the arrow slit.

"Luca," I said. "Luca?"

I thudded down the back stairs, coming out into the kitchens. I checked Luca's laboratory, a converted pantry where he kept all of his scientific equipment. Moonlight polished Luca's specimens. Vials winked at me in the dark. The table was covered in bits of rock from different parts of the Uccelli, shells from the Violetta Coast, dead insects pinned on cards. The tiny room looked as though it had been troubled by a fresh wind. Luca had grabbed what he imagined he'd need in Amalia, and dust outlined the brass microscope's place of honor. Below where it used to sit, a line of slides had been dotted with Father's blood.

"Luca?" I tried again, though he'd clearly come and gone.

I gave the kitchens a quick scour, picking up food as I went and stuffing it into my pack. The cornetti were still rising on the table. I wished I could stay long enough to claim one as Fiorenza pulled them from the oven, crisp and buttery.

I rushed through the dining hall and paused outside Father's study. When I pushed in the door, the room appeared empty. I walked around Father's desk, and a flash of white in the grate caught my eye.

White, with a cutting edge of gold.

The letter that I had thought I'd burned was lying there for anyone to see. I had been so distracted by the strega that I'd forgotten it. I had seen it coated in odd-colored flame but not turned to ash. Whatever magic had turned it poisonous must have made it impossible to burn.

Here was the message, clearly inked. *A representative must report to the Palazza in one week's time.*

A cold mist of fear settled over me.

I started toward the back staircase and my own room, to be sure that Luca hadn't gone looking for me.

That was when I heard it.

A brutal cry. Ridged like a knife for cutting bone. High as a wind ravaging the tree line. I dropped to my knees and put my ear against the cold stone. The sound was rising from beneath my feet.

Luca once taught me that light moves faster than anyone can see or understand. That was how I ran, feet blind, muscles burning. I rushed down to the cellars, past the wine casks, into dark, winding cells that smelled of earth and minerals and, underneath that, rot. I didn't need light; I had that jagged, hopeless cry to guide me.

The walls pinched tight as I headed for the dungeon without thinking. The lesson that Father had given about the history of torture must have lodged in Beniamo's mind like a challenge, or a promise. A torch's stuttering glow led me to a hunched doorway.

Beniamo stood over Luca, naked to the waist. He had tied our little brother hand and foot, trussed like a hare. Bare patches on Luca's hands glistened red. Beniamo had peeled the skin off his palms, and Luca was bleeding freely. The sight called out to my own blood, turning it sickly hot.

Beniamo didn't need torture devices. He was skinning Luca alive.

My older brother caught sight of me and stepped back. Guilt darkened his face—then anger spread over him like torchlight, oily and glaring. "No arteries, see?" Beniamo waited for me to inspect his work, how he had started with Luca's hands before moving on to more deadly places. "I want this little traitor to live as long as possible before he dies."

My eyes met Luca's. He mouthed, *Run*.

I tilted my chin away. Luca would be upset if I disobeyed his dying wish, so I would have to pretend I had never been aware of it.

"You have no right to hurt anyone," I told Beniamo, words that had waited years to leave my body. "Besides, Luca is a di Sangro son. He's done nothing but his duty. He doesn't even *want* to be in charge!"

"But here we are," Beniamo said, spreading his hands wide. "Since the day I was born, I've known my fate." I heard the dark shadow of Father's words that night so many years ago. *Family is fate.* "Fiorenza can't change things because she wants her son at the head of the family."

"Do I need to remind you of your lessons?" I asked. "Father's seat belongs to the person he chooses to pass it to."

"Father isn't here," Beniamo said. "Now turn around."

I tried to master the shivering that came over me in fits. I had Father's knife in my sleeve, and I thought about drawing it, but I couldn't fight Beniamo and win. Not that way.

The smallest, bitterest wisp of a smile came over Beniamo's face. "You want to watch? Maybe you really are my sister."

Like a silver wing, the knife flew toward the delicate veins in Luca's wrist. The magic that had been waiting to have its way with Beniamo since the nursery exploded from me. I had no time to think, to ask for anything. Beniamo dropped the knife. Luca, who had been pouring himself out of his lungs, went silent.

A new sound filled the chamber—throaty, hollow, in-human.

Where Beniamo had stood a moment before, an owl thrashed. It clearly didn't know how to work its enormous wings, mottled black and brown. Orange eyes, as bright as every moment of pain Beniamo had given me, froze me in place. With fresh confidence, the owl sped at me, tail fanned and talons curled. I crouched to avoid being slashed. Beniamo passed me with a gust that could have blown out a hundred candles.

I had transformed my brother. Even if he had hurt me, even if he had wanted to kill Luca, he was my brother. I took this new guilt and ripped it out of me. I'd done what I needed to do. I had kept Beniamo from taking Luca away. I couldn't lose him, not after Mother had left me, not with Father on his deathbed.

But wasn't that what Beniamo had said? He only wanted to protect what was his?

I clamped my arms over my stomach, sick at the notion that I was no better than my brother. No. That couldn't be right. I had tried to keep Beniamo from hurting countless other people.

Of course, I might have failed at that too.

"An *owl*?" I asked the magic. "You've given him claws, a beak, and an excuse to be heartless."

When I turned around, I found Luca pointing one hand at the place where Beniamo had changed. Blood dripped from his fingers, but he barely seemed to notice. My little brother stared at me as if I had picked up the entire world and moved it an inch to the left.

Two

Every Drop of Magic

Luca and I rushed up a narrow path.

The trail met with the dirt road that pulled travelers across the Uccelli. Trees closed in above us, splintering the moonlight. I could hardly tell shadows from sharp ruts, and yet I kept a breathless pace. I knew the turns of this path as well as I knew my own body. But hours passed, and each step grew less familiar. The road became a stranger.

The owl that used to be my brother sounded its hollow call in the trees. Before leaving the castle I'd raced up to the kitchens and chased him out with the good saucepan. I hated to loose him on the world, but I couldn't leave Father, Fiorenza, and my sisters locked up with a monster, especially one of my own making.

"We'll rest after sunrise," I told Luca, not wanting to stop with Beniamo so close. Every time the owl's sharp, empty cry spread through the forest, my body readied for an attack.

I kept one hand on Father's knife.

At some hazy point, after so much walking that my feet became the high note in an aria of discomfort, one spot in the sky turned raw pink. A procession of colors followed—gold, poppy, crimson—before the sun made its grand entrance.

In the distance, the Uccelli's highest peak attempted to conquer the sky. White veins of marble, thick as tears, ran down the sides. With Weeping Mountain in sight, I believed for the first time that we might reach Amalia. "We came a good way," I said, dropping my pack at the side of the road. "Let's rest while we can."

"Now," Luca said, giving me the grave look he usually reserved for disagreements with Father. "Are you planning to tell me about your secret life?"

Outrage and confusion fought for the right of place, and outrage won. "You're upset with me?"

"How could you keep this to yourself?" Luca asked, falling out of his anger like a loosely tied knot. "I was *right there*, Teo."

I knelt beside my pack and rolled out my traveling cloak on a patch of stiff grass, too tired to seek out a better place.

"I didn't want to force you to play the role of secret keeper," I mumbled. "It wouldn't have been fair."

"Fair?" Luca asked, a little-brotherly tone creeping into his voice. "I've told you everything, all my life. And you sit right there with the most important scientific discovery in ages in your pocket!"

"That's what you're thinking about?" I shouted into the brightening sky. "Science?"

I pulled out a round of bread from my pack, and Luca immediately sat forward. This was the truest magic in Vinalia at work—any problem, no matter how large or small, could be solved with food. The bread broke into tempting pieces, scorched dark at the edges and frothy white at the center, but the bandages I'd torn for Luca from the bottom of my spare dress proved too thick, and he couldn't grasp the handful I offered. His breath thickened with frustration. I finally tore off a mouthful and fed him. Luca talked right over it. "I can't believe you hoarded this knowledge," he said, turning thoughtful as he chewed. "So you're able to change people. . . ."

"Not just people," I admitted.

"My guess," Luca said, working himself into a theoretical fever, "is that magic works in a kind of symbiosis."

I tried to pick apart the unfamiliar word. "A . . . symbolic rash?"

Luca snorted. "It's a sort of coexistence. In all the stories, magic and streghe go hand in hand. It takes on a particular form, because you *are* the form. Magic needs a strega to work," he said.

And a strega is incomplete without her magic. I repeated the thought aloud to Luca.

His neck bobbed with an eager nod. "It needs a person to settle in. A home, if you like. You give it a place to put down roots and it gives you . . . well . . ."

"The ability to change brothers into owls," I muttered.

"Yes, but think of what else you might do!" Luca said. "Think of the old stories. There were evil streghe, sure, but most were trying to solve some problem. They used magic and cleverness for the common good."

"What do you think I've been doing?" I asked darkly, standing up and wiping crumbs from the lap of my dress onto the starved late-summer grass. I turned out my pack, dumping everything I had put in so carefully the night before. "Look," I said, brandishing the mirror, the rose plant, the beads. "This was a man who wanted to kill Father because he thought it would be easier than paying his taxes. Here is a woman who wrote a letter threatening the lives of the di Sangro children, because she lost one of her own. Oh, look! The Uccelli priest caught stealing from his church-goers, lire that none of them could afford to lose, and using the money to buy wine and women. This is what I've done with my *selfish magic*."

Luca's eyes skipped away from me like a hastily thrown rock.

"My secret kept you alive in the dungeons," I said, "and that's only the beginning." I summoned confidence and pushed it into my words. I needed my little brother to believe, not just in magic. In me. "I'm going to change into a boy by the time we reach Amalia. I'm going to answer the summons."

Luca stared down at his hands, the bandages fraying to feathery ends. "And how exactly are you going to do that?"

"I've seen it before," I said, supplying the details a little too eagerly. "A person who could take different forms. The strega had a book that seemed to control the changes."

"We need that strega," Luca said.

The magic trembled. "Maybe . . ." I said, giving the word the full weight of my doubt. I didn't want to believe that the person I'd accused of killing Father had become our best chance of saving him.

I curled tight on the ground and tried to sleep, throwing my arms over my face to defend against the daylight. It attacked from all sides, prickling my neck and searing the back of my eyelids. After an hour of useless striving, I stomped to my feet. Luca slept, but not restfully. He whimpered and thrashed. I sat with my knees in a peak at my chest, caught between releasing Luca from the net of his dreams and marching forward with no real plan, and staying here as time slid away from us.

I heard a sound, a great *flick*. I knew what that meant as surely as I knew the slender form of my strega as he rounded a corner in the path. He was back in boyish form and fully clothed. The greenish-purple cloak swirled around his shoulders, tossed by high mountain winds.

Hope and fear tangled in my chest like worried bedsheets.

Luca rolled over, blinking fretfully against the sun's glare. "Who is this?" He looked up as the strega neared. "Who are you?"

Instead of answering, the strega pulled out the book I'd seen by the ravine, leather binding worn soft by touch. As he opened it, I leaned forward, and my curiosity was met with an expanse of white.

The pages were blank.

Bravado stretched from the strega's broad smile down to the quick, sure movement of his hand. *Flick, flick, flick.* He ruffled the edge of the book.

"You could just say good morning," I said.

"Is this the other strega you told me about?" Luca asked, standing and beating dust off his clothes with his forearms, avoiding the flats of his hands. I nodded, but when I went to tell Luca more about the stranger I'd met on the mountain, I found my mind barren.

"Who are you?" I asked.

"Answering that would take my entire life," he said, as if that much should be obvious. "Every moment, I'm a different person than I was the one before."

I shook my head at the strega's answer. We could not afford to waste precious heartbeats before we reached Amalia. "What's your *name*?" I asked, hoping for a straightforward response.

"Cielo," he said—a single word, made soft and lovely by his accent, which seemed to flutter from one end of Vinalia to the other.

"You're making that up." I had never heard of anyone named after the sky. It sounded like the strega's own invention. And he had skipped the family part entirely.

"It's true I picked Cielo for myself, but every name is made up by someone," he said softly. "They are all lies, or none of them are."

Luca tipped his chin toward the strega's book. "Are those spells?"

The strega clapped the book shut as if closing a door in our faces. "Have you been feeding this boy nonsense for breakfast? Spells are tricky and often spill trouble everywhere. Rhymes are best kept in their fairy-tale cages. Magic runs much deeper than spells."

"How do you know that?" I asked, my voice windswept with jealousy.

"I know all kinds of things about streghe." He gave a small, victorious smile. "That is why you need me."

I already regretted lending him the idea. But what if the strega *could* teach me to change?

"Luca, will you walk ahead?" I asked.

"I won't be far," he said, casting an eye backward as he headed down the dusty road, as if he had to protect me and not the other way around.

"Why did you send him ahead?" Cielo asked. "The boy clearly wants to know more. Shouldn't we reward that sort of thing?"

It's not his to know, the magic said. *It's yours.*

It was more than that, though. "My worry isn't Luca

knowing more about magic. It's *you* knowing more about *him*. You were following us, weren't you?"

"Traveling alongside you," he corrected. "And I wasn't the only one. You had an owl on your trail. Two great brown wings. Eyes like pumpkins on fire."

I pressed my fingers to my eyes as if I could squeeze away all the trouble I'd created. Even if I found an antidote and Father woke up, there was no way I could face him. I had taken away his son.

"Are you all right?" the strega asked in a soft tone.

I wished the weakness I'd shown was something I could touch, because I'd have torn it to pieces. "I have to get to Amalia as quickly as possible and answer a summons from the Capo. As you might have heard, I need to be a boy."

I felt the strega's eyes on my body, taking in my softness, my roundness, my obvious breasts. I was sure he knew the stories about slim girls stuffing their bodies into clothing meant for boys, lowering their voices to a pebbly pitch. That would never work for me.

"Magic is clearly the right choice," Cielo said.

The road thinned along the edge of the mountains, turning into a series of ledges. On one side rock rose up in gashes. On the other, a boundless fall. The strega and I barely had enough room to walk side by side. His shoulder pressed against mine, and my heart skittered like a rockslide. "I would ask for your help, but I don't know anything about you, except that you are an attempted murderer."

"I carried a letter," the strega said. "The last time I checked, that makes me a postman."

"There was magic bound to that paper. You're telling me you carried it all that way and had no clue?"

Cielo winced. "I've never been good at finding magical objects. People, yes. But objects are so dull and lifeless."

"Not mine," I muttered.

We reached a bit of ledge so thin that I couldn't imagine us both traversing it at the same time. I wouldn't let the strega go first, putting him closer to Luca. I also didn't want him behind me, in an easy position to push me off a cliff. I settled on walking with my back to the rock and scuttling sideways. Amusement tugged at the strega's lips. "What?" I asked sharply.

"Are you sure you can't change form? You'd make a magnificent crab." He strode over the narrow finger of rock as if hurtling to his death had never occurred to him.

"You took a job from the Capo," I said. "Why?"

"For a variety of reasons, none of them to do with your father," Cielo said. "Well, none to do with *hurting* your father."

"You see!" I cried. "The longer you speak, the less sense you make. I need some thread of truth to hold on to, otherwise we'll both fall." It wasn't quite one of Father's sayings, but I thought he would approve. "I will ask questions and you will give answers. *True* answers. If you refuse or lie, I'll turn you into a . . ." The magic wouldn't give me any ideas, so I had to go digging for one. "A briny olive."

"At least I'll still be delicious," the strega said, dark eyebrows lofted. His sense of mischief never slept.

"How did you keep up with us?" I asked.

"I've been in a blustery form," he said, twirling his fingers.

"That first time I saw you on the mountain—*you* were the cloud."

He smiled, seeming proud of me for catching up, which made me want to rattle the superiority out of him. "It's not an easy thing, being weather. Very . . . moist." He twitched from head to toe, as if casting droplets from his body. "But it does get a person across mountains in a hurry."

"How do I know that the letter you brought to the castle wasn't poisoned by your own hand?" I asked.

"Because all I do is change form," he said, stepping lightly over rocks that had slid and scattered across the ledge. "So unless I *was* the poisoned letter . . ."

I shifted my pack so I could hold a warning finger up to his face. "If it has somehow escaped your notice until now, this is not a whimsical matter." I pulled Father's knife out of my sleeve, using the promise of its sharpness to push Cielo a step backward. He balanced between the tip of the blade and the fall.

"Teo!" Luca shouted from farther down the path. "What are you doing?"

"Yes, Teo," the strega echoed thinly. "What *are* you doing?"

"Proving that if you treat my family's lives as a game, you will lose." The point of the stiletto trembled in the air between us as I held it to the soft place where his neck met his chest. The strega's eyes glistened as bright as the sky behind him. As sharp as the rocks beneath.

"Can you help me?" I asked.

"I never really learned how to change," Cielo admitted. "Only to control it. But you do have magic. Perhaps you can be taught."

"That would make you my . . . tutor?" I asked. I'd never had a tutor before. I didn't think they were people you held at knifepoint.

"A magic tutor." Cielo's voice played over the words. "I'm not overly fond of titles, but I do like that."

"What do you want in return?" I asked, prepared for him to demand money, favors, the protection of the di Sangro family.

"It's nothing, really," Cielo said, but the grave look on his face cut against the grain of his words. "You're going to answer the Capo's summons. I want to be with you. In the Palazza."

"I don't see why you would need my help there. Don't they know you? You delivered a letter for the Capo."

"I delivered a letter to your *father* in the hopes of gaining an audience. It's possible the original messenger was . . . convinced to give his charge over to me in return for a trifling bit of magic. It is rather convenient to have your own personal raincloud for a day. And I'll admit that drenching people isn't bad work if you can come by it."

I twisted my lips, considering. If the strega spoke the truth, he wasn't working for the Capo. It didn't mean he could be trusted, but at least I had a thread to hold on to.

"Agreed," I said, withdrawing the knife slowly.

"You know, streghe don't seal their bargains with blood," Cielo said, skimming past me on the ledge.

"What do they use?" I asked, eagerness breaking through my voice.

Your first lesson, the magic said.

"Can't you guess?" the strega asked. "They kiss."

He must have gotten the startle he wanted, because his mouth bloomed into a full smile, as bright as a whole field of poppies.

❧

THE DAY TURNED HOTTER AS WE WALKED, BUT I PUSHED US forward into the folds of the Uccelli without stopping. Every time Luca stumbled, I became more determined to save him from the fate waiting at the end of this road.

Just as the sun capped the sky, Cielo disappeared, striking off into the brush.

"You've lost your strega," Luca said.

"He's not *my* strega," I insisted, even though that was exactly how I'd thought of him when he appeared on the path.

Brush rustled, parting like a curtain to reveal a girl, as brightly pale and inescapable as the sun overhead. Cielo wore the same clothes she had a minute before—trousers, a loose white shirt. They hung differently against her skin, but it didn't feel like seeing a different person. It was more like reading the same word twice and finding a new shade of meaning.

"So you *are* a girl," Luca said, staring at the strega.

"Is that what your sister told you?" Cielo asked, her bootheels hitting the path briskly, her voice as sweet and low as honey stuck at the bottom of the jar.

I rushed to defend myself. "That's not what I said."

"And what did you?" Cielo asked, a challenge in the way she slung her night-black hair behind her shoulder.

"Sometimes you appear as a girl, sometimes a boy." I watched Cielo's backside as she strode ahead, and more words came. "When you're a girl, you have a bit of boyishness about you. And when you're a boy, the girlishness stays."

We reached a fork in the road, and the strega pointed us down the right path, her broad hands stretched into knuckled hills and valleys. "It's true that I contain more than one thing," Cielo said. "And sometimes the balance shifts."

Understanding rustled through me, soft as leaves. It wasn't quite the same, but I'd often felt I didn't fit inside the boundaries of the word *girl*. It reminded me of a country I could happily visit, but the longer I stayed, the more I knew I couldn't live there all the time. There were moments when I sorely wished to be free of the confines of this body, the expectations it seemed to carry. I'd looked to Mirella for a sign she felt the same way, but she seemed perfectly settled in her kingdom.

It helped when the magic arrived. It wasn't male or female. It simply *was*.

"I can't figure out if I should be using the word *he* or *she* or something else entirely," Luca told Cielo, as if admitting to a small crime.

"Either will do," Cielo said with a warm laugh that melted the nervous, penitent look from my little brother's face. "Though all of those words feel a bit like coats that are too tight in the elbows."

"And the other forms you take?" Luca asked, back to his scientific inquiry. I could see him jotting notes, though he had no paper or ink.

"Those came later," Cielo said. "All things I learned or chose."

"So you *do* know how to stretch your magic?"

"I suppose," Cielo said, holding out her hand to me. "We are about to find out."

"You mean . . . a magic lesson?" I had always thought I would boldly cast myself into the study of magic, but with the fate of the entire di Sangro family in the balance, any excitement I felt quickly tumbled into a pit of nerves.

"We should get started," Cielo said, weaving her fingers together in anticipation. "Only two days left to Amalia."

I nodded at Luca to keep walking. "Don't stray too far."

My little brother sighed. "You know, if this works, and you take my place, you're going to have to let me go off to Gravina *by myself*. That's a bit farther than just down the path."

Before I could decide whether to outline my fears until Luca saw them clearly or apologize to save time, he tramped off.

Cielo frowned at me with a little knot in her forehead.

"What?" I asked. "Don't you have any brothers or sisters?"

"That boy is right, you know," Cielo said, stepping around the question like a particularly sharp stone on the path. "You can't protect him forever. Now, shall we start?"

The magic burst through me like flowers that had been waiting for the right season. "Yes," I said, breathless and ready.

"Tell me what it feels like when you work magic," Cielo said, her tone less harsh and narrow than Father's teaching voice. It left room for me to give, not just a right answer or a wrong answer, but *any* answer.

As long as it was true.

"Veria, help me," I said, invoking the old goddess of truth in a whisper. I had never faced such a question. All my life, people had told me how I felt. They told me what they saw when they looked at me and how it compared to what they should see. Everyone treated me like the odd second daughter of the di Sangro family. No one asked what I *felt*.

"When there is no way forward, I find one," I said. "I close my eyes. . . . There's a comfort in that kind of darkness. Luca once told me scientists say the beginning of time was darkness, like in God's Book, but it wasn't empty. Everything in creation came out of it. That's how this feels. Potent and brimming. I open my eyes, and anything could be there."

Cielo stared at me, unblinking. I had never been an object of fascination before. "Your power changes the world around you, but now you need to change *yourself*. Somehow." The last word was a stumble, reminding both of us that Cielo couldn't see a clear path to changing me into a boy.

"Your magic is turned inward," I said. "You are the one who changes. Can you tell me how *that* feels?"

I thought Cielo would inform me that magic tutors didn't appreciate their students twisting the lesson and pointing it back at them. Instead the strega closed her eyes, her lashes the soft lines of a charcoal drawing. She spread her arms and arced her chest to meet the mountain wind. "It feels like catching a breeze," Cielo said. "Or letting a cold stream play over your fingers."

She took out her book and held it loosely in both hands. The bravado that usually painted over her features, bright and glorious, was gone. Her eyes softened, barely focused, her lips parting as if more truth might fall at any moment. She was trading her experiences for mine, letting them mingle together to see what came of it.

I had never been taught like this.

I turned away, afraid she would catch me blushing, which would only feed the fire in my chest.

"Let's try something," Cielo said, pocketing the book as she started us walking again. Little white flowers pricked the side of the path, tiny stitches in a dark green blanket. "Look around you."

"Just . . . look?" I asked. For all that I wanted to learn about magic, impatience blazed. I needed to learn *fast*.

"Smell what there is to smell," Cielo said. "Feel everything that can be felt. But do not attach names to anything. Do not tell yourself, 'That is a rock and that is a twig and I am a mighty di Sangro.'"

I pursed my lips, pursed my entire face. "What do you believe that will accomplish?" I sounded like a small, girlish echo of Father.

Cielo shook her head softly. "If you are thinking like that, you have already failed."

I faced the path. For the first time all day, I saw more than a line leading us to Amalia. Pebbles studded the path under our feet, and many held crystal flecks that Fiorenza would have noted for their beauty. Flowers lined the path, but also mosses and ferns and tiny trees that took their chances against the hard, stripping winds. Cielo walked behind me and off to one side, and my awareness of the strega felt slightly stronger than my awareness of everything else.

When we had been walking at this pace for an hour, drinking in the world, she whispered, "Now you may think the names."

Rock, I thought as I stepped over one. *Branch*, I thought as one crackled in the brush.

"Out loud, please!" Cielo called, her voice clanging against the mountains.

"That is a rock and that is a twig and I am a mighty di Sangro," I said, pointing at each. But it sounded absurd. "I might as well say that is a rock"—I pointed at a tree—"and *that* is a twig"—I pointed at a deer off in the woods—"and that is a mighty di Sangro." I capped it off by pointing at the Weeping Mountain itself.

"Good," Cielo said, stepping in line with me.

"You want me to spin my brain in circles?" I asked. "You want the world to be dizzy and meaningless?"

Cielo swirled so that she walked backward, facing me. "I want you to see that the world is not such a fixed thing, Teodora." It was the first time the strega had said my name. I heard it as something familiar made new, a view I had been looking at for so long without truly seeing.

"Now try your magic," Cielo said.

"*I need to change into a boy,*" I said on a ragged breath. I couldn't remember the last time I had spoken to the magic out loud. It had never felt safe in Chieza, or the castle, where someone might overhear me. But since I knew that Cielo was a strega, a trickle of freedom worked its way through me, like sunshine finding its way through the cracks between tightly woven branches.

Cielo tilted her head deeply. "You do realize you're speaking the old language."

I looked up, losing half my focus. "What?"

"The words that came from your lips weren't Vinalian. Not any dialect I know, and I know"—Cielo counted on her fingers—"nine."

I had never learned the old language. I'd heard the words twice a week, during mass and novena, but they were more ancient than the church in Prai. People had used them in the time of the old gods, well before the worship of a single one swept the land like a fever. "This will never work,"

I cried. "I don't know the language I'm speaking, let alone how to use it!"

Cielo breathed, in the deep, frustrating way of people who have all the time in the world. "Don't make me tutor you in patience as well."

The sun had taken on a hint of flame that meant another day would soon burn itself out. "If I am not a boy in less than two days, the Capo will claim Luca. My father will die of the strega poison in his system. My stepmother, my sisters will be at the mercy of—"

"*Stop*," Cielo commanded.

"I can't," I said. "I need to save them."

"My mother disappeared when I was an infant," she said in a small, tight voice. "My father, either dead or gone." Cielo looked up to the sky, the colors in her eyes kindled by the dying sun. "I thought losing her was enough. I thought it would never happen again. Now . . . streghe have begun to disappear from Amalia."

I shifted on sweating legs, unable to speak.

"That's why I came to the Uccelli," Cielo said, "following a rumor that my mother was seen in these mountains shortly before she vanished. I wanted to check the ledgers of the legendary Niccolò di Sangro. I thought if I knew what happened to her eighteen years ago, it would give me a place to start."

"What did you find?" I asked.

"I don't believe you care," Cielo said. "It has nothing to do with your *di Sangro business*."

I could tell from the hard seal of her lips that she wouldn't be moved. "You mentioned other streghe," I said. "How many are there? Why haven't I met one?"

Cielo shrugged. "We aren't very interested in being

numbered. The last era of magic in Vinalia ended five hundred years ago, when the church buried a great number of streghe without bothering to kill them first. That's how the Order of Prai was formed." The origins of the harshest branch of the church flooded my mind, vile and yet unsurprising. The Order of Prai had gone through long bouts of executing heretics. Apparently streghe were first among them. How had so much I needed to know been left out of my lessons?

I scrabbled backward in time. Five hundred years. That lined up with the strega stories. "Magic was truly part of life in Vinalia?"

"As common as breathing and dancing and dying," Cielo said.

It felt like I was eating ripe fruit by the handful and somehow growing hungrier. I needed to know more. "Did you learn all of this from the streghe who raised you?"

"Yes, I was raised by a pack of wild streghe," Cielo said with a humorless laugh. She rubbed her eyes with both hands, blocking out a sunset that poured over mountain peaks like thin, watery blood. "Every time you tell me your troubles, all I can think is . . . you still have a family to save."

6

The sun disappeared behind the mountains, tossing a hard line of cold. Cielo spread her cloak at the side of the path like a shimmering puddle. When Luca and I didn't stop, she called out. "People traditionally rest at night."

"We can't," I said.

"Because getting to Amalia is so important, you'd rather die of sleeplessness?" Cielo asked, sitting down cross-legged. "That makes sense."

Exhaustion broke me into small cold pieces. I wanted nothing more than to set my pack down and inch toward the strega's warmth. "It's not that," I said. "Beniamo is following us."

"Who is Beniamo?" Cielo asked.

"The owl," Luca said.

"Our brother," I answered in the same moment.

Cielo whistled, low and impressed. "You changed your brother into that lantern-eyed beast?"

"I didn't mean to," I said. "Well, I *did*. The wings were a last-second mistake."

Luca fiddled with his bandages. "Teo only used her magic because he attacked me."

Cielo tilted her head, considering me from a new angle. She sprang to her feet. "I have an idea. Do you mind if I borrow your sister?"

"She belongs to no man, woman, or strega," Luca said. "But you're welcome to try."

Cielo pulled me toward the woods.

"I can't leave Luca," I said.

My brother threw his cloak on the ground. "We haven't heard the owl since we were near the castle. Maybe Beniamo gave up. More likely, he couldn't find the road. Our brother wasn't smart even when he had a much larger brain."

Luca's well-reasoned truth melted the iciest of my defenses. "When I come back," I said, "I'll be your brother."

"If you take my place in Amalia, you'll need to be *me*."

I hurried to set up a small camp for Luca, unable to leave him without taking care of everything first. I wrenched the hardened bread into pieces, tore the last chunk of cheese from the glue of the rind. "You really think that will work?"

"Better than inventing a new di Sangro heir out of flimsy cloth," Cielo said.

"I'm not *flimsy*," I muttered.

Luca picked at the food with his bandaged hands. They were still healing, but he'd gotten better at working around the pain. "I haven't been over the mountains since I was seven. Everyone will see the resemblances between us and believe I grew up into . . . you."

I turned to Cielo, as close to an impartial party as we would find. "Do we look enough alike for that to work?"

The strega huffed a breath as she squinted from me to Luca. "You both have bitterly dark brown eyes and a special way of glaring out of them."

I grabbed her arm and headed for the woods. As they greeted us with leafy darkness, I called back, "If I'm Luca di Sangro, who will you be?"

My little brother looked up at the stars—so many and so close here in the mountains. "A student at the university. A scientist in Gravina. Anyone I please." I tried to imagine what that would be like, but my mind went as blank as the darkness between the stars.

※

"I'M GOING TO ATTACK YOU," CIELO SAID.

"What?" The trees above us cast long, toothy shadows. Cielo looked strange in the silvery light, and when she smiled at me, the deep curve of her lips carried the promise of trouble.

"That story about changing your brother into an owl . . . You use magic to defend your family, don't you?"

I nodded. It was the thing I knew best. The skill I had practiced and honed to a sharp edge.

Cielo walked through the woods, drawing the boundaries of a space with rocks and twigs. Soon we had a small hand-made battlefield. The strega came full circle and stood in front of me. She looked me over, her eyes barbed with doubt. "Hopefully, when you feel the urge to defend a di Sangro, your magic will put on its best show."

I cast a confused look around the grove. "There is no di Sangro here to defend."

"I didn't think you would approve of using Luca for magic practice," Cielo said.

"You're a quick study," I said flatly.

Cielo tapped the spot halfway between my chest and my shoulder, an unnamed territory that I had never been truly aware of until she lit it on fire with a touch. "In this case, the di Sangro will have to be you."

I was about to admit that I didn't care about my own safety nearly as much as Luca's, but then Cielo stepped closer. I could see the dark pits at the centers of her eyes. I started to ask what she meant to do to me, but the bridge from my mind to my tongue felt broken. Her lips touched my cheeks, swift and light. The kisses didn't vanish—they wandered down the length of my body.

"So streghe really do seal their agreements with a kiss," I said.

"I told you I'm not a liar," Cielo whispered.

"My turn." I stepped in and kissed the highest peak of Cielo's cheekbone. It looked sharp, but her skin felt softer than morning air.

"Ah," Cielo said. "So you are learning."

She drew the book from her pocket.

It seemed an unfair balance, one strega with an enchanted book to help her change and the other with only stubborn magic and a great need, but before I could open my mouth to protest, Cielo peeled out of her clothes with haste and purpose. I had seen bodies before, in all states. Bathing, sleeping. On long walks through the woods near Chieza, I had passed more than one couple in the deeps of lovemaking. There was no shame in bodies.

Still, I angled my cheek slightly, and swallowed the impulse to look as if I'd taken a long, heady swig of wine.

Flick.

Instead of a boy or a girl or even a bird, I faced a tangle

of snakes. They poured over the leather cover of the book, scales black with a green-purple shimmer. They moved toward me fast, bodies spilling over each other.

"*Change*," I told the magic, the old language reaching my ears, powerful and strange.

How will being a boy help? the magic argued. Apparently speaking out loud wouldn't be enough to convince it.

"*Change into anything.*"

But my magic had its own ideas. It left me like a rope cast outward, reaching through the grove. The shadow of a tree branch became a snare, stretched long and then pulled tight around the batch of snakes.

They hissed in unison.

"Well, that's what you get for choosing something poisonous," I said. The word carried me back to Father.

I drew a hard breath.

A single snake tugged out of its shadowy hold and worked its way back to the book, knocking it open to a new page.

Flick.

Standing on the cloak, padded feet rough on the silk, was a wolf. It could hardly be compared to the Uccelli's wolves, their gray coats so thin they looked balding in places, bones sticking out at desperate angles. This wolf had a rich black pelt and steady eyes marbled with many colors. Cielo's eyes.

The wolf bared its long throat, pointed its nose toward the moon, and let out a slippery howl. My body remembered how to be afraid all at once.

"*Change*," I told the magic.

The wolf ran at me, feet tearing at the ground, fur rising. My magic reached and grabbed at a fallen tree branch. With a dry snap, it became a bone the color of whitewash, a meaty scent pulling the wolf's attention away from me.

I dropped to my heels and reached out to Cielo. The wolf drew back, howling again, putting on a show, but the strega's intelligence shone through the wolf's eyes even as it bayed and snarled.

The strega was trying to scare me.

To help me.

I reached for the place behind the wolf's ears—an old instinct, from the time when we kept hounds in the castle, before Beniamo took them out to hunt and never brought them back. We found their bones a year later in the woods between the castle and Chieza.

I moved on to the fur at the wolf's neck, kneading its pelt, and Cielo let out a low rustle of a sigh. The strega pushed into my hand, a sudden wave of pleasure that almost knocked me backward.

"Does turning you into my pet win the round?" I asked.

Cielo's wolf eyes narrowed. The strega stalked away, hackles up. One paw to the edge of the book, and *flick*. Cielo was a boy again, perfectly naked.

"*Like that*," I told the magic, challenging myself to keep my eyes on the strega as his long body unfurled in the moonlight. He caught me staring and raised one potent eyebrow. *If Cielo can do it, so can you.*

"So," I said as Cielo pulled on his trousers, his shirt. "Did I win?"

"The point isn't to trick me," Cielo said. "The point is to change, and you haven't."

The strega's argument came to pieces in my hands. It might be true that I was nowhere closer to being a boy, but

I *had* changed, even if no one else would notice the shift. I didn't fear the strega anymore. Which meant this little game would never work. I didn't believe that Cielo would hurt me, not even to bring my magic to the surface.

Cielo walked around the grove, sniffing at the air as if it held untold secrets. He had a bit of the wolf in him, a set of instincts that stayed in place. I wondered what would happen if I set my hand to his sleek, dark hair.

He raised his nose, as if catching a thread of scent. "There's someone near."

"Luca?" I asked.

"No," Cielo said shortly, but his eyes betrayed him. There was more.

"You're being followed too?" It wasn't fair to be irritated with Cielo for drawing trouble, since I had plenty of my own, but I couldn't stop anger from prickling up and down my skin.

"The use of magic must have pulled him toward us," Cielo said.

"Who?" The strega kept his silence, and I thought of what he'd said—that I didn't care about anything but di Sangro business. "Please tell me," I said. "I can help."

"A strega named Adolfo who lives in this part of the Uccelli," Cielo said. "I stayed with him when I was a child."

Cielo had mentioned living with streghe all over Vinalia, but I'd never dreamed one could be close to the di Sangro castle. Pain knocked at my heart, like a door I didn't wish to open. I could have known Cielo for most of my life, instead of a few short days. "No one lives up here," I said stubbornly.

"Which is exactly why he likes it," Cielo said.

"Why doesn't he come greet you, then?"

"The last time we parted, it wasn't pleasant. He knew something about my mother he wouldn't tell me." Cielo wiped a hand over his forehead, as if rubbing sore memories. "It feels like I've been asking about her my whole life."

In that moment, I felt a *flick* as sharp and clean as the turn of a page. The bargain I had made to get Cielo into the Palazza wasn't enough. He had given me hope of saving my family; I had to give him something just as valuable in return.

It was only fair.

"If that strega knows something about your mother, we have to get it from him," I said.

"And how do we do that?" Cielo asked with a wolfish snap.

I didn't have time to explain my di Sangro lessons. "Take me to Adolfo. I'll do the rest." Wariness caught in the strega's eyes, as if he didn't trust the help I'd offered. As if he didn't dare. "Are we following his scent?" I asked, marching into the woods.

"No need." Cielo caught up quickly. "Just listen for the sound of him tramping around. He's gotten used to moving without being seen, and it's made him sloppy." Cielo offered an explanation over his shoulder as branches stung me in the dark. "Adolfo's magic allows him to make anything invisible, though occasionally he does it the other way around."

"He can make people *see* the invisible?" I asked. "How?"

"Oh, he turns time into handbaskets," Cielo said. "Worries into slippery fish. That sort of thing."

I nodded, trying to pretend this was all normal.

"There," I said, pointing at a dim flicker of movement. Branches crackled, and the sound exploded into quick, thudding steps. Cielo started to run. The ground sloped upward, but the strega's feet fell as easy as a light rain. I'd been raised in the Uccelli and I found myself struggling to breathe, to keep pace, to stay at Cielo's shoulder so we wouldn't be parted in the dark.

The woods broke open, and I skidded onto stone that ran with rivers of sparkling white. We had reached Weeping Mountain. We picked our way over a field of rock that led to the buckled walls of the mountaintops. Cielo pointed at a place where the rules of the world seemed to fall away.

Moonlight drifted down, fragile and pale. What mattered more was where it *didn't* shine. I followed the lines of light as it fell, and found that in certain places it was strangely lacking. I picked out the shape of a house.

"Come out, Adolfo," I cried. "Or we'll come in. And from the way that you live, it seems you don't care for company."

Footsteps stirred. A man appeared from behind a thick wall of nothingness. He was slight, gray-haired, and barefoot, wearing endlessly patched old clothes. He worried his hands, sliding them over and over each other with a dry, rasping sound.

"Cielo," he said. "You look . . . older."

"Funny," Cielo said. "You look precisely the same."

"My friend tells me you have knowledge of his mother," I said in a tone like a rope that I tightened around his neck. "Knowledge that might prevent more streghe from disappearing."

"It's happening again?" Adolfo asked.

Cielo's head fell forward, a half nod. In that one small bowing of his neck I felt the weight of what Cielo had lost. His pack of wild streghe might not have been a perfect stand-in for his family, but they were the closest thing he had.

I thought of Mother, gone on the same day I was born. I had told myself that I would never again trade anyone I loved for a dull, aching pebble in my heart. And now I stood to lose them all.

"If you don't tell us, I'll let my father, Niccolò di Sangro, know there's a strega up here." I didn't bother to add that my father was trapped in a poisoned sleep and he might never wake.

Adolfo's lips twisted into a smile as sharp as a single thorn. "How would he find me? How would he even believe I existed in the first place?"

"Fine," I snapped. "You can deal with me instead." I turned to Cielo, but the strega looked far away, adrift in memories, or fears. "Shall I turn this man into a hare? We need something for supper."

"No," Cielo said, clearing his throat and playing along. "He would be stringy."

I stared at Adolfo, from his bare toes to the tattered ends of his hair. "What about wine? He'd make a fine old vintage."

"No doubt I'd be acid on the tongue," Adolfo offered. The first hints of fear snuck into his tone, and Father's voice came back to me. *Once a man has lost his footing, it's much easier to work him into a corner.*

I strode toward him, wanting him to feel my presence, my closeness. "All you need to do is tell us what you know about Cielo's mother, and you can live your invisible life for as long as you please. Unless you'd like me to turn your little cottage into gold and draw travelers from all over Vinalia."

A bolt of true fear shot through Adolfo's eyes. "You couldn't."

I pointed at a plain gray pebble on the ground. "*Gold,*"

I said in the old language, a word that glowed rich on my tongue. I picked up the pebble and then grabbed Adolfo's palm, setting the proof between us.

The gold bent the moonlight toward it, greedy.

"Of course, you wouldn't want to leave your home, but I could turn you into a statue to adorn the grounds. Gold plating would be nice. If you're made of pure gold, you'll be too soft and the littlest thing will melt you."

Cielo looked at me, mildly stunned, and I felt the brush of victory. If only I could face the Capo in Amalia like this.

But Adolfo wasn't done with me. He reached out one hand, slightly curved, as if he would cap my head with his palm. It shivered an inch away, harder and harder. "Oh, look," he said, curling his palm closed and then flashing it open to show me a smooth, dark stone. "Here is a fear." He closed his fist and tapped my head with one spiked knuckle. "Here is another." A new stone appeared next to the first. "Another." Dark stones rained from his closed hand, falling to the ground at my feet. They piled until they were higher than my ankles. "You can walk away without any of these," Adolfo said, his voice gilded with promise. "You don't have to carry them anymore."

I felt strangely light. Cielo watched me with one hand on his face, as if all were lost, but I couldn't understand why.

Everything was wonderful.

"What about your father?" Cielo asked. "Luca? Your stepmother, your sisters?"

His chant left a scratch in my happiness, but it healed over quickly. "They're fine," I said. No—that was a lie. "They'll be fine without me." That felt slightly more true, so I nodded to hammer the notion in place.

I knew, vaguely, that Father had fallen ill and Luca was unhappy. My stepmother and sisters had been left to run the castle alone, and they were afraid of—something. When I tried to remember what, it seemed as far off as the light from a faded star.

"Don't worry," I told Cielo. The strega's look pierced my skin, and his fears traveled straight into me.

Cielo's mother.

He didn't even know if she was dead or not.

When that fear found a place inside me, I felt the space where the rest of them should be, rubbed raw and empty.

I knelt and picked up the stones. They weren't as smooth as they'd first looked, but gritty. They caught on my skin, threatening to rip me open. "You have to put them back inside of you, where they belong," Cielo said.

"How do I do that?" I snapped.

But the magic already knew. Its certainty moved straight to my fingers, telling them to pick up the stones. I slipped one into my mouth. It felt impossible to swallow. I pushed and pushed until it went down. I shoved more stones into my mouth, battled each one down my throat, my eyes thick with tears that I didn't remember summoning. I couldn't let them spill, though. Father wouldn't have wanted that. Father needed me to take care of Luca. To keep the Capo and his armies away from our home. Fears that I'd been feeling ever since Father had collapsed came back to me, a dark weight that lined my muscles and settled into my gut.

My eyes dried as they settled on Adolfo, who had dared to take this pain from me. It was horrible, but it was *mine*. "Now," I said, wiping my mouth with the back of my sleeve. "About that statue."

"Fine," Adolfo muttered. "You'll have your precious truth, and you'll see you didn't want it to begin with. You'll leave here *thanking* me for the years when you didn't have to carry it. There are things you don't tell children. Not when you . . ."

"What?" Cielo asked, taking a jagged step forward.

"Not when you care about them," Adolfo said, holding his chin high.

Cielo pursed his lips in bored disbelief, but I could see that the words had found their mark.

"If you love someone, you give them the truth," I said. The words burst out of me, bright and confident. Then I dimmed, remembering how long I had kept secrets from the people I loved most.

"You speak as if truth is the only gift that matters," Adolfo said. "You're young yet. Survive here long enough, and you'll learn that hiding is part of the price. Nobody wants to see all of a person. Human minds are too small to stretch around such a thing." The old strega turned toward his cottage, and Cielo and I moved to follow. Without turning to look at us, Adolfo called, "Leave the little di Sangro outside."

I crossed my arms, barely roping in my anger. "I'll be right here. Waiting."

Cielo looked at me as if I had done far more than threaten an old man with a golden cottage. I mustered a smile, letting the strega know that making the lives of dishonest men difficult was my pleasure. The two of them walked off together, and soon they were gone behind walls I couldn't see.

I crouched by the door and let my eyes fall heavy. Luca had taught me all about gravity, and I could feel it now, a strong hand pressing me down. But I couldn't rest—not yet. I started myself awake.

The night had grown into its shadows. The less I could see, the more each sound loomed large with importance. I heard the harsh scrape of insects, the tossing of wind in the high trees. Through the layers of night music, I listened for an owl.

Nothing.

But when I looked up, great wings tore open the sky.

7

It's your brother, the magic said.

The owl traced circles high above. I waited for him to dive at me, but his wings stayed outstretched. Weeping Mountain, the highest point in the Uccelli, offered a perfect view. Beniamo was looking for something. When he found his quarry, the owl broke the circle and cut a clean, dark path.

"Cielo!" I cried. "Cielo!" The strega didn't appear, and I couldn't wait for him to leave Adolfo's cottage.

My feet scraped over stone. I ran with my neck craned toward the sky. As I rushed back into the woods, tree branches and darkened leaves bit into my view. I tripped, fell to the path, and split my hand open on the blade of a rock's edge.

All I could think of was Luca, sleeping. Luca, with his hands not yet healed.

The owl soared out of sight, and no matter how quickly I ran, I couldn't track him. If Beniamo had set a course for Luca, there was only one way I might reach my little brother before he did.

I gave orders more firmly than I had in my entire life. *"Change me now."* My magic rose in stunning waves. This was what Cielo hadn't been able to give me in the woods when we fought: true fear.

Make me faster, make me fly. I could have been a wolf or a bird or a flutter of wind, anything that got me to Luca, but the magic poured out, and changed nothing.

"*Please,*" I said, no longer giving orders. Begging.

My feet kept hitting the path. My breath kept scratching uselessly at the night. I was still myself. Always myself.

When the woods spat me out onto the road, I spun to find Luca. There was his bedroll, his curled, sleeping body.

The owl circling above him.

I closed my eyes to summon magic. "*Change him into something minuscule this time,*" I told it. "*Tiny and powerless.*" Anger lashed through me, but not magic. I had used it up trying to transform.

I screamed. A raw, wordless sound. Beniamo changed direction, wings cutting the air silently. Eyes searing the dark.

The owl's claws tore at my midsection, one talon hooked into my breast, another sliding across my stomach. I hit the ground with a cry that seemed to fill every ravine, every sudden drop, every darkness in the Uccelli.

I touched my wounds, stinging and sticky with blood. I wondered if this was what men felt like when I pointed my magic at them. I didn't put them through pain like this, though. I didn't slash at them in the hopes of hearing them scream.

"Teo!" Luca cried.

I picked myself up.

"Teo!"

He fought the bird off with his feet, using his wounded hands to cover his neck and his chest. I reached for Father's knife. Luca's blood was already coursing through the dust, little rivulets and larger streams that ran down Weeping Mountain. That blood should have been red, but it turned black in the moonlight.

With one monstrous push of its wings, the owl lifted away from Luca, leaving him there on the ground, neck sliced to pieces. Blood draining fast. He gasped and looked up at me.

"You're not allowed to go," I said. "I've already promised to take your place." In the wild spin of losing him, I thought that I might be able to argue Luca out of dying.

It was what Father would have done.

"I'm scared," Luca said, reaching for me. I wondered how I had thought he was nearly a man. He was my Luca, my little brother. After Mother had died, I thought I would be wrapped in a thick gray sadness forever, and then Luca arrived, a child so serious, all I could think to do was smile at him.

I tried to smile now, but my mouth proved as useless as my magic. I looked from the gouged mess of his neck to his face, soft and perfect. I kept my eyes on his as the moonlight washed over him, stealing back years.

Until they were all gone.

Luca was gone.

Rocks gnawed at my knees, Luca's blood darkening my dress, a single thought slicing my mind. I had been waiting for his death. Not just for two days, but for so long. When I looked at my little brother, I'd seen a boy standing on the verge of the world and its cruelties. I had treated him like a soft creature who couldn't stand without my help.

Beniamo had killed Luca, but I hadn't saved him.

I hadn't believed he could save himself.

I screamed, because there was no use in keeping quiet anymore. I tossed myself against the rocks. Smashed my palms. I cried into the dirt, turning it black with tears. I called on the dark mercy of pain. I could live with a few more gashes. I couldn't bear to face Luca's death.

I pushed the air out of my body and the thoughts out of my head. I screamed into the night. "What will you do? Fly to the Capo and take your *rightful place?*" Each word was a wound, open to the night.

Cielo broke through the trees in boyish form, hair tousled, eyes sharp and restless. I wanted to scream at him, to blame him for Luca's death like I had blamed him for the letter that had poisoned Father.

But this wasn't the strega's fault. I had chosen to strike out into the woods, to chase Adolfo. I had wanted to help Cielo. I had wanted more selfish things too. To impress the strega. To learn about *magic*. I blinked against a rush of hate. It stung the backs of my eyelids.

Cielo took in my torn dress, Luca's body on the ground. He looked at Luca's neck with a certainty I wanted to rip away from him with both hands. "There has to be a way to bring him back," I said. "Magic that can—"

Cielo shook his head. "If he had died of magic, perhaps. Not this."

I got close to Cielo. The strega had a warmth that I both craved and hated. The warmth of a living body. "You can't know everything," I said. My voice sounded like raked coals. "This is what magic is *for*. To change things."

Cielo pressed his lips together. He wouldn't give me a way to bring Luca back. He only stared at me as if he understood.

I closed my eyes. I didn't want Cielo's sadness. I couldn't bear for there to be another drop in the world.

It would overflow.

"Teodora . . ." Cielo said. He was just a voice in the dark. I would not let him be more than that. "I'm sorry."

"Don't be," I said numbly. "This is what it means to be a di Sangro."

THE SUN BROKE OVER WEEPING MOUNTAIN, TURNING THE ROCK black as night, the white streams a pattern of lightning strikes. I sat on the road, unable to move from Luca's side.

"He needs a resting place," I said.

"Yes," Cielo said. "Of course." The strega had turned quiet and helpful in the wake of Luca's death, and I found I wanted the other version back. The Cielo who teased me and taught me magic. "What do you think is best?"

There was no simple solution. I couldn't take Luca back to the di Sangro castle. We would never make it to Amalia by the Capo's summons. We couldn't carry him on with us, not through woods thick with wild animals, not in summer when his body would start to give in to heat and the strangeness of being dead.

"We need a grave," I said.

Use me, the magic whispered.

It had returned to full strength, a fine thing now that Luca was dead and Beniamo flown. "Should I start digging?" Cielo asked softly.

I stood up roughly. Cielo had the good sense to stay silent as I walked around Luca and prayed. It was too late to invoke

Melae, so I kept to church prayers, taking out the string of beads I had packed, rubbing each in turn as I sped through the words. Numb words for a furious heart.

I vowed that if I saw Beniamo again, he would not live to scratch another soul. I would use magic if I could—and if I couldn't, there were other ways. Blunt, cruel ways, like the ones he had used on our brother.

I knelt and stared at the hard, rocky ground. I needed magic to do another impossible thing. I needed it to change packed earth into a hole.

How could I ask for that?

"*Turn the ground as empty as my heart feels,*" I told the magic.

I put my hand to the spot I had chosen for Luca, a shady bit of ground under the widespread leaves of a tree. When I blinked, the dirt was gone, leaving a hole that stretched from my feet. Cielo and I placed my brother inside, his body slipping and thumping to the ground, rolling slightly. This was not how we buried a di Sangro. But Luca had never wanted to be a di Sangro. In death, his wish had finally come true. He would rest here, nameless and forgotten.

"*Turn the air back to soil.*"

Luca's brown curls were already clotted with dirt, his skin a lacework of scratches. I closed my eyes, unable to face the knowledge that I was seeing him for the last time. When I looked again, the ground had turned solid. I grabbed Luca's pack, shouldering it along with my own. The doubled weight bothered me less than the obvious shape of the microscope Luca had packed with hopes of bringing it to Gravina. Before we left, I patted the prayer beads into the dusty earth so Luca would always have something of mine, and a lingering trace of magic.

And I left my little brother behind.

꧁✦꧂

CIELO AND I DESCENDED THE FAR SIDE OF WEEPING MOUNTAIN, emerging from a scruff of the woods onto a wide plain. It wasn't just the scenery that changed. Mountain air in the Uccelli felt as sharp and clean as a newly washed blade; it carved into a person's lungs. Here the air was soft and slightly perfumed, as if it had been dunked in soap and washed by hand. The road grew broad and the land around it held countless rows of grapevines twisted onto trellises.

"Amalia is less than a day's walk," Cielo said.

I nodded tightly. "I didn't need a reminder." With Beniamo in his new form, and Luca gone, no one else could possibly answer the Capo's summons. The fate of my entire family rested on this plan—on a change I still didn't know how to make.

When I cracked the silence between us, I didn't say any of that. "What did you learn in Adolfo's cabin?"

Cielo kicked at the dusty road. "Perhaps we shouldn't talk about it."

Everything in me, from my reason to my magic, objected fiercely. "We went all that way and I used my most terrifying voice and—"

"My mother is dead."

The strega's words were a dull blow. "Why didn't you say anything?"

Cielo shrugged his fine shoulders. I was starting to learn

the language of his gestures, the ways he formed meaning. A quick shrug meant the strega wanted to show how unbothered he was. But a lingering shrug meant he had too much to say, too many feelings piled, and no way to sort them.

"Tell me what Adolfo said," I insisted. "Everything." The strega had kept quiet this whole time, probably to avoid stepping on the raw heels of my grief. But I needed to believe that the guilt I felt over leaving Luca wasn't completely hollow.

"Adolfo said my mother's death was shadowed," Cielo said, treating the words like dirty rags, barely touching them with his voice. "He doesn't know the details, but there are streghe who do, and they won't even speak them."

The sun pressed down on us, with no mountains or trees for shade. I tugged down the shoulders of my dress, letting the heat perch on my shoulders like a firebird. "How can Adolfo be certain she's gone?"

"I asked the same question," Cielo said. "He told me he was absolutely sure, and when I reminded him of your threat, he gave me three words."

"Silly little di Sangro?" I asked.

Cielo laughed shortly. Then he went quiet for a moment. Even silence was different here, on the far side of the mountains. In the Uccelli, birdcalls and animal sounds and winds rushed to fill every gap. Even the quietest second bristled with life and death. This was the perfect, promising silence of a book opened to a new page.

"He said, *the brilliant death.*"

"Do you think that has anything to do with *the brilliant life*?" I asked as we passed another field of grape arbors.

"I have no idea," Cielo said, but from the lines carved

across his forehead, I could see the strega was set on finding out.

☙❧

AN HOUR LATER WE CAME TO A POND LIKE A JEWEL SET OFF-center in the fields.

"Shall we swim?" Cielo asked. The heat had been trying to kill us all afternoon. It was layered thick on top of us now, slowing our steps.

I looked down at my skin covered in dust and blood. I couldn't imagine storming into the Palazza like this, girl *or* boy, and expecting to be taken seriously. I walked to the pond, knelt at the shallow dirt edge, and scooped water as clear as quartz stone.

By the time I finished washing my arms and neck, Cielo was unclothed and wading, the water lapping at his hips. Everything that could be called *sinful* was covered, but I found the idea almost as tempting at the sight itself.

"You're still coming to the Palazza?" I asked, hope embedded in my voice. I'd thought that learning of his mother's death would be the end of Cielo's path.

"Of course I am," the strega said, dipping lower. He ducked under the surface and came back up with wet hair and a deeply pleased look on his face. Now that he'd cooled himself, he offered his skin to the sun.

"But why?" I asked.

"That's what I found in your father's ledgers. My mother was sent to the Uccelli by the Capo, well before he unified Vinalia. Whether she was his captive or his willing partner, I don't know."

"So you believe there's more to find? The specifics of her death? And how they connect to the disappearances of these other streghe?"

Cielo nodded.

I unlaced my boots and stepped out; it felt as though my feet had taken a breath for the first time in days. I pushed my toes into the shallows, but the more grime I stripped away, the more the unwashed bits of me grew jealous. It didn't help that Cielo had given in to the lure of deep water, chasing the patches of glitter on the gentian-blue surface as I roasted on the shore. I climbed out of my dress all at once, as if escaping a burning tower. I waited until the strega dove beneath the water and worked myself out of my underclothes. Then I cast myself into the pond. Cold shattered me, and I felt awake all through my skin, the edges of everything as bright and focused as if I'd downed ten cups of coffee.

Cielo nodded me out to where he swam at the center of the pond. "Now that you're here, why not come out all the way?" I marveled at how the strega could tell me about his mother's dark fate in one moment and in the next be darting around like a pale, delighted fish.

I pushed forward in a few neat strokes, making as little splash as possible. "What if your mother practiced *the brilliant life*, even to the end?" I asked. "Could that be what Adolfo meant?" The idea had always made me think of Fiorenza, but I could see the same principles at work in Cielo. The strega walked a path of death and loss, but still noticed the trees and drank in the brightness of flowers.

"It doesn't explain his certainty about what happened to her," Cielo said, tipping on his back to float. "What makes a death *brilliant*?"

I shook my head. Life could be brilliant in so many ways, a gem with hundreds of facets. Death had no shine to it, at least none that I could see. All I could think of was Luca, his brown eyes gone so dull that I couldn't find him anywhere in their depths.

We swam for another minute before I felt the push of time, always at my back. I worked my way toward the shallows, where I crouched to finish up my washing. It had been days since I'd seen my own reflection. The girl in the water had shoulders spiced with dark brown marks, her brown eyes set far apart in a slightly displeased face.

"Is it strange?" I asked. "To change so much? To look at yourself and see so many different things?"

"Is it strange to be stuck as one thing?" Cielo asked just as quickly. "To look at yourself and see the same face, over and over, when you're constantly changing?" Cielo had only asked a question, as playful as the others, but it felt as if the strega had pushed on a tender spot. I *was* stuck.

"I need a book like yours," I said, nodding at the leather tome Cielo had left on the shore. "That would solve my problems."

"It took me three years to forge, and the strega's workshop where I made it has burned to the ground."

"An accident?" I asked.

"The Order of Prai raiding a strega's store of magic is hardly an accident. Neither is setting a man on fire in front of his student." Cielo closed his eyes, and I felt certain it was more than sun he needed to block out. "They caught me using the book in public. Changing. The priests didn't take me right away, though. They followed me home."

Cielo ran his hands through his hair again, this time

clutching hard. The small amount of pain seemed to work like a lens, focusing his words. "I only escaped because the priest holding me in place didn't notice my foot reaching for the book, which had fallen to the ground. I wanted to change myself to water and put the fire out, but nudging a book open with a boot is . . . clumsy. I turned into a mouse instead and scuttled over the priests as they ran from their own smoke. Then I lived in the walls of the head priest's church for a week. I made his life wretched." I laughed, unexpectedly, and Cielo looked like he wanted to join but couldn't quite manage it. "Revenge didn't really add up to anything. Malik . . . my teacher . . . was gone either way."

I wondered if any of what came next would matter now that Luca was gone. But I didn't have the luxury of stopping. "Why work so hard for the book if you already knew how to change?"

"A good question," Cielo said, battling his way back to a charming smile, though his cheeks stayed tight with pain. The strega swam up to me and set his hand on my chest. His longest fingertips grazed my collarbone, the base of his palm perched over my heart. "There is magic that comes easy, magic that is like breathing. And then there is control."

I felt powerfully aware of the strega's body under the water, so much of him beneath the surface. I looked down at the wavering, incomplete pictures of our bodies. I could reach out and touch Cielo so easily.

Was it the nearness of death that made me want to step closer? To feel alive in ways that I had only heard about?

I slid forward in the water, easier than taking a step, and

let one hand rise to meet the hooked bone of the strega's hip. "Control?" I asked, pressing my chest forward against Cielo's hand. "I already have too much practice with that."

I waited for the strega to melt the distance between our bodies to nothing, or to remind me that I was his student and certain lines were best drawn firmly and powdered to set. Instead Cielo swam away, flickering off to the deep part of the pond.

I put my hand over my heart. I ordered it not to beat so fast.

"What happens if someone steals your book?" I called out, the teasing taking on a knife's edge.

"I'm the only one who can touch it," Cielo said. "That was part of its making."

"I could change it into a brick," I said, "and then where would you be?"

"Go ahead." The strega's metallic smile made me think I was being led into a trap.

I marched out of the water, giving Cielo a full view of my naked backside, and walked straight over to the book, dripping water, a handful of droplets darkening the soft leather cover.

Turn Cielo's book into a useless lump.

Magic slid out easily, relieved that I had finally asked it for something it wished to do. In a single blink, a hard clay brick sat before my feet. I nodded once in satisfaction before quickly getting dressed.

Cielo walked out of the pond, dripping, dripping. He picked up the brick and closed his eyes.

I tried to ignore the great expanses of his skin, still slicked with water. I watched his hands instead, feeling the cold shock of the moment when the brick melted back into a book with a soft leather cover.

꩜

THE SKY SPILLED ITS BOTTLE OF INK, BUT THE MOON ROSE BRIGHT enough to show the path to Amalia. As soon as Cielo spread his cloak on the ground, I stopped, without bothering to argue. I needed to rest before I faced Amalia.

Cielo slept like a snuffed candle. I spent my first night without Luca in the world tossing on my bedroll, feeling the hard ground more than the soft cloth. The slashes Beniamo had given me had scabbed over fast, and I balled my hands to keep from scratching at the tight pucker of healing skin.

I kept seeing the leather of Cielo's book—gone, then back again—restored by a strega who didn't have that kind of magic.

I shook him awake.

"How did you change the book?" I asked. "Back at the pond?"

"It's a reversal," Cielo said, sleep clinging to his words. He waved me off with a vague hand. "I'll show you in the morning."

"You'll show me *now*," I said, standing up and pacing under the hard light of the moon. "Magic tutors can't expect normal hours."

"Then I'm giving up the position. You can be my student again in"—Cielo peered at the moon—"five hours."

"If I don't figure out how to do this, you're never getting into the Palazza," I said, dangling the threat over him.

Cielo peered up at me through a thick frown. "Reversals

are tricky. Every strega's magic seems to contain its opposite, but actually it's a variation of the original. That's what Adolfo did, when he changed your fears to stones. He normally hides what most people can see. He could see your fears, and he hid them in a new form." It scorched to think that my fears were that visible to someone who barely knew me. I would have to do a better job of hiding them once we reached the Palazza. "The same logic applies to what I did at the pond. Normally, I change myself. To change something else, I have to see it as part of me. Which is easy enough with the book, because I made it. I put blood and time and toil into those pages."

"I can change anything but myself, but if I can look at myself the way I would look at someone else . . ." I thought of the snarled, stubborn girl reflected back at me in the pond. "Maybe I can use a reversal to become a boy."

Cielo sat up. "You would need to gain a proper distance . . . but yes . . . that might work. . . ."

I drew back at the strega's excitement. "It might not, though."

"Why do you always meet good news with bad faith?" Cielo asked, latching on to my reaction.

"My father," I said. "He taught me to distrust people, motives, weather." Due to his influence, I looked at the world with a shrewd and judging eye. Due to his influence, I was alive, and I had a chance to save him.

"Don't think of your father right now," Cielo said. "Don't think of *any* di Sangro. They'll lead you back to yourself." The strega stared at me, waiting. As he leaned forward, his eyes glowed with moonlight and anticipation.

"It's not going to work if you hover like that," I said.

"Fine," Cielo said, falling hard onto his cloak. "If you insist." He grunted once and fell asleep within moments.

I dug through my pack for the mirror at the very bottom, the heaviest of all the items I had brought. It might have some value in Amalia, but I had chosen it because it was the first person I had ever changed. Sentiment, pure and simple.

I could barely make out my face in the dim light. If this was going to work, I would have to look at the girl in the mirror the way I would look at a stranger on market day. If I was being honest, she looked a mess, face smudged and hair taking flight in every direction. There was nothing lovely in this girl's expression, but it told me something I needed to know.

She was not going to be defeated easily.

I touched my fingertips to the mirror's surface. *"Can you change her?"*

Slowly, reluctantly, it told me, *Yes.*

"Why aren't you doing anything?" I muttered.

A rush of sound came. At first I thought it was the magic going to work. Then I realized it hailed from a point farther away, on the road to Amalia. Torches bobbed over the rise, and in the darkness I could see the lights but not who carried them. Three torches, at least, and voices like rough stone that scraped against the night.

Fear rushed over me like flame traveling up dry brush, setting my magic on fire. I stared hard into the mirror. *Change this girl.*

The magic moved through me with a cold fury that I had never felt before. Instead of the usual warm rush, prickles of ice filled me, spreading outward like frost crystals. I started to wrench my clothes off. I had no idea how much my body would change, and I figured it couldn't hurt to follow Cielo's example.

When I looked down, I was still sharp-faced Teodora.

And now I was naked, to make things complete.

The torches stopped on the road, three pinpricks of light. "Do you see someone over there?" A carriage clattered over the rise, stopping close to the men with their torches. This was worse than I had thought. If I started to run, there was no guarantee they wouldn't catch me.

Now, I told the magic. *Change me into a boy, or we are lost.*

Magic rushed through me, the harshest of cold winds, sapping what strength it found, burning me from the inside. I wondered faintly, through an inner scream of pain, if I could die of it.

I doubled over. Dropped the mirror. Scrambled to grab it again.

I noticed my hands first, how different they looked gripping the mirror's gilt handle. Heavily knuckled and broad, the lines deep, as if someone had drawn me with a firm hand where before I had been lightly sketched. And then I looked past my hands to the face in the glass. I had the same solemn brown eyes, set in cheeks that had been stretched and angled. My nose was proud and peaked, my wide lips parted. I even had different teeth. They were more square, somehow.

I was a boy.

And then I looked down.

I found long feet with bones that I could pick out even in the moonlight. Startling muscles lined my legs, and between them sat something that looked like a close cousin to a large, undercooked noodle.

Cielo woke, flustered by the sound of men approaching, and the sight of me above him, naked and frozen.

"Get up," I said, startled by how my voice seemed to have been dropped from a great height.

"Teo?" he asked.

"Not just me," I said grimly.

"Company?" He sat up and finger-combed his hair, snagging on a knot. "Have none of you heard about the miracle of sleep?"

I nodded at the men as they drew close, the overlapping circles of their torchlight a snare we would soon be caught in. Cielo stood up and went on his toes, peering at the approaching figures. "What are we facing? Bandits?"

"Worse," I said. "Nobles."

I had used every drop of magic to change myself, so I crouched over my dress and snatched Father's knife out of the sleeve. If a bandit slit your throat and stole your things, at least he would do it honestly. A noble would make off with your dignity as well as whatever else he fancied.

The smear of torchlight finally touched us, and the boy at the head of the pack stepped forward, revealing a face as smooth as cream. "A fine night for a . . . Well, I'm not really sure what you're up to."

"We're on our way to Amalia," I said.

"In that city, they generally prefer their visitors *with* clothing," he said, and the other two laughed as if he had made some grand joke. So he was the noble, and these were his flatterers.

The boy's eyes fell on Father's knife. "That stiletto looks like it belongs to a great man." My hands still weren't quite sure of themselves, and he tore the weapon right from my fingers. He turned it over with care, showing the knife much more respect than he gave me. "Di Sangro made. Now, what is a mountain boy and"—he looked Cielo over—"his special bedfellow doing with this? I'm afraid I'll have to take it, for your own good. There are some in the di Sangro family who would give you worse trouble if they discovered your thievery."

There was no convincing this boy that I *was* a di Sangro. The last di Sangro son, as of tonight.

I told myself that it didn't matter. I would find another knife in Amalia. I had to get to the Palazza, to the Capo. Saving Father was a hundred times more important than saving his knife.

I told myself all of that, and then I rushed at the boy, howling.

Being attacked headlong by a naked stranger should have encouraged him to drop the knife, but he held fast, curling it up in his fist. Then he smacked me across the face with the handle. I had just gotten this face, and already it felt a bit shattered. The boy spat to one side and looked back to me with a smile. This was what he had hoped for all along: to stir a peasant into fighting.

I pushed at this stranger, and he pushed back, wrestling me toward the ground. I had to be careful, since I was so exposed, and yet I wouldn't have traded this feeling. As a girl, I had been given rules and restrictions and responsibilities. I drank my new freedom recklessly, like tipping an entire bottle of liquore genziana down my throat.

I swung at the boy's stomach, and he released a satisfying grunt.

"Now, boys," Cielo said dryly.

The two on his side only cheered him on. "You are bound to win, Pasquale."

"Kill him!"

I did not know this Pasquale well enough to know how far he would go. He certainly wasn't holding back his punches, although half of them bruised the sky instead of my skin. But when I thought of dying this close to Amalia, I drew a step back, which opened the door for him to kick me squarely in the gut.

I fell back, into Cielo. The strega held on to me gingerly.

"Pasquale!" came a voice from the carriage. A girl's head slid out from the window into the night. She had a copse of curls and a high forehead that shone in the moonlight. When she caught sight of me in my unclothed state, her eyes went as wide as two centesimi. "Pasquale, these young men have done nothing to you."

"You're right," the young man said, chuckling. He strode off toward the carriage, Father's knife held up so I could see it clearly, every step of the way.

I collapsed back onto the ground, staring up at the sky. Now it was Cielo's turn to loom over me, blocking out most of the stars. He walked around me in a circle, and for the first time since I had looked down at my new body, I felt a twitch of nerves.

Only a minute ago I had been howling under the moon. Now I sat up to fold myself, plagued by modesty.

"What do you think?" I asked, shocked again by the depths of my own voice. I had been to the ocean only once, on the Violetta Coast, with Father and Fiorenza and Mirella, when Luca was a small boy, before my little sisters were born. I remembered the moment when the light-drenched shallows turned dark, when I took a single step into deep water and the world slipped away.

Speaking in this new voice felt just like that.

"You really have managed it," Cielo said, with an approving nod. I wondered if I imagined the sliver of sadness in his voice.

The strega tossed his cloak around my shoulders, the silk so fine, it felt like mist. But not a cold mist—it held warmth from Cielo's sleeping skin. "The nights are growing harsh," he said, pressing his hands on my shoulders, sliding to my collarbone, where his fingers stayed for a moment, at the northernmost reaches of my broad boyish chest, before he snapped the cloak tight.

Cielo shook his head, lips slowly heating into a smirk. The night seemed to hold its breath for us. "Yes, it's getting cold," Cielo whispered. He nodded at the newly filled space between my legs. "You'll want to keep *that* covered."

Three

Sons of Vinalia

I walked for hours in my shifted form, growing used to the thickness of my legs, adding a dash of manly pride to my posture that made Cielo burst with laughter. "You don't need to parade around like a Ranian stallion."

The moon set on me swaggering and swearing like the worst commedia actor in the secret hopes of winning another laugh. When the strega only pursed his lips, I went back to the work of forging a character to match my new form. The harder I tried to hammer my personality into a new shape, the worse it felt. Exhausted, I slid back into acting like myself.

"Much better," Cielo said as we crested a ridge lined in the brightness of sunrise.

Our first sight of Amalia paired well with the dawn.

The Estatta Valley held the new capital in cupped hands. From where Cielo and I stood, looking down, the roofs formed a wild garden of orange, pink, and red, an overlap of tile and domes.

As we made our way down the slope, the city grew larger and larger, but I didn't believe it was real until we crossed one of Amalia's many tile-covered bridges with open sides that offered a generous view of the Estatta River. It wrapped around the whole city like a green silken necklace—and, like a woman's neck, came wreathed in perfume. It smelled of fish and the forges downriver, and underneath that, a whisper of churches, the thick, hot breath of incense.

"We made it," I said on a gust of relief. And then I remembered the journey across the mountains was meant to be the simple part. Now I would have to find an antidote for Father. Now I would have to look the Capo in the eye.

There was also the matter of convincing him, as well as the other four families, that I was the di Sangro son they had been waiting for. To magic myself into a boy's body and to manage a complete deception were two different things.

One would leave me dead if anyone discovered the truth.

Cielo and I descended into the outskirts of the city, mucking through narrow, crowded streets. How many of these people saw a boy when they looked at me? How many were able to sense the traces of the girl I'd been only hours ago? How many only stared because I had Cielo's cloak on, and little else?

Carrying a pack on each of my shoulders turned me almost twice as wide, slowing our progress and drawing shouts from more than one person who caught a canvas cannonball in the shoulder. After a solid minute of frowning down at me—I was still shorter than most men, though I'd gained an inch or two in the transformation—Cielo grabbed Luca's pack without a word. He slung it behind him as if the weight of my dead brother's possessions amounted to little more than a stack of feathers.

"Thank you," I mumbled, rubbing my sore shoulder, hating how relieved I felt not to carry that burden.

Now that I could walk more freely, I looked up at the city instead of down at my feet. Amalia pressed in on all sides, with its rusticated stone, milk-white statues, bronze decoration, and buildings in every color of marble—green, pink, white. Instead of the one church we had in Chieza, there seemed to be dozens. Where we had a bakery and a butcher, here were shops dedicated to bread, sweets, cheese, and the bounty of the river, including live eels writhing in baskets. The noise of the carts and the clang of the forges overtook my body, forcing their way into the beat of my steps.

"Is it always this *loud*?" I asked, shouting up at Cielo, his face a few inches away.

"You don't like the Amalia symphony?" Cielo's long, fine hands took to the air and darted like frenzied birds as he conducted. "The clatter of the laundry carriages with their ashen loads? The catastrophic din of the forges? The wail of babies? The passionate arguing of anyone larger than a baby? Soon, when you take a stroll on a fine day, you will hear nothing but music."

I swallowed the dust in my throat. "It sounds more like a battle."

"Some people hear symphonies in war," Cielo said. "But you have to watch out for them."

The very mention of war caused me to notice the Eterrans in the street. Vinalians weren't identical by any means—we were a tangle of bloodlines, close to two different seas and three great masses of land—yet I could easily pick out the Eterrans in the crowd by their sun-starved skin, the muted expressions on their faces, and the muted clothes they wore to match.

Vinalia had been invaded by nearly every great power in

history. The Eterrans were the most recent to try their hand. In the Uccelli, parents used them as a bedtime story to scare children, more potent than strega stories because they were obviously real.

Alleys twisted away from the main streets, flung in all directions, and Cielo turned so briskly, I had to run to keep up. People cleared the way for me, even though I was a stranger, not their lord's daughter. I couldn't imagine them doing the same for the girl I'd been a few hours ago. Being a boy certainly made it easier to walk down a city street. I wondered what else it would simplify.

We reached a market that lined the city side of the river. Open-air stalls made a bragging show of wares, everything from leather goods to Amalia's finest glasswork, as well as cheap imitations of Amalia's finest glasswork. Cielo picked one of the finer-looking clothing stalls, decorated with brooms at the door and tight bundles of dried sage in the rafters.

He ran his fingers over the weave of a few shirts with a practiced air. "This should do." Cielo cast aside shirts that displeased him and haggled with the merchant, whose bald head prickled with sweat as Cielo drove the prices down.

"Just pick something and let's go," I said, feeling the nearness of the Capo, the violence of his summons.

"I know you're in a hot, sweltering hurry," Cielo said without a hint of exaggeration—Amalia was nothing short of a bread oven. I picked at the strega's cloak with clothespin fingers, holding it away from my chest to keep it from sticking. "We need to make sure you can fool the people waiting at the Palazza."

He tossed a pair of pants at me, and I caught it with

clumsy hands. I wondered when they would stop feeling like gloves that were a size too large. "Look, Teodora," the strega said. "*Truly* look."

I took in the fabric and the seams with a frown.

"Not at the pants! At the truth! It's necessary the Capo believes you are who you claim to be. Do you think Luca would have you stride in and call yourself the di Sangro heir looking like that?" I fell silent at Luca's name, touching the coarse fabric and thinking of the bandages on his hands. My little brother should have been healed and on the road to Gravina by now, instead of in an unmarked grave.

Cielo must have been able to sense that bringing up Luca was a mistake. He stole around the tables and touched my back lightly. "Listen," he said in a low voice meant to recapture my attention. "How much of being a noble or a peasant is in the presentation? How much of being seen as a man or a woman is cut and color and tailoring? You think I want to put frills around your neck, when I'm trying to keep it from being rudely detached from the rest of you."

I slid the pants on beneath Cielo's cloak. They fit shockingly well. "How did you . . . ?"

"I started changing form before I could walk," Cielo said with a quick shrug. "I can size up most bodies in a second or two."

"Right," I said. "Of course." I tossed aside the possibility that the strega had been looking at me closely, giving his attention to *my* body in particular.

Cielo made his final purchases, including a shirt of wine-colored linen with gold patterned cuffs and a slightly open collar. I had to admit that I felt more noble when I pulled it on. I also felt ridiculous.

We rushed back into the crowds, which thickened like cream as we neared midday. "The Palazza is close," Cielo said, fear cutting into his voice.

The streets opened into a series of squares, the first one filled with great hunks of marble hewn into the shapes of the old gods. The Order of Prai used to destroy statues like these, to keep them from drawing people toward the mistakes of the past. The Order of Prai had buried streghe, too. But they hadn't been able to rid the world of gods or magic, because I stood beside a likeness of Veria, the goddess of truth and mischief, with her ripe smile and half-bared body.

A pair of small suns, made of marble but somehow illuminated, spun around and around each other in the palm of her hand, blazing with such fury, I almost believed the statue had plucked them right from the sky.

"But that's . . . that's . . ." I whispered, as if someone might overhear me. As if Cielo didn't already know.

There was magic in Amalia.

WHEN I RECOVERED FROM A BLANK MOMENT OF SURPRISE, I looked around the square and saw Elia, goddess of food, beauty, and all pleasures of the senses, bending forward to offer a stone round of bread to the passersby. Cecci, god of wine, bore a drinking horn that he raised to his lips. Erras, god of judgment, sliced the air with a knife as long as his forearm. And Melae, goddess of death, held rich, dark soil in one hand and a sparrow in the other. The soil crumbled through her fingers as the sparrow lifted toward the sky. These were the symbols of body and spirit, parted at the moment of death.

Around the statues droves of people, mostly travelers, stared at the stonework, but it wasn't the mastery of artists that drew them.

Even through the strain of holding myself in a new form, I could feel my magic leap to the surface. Cielo, on the other hand, looked subdued, slightly hunched and gray in the eyes, like a gloomy portrait of himself. "Why didn't you tell me about this?" I asked. We'd had plenty of time crossing the mountains.

"I thought it might scare you off," he said.

"Maybe some, like Adolfo, prefer to hide, but don't you think that most of us would rather live openly?" I was whispering, but even speaking of magic in a public place was new to me. It brought a thrill, and a dark drop of fear. "This looks like change to me." I heard Luca's voice in my head, calling it by its modern name. *Progress.*

"The night after these statues were placed in the square, ten streghe disappeared," Cielo said, snatching the smile from my face.

He moved us ahead quickly.

"Things will improve," I argued. "What if Vinalians need to become used to the idea of streghe, to seeing us as people who are just like them?"

"But that's it," Cielo said. "We're *not* like them. Or rather, we are and we aren't. People hold a deep fear of complication." I knew that Cielo spoke from experience. As he moved us forward, I saw anger in each strike of his foot against stone. "When streghe are visible, the world becomes doubly dangerous. I've seen it happen," he said in a way that warned me not to plunder the story for details. "The more magic there is in Amalia, the more we will be hurt for it."

"So you're like Adolfo?" I asked. "You'd rather hide?"

"No," Cielo said under his breath. "But I don't believe we should hide the price of this either."

Suddenly the churches in Amalia took on a harsh quality, sky-skimming domes everywhere I turned. As quickly as I'd gotten used to the idea of using magic openly, I shrank from it, growing small within my skin.

The second square leading to the Palazza was newer than the first, dedicated to the Capo and his family, as well as the glory of a unified Vinalia. It was all boring and proud and predictable. I passed the running-wolf crest of the Malfara family and a statue of the Capo with his chin held so high, it almost scraped heaven. The hands on the statue weren't finished yet, just rough stone. I recognized the glittering whiteness in its raw state.

"I don't think Father would approve of Weeping Mountain's marble being put to this use," I muttered.

"I don't think the Capo would care, at least half the time," Cielo countered.

"What would he do the other half?" I asked.

"Have your father killed in some public way."

"How is anyone alive in this city if the Capo has such a temper?" I asked, seething in a manner that I would have to control before I saw the Capo in person. Father's voice counseled me, an echo from childhood. When I was little, he had told me, at least twice a day: *See to your anger before it becomes your master or another man's servant.*

"I don't think it's temper that pushes the Capo from conquest to conquest," Cielo said, winding a tricky path around a statue of a terrifyingly noblewoman, probably the Capo's mother.

"If it isn't anger that drives him, then what?" I would collect information about the Capo. Slowly. Carefully. The way that I always did before unleashing di Sangro punishments.

"The Capo craves loyalty," Cielo said.

I wondered if it was so different in the Uccelli. Father needed people to heed the family. When they didn't, I pulled men up the mountain and added new items to my ever-growing collection.

I pushed away the blasphemy of comparing my father to the Capo even for a second. And then the Palazza came into sight, dun stone in three stacked tiers. Every window was set in an arch, and the arches marched down each tier, an unbroken line. The Palazza stretched as long as the entire village of Chieza, striking without being lovely.

Fiorenza would have hated it. Father would have laughed. I couldn't even ask myself what Luca would have said. That wound was much too fresh.

"Luca? Luca!"

Someone called my brother's name, over and over, in a bold voice. There had to be a hundred Lucas in Amalia, and yet I found myself stricken.

"Do you know that young man?" Cielo asked, pointing across the square. I capped his finger with my hand, but it didn't stop the young man in question from waving at us. He wore the green of the Otto family, a lively color said to match olives that grew on their lands, and nowhere else. His shirt matched mine in cut and fabric, with a few embellishments at the hem, the dark silver of mercury.

It hit me, how expensive the clothes Cielo had bought

me in the market must have been. Had the strega used the money he'd gotten for delivering that vile letter? Of course, I was meant to sneak Cielo into the Palazza.

He was simply paying his own way.

"Luca!" the young man shouted, rushing over the moment I returned his glance. What convinced him I was Luca? The solemn brown eyes, a gift Father had given us both? The di Sangro red?

"There you are, Luca," the boy said. My brother's name, given to me so freely, felt stranger than looking into a mirror and seeing a new version of my face stare back. Knowing I must take my brother's place had been an idea floating through the fog of my mind. This young man and his words were as solid as one of the Palazza's endless stone arches.

"It's Ambrogio!" he shouted, clapping me to him, saving me from an awkward moment where I pretended to remember his name. "Don't you know the man who is soon to be your brother?"

"Of course," I lied. So this was Mirella's betrothed. With the concerns of a sister in mind, I studied him again. He was handsome, with bronze hair, wide-set brown eyes, and tan skin that gave his smile a dose of radiance. And yet what I had noticed first were not his looks but the way he spoke, a braid of eagerness and confidence and good humor.

"And who is this?" he asked, nodding at Cielo.

"This is my loyal servant," I said, confident I had come up with the best way to slip Cielo into the Palazza at my side. There was also the matter of returning my debts. I wanted to tease the strega as fully as he teased me. "Really, he's nothing but deference and duty. All of the scraping and bowing. It's almost embarrassing sometimes. But he lives to serve."

Cielo's eyes grew narrower and narrower with each sentence, until they were little more than trapdoors.

"I didn't think they made them so tall in the Uccelli," Ambrogio said, the laugh in his voice leaping out.

"They don't," Cielo said, with a grin like soured wine. "I'm imported."

I searched through my pack and thrust Mirella's letter at Ambrogio. It would give weight to my claim. "From my sister."

"Your dear, dear sister," Ambrogio said in a silky tone. My sister claimed she loved and admired this boy, but I heard a hint of something else. Had they already shared a bed? Mirella had never said a word about it, and I fought to keep the sting off Luca's face, because it belonged to me and me alone. This was a pain only Teodora could feel at being left out of her sister's life so completely.

"I hate that we must put off the wedding for *this*," Ambrogio said, with a rough nod at the Palazza. "But there is no question about it, of course. And then there is the other matter." I felt a shadow fall over our conversation without being able to see which direction it had been cast from.

"Which matter is that?" I asked.

Ambrogio cocked his head and blinked a few times before he said, "We must bury our fathers."

"May Signore Otto fly straight to heaven," I intoned quickly and dutifully. Beneath the cover of a mournful face, I rushed to catch up. Was Father the only one who had survived the attack? Had there been less poison in his system? Was he the healthiest of the five family heads? I thought of his piling years, his draining vigor.

Ambrogio led me toward the main arch, strolling into

the slate-dark shade as if he did this all the time. Cypress trees trimmed in the most severe style stood at attention around a central courtyard. The noisy, overstuffed beauty of Amalia fell away. We were in the Capo's territory now. Cielo trailed behind, taking my pack like the good servant he most definitely wasn't. Ambrogio threw an arm around me. I had never been touched so easily by a young man before, and it made me start. "So," he said in whispered confidence, "Beniamo chose not to grace us with his presence?"

"Right." I thought of the owl, eyes orange, wings spread as he lifted away from Luca's body. "Something of that nature."

My brother slept through the daylight in the folds of the Uccelli, waiting for darkness to stir him awake. Would he follow me here? Would he go back to the castle and try his luck with Father?

I told myself that I had done the right thing keeping Beniamo away from the Palazza, especially with Father the only family head left alive. Beniamo would have only cared about his own fate, the rising tide of his fortunes. If I saved Father, it meant more than his life. It would decide the balance of the five families.

The future of Vinalia.

9

The high-ceilinged rooms Ambrogio led me through had the stark beauty of caverns. I waited for the Capo to betray a weakness for gold and jewels, the lavish and lovely. But on the inside the Palazza featured marble floors and columns, death-strewn tapestries that sang the praises of war, and little else. Our steps rang so loud through the empty halls that a party of three sounded like an invasion.

"In here," Ambrogio said, pulling me toward a paneled wooden door. "You're the last to arrive. The Capo made us wait until everyone assembled before he would give us an audience. I arrived nearly a week ago, but then, I had the shortest distance to travel. Vanni has been here for days, stamping around in a highly nervous state. Lorenzo came in only this morning." I matched these names to vague memories. Vanni Moschella. Lorenzo Altimari. Mirella had been paraded in front of all of them, at one time or another.

"What of the Rao boy?" I asked, unable to remember his name. Maybe it was better that way. *The Rao boy* had a condescending ring to it, a bit of mockery to start Luca out on a strong footing.

"Ah." Ambrogio's hand made a slow journey up a jaw

darkened by stubble. Did I have those little dots on my face too? My hand flew to the newly rugged coastline of my chin. Nothing seemed to be springing out of my face. Thank whatever gods looked over this place, I didn't have to deal with a beard yet.

Cielo smuggled a smile and a flare of the eyes over Ambrogio's shoulder.

"He came in the middle of the night," Ambrogio said finally. "Awakened half the Palazza, stirred up trouble, and surprised no one."

I nodded, doing my best to look confident. But an ill-tempered family head didn't bode well. I had watched Father long enough to know that dealing with the five families would turn me old before my time. If I made a single wrong move, it might kill me.

Ambrogio set his hand on Cielo's arm, and Cielo looked down as if a vulture had perched there. Ambrogio laughed. I could see why Mirella liked him. He had an open way about him that she lacked. My sister had been born cautious. "You can go to the third floor and settle in," Ambrogio said to Cielo. "The servants up there will help you. Come on." He turned to me. "Let's not keep the Capo waiting."

We walked into a small room, paneled all the way around, one half filled with a polished walnut table, the other half left bare. No windows graced the walls. This deep in the Palazza, sunlight felt like little more than a rumor.

Ambrogio closed the door, and the three young men at the table stopped whispering. I wondered, for a second, how much of their lives had been spent whispering. Plotting. Pretending to be their fathers.

They looked up at me, and I studied them each in turn.

Vanni snatched my attention first, probably due to his curls, red as iron on the forge. His skin was olive in tone, but pale. According to Mirella, these family traits ran strong. *Moschellas have red hair and variable temperaments. They are utterly merry . . . until they are not.*

Next to him sat a young man I guessed to be Lorenzo Altimari. Mirella had once told me, *I could never get a clear sense of Lorenzo. He is a closed book. No, he is an entire locked-up library.* He had curls tighter than Vanni's; a deep brown, near-black complexion; and brown eyes with hearty lashes. The Altimari family ran Salvi, the largest island that had been made part of Vinalia in the unification. Salvi had been neatly self-governed for ages, and I could imagine how little they enjoyed the new arrangement. But I could find no anger in the line of Lorenzo's mouth, no urgency in his long hands folded on the table.

That left the Rao boy. When I turned to him, I almost gasped. I had looked into those hard eyes before. I had swung at that lean body with bare fists. The moonlight had coated him in silver; now his skin proved to be a straightforward beige, his hair dusty brown. The dark yellow favored by the Rao family showed at the collar and cuffs of his shirt. He wore the finest clothes money could produce; his shoes were made of the supplest calf leather in Vinalia. No doubts stood between me and the truth—this was the noble who had stopped his carriage on the side of the road.

The one with Father's knife in his pocket.

In a rush of memory, I grabbed at whatever Mirella had told me about Pasquale Rao. *He has roving hands, but his only true feeling is for a fine vintage in a large bottle. Of all the nobles and their sons, he is the one to avoid.* And I had already gotten in a fight with him, naked and howling.

His face flared with recognition, but the Capo picked that moment to enter from the far side of the room. He had a short stride and a simple costume, a sort of soldier's uniform mixed with elements of noble dress. I'd thought he would be older than Father, but he sat between us in age, no hint of white in his short brown hair or close-trimmed beard. I'd expected a train of admirers and fine ladies and priests, but he brought only a small retinue of soldiers.

Everything I had guessed about this Capo, everything I had imagined, was wrong.

He stood in front of us and waited.

And waited.

Magic rose in me as strong as bile, burning the back of my throat. *Say a word and this story is over.*

But using magic would mean revealing myself. Not as Teodora, Niccolò's di Sangro daughter, but as a strega with enough power to wish herself into this room, where only the most important men in Vinalia were invited to sit.

I could not look at the Capo for a second longer. I turned away and faced the rest of the boys. I took some comfort in finding that murder lined each of their faces, even Ambrogio's. In that moment, we all wore what we wanted on the outside, as plain as our clothes.

The Capo smiled broadly. "Well, we've gotten through the first minute without an assassination. I think that's a fine start, don't you?"

Vanni chuckled and then seemed to remember who he was chuckling at. He dropped his amusement like a hot coal.

"The new leaders of the five families," the Capo said. "A

strong lot. A *young* lot." He sat down at the table with us, acting more like a noble at dinner and less like a self-appointed leader who had tried to kill our fathers. And, in all cases but one, succeeded.

He seemed to know exactly where our minds were. "You have a great deal of respect for your fathers," the Capo said in a smooth voice that reminded me of water moving over stone, using its power to shape what it touched. "You should. They have done the best they could with the world they were handed." He leaned in and smiled again. At me, this time. I was sure of it. "The world is always changing, though, isn't it?

"Some of you will be surprised to find that I offered many peaceful invitations to your fathers, invitations that would have benefited you greatly. Invitations they chose to ignore. You, instead, have come at great risk. That spirit is exactly what I need. I'm not looking for mindless followers, but men who want to have a hand in making this country. Vinalia *is* a country. If we put aside differences and squabbling, we can make it a great one."

This Capo was smarter than I thought. The boys in this room had long dreamed of being caught up in moments like this, alone with great men, trading secrets, making bargains, power passed from hand to hand. But I was a second daughter, not a firstborn son.

"Our di Sangro has finally arrived," he said, turning to me. He took me in briskly and I tried not to stiffen too much. "This can't be Beniamo."

I quietly thanked God that even as a boy I could not be mistaken for Beniamo, but it was not a good sign that the Capo disbelieved my claim to be the di Sangro heir. I tried to speak but found that my throat had sealed itself.

"This is Luca," Ambrogio said.

"Luca," the Capo said slowly, giving away nothing. Then he burst into another smile, as bright as the noontime sun. "Luca di Sangro, you have no idea how glad I am to see you. I have heard that you have scientific leanings. We need men like you. In a moment, you'll see why."

He raised both of his hands and twitched his fingers in a sharp signal. Doors at either side of the room flew open.

"It cannot have escaped your notice that we are invaded so regularly, we could set our clocks by it. By land from Eterra, from over the seas, they come and pillage, and we are left to wait patiently for the next attack. For centuries, we have been called weak and backward. Yet we are ahead of the rest of the world, in science, in religion, in art. We need a chance to show the rest of the world our glory." Those words rang through me like a bell that drew me to some sort of church I had never heard of before. "Unification was only the beginning."

Two girls marched through the open doors. My best guess put them a few years older than I was, with black hair piled on top of their heads and skin gone sallow. One had blue-gray eyes like the sky before a storm. The other's were green-gray, the underside of leaves troubled by a strong wind. They had to be related in some way. Cousins? Sisters? They were both beautiful, but instead of velvet and silk, they wore the black and green of unification.

They were dressed like soldiers.

"An army of girls?" Pasquale laughed so hard, I thought he might die of it. "If that's the future of Vinalia, you might as well bury us now."

I thought of my sister, my mother, Fiorenza. Words cut

their way out of me, sharp and unstoppable. "A woman brought you into this world, bloody and screaming. Every birth is a battle. An army of women raised you. Who would you be, if they had not taught you, trained you?"

"Don't put Luca in charge," Pasquale said to the Capo. "Soon God will be a woman." I thought of the statues in the square outside, the old gods that had been tossed aside by the Order of Prai. Half were women. In the past, Vinalians had seen women's power, believed in it. Pasquale leaned toward me and dropped his voice. "Strange. From what I saw last night on the side of the road, Luca di Sangro doesn't enjoy women at all."

"All you saw last night was a peasant from the mountains," I said. "How does it feel to be so mistaken?"

"Our Luca isn't afraid of a fight," the Capo said. I swelled with something that felt uncomfortably like pride. I thought of Father, that night in the kitchens. How pleased he had been when I didn't draw back from the knife.

"Now," the Capo said, turning back to the two girls, who had ignored the bickering of the boys at the table and waited with cold patience. "Let's show them what Vinalia has in store for the rest of the world."

The girl with the blue-gray eyes stepped forward. She pushed up her sleeves and took in the line of us with a rough, uncut disdain that I had only seen on the faces of small children and powerful men.

She moved along the row, lifting one hand as she went, dangling her fingers in the air, twitching them in a dance that reminded me of the frantic steps of a saltarello. I felt a tug at my pants and looked down in dismay. My pockets were working against the rules of gravity. My pants from the market were utterly new, and only a few stray threads rose into the air.

Vanni and Pasquale laughed at my poor showing as the strega girl moved on to the next boy. Small items rose from Ambrogio's pockets, then Lorenzo's, knives and coins and handkerchiefs. Vanni's coat produced a dueling pistol with a wooden handle and a brass barrel topped with dragons like cresting waves. The pistol's thin snout pointed up toward the ceiling as it floated away. When Vanni tried to snatch it back, the strega's fingers moved, as quick as a puppeteer's, and it sailed halfway across the room.

By the time the strega reached the end of the row, Pasquale's features had settled into a studied boredom. I expected Father's knife to rise, tempting me, but after a long moment of silence Pasquale spread his empty hands.

"Nothing for me?" the strega asked in a harsh voice with a slight playfulness at the edge, like lace adorning metal.

"When you put it that way," Pasquale said, nudging his legs open, "I do have something." Without taking his eyes off the strega, he grabbed himself. My eyes rolled away from the ridiculous scene, toward heaven. Vanni roared with laughter, and Pasquale made it a duet. The Capo's face lit—not with delight.

Anticipation.

The girl's hand spun in a lazy circle. Pasquale's belt slithered from his waist and rose in the air. Her eyes went hard, and the assortment of knives hanging in the air flew at Pasquale's throat. The pistol shot, the ball flying so close to his shoulder that it nipped the shirt and left a smudge of black powder. Pasquale's belt slid around his throat, tightening. Two coins covered his eyes, as if he were already a dead man.

The Capo tapped her shoulder. "You've proven your point."

But she tightened the belt one more inch, until Pasquale's breath pebbled. The other girl looked on, her mouth drawn tight. Then the first made a motion like she was scrubbing her hands clean, and when she stopped, everything fell to the floor.

She moved back to the Capo's side. "I haven't introduced you all properly," he said. "This is Azzurra, one of Vinalia's finest weapons. She can loose a hundred flaming arrows with the turn of a hand. She can jut her chin and cause an avalanche."

"She can disarm soldiers," Lorenzo said. It was the first time he had spoken, and the room went quiet at his words.

"We have a man of peace among us," the Capo said.

"Or strategy." Now that I was a boy, words flowed out of me with no obstruction. As a girl, I'd had to swallow at least half of what I wanted to say. Being allowed to speak my mind felt like running wild down a mountain slope; I might fall and break myself on the rocks at any moment, but for now all I felt was a heady rush. "If we kill an entire army, their brothers and sons will be back to avenge them. If we humiliate our foes, we might win for good." The Capo looked impressed, which immediately shut me up.

"What do you think?" I asked Azzurra.

The boys laughed again, even Ambrogio this time. I had made another mistake. I'd asked a girl for her opinion, as if it mattered as much as the Capo's. Even though they hated this man, they still gave his words more weight.

"Well?" I asked the strega, not wanting to bow to their ridicule.

"What does it matter?" Azzurra shot back. "As long as I get to use *this*." She flicked all ten fingers, and the table we had been sitting at rose above our heads and burst into splinters. They filled the air, the pieces weaving themselves into a tapestry of wood, a table again. It settled gently on the floor.

"If you've come through the public square, you've seen Azzurra's magic at work," the Capo said. My own magic seethed with jealousy, as if I had turned from a strega into a basket of snakes. She had given life to the statues of the old gods. She was the one changing the face of Vinalia.

One girl, one strega, could do that.

I looked to the girl at the back of the room, the one who lingered. "What about you?"

She took a few careful steps to join the Capo on his other side. If her sister splashed magic everywhere, this strega was as shy as a night-blooming flower. "This is Delfina," the Capo said. "You will know her power soon enough."

❦

I CLIMBED TO MY ROOM ON THE THIRD FLOOR. WALLS THE color of raw linen had an immediate soothing effect. A set of windows sighed out the trapped heat of the Palazza. Air touched my neck and stirred fine sweat-covered hairs.

The Capo had given the five families a set of rooms as blank and satisfying as a mind after confession. Did he believe that would erase the memories of our fathers, dying in other rooms?

Everything with the Capo was a move in a much larger

game. I couldn't let myself rest, couldn't be tricked by a well-staged breeze and the temptations of a feather bed into setting down the distrust that kept me alive.

The door clicked open and I braced myself for a visit from one of the five families' sons. Ambrogio seemed to think we were already great friends.

But it was Cielo, in boyish form. "What do you think of our new quarters?" the strega asked, sitting down on the larger of the two beds, the one with the beechwood frame. It was clearly meant for the di Sangro heir. The mattress dimpled with Cielo's weight, and he shifted to a seat in the center, crossing his legs loosely at the ankles, making himself comfortable in my space. I had asked to be put in close quarters when I called Cielo my servant, but this was a bit much.

The strega drew out his book, and I turned without even thinking.

I faced the view of Amalia's rooftops, cluttered and endless. I kept my eyes on the red-pink tiles, pretending they were of the deepest interest, but my mind kept slipping back to Cielo on the bed. Cielo, naked and changing. "How can you use magic so casually, knowing anyone might burst in and see us like this?" I asked, more frustration in my voice than the moment truly called for.

"Lock the door if you please," Cielo said. "You should have done it in the first place."

"I can't look as though I have secrets to hide," I said.

"But you *do* have secrets," Cielo said. "I'm the least damning and the nicest to look at."

Cielo tapped on my shoulder to let me know the magic was done. I turned and found her in girlish form, wearing nothing but a white shirt that whispered against her legs. I couldn't help noticing they were as long and smooth and perfectly molded as a pair of taper candles. I snuck a look at the curve of her breasts pressed against the cover of the book. My breath went ragged at the edges.

This must be the boy's body taking over, staking a claim on my feelings. There was also the small matter of what was happening between my legs. I thought of the rules of gravity, and how easily they seemed to be defied these days.

Cielo looked, not at my trousers, thank God, but my chest. "You're heaving." Her lips spread into a knowing smile.

My cheeks became two small suns. I burned and burned until a cold memory came over me. The strega might smirk and tease, but the moment I had dared to move past flirtation at the pond, Cielo swam away at great speed.

"I assume you've taken advantage of my meeting with the Capo to search for evidence of your mother," I said, sitting abruptly on the small cot. Far, far from the strega. "What did you find?"

Cielo leaned forward, the loose collar of her shirt sliding downward. I scattered pinpricks of desire, like the hard itch of a sleeping limb. "I worked my way through the servants' quarters, asking ridiculous questions. Where's the silver polish, my lord needs a boar-bristle brush, do you have some coarse mustard, that sort of thing. I found an old strega in the kitchens."

"How did you know she was a strega?" I asked.

"There are ways," Cielo said.

"That's both helpful and specific." If I could learn to pick streghe out of a crowd, I wanted that skill. "You knew I had magic that day on the mountain, didn't you? How?"

"Oh, that one was easy." Cielo crawled forward slightly, stretching out to her full length on the bed. She spread her fingers and closed her eyes. "When I'm a wind, I can feel any great force. Rain gathering, storms colliding, the gentle sway of trees and the waves when they *slap*." She hit the mattress.

"You . . . felt me?" I asked.

"Yes," Cielo said. "Your presence was so strong, Teo. Stronger than anyone I've felt. Why do you think I was so eager to meet you? How did I come out in that exact field? You pulled me over the mountain."

"Oh," I said softly.

Cielo turned over onto her back, as if she could stare through the ceiling, straight to the sky. "I've been looking for other streghe for so long that now I can't *help* but see them. The old woman in the kitchen had the smell of someone who is often out at night, collecting herbs and secrets. I asked one of the lovely young baker girls, you know, the ones with flour dabbed on their chins, how long the old woman had been in the Palazza, and she said ages and ages, since her own mother was a child. If my mother was here, the strega must remember something."

"That's perfect," I said, the words wafting out on their own. All I could think of was the sweet baker girl, Cielo chatting at her until she handed over stories like a basket of sugared bombolone. It seemed that Cielo couldn't help flirting. It was how the strega moved through the world, as surely as I scattered threats and bribes everywhere I went.

It didn't mean anything.

"It won't be easy getting this old woman to talk," Cielo said. "You should have seen her face. A single one of her stares could kill a cat and mummify it. Besides, many old streghe don't appreciate being thrust into the light. They grow used to their shadow lives."

I thought of my own shadow life at the castle, hiding the better part of myself, pretending to be the same as my brothers and sisters. Things had changed, I told myself. I was the di Sangro heir, and I got to use magic, even if all that meant was turning myself into a false Luca.

"I learned something too," I told Cielo. "The Capo has dressed up streghe in army uniforms and claims that they are his . . . well . . . *his*."

Cielo sat up, as stiff as dead grass. "He has his own streghe, entirely at his disposal?"

"Two girls. Close relations of some kind."

"Sisters?" Cielo asked. "Eyes like bad omens, black hair, corpsy fingers?" She danced hers in the way Azzurra had. "One of them speaks as if she owns half the world, the other is as silent as the grave?"

"You know them?" I asked.

"No, not personally," she said. "But I have run into stories about how ruthless they are. The young one tried to join the soldiers of Erras, but they wouldn't take the older sister. At least, that's how the story goes."

"The soldiers of Erras?" I tried not to show my frustration at how little I knew about the world of streghe. It felt like I had *two* shadow lives, and the sum of two shadows wasn't one girl. It was twice as much darkness.

"Oh, the soldiers of Erras believe that magic must be used at all costs, because it is a right given by the old gods," Cielo said with fake solemnity. "They punish anyone who chooses not to use their powers."

Cielo sat down next to me, so we were both stuffed onto

the small cot, the rest of the room wide and empty. A single glance at the strega's pink-stained cheeks and the slim bridge of her ankles sent my gaze skittering away. "Keep a good distance between yourself and those girls," Cielo said, and I told myself I was only imagining the soft concern in her voice.

"They are exactly the people I need to speak to," I said. "Isn't it likely they're the ones who poisoned the letter? If one of them created the poison, she'll have the antidote. Or know how to make it."

Cielo's dark brows slanted deeply, but before she could bring the argument to a head, a knock sounded.

"Hide!" I whispered.

Finding a woman in Luca di Sangro's quarters wouldn't be nearly as scandalous as finding a strega in the middle of a magical transformation. Still, it might be considered *odd* that the girl in question was almost identical to the servant boy who attended me. Cielo flattened herself to the floor behind the cot, looking up at me with mischief stitched into her expression, as if we'd actually been caught in the act.

My head swarmed with lightness that threatened to become a faint. Luca di Sangro *could not faint.*

"Signore di Sangro?" a voice called in the dull, uninterested tone of a servant. I opened the door to find arms holding out a new set of clothes.

Black trousers and a sullen green shirt.

Unification colors.

Ten minutes later I stood in the harsh sting of the sun just outside the South Gate of the Palazza. The other heads of the families milled nearby, dressed in the same outfit I had been gifted.

Vanni kept glancing down at himself and spitting into the dirt. Lorenzo stared off into the distance, like he was trying to see Salvi from here. Pasquale winced as if a night of drinking had pitched him headfirst into a foul mood.

Even Ambrogio's spirits had plummeted. "What is the Capo aiming to do?" he asked. "Kill us off in battle?"

"Or just show us off in the street." As I had changed out of my di Sangro red, I'd remembered what Cielo told me. The Capo craved loyalty above all else. If I put on a good show, I could work my way closer to his streghe. I was here for the antidote. I might be able to ask about Cielo's mother into the bargain.

And then there was *the brilliant death*. My magic told me those words were important; it grasped for what they meant but came back empty, a bucket sent to the bottom of a well to draw water and finding only air.

I silently vowed not to stop learning about magic now

that I'd made it over the mountains. It felt, in some important way, like learning about myself. Cielo didn't know about *the brilliant death*, but maybe those girls did.

The Capo strode out of the gates with a slow, simmering confidence. The sun touched his brown hair and gave him the kind of halo that would have converted lesser men to his worship. Behind him trailed another man, tall and disapproving, the Capo's threadbare shadow, dressed in stark gray robes.

A priest.

And not just a priest, but a man in the charcoal robes of the Order of Prai. Here was proof that the Capo had the church on his side.

What did they think about streghe in the Capo's army? Magic outside of his Palazza? Was that why the sisters were being kept secret? Could the church be behind the disappearances?

I set one tiny shiver against the massive heat of the day, and then I forced myself to look away. This man couldn't know that I had reasons to turn cold at the sight of him. Luca di Sangro had nothing to fear from a priest.

"Today we're having a parade," the Capo said as troops streamed out of the gate behind him. He nodded as each row filed into place, one hand against his forehead to blunt the sun. "I thought you would rightfully object to lending your family's colors until I had given you reason to do so. You are dressed this way so you might walk and observe our new country firsthand. You were born sons of Vinalia, but there comes a time in each man's life when he has to choose this place for himself."

And women? I wanted to ask. *When did they get to choose?*

But it wasn't something a family head would care about, so with a great deal of inner writhing, I kept silent.

The Capo tapped Vanni's shoulder. "Walk with me." After a stubborn moment of hesitation, Vanni rushed to join him at the head of the parade. His red Moschella curls glowed fiercely in the sun, so bright that I could barely look. A brigade of soldiers swallowed the rest of us. I stayed close to Ambrogio, thankful for a familiar face.

We marched first through the Capo's square. The man should have looked vain surrounded by marble versions of himself, but it only made him seem larger than the rest of us, as if he had been hewn by an unseen hand for some great purpose.

As we passed through the courtyard filled with the statues of the old gods, the priest looked at their near-naked forms with disdain. Part of me expected him to stop and destroy the statue himself, break it apart with his bare hands, which, along with his face, were the only parts not trapped beneath dark, heavy robes. He gave the statue of Melae a glare as hard as a chisel, then moved on.

The Capo smiled and made commentary on everything they passed, and soon Vanni's laugh drifted back to us. "The Capo is a military man to the last," I muttered to Ambrogio. "He is trying to divide and conquer us."

"He knows we're more likely to attack him if we band together," Ambrogio admitted.

The Capo's strategy ran even deeper, though. I watched Vanni walk at his side, transforming from a foul-tempered boy into a young man with an easy stride. The Capo had picked out the perfect way to make Vanni feel important. It felt a bit like he was wooing us, but I hadn't come to Amalia to be won.

The parade wound through main streets, and even those were barely wide enough to fit the crowds. They cheered with a vigor that I understood, even if I didn't believe in the Capo's cause. Vinalia was a land of parades—every time a leader took power in the provinces, parades stretched out for a season, each more elaborate than the last. Weddings and holiday feasts came dressed in their own parades. A funeral demanded one with mourners trailing the coffin, wearing black to their necks and weeping to show the world every shade of loss. That was what should have happened after Luca's death, the whole town of Chieza turned into one long sigh of grief.

"Luca?" Ambrogio shoved my shoulder in a way that I gathered, from my study of boys, was meant to be friendly. "Are you all right, brother?"

He would never be this cheerful with me if he knew that I'd buried the real Luca without rites. I was the best chance the di Sangro family had, but that didn't change the thinly covered truth. I was a liar. A strega. A thief of men's lives.

I had stolen my own brother's.

"I'm thinking of my family," I said, my voice cracking like dried-out mud. These new vocal cords were unpredictable.

We twisted around a corner, met with a new set of cheers. "How is that sister of yours?" Ambrogio asked.

"Which one?" I played innocent as I waited for Ambrogio's carefully tempered smile. The heat with which he said, *Mirella.*

"Teodora," he said, and I went colder than January.

149

"Why do you ask?" I picked my way over a puddle, delicately. Then I guessed it wasn't a very boyish approach to the problem, so I splashed through the next one and was rewarded with yellow muck all the way to my shins.

"Mirella mentioned Teodora in the letter," Ambrogio said. "She seemed . . . concerned."

I had no idea Mirella worried about me. What cause had I given her? And then it struck me as bold as lightning—what would happen if someone at the Palazza figured out that Teodora was meant to be here too?

"She was right to worry," I said hastily as we passed an old weather-stained church. I promised myself I would pray for all of this lying later. Even if the Order of Prai hated my kind, God would still have to listen. "Teodora has gone missing."

"Really? Mirella worried that Teo would be too ferocious and shred the entire court to bits."

"That's why she ran off," I said, twisting my answer to suit Ambrogio's words. "She couldn't stand to face the Capo after . . ." I almost said after he *tried* to kill Father. That one word, *tried*, would have given it all away. I lowered my voice. "After what he did."

Ambrogio shaded his eyes against the bastard sun. It grew hotter and hotter in Amalia, and I wondered if there was ever any relief before the snows set in. "Odd that you didn't mention Teodora's absence earlier."

Odd. That one word had plagued me all my life, and now it had followed me across the mountains. I couldn't have Ambrogio looking too closely at this story. Even one person bent on the truth was dangerous.

"I hoped I would find my sister and bring her home before

anyone noticed," I said. "No need for her fit to turn into a scandal." In many countries in Eterra, even the whisper of a girl running off would scatter her virtue to the winds. In Vinalia, everyone knew these things happened. In some circles, having people gossip about your secret love life was prized above all virtues. Of course, those circles were more likely to overlap with families like the Malfaras than the di Sangros.

"This is a wide city, and there is a sort of privacy to be found in crowds," Ambrogio said as he took in the seemingly endless houses and shops around us. "Teodora has been stuck in that castle for so long with no worthy men in sight. Do you think she ran away to satisfy . . . certain desires?"

I almost choked on a dusty breath. *Certain desires.* I thought of Cielo on my bed that morning, wearing nothing but a thin breeze of a shirt. What would happen if I had kissed the strega? What could possibly come of it, besides frustratingly obvious pleasure? What if I let *certain desires* carry me away from my purpose? "I think Teodora is a girl of rampant wants and needs and she must be reined in before she destroys us all."

"She's only human, this sister of yours," Ambrogio said. "Isn't that a bit harsh?"

I tramped through another puddle. "Not if you know her as I do."

In the distance, the famed gates of the Giardino Chiaro came into view. The city gardens of Amalia held fountains, mazes, and grottoes, but what I longed for most was their shade. We marched under the petals of flowering trees, and the soldiers began to sing, a song I didn't know. It had the soft swell of the hills beyond the Estatta Valley. After a few minutes it built to a crashing chorus, like the waves along the Violetta Coast.

"The new anthem," Ambrogio whispered as the crowd added its voice. These people knew the words, belting them out with more passion than tunefulness. They followed us through the Giardino Chiaro, and the line between the parade and the city fell away. The rush of bodies caught me up. The Capo looked back, settling his eyes on me, making sure I noticed exactly how beloved he was.

A threat snaked its way through the high spirits of the day. A voice told me, in no uncertain terms, that standing against the Capo would be foolish. Doing anything but following in his wake would be fighting the tide.

We stopped at the entrance, one of the highest points in Amalia, the rest of the city spread out below us like a beautifully laid table.

The priest stepped forward, and everyone's heads dipped low. His voice surprised me, younger and more familiar than I expected. The prayer was one that I had heard at any number of christenings, mumbled over the soft heads of babies. It felt like a strange choice, until I remembered that this, too, was a birth. The beginning of a country.

At least, that was what the Capo wanted us to believe.

The prayer went on, the old language calling to the magic inside of me.

Keep quiet, I thought. Blurting out magic in a dead language in front of half of Amalia wouldn't help matters.

"Thank you for blessing this gathering of the Vinalian people, Father Malfara," the Capo said.

Malfara?

That name was the flinty sound of a church bell struck in

the wrong place. How could a Malfara be a priest, if the family was known for its decadent ways? Had the Capo turned one of his brothers into a priest to gain the needed backing of the church? Would the Order of Prai really accept a Malfara, if they were so terrifyingly strict? Something about this didn't feel right. But I didn't need magic to trace the lines in the priest's face and match them to the fuller, broader features of the Capo.

They were family.

ᘎ✿ᘺ

By the time we made it back to the Palazza, a plan was ripening in my head. I ran up to my room on the third floor. Cielo had vanished, probably back to the kitchen and the delights of the baker girl.

I grabbed Luca's pack, still overstuffed with his possessions, and rushed back downstairs, where I almost blasted through a gathering: Vanni, Ambrogio, Lorenzo, Pasquale. Each one held a hearty goblet of wine.

Ambrogio offered me a cup. "We're going to discover the delights of Amalia," he said. "Care to join us?"

I waved off the drink.

Vanni bounded over to me, wine crashing out of his glass. "They have a soprano who is supposed to be able to reach an octave above high C when she is in"—his voice reached for the falsetto range—"ecstasies." He clapped my shoulder. "Apparently, she loves young nobles." When I poured my exasperation into a sigh, he shouted, "It's a joke! Do they have those where you're from, or is everyone as solemn as great hunks of stone?"

Pasquale had been drinking like the boys were in a race and he wanted to win by a stretch; now he set his cup down on the nearest table. He stared at me with a hard smile, driving my heartbeat faster as easily as he would kick a horse into a gallop. "Either Signore di Sangro doesn't like jokes or he doesn't like what you're joking *about*." He took a step closer. "Where is that servant of yours? You'll need someone to keep you warm while we're gone."

I kept my mouth shut. I didn't want to disavow whatever it was I felt for Cielo. Even if the strega didn't feel the same. Even if it would never amount to more than a few mischievous glances.

"Come with us," Ambrogio insisted. "It was the Capo's idea." That made me more determined to stay. If the Capo wanted us out of the Palazza, there was some hidden reason. "He heard I've always longed to see the opera house of Amalia, so he commissioned a performance of Il *Sole e la luna*. Mirella will boil over with jealousy."

My sister loved the opera, but she had no time for such fine things. I thought of her at home, her voice shredded with too many prayers, knees turned the tender purple of bruised plums with so much kneeling. That was a girl's lot in life. To listen, to want, to wait.

"Not an opera man?" Ambrogio asked, misreading my silence. "Don't worry. We'll make the most of every tavern on the way home. Who knows? Maybe we'll find . . . that *thing* you lost." He referred to Teodora, managing to be both vague and unsubtle at the same time.

"What I've lost is gone forever," I said. The truth in my words lingered like smoke after a candle was hastily blown out. If I succeeded, Teodora was as good as dead. My family would have to keep pretending I was Luca. The people of the Uccelli would be bribed or threatened into silence. Maybe some kind of magic could make them believe I'd always been Luca.

My mind reached outward in frantic circles.

"Say you'll come." Ambrogio's friendship, which had felt solid a moment before, swayed in a hard breeze.

"I'm sorry, friends," I said. "You'll have to listen and love and drink in my honor today."

Pasquale let out a snort that would have made a Ranian stallion proud. I took a half step forward, a movement fashioned from pure anger. As quick as I had been to start things, though, when Pasquale shoved my shoulders, I danced away. I didn't have time for the selfish foolery that boys had been taught was so necessary to life.

My decision *not* to fight angered Pasquale more than anything. He tightened his fists into ridges of bone.

"Come on," Ambrogio said, herding Vanni like a barn cat, urging the others down the hall. "We'll miss the overture." He looking back at me with disappointment in his wide brown eyes. "You're sure?"

"Absolutely," I said. "You go on." I gave them a smile, but there was dread sewn in the lining. I had set myself apart from the rest of the boys, and there would be a price. There was always a price with the five families. It was simply a matter of whether or not I would be able to afford it when the reckoning came.

I ASKED THE SERVANTS WHERE TO FIND THE CAPO, AND THEY said he was in his staterooms, not to be disturbed. I had suspected as much. He was busy with some plot he didn't want the sons of the five families to know about.

Back in the di Sangro castle, I had been taught how to threaten and coax. But there were other skills I'd needed: to sew myself into the darkest corner of a room, to listen at doors, and to snatch whispers from the currents of the air. *Lurking*, Father said, *is for shadows and unworthy men.* But I wasn't a man, and important conversations always seemed to be taking place without me.

So I'd had to teach myself.

How else would I have conveniently overhead Father when he told Beniamo about who had freshly displeased the family? How could I have been Niccolò di Sangro's right-hand man without hearing the meetings in his study, secrets shuffled and handed out like so many playing cards?

I walked past the Palazza's staterooms, a long string of empty, gilt-lined boxes. Each held plush velvet furniture, ivory, rich wood, a riot of embellishments to impress visiting kings and other important figures. A massive door at the end of the hall had been pulled shut. I would never get in, not as Luca di Sangro, and I didn't know the Palazza well enough to guess which tapestries would hide me, which corners I could tuck myself away in. I envied Cielo's ability. A mouse would have been the ideal form, though I didn't love the idea of scuttling through the walls.

I only had one other body. My original one. A short, ample brown-haired girl from the Uccelli.

I told a servant to come to my rooms on the third floor as soon as the Capo could see me. "One other thing," I said.

"I missed the excursion into the city this afternoon, and I thought I might venture out tonight, but I seem to have misplaced my cloak. Could I borrow one?"

"We only have them in green and black," the boy said.

Perfect, the magic whispered.

"That will have to do," I said with enough disdain to sour milk. The boy fetched me a cloak. "This is poorly stitched and my servant will have to tailor it, but with no other real choices at hand . . ."

The servant kept his face impressively blank as I threw a noble fit. As soon as he disappeared around the corner, I walked straight out the front arches of the Palazza and into the gardens.

A short way from the entrance, I spotted what I needed most: a hedge that would conceal me. It was molded into the shape of the Malfara wolf, and I thought of the day Father had held out the Capo's letter bearing the same icon.

Anger, guilt, and fear rose like a flock of birds. They perched at the edges of my mind as I stole behind the hedge, closing myself into the space between the rough stone walls and the slight prickle of the shrubbery.

If it had been a matter of hard work and great difficulty to change into a boy, this was the opposite. I melted back into my girlish body with a stunning lack of effort and a lavish sigh. I ran my hands over the outer curve of my breasts, the flare from waist to hips, down the plane of my thighs, taking stock of myself in a way I never truly had before.

The sun blazed through the thin fabric of my summer shirt, and I pulled the cloak tight, despite the heat, making sure it covered the noble boy's clothes beneath. My body pushed at the seams with every step.

I worked my way around the walls to the gardens that happened to be directly outside of the staterooms. The scolding heat of Amalia sided with me, for once. Diamond-paned windows stood open, allowing a breeze to travel inside.

Voices could just as easily leak out.

I followed the harsh peaks of an argument—always a good sign—and planted myself like a fixture in the dirt. If anyone came by, I would tell them I had been sent on strict orders to weed the gardens. I was wearing the Capo's colors, and so many servants rushed around that I should be able to get away with saying I was new to the Palazza. In all truth, I *was*. The only brazen part of the lie came in making someone believe I would serve the Capo.

I walked in a crouch toward the closed stateroom, stopping below the stone lip of the window. I caught the strains of two voices, distinct and yet similar, like two instruments in the same family, playing a furious tune.

"It's outrageous, and what's more, you both know and enjoy it."

"A bit. But I don't see how that changes anything."

The first voice belonged to Father Malfara, who sawed away at his words with a surprising amount of passion. The second was the Capo, rich and deep and perfectly sure of each note he hit.

"You have to stop," Father Malfara said. "You're going to confuse the people, all to thumb your nose at Prai."

"Is that what I'm doing?" the Capo asked. "I thought I was running a country."

"A country that has been under one rule for far longer than you like to admit. You want Vinalia to be a single nation, recognized by the great forces of the world, and you have it, but shifting allegiances and petty politics will never replace the church. God is eternal."

"Then he won't mind taking a nap," the Capo said. "The old gods certainly seem to be waking up."

"This cannot continue." Father Malfara's words shivered with warning. "Your obsession with the old gods is a blight on our family."

The Capo's voice rose over the priest's. ". . . our family is a blight, I believe I've made us respectable again. . . ."

"And this *magic* you insist on using will be your downfall." The disgust in the priest's voice rang clear. This man believed my very existence was a slap in the face of God. That I was a walking heresy. But I had gone to church every week and listened to the stories of God, who changed stones to oranges, and death to life, who gave himself a human form because he loved people so much, he wanted to be one of them. I had delighted in those words, almost as much as I loved the strega stories.

I'd always known that there would be people who didn't understand magic, who felt confused or afraid, or envious of a power they hadn't been given, but I staggered under the burden of this man's hatred.

"I unified Vinalia without the help of streghe," the Capo said, sounding almost bored by the argument, as if the two men had paced down this hall a hundred times and they always ended up in the same place. "That is what I promised; that is what I've done."

"And now you've let the filth in through the front door," Father Malfara said.

I had to leave. I couldn't listen to another word of this. If I kept silent and still a moment longer, I would cease to exist.

"*Stay,*" the magic insisted, the word ripping out of me, much too loud.

"What was that?" Father Malfara asked. His chair scraped the floor as he stood, and his feet fell in a pattering circle as he looked for the person who had just cried out. "I heard someone speaking the old language."

I bit my lips together, too late. Crossing the mountains, I had grown used to giving voice to my magic. A small freedom . . . I had never thought how much it might cost me.

"You're mistaken," the Capo said. "I told my servants to leave us in peace. And besides, they speak Vinalian."

"It came from outside," Father Malfara insisted.

The Capo sighed, but I heard the tap of shoes on marble as he moved toward the window. If I ran, the Capo would see me. Would he punish me for tricking my way into the Palazza with magic? Toss me into his army? Or give me to his brother, one strega that the Order of Prai would be allowed to hate openly? To bury and forget?

The Capo looked out the window. I folded myself painfully small under the stone lip, tucked out of sight.

Change him, I told the magic, careful not to speak.

It rose in a ready tide.

Change him for Father. Make him into a poisoned needle. Something that his brother the priest will prick himself on.

Magic lashed out of me, and I waited for Father Malfara to cry out, seeing that the very power he feared had entered the Palazza and claimed his family, as it had claimed mine.

Shoes tapped softly, away from the window.

The Capo hadn't changed.

My magic had left me in a great wave and done nothing. Had it been weakened by the demands of constant use? I was tired, but not fully drained as I'd been when I'd run toward Luca, tearing through the woods.

So why was the Capo still breathing?

"It must have been some old servant wandering the grounds, muttering prayers," the Capo said. "Vinalians do cling to their traditions. Your god is in no danger from me, Oreste." That name, the weighted familiarity of it, sounded so strange.

The Capo had a name too, but I couldn't imagine anyone using it.

I couldn't even remember it.

"Now that you have power, you believe you don't need God's grace or our protection," Father Malfara said, picking up his old tune. "You cannot flout the church at every turn and hope to rule without trouble."

The Capo paused, so long that I thought he might be done speaking. "If you withdraw support now, I will tell the precious Order of Prai *exactly* what you did."

I held perfectly still. What had Father Malfara done? What could be so bad that the Capo counted on it to keep the Order of Prai on his side, even as he defied them? Had Father Malfara used his power in some underhanded way, to help his brother rise to power?

Because I had listened to the scenes of so many guilty men in the di Sangro castle, I understood what followed. The heave of Father Malfara's breath, as if he could move boulders with his anger. And then the precarious moment when he stared down his brother before he left the room, his steps quickened with fear.

❧✦☙

I skimmed around the walls of the Palazza and back through the front archway as a girl of no importance, wearing the colors of the house and darting like a servant would, from task to task. I climbed the stairs, knocked politely on my own doors, and, after checking the halls on every side of the central courtyard, slipped in.

I grabbed the mirror from my pack.

When I looked down into the glass with its silver backing, I saw a girl with the deep, sticking lines of a frown, her cheeks and forehead polished with sweat. This face belonged to me; other people believed it *was* me, but it could change by tomorrow.

I had already been a screaming baby, torn from her mother too early. An uncertain little girl, watching Father from the shadows. A di Sangro daughter who did not always feel like a daughter but would never be a son. A young woman hiding a knife in her sleeve and magic in her heart.

I was all of those things, and I would be more. I stared at the mirror and found a boyish smile waiting. My lips were a dusty brownish pink that I knew perfectly well, and even in this form I had one freckle trapped in my upper lip. I settled into my broad shoulders and flared my strong hands. Everything felt strangely not-strange. This was another version of me, not a disguise. I didn't feel *odd* within my skin.

I'd never felt odd. That was everyone else's word.

A knock came, and I shoved away the mirror. When I opened the door, I tried to make it look like I'd been waiting the whole time. The servant I had spoken to earlier told me the Capo was ready to receive me in his private rooms.

"It took long enough." I made the boy wait as I grabbed

Luca's pack, checking the contents twice, playing the role of the fussy noble as well as he played the one of the obedient servant. He nodded slightly and led the way through the Palazza.

The Capo's private rooms were on the fourth floor, the highest and therefore nearest to God—befitting a leader, but all I could think was how the Capo had scoffed at God as if he were just a king grown dusty and ineffective in his age.

As if his reign in Vinalia had ended.

The servant waited, not even bothering to knock. "He'll know we're here, Signore. He always does."

The Capo was aware of every move made in the Palazza, every step taken in Amalia, and he wanted me to know it. What *he* didn't know was that I'd escaped his keen eye not ten minutes earlier.

"Come in," the Capo called.

I had dreamed up a dozen potential ways to sneak past him and get to the streghe and Father's antidote, but those came with the risk of getting caught. And then I thought of the strega stories, which all boiled down to one sweet truth. Cleverness was the answer. Whoever was the cleverest would win.

I stood in the doorway of the Capo's nearly barren room, trying to look the way I imagined Luca would. Eager, nervous.

"What can I do for you, young Signore di Sangro?" the Capo asked, pushing on the word *young* as if we both knew how untried I was. I held in a smile. The Capo saw what I wanted him to see.

I stepped forward, with a hitch of hesitation. "I assume you've heard about my . . . disinterest in spending my life as the head of the di Sangro family." Let the Capo think that

I didn't have a taste for power. It was true of Luca, so even though I was lying, I hadn't invented a thing.

"I'll admit to some surprise when you arrived in your brother's place," the Capo said. He held up a finger to let me know he had more to add. "Surprise, not disappointment."

Beniamo swept through my thoughts on wings I had dreamed up, burning into me with bright eyes. He might not have made it to the Palazza, but knowing he might be anywhere else in Vinalia didn't exactly put my fears to bed. "Beniamo wanted to be here, but he was . . . waylaid," I said. "And I was the only one left who could answer the summons. I didn't want to let my family down."

All true.

A parade of truths.

"Of course not," the Capo agreed. He spoke with such conviction at all times. It was extremely persuasive, enormously dangerous.

"My true interests lie elsewhere," I said. "As I believe you know. I've been drawn to Vinalia's work in the sciences since I was young, and I . . . I'd like to offer my help with your streghe." I waited for the glimmer of a reaction, but the Capo blinked dully, giving nothing away. "I'm interested in the basis of magic, how it works. There must be underlying principles." The Capo nodded at me to go on, and I tried to summon up what Luca had said on the mountain, the beginnings of a study he would never get to conduct. "I believe there is a symbiosis involved that gives streghe distinct powers. A meeting of mind and magic. It's the reason Azzurra can animate objects with no life of their own, while Delfina . . ."

I waited for the Capo to offer up the other girl's abilities.

What could she do? Turn harmless liquids into poison? Charm a cask of wine or a bucket of milk or a pot of ink? It would explain the letter with its clean black strokes. Its unthinkable words.

The head of your family is now dead.

"Well, she must have a power of her own," I said, rushing over the raw feelings. "I can discover the reasons behind that." The more I spoke, the tighter my stomach curled. Using Luca's words to get close to the streghe had seemed clever a few minutes ago.

Now it felt foul.

"What would be the purpose of this inquiry?" The Capo twisted a ring on his finger, keeping his eyes on me. If he looked closely enough, would he be able to peel back my layers? Would magic melt away under his scrutiny? Whatever boldness I had felt at the start of our meeting left me, and the fear that I'd been playacting as Luca became real.

"The purpose of the study?" I asked, my throat as dry as parchment. Luca wanted to know things for the simple pleasure of it, as if the natural world were a person he could speak to and understand. But the Capo was practical above all else. I needed to be smarter, to think more like Father. He would tell me to make sure any favor had a little something in it for the other party. *Don't forget to sweeten the cake, or no one will want to eat it.*

"Vinalia is already first in the sciences, and this will earn our place for years to come." The Capo's eyes snapped into focus, and I could tell I'd started down the right path. "Perhaps I can find a way to make magic more useful to Vinalia."

He nodded briskly.

And in that small stroke, the Capo told me a great truth. He believed in the glory of Vinalia above all else: family, God, even his own life. The power he had gathered to himself wasn't a matter of pride or even a delusion of greatness. He kept his room as neat and simple as a barracks. He was the first soldier in the army of Vinalia.

If I had learned so much in speaking to the Capo for five minutes, what damning truth had I handed over without knowing it?

I shoved my pack forward. Luca's vials clinked inside. "It won't be any expense or trouble. I have my own tools."

He inspected the wealth of instruments. "It seems you came prepared for the challenge," he said. "But be careful. The streghe of the Palazza are not little girls to be toyed with."

I almost stumbled to hear him speak of these girls with such respect. Would anyone in the five families do that much? Would they defend streghe even against the church in Prai? "I'll tread lightly," I said, and for once, I was telling a complete truth. "Where do I find them?"

The Capo flicked a look toward a door vined with iron bars, a private door in his private rooms. My face must have gone as hard as stucco, because the Capo gave a short laugh. "If I was keeping them here by force, do you think I would tell you so freely?" He worked a ring off his middle finger, a thin band of dark metal stamped with a running wolf. A gold ring adorned the next finger, beside his thumb. It looked close to pure gold, untempered and soft, like a craftsman who barely knew his trade had made the thing. And yet it lived on the Capo's hand, right next to the infamous Malfara wolf. "Show this to the servants along the way."

The Capo opened the door with a harsh cry of metal. "This is for their own safety."

Did he know about the abductions of streghe throughout the city? Was he offering asylum to people with magic? As much as I hated the Capo, the idea tugged at me.

I stepped onto a shadowy landing, then started down stairs so long, they seemed to pinch in the distance. Torches lined one side, striping the steps with darkness. The stone walls breathed cool after the murderous heat of Amalia. I stepped off the last of the stairs into a chamber that swept away from me on both sides. The dungeon was silent.

Luca was screaming.

My breath turned to shards as memories came back in broken pieces. The musty reaches of the dungeon. Beniamo, sweating with the effort of his cruelty. Luca, yellowed by the torchlight.

Luca, telling me to run.

I wouldn't be able to take another step unless I pushed these thoughts away. I forced myself to take a long, smooth breath. I pulled myself up from the depths of memory and kept to the surface of things.

Walking toward the strega sisters, I chanted two words under my breath.

"The antidote.

"The antidote."

I told myself it was the only thing I needed.

11

I made my way through the false night of the dungeons, each step taking me farther from the daylight and anyone who cared if I went missing. No one but the Capo knew I was down here, and the only path back went through his private rooms.

I had cornered myself.

The dungeons of the Palazza were laid out in a series of concentric circles. A guard stood at the entrance to each circle, and I counted eight before I reached a final wooden door with iron hinges. Like the rest of the guards, this one nodded silently and stepped aside when I showed the Capo's ring.

When I reached what appeared to be the center of the rippling dungeons, I found the girls in a small circular room with two bare feather mattresses on the floor, plates of rich food scattered around, and a pile of storybooks spread wide at the bindings, their illustrations drenched in color.

Strega stories.

The girls no longer wore their green and black, but simple white dresses that rushed down to their ankles. They looked even younger than before, dark hair curling against their long necks, cheeks yellowed by the torchlight. If this had been an illustration in a story, I would have called the girls sweet, delicate, innocent. But I knew from experience that power and the look of power were two different things that only sometimes overlapped.

"Azzurra," I said, bowing slightly at the waist. I turned to the other girl. "Delfina."

"Not royal, the last time I checked," Azzurra said, rubbing her bare forehead as if she might find a crown.

"I'm only showing respect for your abilities," I said, keenly aware of how they outweighed mine.

"Power." The word sounded bitter in Azzurra's mouth. "Where does it lead a person? Here. To hell." She waved at the walls, gesturing grandly at the bare flagstones. "Did you not notice?"

"The Capo said you were here by your own choice." The stones threw my voice back at me, merciless.

"Oh, we are," Azzurra said. "There are worse places than hell, and we've visited a few."

Delfina nodded, her black curls jangling behind her. She held a cloth-bound book firmly in one hand and sketched with the other.

Did she use that book to control her poisons? Did each page contain a different one, like Cielo's book? When I inched closer, all I saw were sketches, the sort that Carina and Adela liked to do on a fine spring day. A perfect rose. A batch of lavender. Another rose, wildly blooming, petals loosened by the wind.

"Do you have an interest in flowers?" I asked, my mind speeding toward new possibilities. What if Delfina turned flowers into poison? Could a certain bloom contain the antidote I needed? I tried to catch Delfina's eye, but she stayed in her world of charcoal and paper. "I might be able to bring you flowers here, if you'd like."

"I wouldn't make any promises you can't keep," Azzurra said. "And I wouldn't step closer." She slid her body between mine and Delfina's. The smile she gave me looked deeply wrong, as if she'd seen so few smiles in her life that she had to make one from scratch. "So, you are a *scientist*," she said. "We've never had one of those. Our village saw no use for such men."

"I'm from a small place too. A town fastened to a mountainside." I wanted to spill the beauty of the Uccelli and the di Sangro castle and Chieza all over this dark room, but my words stopped, half-formed. I thought about the first meeting with the Capo, how easily Azzurra turned all of our weapons against us. I didn't want to give her anything new to play with.

"Tell me about your science," Azzurra said, and her smile glowed brighter, like a knife catching the light.

I dug up Luca's ideas again. "I believe magic lives in you in a kind of symbiosis. . . ."

"And I believe those fancy words cover the dark pit of your heart," Azzurra said. "Now that we've traded opinions, you can go."

She swayed on her toes, but it wasn't just a bit of tuneless dancing. She was blocking Delfina, protecting her sister from me. It took me a moment to remember my boyish body. If a strange young man came to speak to Carina or Adela, I would stand between them, too.

"Don't you want to know how magic works?" I asked.

"You came here to tell *me* about magic?" Azzurra asked

with a laugh so raw, it was bloody. "Trust that I know a great deal more about it than you."

"Please," I said, holding up the pack, carefully removing a vial. "Just a few small samples. It could lead to great discoveries." I thought of Father's words again. *Sweeten the cake.* "Ones that could help you and your sister."

"Help! You want to help us?" She looked to Delfina, who shook her head, curls clashing. When Azzurra spoke again, her eyes stayed on her sister. "Our childhood was as simple as a story. We ran barefoot in the woods, told each other pretty tales, slept under warm blankets. Our parents loved us. Even after they saw what we could do. They took care of us. Kept us safe from everyone else."

"Mean eyes and meddling," Delfina added, her voice a thin shadow of her sister's.

Then she shut her lips tight.

"The village knew there were pretty girls locked up in our house, and pretty girls belong to whoever can claim them. Delfina was barely twelve when the first men came. They ended up dead. She and I dragged them to the woods, but our parents could feel the truth. One day a man came and said he didn't crave our magic or our bodies. He didn't dream of ridding the world of our kind. He just wanted to understand us. He just wanted to *help*. Our parents saw his sweet eyes and our dangerous ways and they thought, yes. *Help.* The first time a man was brought to take us, Delfina made short work of him. He sent more men, and I made longer work of those."

My hands tightened a notch for every word she spoke.

Azzurra made her way around the room, flitting in and out of torchlight. Her sister stayed crouched behind her, never looking at me. "When we were too tired to fight, he took us to an abandoned house outside the village, locked us up in a room below ground. He would come every few days. Give us a bite of food. A dab of water on our lips. A trickle of sunlight. In return, he wanted answers. How did we come by magic? Where did it live? Could he cut it out of us?"

"That's not science." Sadness raked its long nails over my voice, my skin. "That's barbaric."

"I'm sure you're very different," Azzurra said. "And I'm sure that's what everyone tells themselves at night before they fall asleep." Her fingers drifted back and forth, as if conducting a lullaby.

Vials from my pack rose into the air, dancing back and forth. Azzurra dropped her hands and smashed them to

pieces.

"You're wrong about me," I said. The truth pried at my thoughts, loosening my tongue. I wanted to give them my secret. I was a strega. These girls could trust me. But I couldn't take such a risk—Azzurra was clearly dangerous.

I asked my magic for an idea, some way to prove I hadn't come here to hurt anyone, but to learn the truth. "Tell me about *the brilliant death*." The words slipped out, the ones Cielo and I had found in the woods, so heavy with magic that I could barely hold them.

Azzurra turned to me in one sharp twist. "Where did you hear that?"

"An old strega in the woods of the Uccelli," I said. "I want to know what *the brilliant death* is, exactly. How it works. The intricacies. I believe it will help me understand the nature of magic. Delfina, will you show me?"

Delfina shook her head.

"She doesn't like to use her power," Azzurra said.

I thought of what Cielo had told me about the soldiers of Erras, how they wouldn't let the sisters join because they demanded all magic be put to use. How poisonous was Delfina's power that she didn't even want to claim it?

Azzurra darted forward and grabbed the collar of my shirt. Her blue-gray eyes filled my view, dangerous skies before a storm. "My sister won't show you the brilliant death, but I will." She curled her fingers through the air and the broken pieces of glass on the ground lifted, hovering. They flew at me, prodding sharp points into my back.

I cast a look at Delfina, but she had gone back to her drawings, and the glass sliced into my back viciously until I followed Azzurra. She marched through the gate of the center ring without being stopped by the guard.

The Capo had told one truth, at least. These girls weren't being kept here against their will.

"This way." The cells along the ring were empty, their silent stones and their neat straw cots patient, as if waiting for prisoners. We stopped in front of the only cell that seemed to hold one. A woman, with hair the color of red-orange roof tiles, lay curled on her side, but as soon as she saw Azzurra, she pricked up to sitting.

"What was her crime?" I asked.

"She wasn't brought here against her will," Azzurra said. "She agreed to this, the same as I did."

"Please." The woman drew breath so heavily, it sounded like the hiss of watered coals. "Please, don't."

Those three words visited me again. *The brilliant death.* What could it have to do with magic? With Cielo's mother?

With this woman on the floor of the dungeon, her eyes forced wide with fear?

"It's too late for regrets," Azzurra said, stroking the woman's face through the bars. Her hair color changed under Azzurra's fingers, dun red to crow black. Her eyes flashed violet, then brown, then a bright, cutting green.

"She's a strega," I said.

The shards at the small of my back whipped away, leaving a sting. They parted around Azzurra's body and found their way through the bars. The sight of the glass seemed to gather the woman's panic to a single, hard point. "How can you do this? How can you bear it? We're the same."

"You are nothing to me," Azzurra said, smiling through the bars. "But your magic . . ."

The glass flew at the woman, shards landing in her chest, her stomach, her neck. She struggled against them, which only seemed to make it worse. Her blood ran in trickles and gouts.

She screamed and screamed.

I was back in the dungeons.

I was watching Luca die.

The woman's neck drooped, and as her heart weakened, the blood stopped rushing with such force. Her breath shivered to a stop.

Azzurra closed her eyes, looking refreshed, as if she'd taken a drink from a clear mountain stream. "The body falls away, but magic can't die. It simply finds another strega."

The magic inside me stopped like frozen rivers. "And it . . . always works like that?"

"No exceptions," Azzurra said.

Which meant my own magic came from someone who had died.

Mother.

That was the truth I'd been grasping for. I had it in my hands now, shiny and obvious. My mother must have carried magic in her body, and when she died in childbirth, I had been the one to take it in, to give it a new home.

That explained why Father refused to speak of magic. Why he hated strega stories. Though he loved Fiorenza, he missed my mother, every day, and those stories mocked him, promising magic when it had already fled from his life. My father must not have heard about *the brilliant death*. He couldn't have known her magic would pass to me.

Maybe the same had happened to Cielo's mother. Maybe it was *meant* to happen. Childbirth, sickness, old age, those were the ways magic was supposed to be passed down. Azzurra had taken the idea and, like melting down metal, forged it into a new shape. One with a vicious edge.

"You look sickly, mountain boy," she said, and I blinked away the thoughts of my own magic. I tried to bury it deep inside me, as if that could keep me safe. Azzurra *couldn't* know I was a strega. She would do the same to me that she'd done to the woman in the cell, slumped on the stones in a ring of her blood.

"Thank you for showing me," I said, the fear in my voice carefully covered in a thin layer of manners. "This is a great discovery."

Azzurra dropped her hands, and the glass—the bits of Luca's vials—fell to the ground with a pretty, harmless sound. "Streghe have been doing this in secret since before the invention of time. You can try to wring some personal glory out of it, if you want, but everyone will know how this works soon enough." She spun on a bare heel. "You were right about one thing," she added over her shoulder. "I do like showing you how magic works."

༄༅

AZZURRA SEALED HERSELF BACK IN THE INNER DUNGEON WITHout a word. I ran up the long stairs, through the trapped air, and emerged back in the Capo's rooms. He was still there, reading from one of the history books that lined the single shelf above his bed.

"Make any new discoveries?" the Capo asked, as if I'd taken a nature walk instead of throwing myself into a lair with dangerous streghe.

The words lumped in my throat.

The Capo must know about *the brilliant death*. He had to be aware of what was happening in his dungeons. Or did he leave everything to Azzurra and Delfina, not caring what they did as long as they grew stronger and used their magic for the glory of Vinalia? Was he the general, plotting every move, or only a soldier, turning his back as they plundered?

"I'll have to come back and continue my efforts," I finally said.

The Capo turned serious as he looked me over. "I'm afraid I can't allow that. They've hurt you." He spun me around to inspect the bloody lines on my back.

"A small miscalculation. It's nothing. . . ."

"I do not wish to see you damaged by the magic of an eager

strega," the Capo said, and strangely enough, I believed him. It would have been easier if he hated me outright. I was used to having simple enemies, not dangerous friends. In his thinking, the Capo really had tried to kill my father for the future of Vinalia, for the betterment of the people, even for me.

The Capo instructed me to go to the kitchens for a poultice, but the cuts lost their sting more quickly than I thought possible. I took the main stairs toward the third floor. The cutout of sky above the courtyard burned an eager blue. All I could think of was Cielo. I needed to find Cielo and admit I knew the meaning of *the brilliant death*.

Within a single breath of my quarters, a voice snared me and held me in place. "Di Sangro! You there, di Sangro!"

On the facing hall, across the central courtyard, a girl with golden-brown skin and hair the color of deep afternoon sunshine waved at me. She had a forehead so high, it resembled a cliff's face. Sharply drawn lips, a long, straight nose. Despite her vivid features, or perhaps because of them, she was beautiful.

She also walked fast—she had already turned the corner and was coming my way. I bowed stiffly at the waist and waited for a sign of how to proceed. I had spent so much time thinking about how changing into a boy would set me in a different position to the men of Vinalia, I had hardly spared a thought for the women.

It gave me a touch of guilt.

"I knew it," the girl said, breathless with victory.

"Knew . . . what?" I asked, the courtly language I should have used falling away.

"My name is Favianne Rao," she said in a distinct accent that could only be from the southern provinces. "And *you* are the boy we saw on the side of the road. The one who had nothing on his . . ." Her eyes flicked down my body.

This was the face I had seen by moonlight, emerging from a carriage window. This was the voice that rang out, drawing Pasquale back to her side when he would have happily beaten me to dust. "I owe you a debt."

Her smile tightened as she took me in. Her eyes were deep water, a dark but clear blue. "Pasquale never told me you were here."

"I don't think I delighted him with my magical reappearance," I said.

Favianne laughed, and it sounded like an ice-fed spring, cold but refreshing. Cielo topped the stairs just in time to see her hold out her hand to be kissed. I grabbed Favianne's hand, a little too roughly, and corrected by gracing her skin with a particularly gentle touch of the lips.

"Pasquale is a fool," she said, setting her hand to her chest. "I am very, very glad you're here. We could do with a bit of fresh mountain air."

Cielo cleared his throat.

Favianne looked back and forth between us. "There is a ball tomorrow," she said, fixing her eyes on me. "Some grand affair for the glittering set of Eterra. If you owe me a debt, I hope you will come and save me from eternal boredom. I couldn't dance another stiff-backed waltz or eat another candied almond if my neck was on the block."

She started off toward Pasquale's rooms, and Cielo frowned openly at the girl's back. I wondered if she could feel the force of it, nudging her down the hall.

"I have to tell you something," I said, the moment Favianne was gone.

Cielo didn't seem to be listening. The strega stormed toward our room, and as soon as the door closed, he started in on me. "Are you sure you've thought through the mechanics of being a boy? Of *staying* a boy?"

"What do you mean?" I asked, surprised by the strega's sudden force.

"It's not enough to saunter around the Palazza with a gruff voice and a manly gait. This is your life, Teodora."

"And it's not yours to lecture me about," I said.

Cielo seemed to be looking for words to toss at me, to see if they'd throw me off-balance. "As the head of the di Sangro family, you'll be expected to kill people."

"Only if they have done great and unquestionable harm." My mind twisted below the Palazza, into the dungeons. That strega had done nothing wrong. Azzurra had even told me she wasn't a prisoner.

Cielo sighed, long and gusty. "It must be nice to live in a fortress of rightness that no one can scale."

I crossed my arms as if that could stop the strega's barb from finding my heart. "I've changed men with my magic. I would have killed them if I could see no other way." The words were ugly and comforting at once. "Do you have any other challenges in mind?"

"Yes." Cielo grabbed his book and turned into girlish form in a whirl of skin and silk. She held her eyes wide with challenge. "What happens when they start tossing young ladies in your direction?"

"Is *that* what this is about?" I asked, gesturing to the

hallway where I'd talked with Favianne. "I'm here to save my family, not to flirt."

"You imagine that if you become the di Sangro heir, a marriage won't be close behind?" Cielo asked. "You'll have to pick a noble young lady and produce—what are those pesky things called?" She slid toward me, close and then closer yet. "Ah, yes. Heirs." Her every-colored eyes glossed with mischief. "Could you do that?"

The strega was testing my resolve. She wasn't *trying* to make my heart skip like a stone across the surface of a lake.

It would have been easy to pull away and give some excuse about fulfilling my duty. The lie shimmered like a dropped coin in the gutter, tempting and mostly harmless. Yet the more I spent currency that did not belong to me, the heavier I felt. I was tired of other peoples' truths.

I put a hand to the side of Cielo's face, the velvet pink just beneath her cheekbone. "I don't think I'll have trouble finding girls beautiful." Cielo blinked at me as if I'd changed the rules of a game in the middle of a round.

In the courtliest gesture I could imagine, I lifted her hand to my lips. Kissed it. This was nothing like kissing Favianne's hand, which was small and tidy and overly scented. Cielo's long fingers skimmed the air as if their touch might pluck music from it. Her skin was soft and warm, and one kiss beckoned another. I turned the strega's hand over and pressed my lips to the lines in her palm.

It wasn't my new body or its boyish ways that made my blood press through me like spring rivers, overflowing their bounds.

This was me. This had always been me.

"Well," the strega said softly. "That's one less thing to worry about." But it felt like she was telling me the exact opposite.

The truth I had given Cielo would most likely prove expensive. We could not afford to care about each other more than we already did. Cielo was a wild strega. I was a di Sangro. We could only lose each other.

"I have something to tell you," I said, still holding Cielo's hand in both of mine as I blinked away this dream.

"I have news too." Cielo moved away like quicksilver. It was too much like that moment at the pond, when the strega dashed away from me—or from feelings that might prove impossible to act on.

"My news first," I said, but Cielo was already leaping ahead.

"I went to see the kitchen strega," she said. "I told her that you'd sent me down to ask about her recipes. The old woman said lies were as easy to see through as onion skin. And then she peered at me as if she were looking through time itself. As if she knew me."

"Did she?" I asked.

"She said she would pack me a picnic," Cielo said, not swerving from the road of her memory. "And that I should come back tonight if I got hungry again. I took the basket from her, went outside in the last of the sunshine, and ate every bite."

"What happened?" I asked, feeling breathless as the story brought us closer to each other. This sort of nearness had little to do with our bodies. I could know the look of Cielo's bare skin without knowing a thing about the person inside it. This, what we were trading now, was a deeper kind of knowing.

"I fell asleep, and she was there," Cielo said.

"The old strega?" I asked.

Cielo shook her head, like she couldn't believe the words she was about to say. "My mother. I saw her walking through the Palazza back when it was first built. Before this was the capital of Vinalia. My mother was there . . . wandering the rooms. Touching things. Humming. She looked like me, if you painted me in watercolors and smeared me to a soft hue."

She must have been beautiful, if she looked anything like Cielo. "What else was in the dream?"

"Not a dream. It was a piece of the past." Cielo's eyes lit on me with an eagerness I hadn't seen since the day on the mountain, when we'd first met. "That strega knows what happened to my mother. She's going to show us."

". . . us?"

"I thought you might come," Cielo said, pruning each word carefully. "The old woman wants a trade, magic for magic, and I can hardly give her my book."

You can help, the magic told me.

I had a pack full of items for such a purpose. If none of those appealed to the strega, there were other ways. The promises I'd learned to make as a di Sangro. The shiny bribes, the shadowed threats.

It had worked with Adolfo. It could work again.

You are what Cielo needs, the magic told me, pushing with the strength of my blood. Leaving behind a burn as fierce as any blush.

Every minute away from the castle was a minute Father grew sicker. He was dying in a makeshift bed, and I was sitting on a fine feather bed in Amalia. But I could not look away from the swirl of colors in Cielo's eyes. I could not deny what Cielo wanted. What I'd always had.

A family to love, even if they were gone.

I shouldered my pack, heavy with the weight of changed men. "Don't worry," I said. "We'll convince her."

12

I nudged a door open to find that the kitchens were a dark, vast country under the Palazza. A great number of servants and cooks inhabited it, working at their tables and ovens by candlelight.

"That's her." Cielo pointed to a woman in the farthest corner, sweeping ashes. Warm light smudged away some of her years, yet she still looked older than anyone in Chieza.

I started to walk, the sea swell of my hips reminding me with each step that I looked like a girl again. I hadn't expected to be back in this form so soon, but Luca di Sangro would have drawn too many stares in the kitchens.

As we neared the old strega, a door in my mind opened onto a snow-filled night. I was back in the di Sangro kitchens, nine years old and clutching a glass that was soon to break. Magic waited for me, and death.

"What's wrong?" Cielo asked as my steps faltered on the stone. His hands flew to my waist, reminding me of how that man, who did not belong in our home, had slumped against Father as he'd died.

"I'm feeling . . . strange." Walking toward the strega was

like walking through a storm of memory, thoughts dark, cold, and swirling.

The strega blew on the ashes of her hearth fire; it sprang to life. "Some people cannot help but remember things when they are near me," she said. The words were clearly aimed at me, even if she didn't look away from the velvety orange flames. "Call it an old woman's gift."

I knew it was more than that, but I wasn't going to point her out as a strega in front of the whole kitchen. Still, I wanted to know why I kept returning to this place in my head. This small set of moments, each as crystalline and sharp as a snowflake. The moth, the sugar, the man dying.

Father telling me my fate.

The strega shook her hands vaguely at the low beams of the rafters, hung with braids of garlic and the long fingers of dried peppers. "I've been in these kitchens forty years. This place is filled with flour dust. Butter and lard smear the air. Rosemary weaves itself in. Little bits of everything I've done are here, and anyone can taste them. For some people, that's enough to help them remember."

I was breathing in her magic—but why did it bring me back to that night?

The old woman shrugged, as if my question made itself plain without a single word spoken. "A memory is like any other story. You can hear it a hundred times and think it is always the same. And then"—she waved her hand in that same vague, frustrating way—"one hundred and one. The transformation comes."

I sifted through the memory again, but all I could see was Father, telling me what it meant to be a di Sangro. A small,

eager Teodora, reaching for a knife. I checked my sleeve without thinking.

Pasquale still had Father's stiletto. The worry that I would never get to steal it away from him brought me back to the Palazza, and the moment at hand. I had too many problems to go digging for more in the past.

"So," the strega said to Cielo. "You're hungry."

He nodded.

The old woman pulled a basket from under the table— pale wood, woven tightly, covered with a dark blue cloth. Cielo lifted it from the old woman's arms, which appeared as strong as they were riven with wrinkles.

"Thank you," Cielo said with a deep nod. If the strega appeared older than anyone I'd seen, Cielo looked younger than I'd ever imagined he could. Getting closer to the truth of his mother was changing him.

"Thank the Palazza, child," the old strega said. "This place has memories. They all do. Homes, cities, countries. You're young; you can only see through your own eyes. I was young once too. Remember that."

"Yes," Cielo said. "We will."

The old woman's hand shot out, trapping Cielo's on the handle of the basket. "Swear to it?"

Cielo nodded more slowly this time.

"Remembering is not an easy thing," the old strega said. "But what we choose *not* to remember can hurt us more than what we do." She let up on Cielo's hand, patting it once. "I put olives in there for you."

Cielo gave her a tight smile.

"Now, where is my payment?" the old woman asked.

I turned my pack over on her work table. The rose plant

and the rest of the items tumbled into a dusting of flour. I fished out the mirror. I would need that to change me back into a boy. "Anything else is yours."

The strega spat on the table. The gobbet mixed with the flour, turning into a foul paste.

"Charming," I said.

"Trinkets," the old woman muttered. "What use do I have for finery?"

The question made me think of *the brilliant life*. The use wasn't always the point. Loveliness could be its own end, a way to twist the thread of life and turn it into something beautiful beneath your fingers.

"They're made from . . ."

"Yes, yes, I see what they are. I see it a deal more clearly than *you*." She waved off my life's work. "What else can you offer?"

I wanted to walk away from this miserable lump of a woman and tell her that she could keep her picnics. But Cielo had the basket in his arms, filled with memories he had chased all over Vinalia.

I could not ask him to hand it back.

"I am at your service, Signora," I said in a dim voice. "If you have enemies, I will transform them."

"Enemies?" She waved the word off as if batting children away from her ankles. "I have no enemies."

"Would you like to borrow a few of mine?" I asked. She glared, her eyes so deep inside their folds that they were almost hidden. And yet I could feel them searching me. "What else can I give you?"

She pointed at the iron necklace I wore. The one that Fiorenza had given me for luck before I left the di Sangro

187

castle. The one that traced a short path back to my mother. I clutched at the circle. "It's only a charm. An old superstition."

She reached out and snapped the leather cord, the back of my neck stinging. She looked down and muttered, "Weak and crude, but it will do." When she looked up at me again she smiled, her teeth rising in harsh moons against her gums. "There's healing in here."

"Is that true, Teo?" Cielo asked.

I had never thought to wonder if the necklace carried anything but comfort. I touched my back and found Azzurra's cuts had already faded. The scratches from Beniamo's claws had become scars so quickly.

My mother had told Father to give the necklace to his new wife, to keep her safe. And if Mother was truly the strega who had died and passed her magic along to me, she must have had a power of her own.

Was there healing in this little ring of iron?

Yes, the magic told me. *Yes.*

"Teo?" Cielo's voice summoned me back to the kitchens. "She's asking if she can keep it."

The old woman was fondling the necklace, the only reminder of Mother I carried with me. "I need this for aches and pains," she said. "Time is your friend when you are young. It will be the only enemy left at the end."

I thought of Father on his bed, dying. Fiorenza and the girls, waiting for me. My mother, who had died waiting for the doctor.

Time had never been my friend.

"That belongs to me," I said.

Cielo's face collapsed. I thought the strega would be disappointed, angry even, but all I saw in the strega's eyes was permission to take it back. Somehow, that was worse. Cielo would come all this way and learn nothing, because of my selfishness.

"It's yours now," I said.

I traced the necklace with my eyes, a quick farewell. I hadn't understood what it was until I stood to lose it. But that bit of iron wasn't the only possession of Mother's that I carried. I had her magic, twined up with me.

I always had.

Still, it hurt to watch the old strega smile as if she'd earned it, settling the charm in the sharp valley of her collarbone. "Nothing is truly ours, but I'll keep it warm for a little while." She went back to the hearth and tended to her precious ashes, as if we weren't even there.

"Let's go," I said. "Before she spits on us again."

BACK IN OUR ROOMS, I REMOVED THE FEATHER-STUFFED DUVET from the bed and spread the contents of the basket on the white sheets. Besides olives, the strega had packed a long crispy ciabatta, blackberry jam, and a small bottle of wine that fit neatly in Cielo's palm.

"How do you think she does it?" Cielo asked, pressing his nose to the sage-colored glass, inspecting motes that fell through the dark liquid. "Does she infuse the wine with memories? Add them to the jam as it cooks? Knead the past into the bread?"

"I have no idea," I said, not really caring about the old strega's methods, only the peace of mind they promised Cielo.

He tucked one long leg beneath him and sat on the bed.

Cielo had taken on many appearances since we'd met, but until now I had never seen the strega look excited and nervous enough to shatter glass.

"I know what *the brilliant death* means," I said quickly. I waited for the pain of holding the secret to be replaced by the pain of saying it out loud. "It's how magic is passed down. A death inheritance. It means . . . Adolfo was right. Your mother is dead."

The strega ripped off a piece of bread and coated it carefully with jam. "Do you want some?"

"I just said . . ."

"I know what you said," Cielo told me, looking up. "But that doesn't change whether or not I need to see her."

I nodded. That much, I understood. I had wanted to know more about my mother every day of my life.

My fingers hovered over the morsel. "What if it's not as strong if you share it? What if you only see half the dream?"

"Magic doesn't work by half measures." Cielo's knowing tone usually drove me to the cliff's edge of patience. Tonight I didn't mind. It felt good to hear the strega sound so sure. I took the piece of bread and chewed slowly. Cielo used a knife to pry the cork from the wine bottle, and raised the bottle over our heads. "To your mother."

"Don't you mean to yours?" I asked.

"I know what you did," the strega said, frowning at the bread in his fingers. "What you gave the old woman."

My hand flew to my neck, rubbing at the spot where the cord used to sit against it. "I never told you who that necklace belonged to."

The wine had done its work, softening the strega's edges. "You didn't have to." Cielo leaned forward, and I could smell the traces of our long night, sweat and wood fires and mingled spices.

I washed the food down with several long drafts of wine. Cielo finished the bottle and drew the back of one hand across his lips, stained dark as the blackberry jam. I wondered if they tasted as sweet.

"Take the bed," I told him. "I'll sleep on the cot."

"There's no real need," Cielo said, without a hint of teasing. I had never seen shyness on the strega's face; it came with a nervous pressing of the lips and a soft gray wash to the strega's eyes. It claimed my breath, turned my heartbeat to a painful staccato.

I almost climbed straight into the bed with Cielo, but then I would never have been able to let him sleep, and the old strega's picnic would be wasted. I crawled into the cot and took a deep breath, facing away from Cielo. I stared at the whitewashed wall and named every flower that grew on the mountain where I'd been born.

🜂⚕🜍

IN THE WAY OF DREAMS, I DIDN'T KNOW IT WAS A DREAM AT first. I simply arrived in the Palazza, in one of the great halls. It was stuffed with furniture, paintings, every kind of adornment. Even the umbrella stand shone with jewels. Whether the sum looked glorious or gaudy depended on the angle and the light and the person looking.

A young woman stood in the center of the room, carrying a small bag. She appeared to be only a few years older than I was now. She had Cielo's long dark hair. She had Cielo's willow switch of a body.

She also had Cielo's laugh.

"You can't be serious," she said.

The dream revealed a person I hadn't known was there before. A young man with stiff brown hair and a crescent of perfect white teeth. He hadn't decided on a beard. He wasn't the Capo yet, just a boy.

"I'm entirely serious," he said in an evenhanded tone. "I want to use strega magic to unite Vinalia." My mind ran ahead of the dream—that wasn't what happened. "I believe in a strong country where streghe can be free. Is that something you're interested in?"

This young woman didn't have Cielo's controlled emotions. They filled her face one at a time, so plain that I could read them like words in fresh ink. Disbelief. Need. Hope.

"Of course, we can't let anyone know that magic is behind this," the Capo said. "Not for now. There will be a day when magic is used freely in Vinalia. You can help bring that about, Giovanna Allegri. But first I need to know: Will you fight for it? Will you die for it?"

"Yes." Cielo's mother nodded. "Yes."

"Will you kill for it?"

A COURTYARD IN THE PALAZZA REPLACED THE GREAT HALL. Cielo's mother stood at one end, faced at the other by a young woman with fire wrapped around her wrists, like two pet snakes. A bucket of water stood in front of her, and when she dipped her hand in, the flame grew stronger.

The girl was an element changer.

She picked up a handful of dust and blew. It became a

great wind tossing Cielo's mother backward. The Capo watched them, off to one side.

Cielo's mother waited. She didn't fight back. She didn't make any great show of magic. Instead Giovanna concentrated on the girl at the other end of the courtyard, her face tortured with effort.

The girl's fire snakes dropped to the ground and went out with a hiss. "What are you doing?"

"You used your magic up so quickly," Cielo's mother said. "And then you wanted to rest. All I did was change your wish into a reality." The Capo kept his eyes pinned on Cielo's mother, his prize horse about to win a race. "If I find the merest hint of rage in someone's mind, I can bend it toward violence. Where there is weariness, I make a person lie down. I spin fear into a show of cowardice."

"You told me I was here to change the future of Vinalia," the girl said, turning to the Capo, her words hot with betrayal.

I thought of the strega in the dungeon, the one whose hair had changed, red to black. Had she been given the same promise? What if Azzurra had spoken the truth? What if the woman I saw die wasn't a prisoner but a willing convert?

"You *are* the future of Vinalia," the Capo said. "Your power will feed Giovanna's, and her power will change everything." He paced, speaking as much to himself as to the young women locked in battle. "I can't keep an army of streghe. It would be unruly. Impossible to command. Too much magic that could be turned against me." He caged the girl with a hard look. "You agreed to be a soldier, and soldiers are ready to die for their country."

So this was what I'd seen play out in the depths of the Palazza. The reason streghe were disappearing.

Everything I watched in this dream was happening again.

"She doesn't care about your glory," Cielo's mother said, the mercy in her voice far more terrifying than the Capo's cold reason. "All she wants is to go home. I am giving her what she wants. I am sending her home."

The young woman, weeping, lay down in the dirt. With a booted foot, she kicked over her bucket of water, and in a rush that burned through colors as fast as cloth, blue to orange to pure white, she went up in flames.

"YOUR FAMILY IS AFRAID OF US," CIELO'S MOTHER TOLD THE Capo. They capped the ends of a long dinner table, empty but for the two of them. Dishes between them had been laden with veal and lamb, soft cheese, red pears so fresh that they glistened.

"What do you propose we do about it?" the Capo asked, not sharply, simply entertaining ideas as he ladled the spring peas.

Cielo's mother beamed at her own cleverness. It hurt to see that look of Cielo's carved into Giovanna's face as she worked out ways to harm people. "They will think it's their idea," she said. "I promise."

"If I wake up in a pool of my family's blood, you will be back on the streets," the Capo said over a mouthful of peas.

"The streets of Amalia raised me better than your parents would have," Giovanna scoffed. "They spoiled you until you were as useless as a blackened tooth. *You* made yourself who you are. You owe them nothing. We should—"

"I *will not* have them dead," the Capo said, slicing across her words. "We begin our military campaigns in the fall. No one must be whispering of what I did back in Amalia. Tell me what you are planning, or I will make the fights in the courtyard three against one."

Cielo's mother stabbed at a piece of lamb. "Your family dreams of escaping to some lovely place where they can forget you, forget all of this. I'll encourage them to leave, that's all." She chewed a stuck mouthful, then spat a white mess of fat onto her plate. She pursed her lips, looking thoroughly disgusted with the dinner, the Capo, herself. "Let's send everyone away but the two of us."

The Capo shook his head. "When the time comes, I will need the people of Amalia on my side."

"One more reason to get rid of your family," she said. "The people don't trust them. They're noble backstabbers, and they've made a sport of putting their cocks in any woman they can find. It might entertain some, but most people are sick of their excess. Or haven't you noticed?"

"Fine," the Capo said. "But leave my brother Oreste. He's the only good one in that pack of wolves."

༄✿༄

THE NEXT TIME I SAW CIELO'S MOTHER, SHE LOOKED OLDER, AS if a few years had passed in the world but centuries had passed behind her eyes. They were darker than Cielo's, a single color, the deep brown of frost-hardened earth.

She sat in her rooms in the Palazza, which had been stripped of extravagance, down to bare walls.

A man who looked like the Capo, with a wider set to his eyes and a softness to his lips, knelt at Giovanna's feet.

Oreste.

He wore the robes of the Order of Prai. At first, I feared what he would do to her, or perhaps what she would do to *him*. But they only stared at each other, a trembling string that might snap at any moment.

"You shouldn't trust me," Cielo's mother said.

Oreste sighed as if he'd heard this many times before.

"I've killed people." She threw the words at him. "I'll kill more."

Oreste was not moved by the outburst. "I've killed as well, for what I once thought was a noble and necessary cause." He reached for her hand, but she slithered back from his touch, curling as if she had some mortal wound in her stomach. "Giovanna, you believe my brother sees what you truly are. He only sees what he can do with you."

"Doesn't that make you the same?" she asked. "You just want to do different things with me." She tried for a cruel laugh, but it died in her throat. "I can make you love me, you know. It would be worse than killing you."

Oreste's smile was a flower blooming in an impossible place. "If I already love you, what will that change?"

Giovanna did not command him away. He moved closer, lying down beside her on the bed. Her face rested against his for a long moment. And then they were kissing and tearing at each other, and the dream turned to soft gray dust.

❧✦☙

A NEW PICTURE SNAPPED INTO PLACE, THE CAPO WATCHING over a scene in the same hidden courtyard. Cielo's mother wore a soldier's uniform that had not been cut to hide the gentle rise in her stomach.

The Capo's brother stood in the spot where the element changer had died.

"I thought you were better than this," the Capo said to Giovanna. "I thought you understood loyalty, power." He pointed at his brother. "If you love Oreste, he has power over you."

Giovanna refused to look at either man. She kept her eyes on the ground, on the fresh coat of snow.

"You speak of weakness and excess, and yet you find the first man who wants to crawl into your bed. Prove that you aren't some weak, ridiculous woman, but a strega." Giovanna shook her head, black hair as brittle as winter branches. "Do I have to fall back on mundane threats? Fine. You should be afraid of what I'll do to the child."

Cielo. I wanted to reach for the strega. We might be watching the same memory, but each of us had to live through it alone.

"Giovanna, you don't have to listen to my brother," Oreste said. "You are not his."

"And if you're *his* instead, what happens?" the Capo asked. "Do you think the Order of Prai will be kind to either of you when they learn that one of their own bedded a strega? Produced a child?"

"I'll leave the order," Oreste said.

"Prai won't let that happen," Giovanna muttered to the snow at her feet. "They'll come for us."

The Capo marched over to Giovanna and put his hands on her shoulders. "You know what you should do."

Giovanna's hands slid to her stomach. She hadn't been staring at the ground, but at the baby, which pushed at her boundaries, giving her a new shape. Changing her from the inside. Like magic.

She looked up at Oreste, her eyes as pitiless as they had been in the moment when she'd killed the element changer. "I tricked you into it," she said. "I used magic to make you think you loved me, to give me a child. You never wanted to touch me. You never want to touch me again."

"No," Oreste said, but he winced as if he could feel himself weaken and crack.

"Say it," Giovanna ordered.

Next to her, the Capo nodded. Not greedily, not happily, but with the grave conviction of a man who believed there was no other way.

And some part of Oreste must have wanted to believe it. "You tricked me into it," he repeated, quick and hollow. "You used magic to make me think I loved you, to give you a child. I never wanted to touch you. I never want to touch you again."

❦

I GASPED IN THE BOTTOMLESS DARKNESS BETWEEN DREAMS. I wanted nothing more than to wake up in our rooms and shake Cielo from his sleep, but light crept in, red and gray, and the kitchens of the Palazza formed around us.

The memories were not done with us yet.

Giovanna walked past the open fires and the bread ovens, a baby held so firmly in her arms that I worried she would harm it with her nervous clutching. This tiny creature with red fists was Cielo.

Another, less-expected figure came into view—the

kitchen strega, tending a different hearth, looking impossibly young. She couldn't have been more than ten years older than Cielo's mother. The years simply didn't add up. The memories she carried, the crush of their pain, must have aged her faster than living would have done on its own. I felt almost guilty for hating her.

"I need something," Giovanna whispered.

The kitchen strega shook her head.

"I'm not talking about magic," Giovanna said with a flare of Cielo's impatience. There could be no argument about it—that was part of the strega, bred into the bone. "I need a potion that could kill someone. Not quickly, though."

Was she planning to murder the Capo for what he had done? I found myself plotting for her, though I knew it would never come to pass.

"How long?" the kitchen strega muttered.

Giovanna looked to all sides, as if she were being spied on. Or hunted. "An hour."

The kitchen strega nodded and went back to stirring a pot. Cielo's mother bobbed the baby up and down in her arms and sang a nervous little song.

❧❖❧

LATER. NIGHT. I COULDN'T FEEL THE COLD, BUT EVIDENCE OF IT showed in the scratches of frost on the windows. White breath escaped from Giovanna's lips as she ran with the baby Cielo bundled in her arms. Had she tried to kill the Capo before she left? Was she racing away from an attempt at murder?

When she arrived on the doorstep of a small cottage, she

knocked loudly and then pulled a bottle from her sleeve.

I understood all at once.

The poison was meant for Giovanna.

My magic thrashed inside me, as if it could somehow change what I was seeing. But it could not touch the past, and it could not overpower death.

"I'm sorry, little one," Giovanna said, lowering her face to the baby's. "But you would never be safe with me." Snow fell and the dream blurred, as if it were difficult for the magic to stretch so far away from the Palazza.

Giovanna set the baby down in a great pile of blankets and pried at the bottle with her cold-hardened fingers. The baby who would become Cielo cried and cried. Dull footsteps sounded nearby, moving toward the door.

The potion was meant to give Giovanna time to escape from the doorstep and die well away from Cielo, to keep *the brilliant death* from taking root in her baby's tiny body. She tipped her head to swallow, but the shouts of men rose in the near distance.

Giovanna knelt in the snow and prayed. Then she pulled out a knife of no particular make, a cheap but well-sharpened blade, and as she stabbed it deep into her own chest, I woke to the sound of Cielo crying out.

I RUSHED ONTO THE BED WHERE CIELO WAS THRASHING LIKE A bird in a net. I tried to hold the strega down, but he flickered in my grip.

The strega changed. A girl. A boy. A girl again. The transformations, which had looked so smooth before, turned jagged, accompanied by small whimpers and great cries. The strega writhed and bucked and stared through me, unseeing. I grabbed Cielo by the wrists, but every time the strega changed, they became thinner or thicker, and with a constant ripping motion, the strega pulled away.

"What's happening?" I asked, though I already knew. When Giovanna killed herself on the stoop of that cottage, the power she'd gained by killing other streghe passed into her child.

Into Cielo.

That much power had turned against Giovanna. She'd killed herself because she believed she couldn't keep her own baby safe. Not from the Capo. Not from herself.

My face crumpled under the weight of borrowed pain, but if I hurt too deeply right now, I was no help to Cielo.

The strega's eyes slid into focus. Her long dark hair was matted with salt water: sweat, tears.

I looked to where Cielo's book sat on the bedside, untouchable. "How do I help?"

"The book . . . it's a tool . . ." The strega gasped. "It only works for me. It gives me focus. I need . . ."

She changed into a boy again, strong legs kicking out against the mattress, rattling the bed frame on the stones.

"What?" I asked.

"*Focus*," Cielo said, exasperated. "I need . . ."

The strega was struck as if by lightning. Another change, back to a girl, her arms flinging wide.

I put a hand against Cielo's forehead, but the strega wasn't sick. She was being tortured by the past, by her magic. "You love to talk," I said. "Too much, if you ask me, which you never do. Tell me a story. Focus on the words."

She groaned and bit her lip until a bead of blood rose. "Words are slippery." She gasped. "Words are fish. Fish are never helpful."

My mind had hit the end of what it could do, and my body took over. I slung one leg across Cielo's slim, girlish ones. My knees pinned the strega down while one of my hands gathered her wrists and held them above her head.

"Look at me," I demanded in my finest, clearest di Sangro voice. "Only me. Not at what will happen in ten minutes. Not at what happened twenty years ago. Not at whatever is in your mind, shredding it to pieces."

Cielo took a deep breath and nodded. The strega's body forced another shift, turning wider and taller and boyish, but I refused to be thrown from my course. I let the moment wash over me like a wave.

I could not change what had happened to Cielo's mother. I could only change what happened now. I put one hand in the middle of the strega's chest and held him steady. "Your heartbeat," I said. "Two sounds, moving you forward. Further and further from this pain. There is a perfect clock inside of you. Focus on it. This is yours."

The strega's breathing slowed. He closed his eyes. I let my hand soften, my fingertips leaving his skin lightly. I pressed a kiss to his chest, and the simple song of his life pulsed through my lips.

"This is yours."

I meant the strega's heartbeat. I meant much more than that. Cielo opened his eyes, and it was easy to name his emotions. Disbelief. Need. Hope.

Cielo pressed up and grabbed the back of my neck; I kissed the strega through a gasp. If Cielo had been shy about asking me to sleep beside him, his lips seemed to have every confidence we were doing the right thing. I felt the brush of wind everywhere he touched. His hands pushed harder, and the wind turned to a rush of fire.

It had been dark when we woke, but now the windows blushed at the coming sunrise, a blue-gray sky tipped with rose. In an hour it would be scalding blue.

"Your name," I said, filled with a soft flood of understanding. "I know what it means. The sky is always changing, but it's always the sky." I didn't touch the second half of Cielo's name. It should be Malfara, to match Oreste and the Capo.

A dark seed planted in my thoughts threatened to grow and cover everything in wild, choking vines. I had seen Cielo's father. Not just in a dream. In the Palazza.

I didn't want to think about that, especially now. It was one thing to help Cielo look for family. It was another to give him up to a priest in the Order of Prai.

"Well?" I asked. "Did I guess it?"

I took the lack of argument to mean yes. I took Cielo pulling me down on top of him as a sign I should get back to what I had been doing before. My hands took on their own life, pulling at the strega's clothes. Cielo twisted a fist up in the hem of my shirt, and I almost begged him to remove it. When he did, fitting bare hands to skin, I lost myself, lost my edges. There was no sharp line left between us. I blurred into Cielo's grip. I felt myself shading into the air, the sheets, the heat of the morning.

I took in the angles of Cielo's hips with my hands. I kissed every one of his cut-glass features. I pressed the heat between my legs against the hardness between his. He let out a sigh that sounded as if it might have been trapped for years.

And then, as smoothly as turning a page, Cielo turned into girlish form. I looked down into her delicate face, her shamelessly red cheeks. "Are you all right?" I asked.

The strega nodded vigorously. "I did that on purpose. Once I'm back in control it's important to, ahhh, test things."

I took her in with greedy eyes and greedier hands. "Everything looks perfect. You're perfect." We fell into a more serious rhythm than before, our hands making constant journeys up and down each other's bodies. I stopped at her breasts, kissing each one with reverence.

Cielo changed back and forth, once, twice, my hands molding and remolding to the strega's body. As Cielo slipped back into boyish form, and the sun rose higher, I thought about letting my hand slip down the front of his trousers. I had spent enough time as a boy to know exactly what I would find.

I was stopped by the sounds of the Palazza waking up around us. I had been frantic to kiss Cielo, to rush as far as we could in the time that we had. Now the strega's eyes went rough and faraway. Everything that had happened in the dream tumbled into the room with us, as dark and icy as a snow-filled night.

I stood up and grabbed the mirror from the bedside table. Being stripped down, close to naked, made things easier. *Change this person*, I ordered, and my body gave way to a slightly different one. I had a boyish body, but I was still Teo.

Always Teo.

No matter what form I took, I had the same heart, the same hungers, and a thirst to punish wicked men.

"Where are you going?" Cielo asked. He looked around as if he could see the shadows cast by everything that had happened in the Palazza. His mother, making a deal with the Capo. His father, falling in love and being ripped out of it.

Streghe dying.

"There's a ball tonight, and by the time it ends, I will be finished with this place," I said, pulling on my boots. I promised myself that when the sun rose again, I would have the antidote and be headed back over the mountains.

But that wasn't enough anymore. Cielo's family was gone, and mine would follow soon. Cielo's mother was dead, and my father was dying. Someone had to answer for all of it. Someone had to pay a steep price for every strega who had hoped for a better life and died to feed the Capo's power.

Father's voice pressed into my ears, reminding me of how I'd stared at his knife.

You don't reach for it, but you don't shy away.

The storm of memory broke, and I could see clearly, the new meaning inside of the old story. Magic wasn't the only power I had. I was a di Sangro, and all those years ago Father had predicted my fate.

I was going to kill the Capo.

Four

The Twenty-Seven-Part Favor

13

When I left Cielo behind in our rooms, I had only the faintest idea of how to begin. But so many years as a di Sangro made it easier to sketch out the shape of trouble. By the time I knocked on Ambrogio's door, I had a rough scheme.

I tugged at the cuffs of my shirt, the only clean one I'd been able to find in our clothing-strewn room.

I thought of Cielo, still in bed. Cielo, half-clothed and shaking.

If the Capo found out there was a powerful strega in the Palazza, bound to him by blood, one whose power the Capo had gathered death by death, no doubt he would try to make a claim on Cielo's life. That couldn't be allowed to happen.

I knocked again. "Ambrogio!"

Vanni's red curls lit the entrance to a door down the hallway. "All right," he said, holding his head like it was a squalling infant. How many casks of wine had he and the other boys laid to waste while I was trying to save Father? "Do you need to be so loud about it? We're all in here." He waved me into his rooms.

I had wanted to start with Ambrogio because he would be the easiest to convince. He already called me family. I wasn't prepared to win the sons of the five families over all at once, but here they were, a grim-faced audience. Ambrogio sat off to one side, his sunny demeanor traded for a batch of rain clouds. Lorenzo stared out the window, always halfway to Salvi. Pasquale, on the other hand, made his presence known, racing from one end of the room to the other like a squall.

"I came because I need your help," I said.

It was a tricky opening. Father would have been able to see the balance, a risk in one hand and a benefit in the other. Putting myself at the mercy of these four boys gave them power they were ravenous for, but telling them I needed help unveiled a weakness. At least, in their eyes.

"We're not really in the mood for scheming," Vanni said. "As you can probably see."

"Why is he in here?" Pasquale asked, giving me a look that could have sucked the marrow from bones. "He's not one of us."

"I'm the di Sangro heir," I said.

The magic whispered, *Liar, strega, thief.*

"What about your brother?" Pasquale asked. "Beniamo might not be much for brains, but at least he's not waiting around the Palazza for a chance to fawn over the Capo while the rest of us plan to bring the five families back to power." So that had been the trip I'd missed in favor of the streghe in the dungeons. Pasquale looked me over as if I were both filthy and predictable. "You probably wanted to get on your knees and show the Capo precisely how loyal you are."

"Pasquale," Ambrogio warned. He turned to me. "That's the last bottle of wine talking."

My lips tightened a notch. I was almost angrier at Ambrogio for defending Pasquale than I was with Pasquale for saying such ridiculous things. The idea of two men to-gether bothered him as much as betrayal.

"Father wanted me to answer the summons, not Beniamo," I said. Those words sliced into my mind, snuck past the defenses of my heart. Father had chosen my little brother be-cause he could see no other way, because Beniamo's cruelty backed us all into a corner, not because Luca was suited to the task of running the di Sangro family.

Father would have chosen me if he could have. The truth had been in front of me since I was nine years old, as plain as that knife on the table.

"Notice that he hasn't denied a special relationship with the Capo," Pasquale said, attacking from a new angle.

"Signore Rao has decided that one of us must be in league with the Capo," Vanni said with an edge of hysteria, as if he'd been trapped in a room with a snake and had no idea when it would strike.

"He's spoiling for a fight," Ambrogio said. He leaned in to me, whispering, "I think he's got a poor hold on his woman. Nothing rattles a man loose like a wife who won't stay put." Ambrogio's smile was as smooth and sweet as but-ter. I wanted to melt that bland, satisfied look off his face. This wasn't the way he should speak of women, whether or not he thought any were in the room.

"I'm sure Favianne has nothing to do with it," I muttered.

"I trust Luca," Ambrogio announced.

"If you'd seen him at the side of the road like I did, you would know there's something not quite right about our little di Sangro," Pasquale said. He kept coming back to this over and over, worrying it like a coin with the face nearly rubbed away.

"You think putting your cock in a woman is what makes you trustworthy?" I asked. "I've met plenty who prove your theory wrong."

Vanni laughed nervously, and Ambrogio added a hearty counterpoint. Lorenzo looked at me with quiet approval.

I had earned my spot at the table, at least for the moment, but the victory had no flavor. I had lowered myself to Pasquale's way of thinking, and I didn't want to spoil the memory of what had just happened.

I had kissed Cielo. Cielo had kissed me. And while I had been drawn to the strega's body, every bit, we'd given each other more than the meeting of skin and the sparring of muscle. I had felt more in those minutes than I had in entire years. The thought heated my cheeks. I breathed twice as hard as usual.

"Are you all right?" Vanni asked. "You look as if you're going to pass out." He kicked a footstool in my general direction.

I caught it under my heel and banished all thoughts of Cielo. I could remove my heart from any matter.

I took a readying breath.

"I'm going to kill the Capo tonight," I said. "And I can't do it alone." A great silence spread. It seemed to push at the walls. Lorenzo, Vanni, and Ambrogio stared at me. "Why are you all looking at me like that?"

"Because you're breathtakingly mad," Vanni said.

"I think it's the first reasonable thing he's ever said," Pasquale muttered.

"We can't," Ambrogio added, as if fate had already decided things for us.

"Luca," Lorenzo said quietly. "We need to think of our

people first, now more than ever. Would revenge be in their name or ours?"

"This is more than paying back a debt. This is our only defense." The Capo was willing to destroy anyone to get what he wanted. The streghe of Vinalia would never be safe as long as the Capo was alive. None of us would. "Perhaps you believe the Capo's power will protect you if you don't stand in his way, but he will do whatever it takes to heap glory on Vinalia. If that means courting the favor of the five families, he'll do it. If it means tossing you off the nearest church dome . . ."

Ambrogio scoffed, but I had caught the rest of the boys.

"Do you really think he cares about our people?" I pressed. "Or will he cart us around, making a show of how loyal we are to his regime? Then later, on some day we don't currently have time to fear, he'll decide we are the old way, and take whatever we have left as easily as he took our fathers."

I swallowed hard against the pain of saying that out loud. I was used to telling stories of the ways men wronged each other, but I'd never had one double back and gut me.

"Are you going to tell us this plan?" Vanni asked, the last traces of his drinking gone, replaced by giddy nerves.

"No," I said. "But I am going to tell you your parts in it." Killing the Capo would be more complicated than taking a fool from Chieza for a walk up the mountain, but the basic steps were the same. I would snare the Capo using his own weakness. Then I would change him, with magic if I could. With Father's knife if I had to. "The less you know about what I've got in mind, the easier it will be to disown me if I'm caught."

"Better and better," Vanni said.

"Vanni, I need you to make sure that the Capo is in high spirits at the ball. Give him plenty of reason to laugh and carouse. Get him as drunk as you can without looking suspicious."

"Oooh, I like my part," Vanni said. "I would do that even if we weren't killing him."

"Lorenzo, I want you to talk to him about Salvi," I said. "Anything, as long as he comes away thinking that you're warming to the idea of being Vinalian. We want him to think that *his* plan is working, so he doesn't see ours taking shape."

Lorenzo tapped his fingers on his knees. He didn't say yes, but he didn't say no. That was all I needed for the moment.

I turned to Ambrogio. "I will need you to draw the Capo away. We'll decide on a spot once we know how the ball is laid out."

"Drag him into a corner?" Ambrogio asked. "It's that simple?"

"The Capo is trying to prove how powerful and beloved he is. We'll use his confidence and crowds against him. Tell him that you need to speak to him alone, that you have to say something you don't want the other boys to hear. Talk about how grand and impressive the ball is, say you can't help but be swept up in the whole affair. I'll be waiting."

Ambrogio looked down as if I'd asked him to do the killing and he was trying to decide if his hands were up to the task.

"Pasquale, I need one simple thing from you," I said, spinning to face the Rao boy. "All I ask is that you return my father's knife."

"I took it in a fair match," Pasquale said. Considering the

nature of our fight, I wondered what he thought an *unfair* match would be.

I wanted Father's knife back, but I couldn't let a personal matter stop me. "The Capo has been watching us closely for days—we'll be an afterthought tonight. No matter how much the Capo wants us to believe he's won over the Eterrans, he'll be paying them close attention. Once a threat, always a threat."

"You think that he's more afraid of the Eterrans than he is of the five families?" Vanni asked, sounding as wounded as a small boy who's just figured out he isn't, in fact, a fearsome warrior.

The truth was that the Capo had reason to dance lightly around the Eterrans, whether or not he truly feared them. They had standing armies, which meant he couldn't poison their kings without bringing a war down on every Vinalian.

"What are *you* going to do?" Vanni asked. "What is your part in all of this?"

"You mean besides making sure the Capo never breathes again?" I asked.

Vanni laughed, a thin sound with a nervous flutter at the edge. Of course, I had more work to do, invisible bits of the plan that the boys would never see. Most important, I had to find out what had stopped me from using magic on the Capo in the garden.

And then there was the act itself. My magic danced at the thought, not a polite or pretty dance, but spinning and breathless. The ball was our chance. I couldn't wait for another one, not with Father dying. Of course, that was one more thing I couldn't afford to tell the boys. They needed to believe that after we killed the Capo, we would all be on equal footing. If they knew that Niccolò di Sangro drew breath, they would see this as a move to put the di Sangro family in power.

"I need your answer," I said.

Silence shrank around us, drawing us together. Lorenzo leaned forward, but Vanni surprised me by grabbing my hand and shaking it first. His brown eyes and blunt features looked more earnest than I'd ever seen. "We're agreed."

"I might have trouble acting the part of a happy Vinalian," Lorenzo said, "but you have my word."

Ambrogio twisted his lips. "I'm worried for you, brother. If anything goes wrong . . . this is no small matter."

"We are no small men," I said.

Ambrogio nodded and clapped me to him. "It's decided, then."

I looked to Pasquale, but he didn't say a thing. His eyes glinted with the same disdain they had when we fought at the side of the road. He had made up his mind about me the moment we had met, and nothing could change that story.

 ❧✦❧

I RAN BACK TOWARD THE SAFETY OF OUR ROOMS. I DIDN'T THINK of them as mine anymore, but the place I shared with Cielo, where we were allowed to be ourselves for a few breaths before shifting, always shifting, to face the world.

I hadn't turned the first corner of the courtyard when a small furry shadow ran over my shoe. Fiorenza had taught me not to fear mice but to kill them with a swift crack to the spine.

I raised my foot.

Look down, the magic cried.

I found small every-colored eyes staring up at me. This mouse was silky black, with a tilt to its head that looked far too human, and a disappointed twitch to its whiskers that I knew well.

I knelt down and cupped my palms. The mouse clicked its feet on the marble, hurrying into my hands. "This is no place for the small and furry," I whispered. I could only imagine how many feet Cielo had narrowly avoided that day, how many poisons in the corners and traps strewn about the kitchens.

But if the Palazza wasn't safe for mice, it was less so for streghe. I couldn't blame Cielo for changing form.

I carried the strega toward our rooms, trying to mask the fact that Luca di Sangro was talking to a mouse trapped between his hands. Cielo's nose twitched toward a tapestry along the hall.

"You want to admire the art?" I asked. "Now?"

Cielo's nose twitched again, insistent.

I stopped in front of a heavy woven rug that showed one of the Capo's great victories, a battle on a shining field along the Violetta Coast. Opposing forces laid down their arms and welcomed their fate as Vinalians. I wanted to pick apart the lie, thread by thread.

Cielo nudged at me with a small pink nose, and when the hall was clear of servants, I slipped around the side and discovered a nook behind the tapestry with enough space for one person, a change of clothes, and a book.

Cielo's book.

I put the mouse down, and it nosed the book open with a *flick* that grabbed my breath and refused to give it back.

My boyish body was stuck to Cielo's naked, boyish one.

I hadn't given myself time to think what would happen when we were this close again, and now I could barely think at all.

"Why did you leave the book here?" I whispered.

"I believe someone is keeping watch on our door," the strega said. Our location now made sense, but on top that, I sensed a dare in Cielo's eyes. The darkness behind the tapestry was murky and incomplete. We were alone here, yet inches away from being discovered.

"I need you to leave the Palazza." It was mostly a matter of keeping the strega away from the Capo. Perhaps it was also a matter of keeping me away from the strega. When I'd kissed Cielo after the dream, it had felt necessary. Kissing him now would be utterly selfish.

I told myself not to look down. Not to look anywhere. "I need to know if there is some way a person can protect themselves against magic. Some kind of counter-magic that can be used."

Cielo nodded. He ran his fingers lightly up and down the sides of my body.

"And I need a knife," I said, in a rough stumble.

"For your bread?" Cielo asked, his smile slicked with mischief. "Or your whiskers?"

I put a frantic hand to my chin. Still smooth. Cielo gave me a smile that should have been a laugh, held tight to keep us from being found. It wasn't even safe to laugh here. How could it be safe to kiss? To take a step past kissing? To lose sight of the path altogether?

"The knife is to keep us safe," I said. "On the way back over the mountains." I had promised myself I wouldn't pull

Cielo into the plot to kill the Capo; keeping the strega safe was one of the reasons it existed in the first place.

"I can't make another trip back to the lovely, murderous Uccelli at the moment," Cielo said. His whisper came easy, but I felt the strain behind those words. "The streghe of Vinalia need to know what the Capo is doing. They will be lured in by the promise of living openly, and then . . ."

Then they would be dead, their magic stolen.

When I removed the Capo from power, maybe Cielo wouldn't have to warn the streghe. Maybe we would be able to stay together for a short while longer.

Would I kill a man for that?

Cielo looked down between us, a smirk decorating his lips. My body was making demands that neither of us could ignore. I had never considered how much harder it was for boys to hide the strength of their interest.

Before I reached the highest peak of embarrassment, the strega pressed against me, revealing a matching state. When he reached for me, the sound I made was as rough as unfinished stone. He put a finger to his lips.

"You know who I would love to see tonight?" he whispered. "That girl I met on the mountains."

I shook my head.

There was more to it than practicality. "You don't like me this way?" I asked, my tone coarse, and not just from what we were doing. I did not wish to be with someone who disliked this version of me. *Any* version of me.

"That's not the trouble," Cielo said, leaning into me harder, his lips on my shoulder, heating my skin with the words. It made me feel on the verge of boundless happiness, or death. The line between them thinned to a gasp. "I thought you might want to spend some time as Teo, rather than pretending at being your brother."

I set my broad hands to the sides of Cielo's face. My lips were different, fuller, actually, than when I'd been in a girlish form. I kissed the strega as if I were learning how all over again. Newness and familiarity swirled together like warm and cold water, each pleasurable in its own way.

"Where is the magic tutor who taught me that having a single form is silly and limiting?" I asked.

Cielo's hands made a study of me as he spoke in a quick, fervent whisper. "It's wrong to fear possibility, but not everything possible is true. Some people hold fast to one form all their lives and feel none the poorer for it. There is most likely a reason you fought so hard for this change, beyond keeping your family safe. After all, you were set to do it while Luca still lived. Perhaps there is a part of you that has always felt different, and that is something worthy of exploring. Exploration is . . . highly encouraged." Cielo's breath thinned as his fingers found the hard curve of my hip. "But I don't want you denying a form you love."

I bit down on my lip to keep an argument from rising up—a grueling task. It was one thing to love Cielo's body, and another entirely to love the one I'd been given at birth. It had caused my mother's death. It had been compared to Mirella's and found wanting. It had never seemed to hold the entirety of who I was, or wished to be. Still, I could not forget the moment in the gardens, and how delightful it had felt to sink into that form. To claim my girlish body and its power on my own terms. Cielo hoped to see me that way again. To press ourselves together in a different combination. I went rampant with rushing blood, the starburst of my pulse in each fingertip.

"I can't appear as a di Sangro girl in front of the Capo and you know it," I said. "But maybe . . . later . . ." I let myself imagine us together in that way, but the idea was a dangerous bauble. The more I played with it, the more I wanted to keep it.

"Yes," Cielo said, his mouth against my neck. "This now. That later."

A liquid moan spilled out of me as Cielo's hands stroked across my stomach and his mouth worked its way back toward mine. This was madness. If anyone were walking along the hall and had an ear for debauchery, we would be found out.

I picked up Cielo's clothes and stuffed them into his hands. "As soon as you have the knife and the truth, come back," I said, already desperate to see the strega again. He pulled his shirt on, and I tugged it down, missing the sight of his chest as soon as it was eclipsed by fabric. "Can you do that?"

Cielo struggled into his pants, a difficult task in the tiny space we shared. "Teo . . ." he said in a way that sounded exactly like *no*.

"This is important." I had just faced a roomful of the most powerful young men in Vinalia and told them, without a knot in my breath, that they should follow me into danger, possibly death. This was different. I didn't want to force Cielo into a quick, rough alliance.

I wanted the strega to be with me. *Truly* with me.

"We have a problem," Cielo said as he arranged his cloak around his shoulders. "Actually, we have a great sea of problems." He whipped the tapestry aside, and though the sun was dull, with no real edge to it, I startled. "You suppose

I don't mind being away from you until this evening." He rushed toward our rooms and I followed, Luca di Sangro dogging his servant's footsteps. "You suppose it's an easy task for me to leave you alone at the Palazza, knowing the dangers." Cielo covered the last of the distance in one long stride, and then we were in the bedroom. As soon as the door sealed, he added, "There's also the matter of favors. You want a secret, a knife, a return to this place. . . ."

"It's too much," I said, my words raw and certain.

Cielo pushed out the panes of the window and stepped onto the ledge as simply as someone would swing open a door and stride through. The strega turned back to me with a flourish. "And for that reason, your next favor to me will be delivered in twenty-seven parts. We begin as soon as I return. It ends on the day that one of us dies."

"That's . . . that's . . ."

"Something *you* would come up with?" Cielo asked, mischief in every crease of his lips. He stepped off the ledge of the window. The book fell to the stone, and where there had been a dark-haired boyish figure, a glossy bird lifted into the sky, cutting it to bright ribbons with dark wings. I waited until the strega was out of sight.

And then I readied myself for the ball.

14

The day shaded into a subtle blue evening, and sounds of a gathering led me through the Palazza like a beckoning finger. I followed the shiver of violins, determined to meet the crowds with a face that suited the di Sangro heir. I didn't have Ambrogio's ease, Pasquale's way of putting himself above everyone else with a simple tilt of the chin, or Lorenzo's voice, which carved a space for his opinions. All I could do was imitate Father, holding my features tight.

At the bottom of the stairs, I was swept into a group of nobles. Women swirled in shades of white and summer green, while men swaggered in their finest white linen. I was wearing di Sangro red, a shirt Cielo had chosen for me at the market, and I stood out like a drop of blood in a garden of white roses.

It felt like everyone who looked at me, everyone who passed by, could sense what I was plotting.

Breathe, the magic told me.

I drew in the spice of bodies, the nearness of others. It did nothing to calm my nerves.

Be invisible, the magic said.

We're not very good at that, I reminded it.

I had always been the odd girl, the one who drew the stares of strangers. They wanted to know what was different about me, to drag my secrets to light. Tonight I needed to be a boy who had no secrets. A boy whose greatest care in the world was a slight worry about whether he should pledge loyalty to the Capo now, or wait to be won over.

I followed the natural movement of the party, as quick and winding as a stream. It led me to a dining hall, where heaps of food sat on tables: great braids of bread topped with edible gold, rabbit and liver and honeycomb tripe, strawberries steeped in wine, pear and frangipane tarts, small cups of bitter chocolate from Masca. And there, in a bowl, were the candied almonds Favianne had said she couldn't stand.

I took a small plate and helped myself to a bit of everything. Perhaps this food should have tasted bitter, dusted with the knowledge of what the Capo had done. But I delighted in every bite stolen from him.

Wandering with my plate gave me a chance to peer into the rooms around the dining hall, to see if any would suit my purposes. I needed a place not too far from the crowds, not removed enough that the Capo would suspect danger. It had to be hidden so that that I could use magic without being seen; I had no wish to reveal myself as a strega. Even if I managed to kill the Capo, I needed to escape without drawing attention. There were plenty who would step in to punish me.

Oreste, for instance.

The rooms off the dining hall contained little but Vinalian nobles laughing and flirting. When I'd emptied my plate and run out of rooms to inspect, I tossed myself back into the motion of the crowd. It pushed me into the largest, most ornate room I had ever seen, packed with people. The walls and floors shone cream and gold, the ceiling covered in painted scenes. Melae stood at the center of a flock of birds that rose up and broke into white clouds. Erras sat on a throne made of open, staring eyes, and reigned with judgment over the rest of the gods and everyone below. Veria danced, naked and twisting. Cecci's horn spilled wine over his body, painting him red. This place barely matched the rest of the Palazza; I felt like I had found the secret beauty inside of a dull seashell.

Look, the magic said.

On the chandeliers above our heads, flames danced and leapt from wick to wick, like slender young women turned to fire. Around the pictures, gilt molding spiked and curved, and instead of staying in one place, it changed fashion, as if it had its own whims.

Azzurra had added touches of magic everywhere.

She stood at the right side of the Capo on a raised dais at the center of the room, weaving her fingers with a frenzy. Oreste stood to the Capo's left, looking as if he would rather die a quick and straightforward death.

What was the Capo doing? Why had he chosen tonight, of all nights, to reveal streghe to the world?

And where was Delfina?

If she'd been left in the dungeons below, this would be the perfect time to catch her alone. I had been telling myself that I was pushing Father's life to the side in favor of killing the Capo, but what if I could have both things in one night—the antidote *and* the Capo's death? I worked fast, layering one scheme on top of the next, like the delicate paper Mirella used for tracing.

There were nine rings to the dungeons. Nine guards. The idea of changing so many of the Capo's men tempted me as much as another bowl of strawberries in wine. But I would need a subtler method if I didn't wish to be caught. I looked to the Capo, fixing on the ring that sat on the middle finger of his left hand.

"Signore di Sangro!" the Capo cried when he caught me staring. He started toward me across the great room, drawing the attention of every noble in sight, as if he had secretly attached strings to their eyes and all he had to do was tug. "How was your afternoon?" the Capo asked, his voice pitched too loud. There were haughty laughs from the Eterrans in the crowd. Among the rest of the world, Vinalia had a reputation for shouting, wild gestures, passion of all sorts.

"It passed as well as it could," I said, keeping my own voice low. I didn't want to put on a show for these people.

I tried not to stare too openly at the Capo's ring. The wolf stamped into the dark band was caught in a swift pose, running without end. Its mouth hung open, teeth bared, each line biting into the metal.

"Please tell any Eterrans you meet tonight about your study of magic," the Capo said. "I want them to know that we're at the front of a new field, and they have some catching up to do." He clapped his hand on my back, and I felt no evidence of loose or blurry motion. Vanni hadn't started on his work of getting the Capo drunk.

I hadn't realized how difficult it would be to stand at the Capo's side, knowing everything he'd done. I looked at his face without meeting his eyes, a trick Father had taught me.

"I haven't learned anything new about magic yet," I said.

Not true, it told me. I had seen *the brilliant death*, the moment when life and magic leaked from the body of a strega in twin streams.

"You will give us some great discovery, Luca, I'm sure of it," the Capo said. "You went down to the dungeons knowing what Azzurra was capable of. I like a man who sees what is stacked against him and walks into the fight, head up, heart pounding. I don't care for men who have always known they were going to win."

"You're going to love me, then," I said.

I thought about the moment we were rushing toward, when I tried to kill the Capo. If I'd known I was going to win, I wouldn't have blazed with anticipation and fear.

"You see? That is exactly the sort of man I need in the new Vinalia." The Capo took me by the shoulders and turned me to face the great tapestry of the crowd. "Who is the strongest man in this room?"

"Why does it need to be a man?" I asked, nodding at Azzurra.

The Capo gave me an amused slap on the back and a broad laugh. I wanted to hold that laugh in my hand. I wanted to stretch it thin and strangle him with it. "Who is the strongest *person?*" the Capo amended.

If Cielo had been in the room, my eyes would have flown to wherever he was standing and given us away.

The nobles of Vinalia and Eterra watched us, their gazes flickering back and forth like Azzurra's dancing candle flames. I turned to the Capo and said, "Whoever isn't afraid that we are standing here, talking about them."

The Capo smiled and made much of my answer. "Signore di Sangro! I should have invited you to the Palazza sooner!"

I held steady, trying not to let loathing capsize me. The

Capo thought I was only grieving my father, and soon the need for power would overcome a fading sense of loss. He had no idea how deep my wounds were and how many of them had been dealt by his own hand.

"I have to go make a speech," the Capo said. "Would you like to come with me?"

I knew what that invitation meant. He wanted me to add the weight of the di Sangro family's approval to his words. If I had been following the narrow path of my scheme, I would have agreed. The Capo needed to believe he was winning me over. But I turned slightly, toward the door. "I have to go find . . . a friend." My mind raced to the dungeons and Delfina.

The Capo smiled.

And then all of the candles in the ballroom went out at once. My heart told me I was in danger, but from whom? The Capo, Azzurra, the Eterrans?

When the chandeliers flared back to life, they burned twice as bright as before. Azzurra's hands were poised above the crowd, her palms two small suns. The Capo had left my side to ascend the dais where he stood with Azzurra. The entire room turned to him, one body.

The Capo looked down at us.

"Vinalia is but an infant," he said, "and I am pleased you have joined us to celebrate her birth. Please make sure to take a turn of the grounds and delight in the touches of magic you will find there. What you have heard is true. Streghe are not stories but real Vinalians who are lending their talents to make this land even richer." If I had been the same girl who had arrived at the Palazza, if I hadn't known about *the brilliant death* and how it had been twisted to violent ends, I might have thrilled to the Capo's tune. No wonder so many streghe had given themselves over to his cause. "Magic, art, and science, these are the pride of Vinalia." He left out the military that, until today, had been the greatest feat of his rule, the way he had become Capo in the first place.

Father's voice drifted to me on the breeze. *Listen to what a man is not saying.*

"Before the dancing begins," the Capo said, "we have a little something to add intrigue to your night." Servants carried in baskets and set them down just inside of the doors. Azzurra raised her hands and masks flew into the air, swirling above us like autumn leaves. They scattered through the ballroom.

A mask cut toward me, settling over my eyes and nose. When I tugged, I found I couldn't take it off. Masked faces surrounded me, some with laughing eyes, others rimmed in mournful black. Some sprouted noses like beaks. Others were dotted with jewels, strung with ribbons. Everyone looked infinitely strange, although the only thing that had changed was a narrow strip of each face.

I almost wanted to thank the Capo for making my work easier. This mask was its own hiding place, a false skin that would make it almost impossible for the crowd to point an accusing finger at me.

The musicians splashed into a new song. Not a stuffy Eterran court piece but a lively saltarello. Dancers took to the floor as I pushed my way through the thick crowd, toward the doors. It was growing difficult to move in a straight line. The ballroom kept shifting into new constellations of revelers. The air filled with rough laughter, jokes that would have made a tavern keeper blush. I heard a bald proposition of lovemaking pass between strangers, and at first I thought my ears had to be mistaken. This was a noble party of the highest order. Then I remembered Eterrans believed Vinalia a place where they could shed the strict ways of their homes and act out the role of passionate fools.

The peasant music, the masks. Eterrans wanted to believe Vinalians were indulgent and weak; the Capo had created a mirror and held it up, not to the truth, but to what the Eterrans already saw. He was toying with them just as skillfully as he had with the streghe, who wanted nothing more than to live in a Vinalia that did not despise them, or pretend they were only characters in dusty old tales.

The Capo had worked his little spell on the five families, too. We had grown so used to violence that we believed it was the way of the world, the only way things worked. The Capo had shown us exactly what we'd come to expect. The call we answered to was not reason or temptation, but the deaths of our fathers.

A great clock struck. Half an hour until I was meant to meet the boys.

She is waiting, the magic said, and for a moment I believed that I could feel Delfina through the layers of stone that separated us.

Right before I reached the doors of the ballroom, I felt a nudge at my side. When the touch lingered, I looked over and found a long golden arm threading through mine. Here was a young woman with a green-and-yellow jeweled mask and hair like afternoon sunshine.

Favianne Rao.

"You will have to excuse me." I pulled away from her arm, my whole body bent toward the dungeons.

"Remember your debt," she said, a lively tilt to her voice that disguised her serious words. Favianne had saved my life. If I walked away, no doubt she would tell Pasquale I had wronged her in some outrageous fashion, and then I would have to answer for it in the middle of the ball, at the precise moment I was meant to be killing the Capo.

"Of course, Signorina." I inclined my head, acting the gentleman when all I wanted was to be the odd di Sangro girl and run away.

"You worried me," she said, hooking us around, heading deeper into the ballroom. "I thought you had fled back to the Uccelli, and I would have to go track you." I believed she would have done it, too. "What do you think of the Palazza's grand ballroom?"

"I think it could hold the entire village of Chieza and have room left over for the goats," I said.

Favianne laughed and blushed so boldly that it spread beyond the edges of her mask. As long as I was caught, I allowed myself a minute to marvel at her. This girl was an artist of flirtation, taking any ordinary moment and spinning it into a memorable one. Favianne's fingers slid along the inside of my sleeve.

I thought of the look Cielo would have given us, a rude little noise escaping the strega's throat.

If I couldn't run, I would have to scare Favianne away instead. "Exactly what shade do you think Pasquale will turn when he finds out I have been escorting his wife through the ball?"

"Oh!" Favianne said, delighted with the game. "The crimson of an overripe plum. And I'm not Pasquale's wife. Yet. We're betrothed."

If that was true, her flirting might be in earnest, and Pasquale was undoubtedly nearby. I took five steps back as quickly as if she had admitted to being ill with a new form of plague. "But you called yourself Favianne *Rao*."

She tilted her head back and laughed, drawing the line of her throat out long so I could see God's artistry at work. "Funny you didn't know. I thought the five families kept their ears forever at each other's doors."

"Yes, well, I've been hiding in a laboratory," I said. "Thick walls."

She peered at me, dark blue eyes narrowed in their jeweled settings. "There's something different about you." I feared she would be the first person to scale the walls of my lies and see what I was hiding.

Be careful, the magic said.

I had discovered a special way that women could be dangerous. They were trained to pay close attention to people. To take them apart, like Luca had done with his clockworks, and study how they ran.

Favianne smiled as if she had cracked one of the great mysteries. "You scrapped like Pasquale at the side of the road, but now, speaking to you, I might as well be talking to another woman." My throat pasted itself shut. "You, Luca di Sangro, are the sensitive man we've all been promised."

"By whom?" I asked with a slight croak.

"The entire modern world. Didn't you know? We're moving out of the age of barbarism and blood. Soon everyone will be educated and soft-spoken, and have opinions about the ballet and whether soaps should smell of lavender or bergamot."

I nodded, but really I was looking around to be sure that

no one had noticed us walking arm in arm. "If you call me sensitive, then you'll see why I can't in good conscience keep company with Pasquale's—"

"His *woman?*" Favianne asked with a laugh, making it clear how ridiculous the notion was. She belonged to Pasquale in the eyes of the world, as if she were a handsome wardrobe or a fine pair of shoes.

I had never fancied the situation either. And it seemed especially bad with Pasquale involved. "If I'm allowed to speak the truth, I don't see how you could marry that boy. If I'm enlightened, he seems to be happily marching backward through the ages."

Favianne sighed in a way that had nothing to do with flirtation. "Pasquale and I have known each other since we were children. He was never kind or gentle, but then again, neither was I." She fiddled with the finger where a ring would have sat if they had exchanged vows. "It's a year since he proposed, and he has put off our wedding at every turn," Favianne said with a slight irritation that I understood too well. It was a girl's anger, bottled because it had nowhere to go. "Since his father died, he's been . . . different."

I thought of Pasquale's eagerness to fight at the side of the road, the desperation that came off of him as thick as cologne.

Ambrogio put on a mask of good cheer, but what happened when that mask slipped? What if Lorenzo's silence was not a matter of character, but of mourning? And Vanni's dance of hilarity and nerves, could that be another symptom of grief?

What would happen to me if Father actually died? Who would I become?

I had to get to Delfina, or else I would be answering that question soon. But first I drew Favianne to the side of the ballroom and stopped in front of the musicians, where the high pitches of the strings hid our talk. "May I ask you something?"

"A man in a mask may do anything he likes," Favianne said, refreshing her smile. "I believe that's the point."

"Are you using me to get Pasquale's attention?"

"Why does this have to be about Pasquale?" Favianne moved closer as the sound of the ball flared to new heights. "I was rather enjoying that a single moment of my life *wasn't* about him." She pressed in until her body locked with mine, her eyes tilting up. They were so deeply blue. I felt like the world had tipped upside down and I was falling into the sky. That was, undoubtedly, what Favianne wanted me to feel.

If I stayed a di Sangro man, I would have to court a woman. Cielo understood, perhaps even better than I did, that any real match between us was impossible. The strega was not part of my chosen fate. At some point I would have to accept that truth. And here was Favianne, making it very clear that I could steal her away from Pasquale, which would have been satisfying on more than one front.

But when Favianne looked into my eyes, no matter how much she saw, there was still magic between us. She would never know about Teodora, and I didn't want to lie to the person I shared my bed with.

And then there was the strega, always the strega, how Cielo's every-colored eyes went searching for mine, looking for new truths when so much of the world seemed content with a single one.

I took a step back from Favianne, ruining our little dance.

"Is something wrong?" she asked, wrinkles of worry around her powdered lips stretching into displeasure.

I snatched up a hand to kiss that instead, hoping that I hadn't earned the wrath of yet another person in the Palazza. As my lips grazed her skin, I caught on the gold shine of her rings.

"May I . . . may I borrow one of these?" I asked.

Favianne gave me that look. *Odd.* It bloomed as ugly on her face as on any other, but she blinked it away. "You may have anything you like from me," she said sweetly. "If I haven't made that clear."

I slid one of the gold rings from her finger and pocketed it quickly, trying to look like a shy would-be lover instead of a scheming strega. Like anyone versed in the arts of flirtation, Favianne made a quick exit, her final glance rich with expectation as she slipped into the crowd.

I headed for the doors again.

"Di Sangro!" The name rang out in a familiar voice, and I turned to find Ambrogio wearing one of the leather masks, pulled into peaks at the nose and eyebrows, tooled in a way that made him look as if he were attempting ten different expressions at once. Vanni and Lorenzo flocked behind him.

"You look fairly wilted," Ambrogio told me. "Drink?"

"Thanks," I said, taking a small golden cup from him and downing the bittersweet liquid. Ambrogio and Vanni cheered. Even Lorenzo looked at me as if I had climbed a rung on some invisible ladder.

"Aren't you meant to be doing this to the Capo?" I asked Vanni.

Vanni scowled. "The man won't touch a drop. At least,

not from me. Do you think he fears we'll poison him?"

"That would be unimaginative," I said, even as I pictured the Capo shaking on the floor, starved for breath.

"How are you going to do it?" Vanni asked, giddy.

"Shhh," I said. "You're going to draw all of Eterra into our plan."

"Oh, they're just a bunch of pale fish!" Vanni shouted. He was drunk enough for all of us put together.

"Did you find a place?" Ambrogio asked.

"Not yet," I admitted.

I followed Ambrogio across the great room on our quest to find a suitable place to kill the Capo. He walked to the punishing tempo of the music, and I almost had to run to keep up. Ambrogio seemed more nervous about our plan than I was.

"Wait," I called out. "Did we already lose Lorenzo?"

When I turned, I found him in a sort of rapture, speaking to a girl with long limbs and delicate hands, rich brown skin and a mask that was white lace turned into a line of poetry, lovely and surprising. Below that, a scar emerged on her right cheek, a long pale line that curved all the way down to her chin.

She led Lorenzo with an outstretched hand, and they found an open place on the floor. They pulled apart and snapped together as the dance demanded, but if their bodies were dutiful to the steps, their eyes told a different story. They stared as if there were no one else in the wide, stuffed room.

Jealousy clutched my heart. "Tell me," I said as Lorenzo and the girl spun tighter into each other. "Did those two meet tonight?"

"Not even close," Vanni said. "Mimì is a girl of Salvi, not noble born, but beautiful and wise and perfect and so on. Her parents are of Ravinian heritage, like Lorenzo's mother, and the family has lived on Salvi for ages. Her mother is a healer. Her father was a teacher of noblemen's sons, including a few in the Altimari family. I could tell you a complete history of Mimì. Lorenzo refused to stop talking about her last year."

"The same Lorenzo?" I tried to picture him saying more than ten words in any given day.

Ambrogio elbowed me in the side. "We couldn't get him to shut up." His smile withered on the vine. "His parents made it clear they would never marry. The Capo must have found out about Mimì and brought her here. If the five families manage to keep power, Lorenzo will have to make a marriage to secure himself to us."

I studied Lorenzo. He glowed, but it wasn't a matter of pure delight. He had the feverish stare of a man who knew his happiness would be taken away at any moment.

Was that what I looked like when I kissed Cielo?

"What about our plan?" I asked. Lorenzo should have been talking to the Capo about the newfound delights of being Vinalian. I thought of Pasquale and his strange insistence that one of us had sided with the Capo. "Do you think Lorenzo would switch his allegiance if it cleared a way to the marriage?"

Ambrogio shrugged, a failed attempt to look uncaring. "Lorenzo had a deeper bond to his father than any of us."

I remembered something Mirella had told me once. *Signore Otto has no love for his second son. No hatred, either. There is a hollow where his feelings should be.* Ambrogio's older brother should have inherited the family seat, but he'd died in a skirmish with the Capo's unification army. The other Otto boys were far too young to take their father's place. Ambrogio was like me, answering the Capo's summons because no one else could.

He and I left Lorenzo to his dancing and Vanni to his drink. We looked around the ballroom and chose a small recess that the guests of the masked ball had overlooked in favor of the brighter, more beautiful sitting areas.

"Bring the Capo here," I said.

"Yes, but give me time. He'll have to be lured away from the flatterers, and the Eterrans, and I don't want to draw the attention of that priest. Or worse"—Ambrogio said with a shudder—"the strega."

I didn't want the storms of Azzurra's eyes thundering over to us any more than Ambrogio did. "Fine," I said. "Make it an hour from now." That would give me just enough time to visit the dungeons.

I was headed for the doors a third time as a young woman burst through them. Balanced on her toes, she looked out over the ballroom as if searching for a sailor lost at sea. She had a fall of straight black hair, a blue dress so bright that it almost hurt to stare directly at it, and a mask of feathers. Blues, pinks, yellows, reds.

Cielo had come to the ball.

I watched as her eyes skimmed the crowd, looking for me. And found Oreste.

15

Cielo moved in a rush of silk and fury.

"She's stampeding you!" Ambrogio locked me around the shoulders with one arm as Cielo neared. "If this was any other night, I'd say I wouldn't see you until morning. As it is, enjoy the hour as best you can." Then he set about destroying my hair in a brotherly fashion.

I shouldered past spinning drunks and laughing couples, and met the strega in the center of the ballroom. Cielo's face swapped out emotions so quickly, I didn't know which one to focus on. She looked around the room wildly, and I could feel she was on the verge of changing.

I needed to touch her, to hold her in place. It had worked before. I grabbed the strega and led her into the thick of the dancing. I pulled Cielo tight against me, leading with the precise, nervous steps of someone who has been cast in the following part her whole life.

Oreste stood there, so close, looking out over the dancers, his eyes marking us all as sinners. I'd seen the way Oreste had talked after Giovanna had used her magic. I'd overheard him only a day earlier, in the Capo's staterooms. He loathed streghe. Giovanna's magic might have led him to that feeling, but he had spent eighteen years believing it.

"What is this dress?" I asked, to keep Cielo distracted.

Cielo looked down at the brilliant blue gown as if she'd forgotten what she was wearing—forgotten everything but Oreste. "This was a gift," she mumbled, "from a strega who turns dreams into clothing. She said this was the best dream she's had in years."

"You look magnificent." It was the truth, but my voice sounded so brittle with nerves that it easily could have been taken for a lie.

Cielo's eyes wandered away from mine. She looked lost in the woods, rather than shining at the center of a grand ball. I tightened my hold on her waist. "That man might be your father," I whispered, "but he is not family." The way the Capo had threatened Oreste taught me more than I wished to learn. Giovanna and Cielo were his greatest shames. The secrets he kept from the world.

"You knew, didn't you?" Cielo shook her head, amazed at my betrayal. "You knew he was here, and you didn't say a word." She spun away from me. I should have let her go, given her time to understand what I'd had several hours to turn over in my head. But I was too afraid to leave Cielo alone in her frantic state.

One *flick*, one change, and the Capo would know Cielo was here.

He stood chatting with a group of Eterrans, Oreste beside them, as still as a statue in a nave. I caught up to Cielo, taking her gingerly by the shoulders. It was a good thing Cielo had come in girlish form, or else I never would have been able to touch her like this. We would have had to stay to the shadows. The unfairness bit into me deep enough to draw blood.

"I wish I had more comfort to give," I whispered, stroking a thread of Cielo's dark hair between my fingers. "Welcome to the delights of having a family."

The dance ended, but the moment lingered, the air still touched with music long after the final note was played. I offered Cielo my arm, and we left the room through one of the high doors. The garden smelled so thickly sweet that walking might as well be swimming through rose water.

I was pointed in the wrong direction again, away from the dungeons and Delfina. Away from Father's antidote. I steered us past a water garden where lovers kissed, with their feet in the froth of a brook, and fountains cut the air with ambitious arcs.

"So this is the Capo's ball," Cielo muttered. "He strikes me more as the tea and beheadings type."

The sounds of merrymaking dwindled until the Palazza was only a set of lights and dark figures in the distance. I claimed a bench and sat Cielo down on the cool marble. She kept silent, but it was not an easy silence.

I let my magic go. My skin delighted in the shifting, the way it arranged itself into Teodora, stuffed into boy's clothes, my hair caressing the wind, my body plainspoken. Cielo smiled at me, as weak as stars at dusk. Still, the pleasure was there, shining through her pain.

"Well." I swept a gesture down the length of my body. "This is what you asked for."

Cielo tried to smile, but her eyes were tugged back toward the ball. Toward her father.

"I should have told you," I said.

"Yes." The strega pulled herself up and faced me, making a grand show of her height. "You should have. But I would have been miserable knowing that you had seen him and I hadn't."

"So there was no winning," I said.

Cielo shook her head. "This isn't a game," she said, forming each word with soft, careful lips.

We still had everything to lose, and that meant the Capo had to die tonight. "What did you find out from the streghe you visited?"

"About magical ways to stop magic?" Cielo asked. "Not a thing. There is almost no one left in Amalia to ask. Those who weren't tricked into the Capo's dungeons have run off, fearing that the city is no longer safe."

So I would have to do this without any magic to help me. I would look into the Capo's eyes and kill him, the way Father had stabbed that man on the stairs. "Did you at least bring me a knife?"

"Tell me what you need it for," Cielo countered.

The strega had chosen the wrong moment to ask for perfect honesty. I could not have anything making this plan harder than it already was. "I'll get mine back from Pasquale," I said. It added another layer of difficulty to the evening, thickening the air until it became hard to breathe.

A cold laugh trickled toward us, and I thought it must have been one of the lovers straying to the edge of the grounds, but then Pasquale strode out of the darkness. He had Father's knife wrapped in one fist.

"Is this what you need?" he asked, holding the stiletto out. "Teodora di Sangro. The wayward daughter. Such a pleasure to finally meet you." Pasquale's grin matched his bone-white mask. "I've been following you all evening, in case your plot to kill the Capo was a ruse. I figured you would get us to agree and then turn us over as traitors."

Cielo put a hand to my wrist, either to give me strength or to keep me from starting another ill-fated fistfight. "That's far too boring a plot for Teo."

"*Someone* in this party is a traitor," Pasquale said, "and I could have sworn it was you. Let's be honest, little di Sangro: you made the whole thing worse, stumbling around in full view of everyone, trying to make love to my wife."

"She's not your wife," I said.

Cielo whispered in my ear, "Wrong answer entirely."

Pasquale only laughed harder, as if everything about me had turned ridiculous. "What will Favianne say when she finds out a strega girl was trying to climb into her bed? What will *anyone* say? Vanni and Lorenzo won't like your dishonesty. Ambrogio will feel especially betrayed." Pasquale ran a finger along the delicate line of my chin. "And the Capo will have all sorts of fun with you."

The magic was slow to gather. I had been using it to hold myself in a boy's form for days, and now the demands had changed. *Change him, please. I don't care what. Change him quickly. Change him now.*

"If you know I'm a strega, shouldn't you be scared?" I asked, taking a step toward Pasquale. "We're far away from the Palazza. People are too busy carousing to hear you. I can do whatever I like."

Pasquale kept his feet square, but his eyes flickered with worry. "If you had any real power, you would have used it by now."

"*Change him,*" I ordered. "*Change him.*" The words came

out sounding like a rushed and ragged prayer. I was filled with memories of the merciless night when Luca had died, when I couldn't drag magic out of me even to save his life.

"Where are your brothers?" Pasquale asked, cutting too close to my thoughts. "What did you do to them in order to take their place here? Did you kill them? Are you that mad for power?" I thought of Beniamo and Luca, both changed, both gone because of me.

I almost fell to my knees.

Cielo put a hand on my back as the magic built, until my fingertips were charged with it and my skin was singing. "Don't let this boy tell you who you are, Teo. You know who you are."

I was Teo, always Teo, no matter what form I took. I was a force strong enough to pull a strega over a mountain.

Change him. Now. All except Father's stiletto.

For once, I kept my eyes open as the magic tore out of me. I wanted to see what I was capable of. I felt a shift in the air, the tremor of lightning without the bright flash.

Pasquale vanished.

On the ground where he'd stood was a long, thin piece of wood, spread into a small fan at one end. Cielo squinted down at the dark item in the grass. "A shoehorn?"

"At least he's useful now," I muttered.

The night was coming to pieces all around me, but there was Father's knife, with the dark glow of a fallen star. I grabbed it and stuffed it inside my sleeve, where it belonged. Pasquale went in my pocket.

"Come on," I said to Cielo. "Before anyone else gets a glimpse of the truth."

CIELO AND I WORKED OUR WAY AROUND THE PALAZZA, TO THE quieter side where revelers gave way to a scattering of servants. Cielo hiked up the skirt of her glorious dress and tramped through the crumbly soil of the kitchen gardens where the smells of thyme and blood oranges rubbed against the night.

We stopped at the door of the kitchens. Cielo's pale skin glowed, like the milky parts of the sky. "They know me as a boy in the kitchens."

"So change," I said. "You can have my pants, although a few inches of your ankle might show."

Cielo stitched her lips together, tight.

"What is it?" I asked. "We don't have the time for—"

"Pasquale said you want to kill the Capo. Were you planning on telling me, or was this going to be another lovely surprise? Like seeing my father standing in front of me?"

I couldn't argue that point. The only responses I could think to give were shame and silence.

"Please think before you pitch yourself headfirst at the most powerful man in Vinalia."

My arms crossed smoothly over the fine silk of my dress shirt. "I have."

"It can't end well, Teo. And I don't know if I can bear that. I've lost everyone I've ever been given."

"You want me to leave the Capo alive because he's your uncle?" I asked. This was one twist of our fates that I hadn't guessed, a bend in the path I never could have foreseen.

"I wasn't talking about the Capo."

My face throbbed as if I'd been struck, but it was only the force of the truth hitting me. The strega didn't care about a blood tie to the Capo, even after so many years of searching for family.

Cielo wanted me alive.

Cielo wanted *me.*

But I couldn't leave it at that. "If the Capo lives, he will find a way to hurt you. I've seen it. I've seen *exactly* what will happen."

I meant the streghe in the dream, the one in the dungeons. But those weren't the pictures that flickered brokenly through my mind. I saw Luca all over again. Father, writhing and gasping on the floor. If I killed this one man, I could set the tipped world back where it belonged. I could keep it from tipping further.

"The Capo isn't the only threat out there," Cielo said. "I don't want you to kill everything and everyone you come across."

"I have to." The words would have sounded better in a boy's deep voice. People believed them more. *I* believed them more. "It's the only way to keep you safe."

"No," Cielo said softly. "It's the only way you *know.*"

"I can't believe you don't see the good in this!" I cried. "You're the one who wanted to stop streghe from disappearing."

"That's not why you're doing it," Cielo said.

"You don't know me well enough to decide that. I'm not a subject you can tutor."

Cielo narrowed her every-colored eyes. "Killing a man is not how you show someone the contents of your heart."

My voice dropped several pitches, as if it knew I meant to deal a blow. "You want to believe you're better than all of this." The anger I'd gotten so good at showing in my boyish form flew out with nothing to temper it. "You think you're above people like me, but the moment you actually care about someone, you'll do what you have to."

The light in Cielo's eyes extinguished all at once. There was nothing left on her face but a crisp, dark stare.

She turned and left.

I sat down in the crumbling soil of the border garden, wrapped in the smell of herbs that reminded me of home. I ached in a way that I had only ever felt in small doses. I'd lost Mother when I was too young to truly feel it. I'd lost Luca when I was afraid that I would follow. I was always on the verge of losing Father.

This felt different. I could see Cielo walking away. I could feel how impossible it would be to change things.

I worked my way up through the kitchens, where they knew me as a girl. If they cared that I wore pants now, they didn't blink. But I couldn't stay this way for long, not unless I wanted to reveal who I truly was.

I ran up the stairs, around revelers who had snuck away from the ballroom in search of places to couple. Lovers fumbled at skirts and belts. I lit with dark fire at the sounds that rose from their mouths like smoke.

I stopped on the third floor long enough to grab my pack. I used the mirror to change into a boy, then grabbed the potted rose that I had brought across the mountains.

My heart flinched at every step as I ran up the long flight of stairs. The Capo's rooms stood open, waiting. The door to the dungeons was locked, but the Capo hadn't made a secret of where he kept the key.

I pulled the ring Favianne had given me from the same

pocket that held Pasquale. The gold of the band wasn't hard with shine, but pure and slightly soft. Changeable. I held the ring in my palm and told the magic, *I need a man's ring, burnished silver, a running wolf stamped into the band.*

I had never been so specific, and the magic gave me a blank-eyed response. I closed my eyes and pictured the Capo's ring. The one that meant I could enter the dungeons at will. *Change Favianne's ring and give me this.*

As I waited in the dark, fear brushed over me—a soft, feathery feeling. It whispered that this was never going to work. But when I called my magic again, it came. The weight in my hand changed slightly, and so did the feel of the metal against my skin.

When I opened my eyes, a perfect imitation of the Capo's ring sat in my palm.

꧁❖꧂

THE WALK DOWN TO THE DUNGEONS SEEMED LONGER THIS TIME, possibly because I was hurrying. I leapt from the bottom of the stairs to the first door of the dungeons, holding out my ring with a steady hand. The guard raised it up to the torchlight, and not a single blemish of suspicion appeared on his face. He handed it back.

I rushed through the door.

This time I counted as I waited for each guard to inspect my handiwork and nod me through another door. Nine layers to the dungeon. Azzurra called this place hell, and the church believed hell boasted nine rings.

Which one would I go to after I killed the Capo?

The final guard looked me up and down before saying, "You're going in again? Be careful. It's just the dangerous one tonight." I had faced Azzurra enough times to know that if her sister was *the dangerous one*, I should turn and run.

Instead I stepped into the center of hell, the ninth ring, where traitors lived. Did the sisters find it fitting after everything they'd done to harm their own kind? Did they feel they were betraying their people when they killed other streghe, or were they delighted to take more than their fair share of power?

Delfina still wore her white dress, the one that resembled a nightgown. She looked up at me with eyes that bruised and begged.

"I brought you something." I took the ever-blooming rose out of my pack and set it on the ground between us.

Delfina rushed to the rose, her hands hovering over the waxy leaves and the shallow cups of the petals. They were a deep garnet. I'd made the rose di Sangro red without even trying.

"I tried to think of why you should trust me after everything that has happened to you," I said, "The world is not always kind to people like us." I watched Delfina's hand grasp the stem carefully, between the thorns. "That wasn't always a flower. I used magic to give it that shape. It needs no water to bloom, and it never stops flowering. It won't die, even down here."

Delfina squinted up at me.

She had been in the dark for so long—first the prison a man had made for her, and now one that she'd chosen for herself. I hoped I hadn't made my worst mistake yet, showing my secret to a girl who might use it against me. I needed what she could do, though, and she didn't trust anyone without magic. So I would be a strega for her.

You are always a strega, the magic reminded me.

"I know what the Capo wants you to do. I know how magic is handed down. *The brilliant death*. Your sister showed me." I was here for Father's antidote, but I couldn't pretend that I cared only about being a di Sangro. Streghe were dying, and no one was stopping it. Streghe were dying, and no one else cared. "I'm going to kill the Capo tonight."

Delfina blinked her green-gray eyes and said nothing.

"We can change this."

The girl's lips twitched, as if she needed to speak. She rushed to the far side of the dungeon and grabbed her notebook and a pencil. She wrote, in a child's unfinished scrawl, *Magic won't touch him.*

"Why not?" I asked.

Delfina hunched over, this time drawing. Lines of charcoal spun into the shape of the Capo's hand, bearing two rings. She circled, not the one with the Malfara crest, but the plain gold ring beside it.

"What do you mean?" I asked. "The ring protects him?"

Delfina started to scribble, but she flung the pencil down and shook her head. "It's a shard of magic," she said in a breathy, barely formed voice. "Trapped inside of an object. When a strega is in great pain, magic can splinter."

I thought about the necklace Father had handed down to Fiorenza. The necklace that foul strega in the kitchen wore now. When had Mother made it? Did her magic splinter when she knew she was dying and leaving us?

Leaving me?

"I'll find another way," I said, feeling light-headed. "But I need the antidote."

The door to the dungeon swung wide, the hinges screaming, and Azzurra stood there in her soldier's uniform, as vivid and sudden as a nightmare. "I thought I made it clear that I don't want you here."

"You were at the ball," I said weakly.

"Yes, well, I've done my little show for the Eterrans," Azzurra said, shucking off her boots.

"This boy is planning to kill the Capo," Delfina told her sister.

"And he thinks we *care*?" Azzurra asked, putting an arm around her sister's spiky, thin shoulders. "The Capo is no better or worse than any man, and he keeps us safe. Can you promise that, mountain boy?" I thought of the five families, and how many people I would have to swear to such a thing. How could I keep Azzurra and Delfina safe when I could barely manage it for myself? "It's the only thing that matters," Azzurra said. "Not unification. Not saving the streghe or helping a great man. I am keeping my sister *safe*. When people see what Delfina can do, their murderous sides come out of hiding." Azzurra grabbed at the spreading ink stain of Delfina's curls and pushed them into a braid. I had done that to Mirella hundreds of times. The motion was so familiar, it made me dizzy.

Or perhaps I was already dizzy.

I stumbled and found myself on my knees, trying to breathe, pulling in a thin thread of air when I needed a great rope.

Azzurra shook her head as if the whole thing were my fault. "I told you not to stand too close. The smart ones never listen." She stood over me, and she was shaking. No, I was shaking, while she stayed perfectly still. "You've gotten yourself poisoned. I have a tolerance built over years. The Capo has his ring. You, on the other hand, are about to die."

My body rioted against the stones. I couldn't control my muscles, or the wild ache that ran through them. "How? I didn't eat or drink." I thought back to Father's letter. "Didn't touch anything."

"You didn't have to." Azzurra picked up the ever-blooming rose from the ground and held it to her sister's face. Delfina pinched her lips tight. When she finally let out a sigh, the petals withered, leaves curling and turning to black. They drifted off like ashes.

Her breath was the poison.

"Your knife," Delfina said, holding out a hand. "Give it to me."

I couldn't imagine my arm making the journey from where I'd flung it on the stones, all the way to Father's stiletto. My fingers shook and shook.

"Why?" I asked on a single wisp of breath. Was she going to kill me now that I knew what her power was? That made no sense. I could feel myself dying already, the pain so intense that I started to numb.

Delfina clutched at her sister. "Do you have anything sharp?"

Azzurra sighed. "You have a heart like a pincushion. Do you want to let people keep sticking you?" The pain renewed itself, and I closed my eyes. It was easier to scream in the dark. Over the sound of my own wailing, I heard Azzurra say, "Give her your knife."

My hand couldn't be trusted. It flew everywhere but my sleeve as I tried to grab Father's stiletto.

"Oh, for the sake of all the gods," Azzurra said, grabbing it for me.

I wrenched my eyes open and watched as Delfina sliced a neat line on the inner flesh of her arm, white as mushrooms from being out of the sun. Red welled in the cut. She sprinkled me with her blood, like I was a rose that needed watering. The drops hit, and a moment later came relief.

Her breath was the poison, her blood the antidote.

"More," I said. "Please."

I didn't know how I would get it across the mountains, but I needed more. For Father.

"You're lucky she healed you and I didn't stop her," Azzurra said, kicking at my side. I pushed against the harsh stones, but I couldn't stand. I ran, folded double, as Azzurra's voice chased me out of the dungeon. "If your plan to kill the Capo hurts my sister, I will find you, mountain boy. You'll wish you had died half this softly."

❦

I SCRAPED MY WAY UP THE STAIRS. I NEVER SHOULD HAVE GIVEN the iron necklace to the kitchen strega. It was more than a reminder of my mother; it was magic. The kind that could have been used to stop my muscles from ripping apart. Delfina's blood had saved me from death, but the aftermath of her poison still felt like a brisk walk through purgatory.

I stopped and gathered breath for the rest of the climb. I thought of every possible way to remove the Capo's ring.

Dead ends, dead ends. I was caught in a labyrinth of failed plans when the door at the top of the stairs opened and a pair of figures came into silhouette, cast in a full body halo by the light in the Capo's rooms. I slipped into the darkness between torches.

Change whoever is up there, my magic said, shouldering between fear and reason. *Before you lose the chance.*

Most likely, one of those men was the Capo. His ring would protect him, and I would be found out. The magic didn't care about consequences. It had gotten sick of pretending to be Luca di Sangro, and it wanted to be cut loose, free to change things. No matter the cost.

I held my magic at bay as the door slammed shut.

What would have drawn the Capo this far away from the ball? Was he bringing streghe down to the dungeons? Could I slide out of the darkness and fit Father's knife between his ribs?

The two men stopped at the head of the stairs. "No one will be able to hear us here," the Capo said, irritation beneath the skin of his words. "Now what is it? You're the one who insisted on speaking."

"You told me you would help," came a voice, one I knew well. It had called out to me on the day I'd first arrived at the Palazza.

Had Ambrogio lured the Capo here? How could he know I would be visiting the dungeons? Had he followed me all night, like Pasquale, a new shadow to add to my growing collection?

"Tell me what is happening in plain terms," the Capo said.

Ambrogio blurted two words. "Luca di Sangro."

I shifted to be sure I wasn't touched by a single drop of

light. The darkness felt like a thin covering that might be ripped off at any moment.

"What about young Luca?" the Capo asked. "I think he's coming along nicely. Though I don't know if offering him a position at the university will be enough. Do you have any insights?"

"More than you know," Ambrogio muttered. "The di Sangro family has some curse on it. That family *is* a curse. First Beniamo doesn't come to the Palazza, so we can't kill him. Then I receive that letter from Mirella. Teodora, the wild sister, goes missing. And Luca is here, which should make things easier. But the boy is nothing like Mirella describes."

I shook against the stone, harder with each word. It felt as if the poison in my body had met its match.

"Luca is plotting to kill you," Ambrogio said.

The magic turned its attention to him. We agreed on one thing—he was a traitor—but it had its own ideas about what form would suit him best. *A grand clock that never tells the true time. A beautiful dress lined in poison darts.*

"An assassination plot," the Capo said. "He never would have succeeded, and yet he was going to try. I like this new di Sangro more and more." My stomach rioted, from the poison or the Capo's approval, or both.

"What am I supposed to do?" Ambrogio asked.

The Capo's feet ground slightly against the stone as he turned to leave. "You, Ambrogio, will go back to the ball. Find some more wine and a girl to bed. Tomorrow you will see another opera. Elettra, that soprano you like so much, is starring in something new, lots of arias."

"And what about this meeting I'm supposed to arrange?"

Ambrogio asked. "In a quarter of an hour? The one where he kills you?"

"You want to run the Uccelli, as well as your own lands?" the Capo asked. "I'm going to need a man who can keep his head from toppling off his shoulders every time a difficulty arises." Ambrogio fell silent. I could almost feel him sulking. "Show up for the meeting. Tell Luca that I was nowhere to be found."

I had trusted Ambrogio too much, right from the start. I had let him lead me around the Palazza, sling his arm around me and call me *brother*. I had felt terrible for keeping secrets, when he was the one cutting deals with the Capo.

Pasquale had been right about the traitor. He'd made the mistake of suspecting the boy he hated. I'd made the opposite, more dangerous mistake of trusting the boy I liked.

"And the other matter?" Ambrogio asked, nerves leaping through his voice. "The one Mirella told me about in her letter . . ."

"That will sort itself out in time," the Capo said, a smile laced into his tone. "Niccolò di Sangro can't live forever."

16

I rushed up the dungeon stairs as fast as the effects of Delfina's poison would allow. I listened to be sure the Capo and Ambrogio hadn't lingered in the Capo's private rooms, and then I took my time working my way down the staircase, because my muscles still disagreed with the concept, and because I didn't want either of them to catch me away from the ball.

I met Ambrogio in the place we'd chosen, a small room peopled with shadows. Ambrogio had found himself a great glass of wine, just like the Capo had told him to.

"Good," I said. "You made it."

My sudden presence caused Ambrogio's hand to tip and his drink slapped from his glass onto the marble floor, crimson against white. He got to his knees like a servant and swiped the bloody drops with his own handkerchief.

Here's an idea, the magic said. *Turn him into a handkerchief that is always stained.*

"The Capo . . ." he said.

"He's not here yet, is he?" I asked, pretending at nerves. I didn't have to work hard. I trembled, but with anger, not fear.

Ambrogio took a measly sip. "The Capo's not coming."

"Maybe that's for the best." I lowered my voice, as if I were afraid of being heard. "I don't know if I can do this."

Ambrogio nodded sympathetically, looking far too relieved that he would no longer have to make excuses for the Capo's absence.

"Can we talk away from all of this?" I asked.

Ambrogio led me upstairs, and we entered his rooms, a tumble of papers and clothing and trinkets. He had every fine thing a person could wish for, and yet he still hoped to steal from my family.

"Now," Ambrogio said. "What's the matter? Have you come up with a plan to—"

"I heard you," I said, my voice a hard slash, cutting him off. "The di Sangro family is a curse."

Ambrogio swayed on his feet. "Luca," he said. "It's nothing as bad as you think."

It's worse, the magic said.

I ground my teeth and waited. "I will give you one chance to explain."

Ambrogio took a sticky swallow. "After Mirella and I made our promises to each other, she mentioned the di Sangro family would have a problem when your father died. Your brother, Beniamo, is a madman." He said that like I didn't already know it. As if, in discovering this fact, he had somehow made it true. "And Mirella said you had *no* interest in running the family, or being part of it, really. Mirella said, when the time came, I might be a natural replacement."

"So you helped the Capo kill my father," I supplied. I imagined the two of them writing letters, holding them out for Delfina to breathe into their fibers and infuse with poison.

Ambrogio waved the idea away. "The Capo came up with that. I had nothing to do with it."

"You had no quarrel with the results, though." Our talk earlier in the night swelled with new importance. "You hated your father."

"No. He hated *me*. He called me spoiled, even though he was the one who raised me this way. He preferred my brother, everyone did, but when Leo died in the unification wars, Father had to settle for his second born." I wasn't the firstborn either; I knew how pitiful our lots could be. But as Ambrogio spoke, every bit of understanding I had for him drained away, leaving me empty. "I wasn't sad to see him go, but I swear I had nothing to do with his death. And it seemed that Niccolò would follow soon. . . ."

"So, naturally you thought to kill my brother."

"Yes," Ambrogio said stiffly. His brown eyes held mine. "You have no idea what he did to my Mirella. How he tortured her."

Of course I did. Did Ambrogio really dream Beniamo had overlooked any of us in his cruelty? "Knowing my brother is unfit has nothing to do with . . . *this*," I said, almost spitting. I didn't want the taste of Ambrogio's plot in my mouth.

"I was never going to hurt you, Luca." Ambrogio rushed forward as if to embrace me, then thought better of it. "This was supposed to be neat, simple. The Capo was going to find you a place in Amalia. At the new university, or the Malfara family's museum. Did you know they founded the first institution for the natural sciences?"

My heart scraped over the notes of a familiar sadness. Luca—the real Luca—would have loved that museum. "You have no idea what I want," I said. "You have no idea who I am."

I let go of the magic, slowly this time. Boyish features melted away, and with a slight shift, I centered inside of my body. Air brushed over my skin, announcing every difference. I wanted Ambrogio to know the full measure of the person he dealt with. The odd girl from the mountains. The self-made heir of Niccolò di Sangro. Liar, strega, thief.

Ambrogio's chest heaved at the sight of me. "What . . . ?"

"Is the story moving too quickly for you?" I asked. "Shall I flip back a page?"

"You're Teodora," he said.

"And you're a traitor with a heart of wood." I savored the sound of my voice, the feel of it pouring from my throat. "You have no claim in the Uccelli. You tried to take over my family through my sister's bedchamber."

"That's not right," Ambrogio said. "I love Mirella. The rest just . . . followed suit."

Anger pitched through me, twisting my face. Ambrogio became a mirror, his dread showing me how frightful I must look. He sank to his knees, looking urgently to the skies, as if he needed a new god to pray to.

One that could stop me from killing him.

There's no such god, the magic said.

"You told the Capo about my plan. He could have easily chosen to kill me." Ambrogio looked about to pick up the thread of his argument, but I slapped it out of his hands. "You told the Capo about my father being alive. Was that another thing Mirella mentioned in her letter?" A guilty silence stretched. "Your betrayal will lead to another murder attempt, and another, until the Capo succeeds. How is picking the di Sangro family apart, one person at a time, *loving* my sister?"

Ambrogio shook his head with great feeling. "She will understand that things went differently than planned. God, is that really you, Teodora?"

"Yes, and I know my sister better than anyone. Her loyalty makes the Capo's obsession with the word look small and mean. She won't want you anymore once I tell her what you've done. You will *never* be a di Sangro."

Ambrogio looked at me steadily, and I could feel the world sliding beneath my feet. "That's already settled."

"But . . . the wedding isn't until spring."

Ambrogio's eyes held the marbled gleam of triumph. "It can hardly be called off now. There's going to be a baby."

"You're lying," I said weakly. Somehow, though, I knew he wasn't. He was too cowardly to attempt a grand deception.

"Send a letter," Ambrogio invited. "Ask her yourself."

I sat down hard on the bed. A baby changed everything. Mirella wouldn't be able to break off her engagement, a thought that had surely crossed Ambrogio's mind as he formed his plans. As he crawled into her lap.

"No," I said.

"I'm telling you—"

"*No*." Magic rushed to my fingers. Power crashed out. Ambrogio fell to the ground without a cry.

He stayed the same—a disappointment to the last. When I approached his body, I found it stilled in a way that made Ambrogio appear more than dead, as if he'd never been alive to begin with.

Spent and satisfied, the magic curled up inside of me.

I got to my knees and took in Ambrogio's paled face, his stiffened fingers.

I hadn't asked the magic to change him. I hadn't given it

any ideas. Then I remembered my words, the ones that had come to my lips so easily.

You're a traitor with a heart of wood.

I set my knuckles to Ambrogio's chest and rapped once. A hard, hollow sound rose.

"WHAT HAVE YOU DONE?" I ASKED THE MAGIC.

It refused to answer.

"*Change him back,*" I said.

You never learned how, it scolded.

There had been no time to learn. I had too much to worry about, too many people to save. The magic didn't care about that. It only wished to be stronger. To know more. To be a greater part of me, even as I starved it.

I sat on the floor of Ambrogio's room, speaking ancient words, beautiful and jagged as shards of glass broken long ago.

"*I need you,*" I told the magic.

Yes, it said. *You do.*

I had denied who I was for far too long.

"*I won't pretend to be Luca anymore,*" I promised.

But the magic knew I was a liar. I would change at the first chance. And I had to bring Ambrogio back. Especially with Pasquale changed, it would be too easy for the five families to follow the line of these events to Luca.

To me.

There is nothing we can do now, the magic said as I stared down at Ambrogio's body, set like wax.

It should have been the Capo.

This was all wrong.

I tugged at Ambrogio's arm. His muscles splayed, loose. In my girlish body, I had certain kinds of strength, but my arms weren't especially hearty. I grunted and tugged until I lifted Ambrogio from the floor, then shoved bit by bit until he reached the bed. I pulled the sheets over him.

He looked like he was sleeping. A hard, uncomfortable sleep, but at least his posture didn't betray that he was dead.

I checked the halls before rushing to my rooms. The door closed with a bang that shuddered through my entire body. I sank to my knees, ran my hands through the pile of items near the bed, and came up clutching the mirror. I looked into the glass and tried, and tried, but I couldn't undo the knots that tied me to that girl.

I was Teodora di Sangro.

No one else would have made this mess.

I pitched the mirror to the floor, and it cracked into silvery pieces. The Capo still lived. Father was dying. The five families had started to break apart. Mirella might never forgive me. Cielo would never return.

I grabbed things from around the room, stuffing them into my pack with no real sense of what I meant to do, only sure I couldn't stay at the Palazza. I took Pasquale the shoehorn from my pocket, pried off the boy's boots that Cielo had bought for me, and replaced them with the ones I'd worn over the mountain.

I grabbed at a rumpled shirt on the floor and felt a lump. Pulling the linen away, I uncovered the soft leather of a well-loved book.

Cielo had left it here.

Which meant Cielo had to return.

And there was the slight chance the strega might be able to change this, to twist it in a new direction before the Capo or the five families found Ambrogio.

That wasn't a plan, though. It was a hope. I threw myself onto the bed, writhing against the sheets, visited by Father's voice and another saying from my di Sangro childhood: *Hope can torture a man better than any dungeon.*

I closed my eyes and waited.

17

I woke before dawn to the sound of wings and a rude cry. Before my eyes were properly open, I grabbed Father's knife and lashed out with one hand, defending my neck with the other. My body remembered what it meant to have a bird attack in the night.

I blinked and focused on a spatter of raindrops on the window ledge as thunder ripped and tore at the sky. A large black bird of no particular species lit on the ledge, feathers thick with rain. When it raised its wings to ruffle the water away, it revealed bright red patches.

I put the knife back in my sleeve.

"I know your brother is a murderous owl," Cielo said, freshly changed into boyish form and kneeling over the cream-white pages of his book. "But please, try to control yourself." He pulled on trousers and the rumpled linen shirt from the floor, then combed his fingers through his hair, leaving shining furrows.

"Speaking of your brother, I might have run into him in the skies over the city. He chased me for a mile until I took shelter in the Giardino Chiaro. I don't usually set down there—far too many pigeons—but one look at your brother's hellfire eyes was . . . inspiring."

"Beniamo is in Amalia?" My voice was as ruined as everything else about me. I sounded terrible. I must have looked worse.

"Well, an owl who hates everyone and everything and wants to slice the world to ribbons is in Amalia," Cielo said.

"That's him."

The strega sat down on the bed at my side.

"Can you bring a person back to life?" I asked.

"You asked me that before," Cielo said, treading softly on what he knew was dangerous ground. "When Luca . . ."

"I know," I said. "But you also said that if the death had something to do with magic—"

"The Capo?" Cielo asked. I thought the strega would be angry, but he only looked sad. As if I had disappointed him—or maybe it was bigger than that. Maybe the entire world had disappointed him, and the strega had finally seen I was part of that world and couldn't be separated from it. "Did you change your mind about killing him?"

I shook my head. I shook and shook.

"Teo, tell me what happened." Cielo leaned in close, as close as he had when he kissed me, but this time he caught ahold of my eyes with his own and refused to let go. "Remember the twenty-seven-part favor we agreed on? I want to know what is happening, and I need you to tell me at once. Let's call this part one."

I HAD CIELO CHECK THE HALLWAY BEFORE WE SCUTTLED TO Ambrogio's rooms. The ball must have died out in the night. The halls had been swept clean of the mess as well as the couples making the most of dark corners.

I pushed in the door and then nodded the strega inside. Cielo spent a full minute staring at the motionless boy before he approached the bed, bending over Ambrogio's body. "I will, at some point, need you to explain."

There was no point in decorating the truth. "I changed his heart to wood."

Cielo face managed at least three expressions at once. He looked impressed with my magic, unimpressed with my decision-making, and nervous about how to proceed. He turned on his heel and went back to inspecting the body. "There is something I might be able to do," Cielo said, leaning over to rip open Ambrogio's shirt at the chest. "It's not . . . certain."

"It either works or it doesn't." I didn't mean to sound so cutting, but fear was a whetstone. It sharpened everything.

"I've never tried this," Cielo admitted. "There are things about my abilities . . . things I don't know because it's safer not to find out." I thought of Giovanna. She had been afraid too. Cielo didn't just have his own magic; he had the power of many streghe packed inside of him. "When I was younger, magic flooded my body, swamped my mind. That was before I learned to control it."

The hope that I'd been gripping for hours felt suddenly delicate. "Don't do this if it's too dangerous."

"I should have taught you something when we first went over the mountains," Cielo said. I felt the old ache to understand. The strain to be more than I was. But that wasn't right: I'd simply wanted to be all the parts of myself at once. To learn about magic *and* master my di Sangro lessons. To enjoy my life as a girl without having to feel like a girl in every moment. To follow the strega, and run home to the castle. "All magic is dangerous," Cielo said. "The question we ask, over and over, is whether or not it's worth doing anyway."

I looked over Ambrogio's body. Without life in it, it became more like a landscape, a series of soft hills. I preferred him this way, quiet and motionless, unable to hurt the people I loved. "And this is worth doing?"

"Of course," Cielo said.

"You owe me no more favors," I said.

"I have other reasons," Cielo said, looking down at me, the colors in his eyes lit by the threat of dawn in the window. "Ones that cannot be written down in ledgers." The strega put a hand to the back of my neck, and that simple touch was a key, quietly turning, unlocking everything I'd felt when Cielo kissed me.

The strega nodded quickly and then rolled his sleeves to the elbows. "Now, if you'll stand back, I have magic to work."

"Thank you," I said, two plain words that would never stand in for the ones I wished to say.

Cielo put his hands over Ambrogio's heart.

He waved in a clockwise circle over Ambrogio's chest and then, in a smooth motion, he reversed the circle, as if erasing what he'd done. The air seemed to warm, and it took me a moment to understand that Cielo was humming. His lips parted slightly as he formed words, the first line of the nursery song Giovanna had sung to him as a baby. Cielo took a deep breath and sang again, a warbling set of sounds that moved oddly.

The same line, backward.

The wind that had flowed into the room through the window was sucked out like a gasp. A flash of lightning showed rain skittering up into the sky.

"That's not good," Cielo said. The words were ripped away from him and then stuffed back into his mouth. They came out backward. He rushed toward the window, but magic sucked at his steps like quicksand.

The room had become a whirlpool of time, and I would never be able to cross it. I would never reach the strega to calm his heartbeat, to kiss him. Everything we did together would be unraveled.

Focus, my magic told me.

I could give Cielo something to focus on. I could look at him and fill my eyes with the truth of how I felt.

Cielo fought against the winds, each step a battle to gain ground. I kept staring, waiting for him to notice me, to remember he wasn't alone. It hurt to look at him so openly. It felt like giving myself a wound that only one person in the world knew how to close.

Cielo caught my gaze, and the room calmed, the night air returning to its normal balance, the rain starting up its reassuring hiss. The strega took a tentative step forward, and his foot stayed where he'd put it.

"What was that?" I asked.

"An undoing," Cielo said, breathless from the effort.

Ambrogio stirred on the bed, letting out a light groan. I backed toward the door on soft feet. "Will he remember that I changed him?"

"I've never brought someone back from a magical petrification, so it's hard to say." Cielo grabbed my hand. "Let's leave before Ambrogio catches the di Sangro fever and decides it's his turn to take revenge."

꽃

THE SKY ABOVE THE COURTYARD HELD THE LAST BRAVE STARS, ones that would not be chased off by a few rays of sun. With the night over, how would Cielo and I get back to the dungeons? A few drops of Delfina's blood were all I needed to cure Father, and then the five families would be able to stand against the Capo.

I pushed open the door to our rooms, ready to forge a new path. There was a man sitting on my bed. A man with dark curls and hazelnut eyes, a man who looked as tightly wound as a music box.

"Pietro?" I said, keeping my voice even, while my insides wobbled with a new sort of fear.

Pietro hummed the frantic pitches of a song I knew well. A fugue. He jumped to his feet, hands twitching in circles, the leftover effects of his life as a tiny musical contraption. The way he looked at me, though—a potent brew of loathing and fear—was perfectly human.

"You," he said. "It's you."

"I think your undoing was *too* successful," I whispered to Cielo.

"I told you it would be hard to control." He stared at Pietro with a thick wariness on his face.

"She's going to curse me," Pietro said. "Again."

"I never cursed you to begin with," I said. Though now

that I thought about it, the situation could have seemed that way, depending on what you thought curses were, and whether you were familiar with other uses of magic.

You sound like Cielo, the magic told me.

"Be quiet."

"Ohhh," Pietro said, "She's using God's language for her terrible magic. Ohhh, it's happening again."

"Be quiet!" I cried, in Vinalian this time.

"The magic couldn't have been undone all over the Palazza," Cielo said into my ear, "or we'd be hearing shouts. Explosions. The usual sort of thing. Maybe it's only *your* magic that reversed."

I rushed to remember what else, *who* else, might have been changed back. The potted rose had died in the dungeons. The mirror was smashed. The rosary marked Luca's grave on Weeping Mountain.

Cielo and I turned to each other at the same moment. He pointed down at the soft leather boots I wore.

The shoehorn.

"Was there another man in here when you . . . woke up?" I asked Pietro. He ignored the question and hummed harder, the fugue growing hot with intensity. "Have you seen anyone else?" I stepped closer, but Pietro shied away, humming so loud that I feared his lungs would burst.

"Tell me," I said. "And I'll never touch you with magic again."

He stopped humming long enough to nod. "Pasquale," he said. "That was his name. Said it a few times like he was trying to convince himself. Then he threw all your shoes out the window and ran off."

A knock sounded at the door.

I was about to be dragged out of this room and made to answer for my deceit. But I wouldn't take Cielo with me. I wouldn't give him up to the Capo.

I shoved the strega toward the window.

"What are you doing?" Cielo asked, pointing a slim finger past my shoulder. "The trouble is at the *door*. You're headed in the wrong direction." I could see, by the stony set of his lips and the defiance in his eyes, that falling in love with Cielo was going to be as much trouble as anything else.

I kissed him as briefly as I could bear. Then I pushed. Cielo hurtled backward over the ledge and into the air, his fingers working to find the right place before he wrenched the book open. Pages flashed white.

The strega vanished.

A ball of fur twisted through the air, a black cat with white boots. It clawed its way into a decent landing position. The book hit the perfectly manicured lawn first, then the cat. It sent up a series of raspy cries. Cielo could complain all he wanted, but I had saved him from an unspeakable fate. With my stomach pressed to the window ledge, I let out a sigh.

Another polite knock, as if whoever stood on the other side of the door didn't mind waiting. He already had me trapped. "Teodora di Sangro?" My name, spoken in that voice, turned my heart to water.

The Capo had come for me.

Five

How to Change Anything

18

I stood in a courtyard with no windows facing it, tucked among the many wings of the Palazza. Though we were hidden from the Capo's court, I still felt exposed, like someone had peeled back my skin. The girlish form that I'd done so much to keep secret was now the centerpiece of the Capo's attention. He stared, not into my eyes, but over every inch of my body, as if I were a field of battle and he needed to draw up plans.

I refused to look at him. I took in the rest of the courtyard to distract myself from the lack of air in my lungs, my throat screwing tight. Long, thin cypress trees lined two walls. On the others, jasmine and wisteria climbed trellises upward, toward the sky. The clouds overhead were perfect strips of white, as if they'd been pruned to match the plants.

No amount of careful beauty could cover the layers of great power here, and great pain.

The Capo had brought Cielo's mother to this place. He had killed streghe, or ordered them to kill each other, which was worse. For every battle I had seen, there must have been dozens more. This was where *the brilliant death* had done its work. My magic shivered through me, leaving shards of ice.

The Capo faced me from a distance, not that he needed one to keep him safe. He twisted the gold ring on his finger, subtly showing off the fact that I couldn't touch him. Now that he knew I was a strega, and Pasquale had told him exactly what I was capable of, he wasn't going to risk me changing half of his court.

He would handle me himself.

"Who did you take that from?" I asked, nodding at his ring. It was a shard of a strega's pain, another stolen bit of magic.

The Capo smiled broadly. "So you noticed my little treasure," he said. "I knew that if I wanted to work with your kind I would need to protect myself. Fortunately, I found a strega who could change magic back into useless wishes."

"Did she die here?" I asked, holding my voice as tight as a fist so it wouldn't tremble.

The Capo's smile never faltered. He didn't care that I knew his secrets. I was going to die here too.

Delfina walked in at one end of the courtyard in soldier's garb, her dark hair drawn back into a bun. She looked reluctant, as always.

"Where is Azzurra?" I asked. I'd expected her to be the one sent to deal with me.

"Oh, I gave her some Eterrans to amuse," the Capo said. "Azzurra will be busy for hours. We don't need her assistance at the moment."

"Of course not," I said with a peppery bite. If I fought Azzurra, I would have been given a fair chance. Faced with Delfina's poison, I would crumple like a flower tossed into a hungry flame.

The Capo paced between me and Delfina. I had no

interest in doing this dance. "Why haven't you killed me yet?" Thoughts of the future came with the speed and smothering quality of an avalanche. Cielo would never hear from me again. My family would lose Father and three children in less than a week.

"I don't want you dead." The Capo's pacing became even more precise. "You came here, a second daughter, doing away with both of your brothers to earn the chance." I shook my head, forcing my eyes shut. The idea that I had *done away with* Luca hurt almost as much as his loss. "You fooled my entire court, talking the five families into a dangerous plot. You gathered strength at every turn. If Luca was a young man I wanted at my side, *you* are what I need."

"You have streghe to your name," I said. I could not imagine living their lives, packed away in the dark, doing magic at the Capo's bidding.

He flicked my argument away with a sharp wrist. "Azzurra would rather burn the world down than build it up. Delfina here has a talent for taking lives but no interest in wielding it." Delfina looked at the ground, frowning so hard that I thought the dirt would crumble.

"You, Teodora, have a beautiful gift." The Capo stopped in front of me. "You could halt an army and make them lie down on the battlefield without a single soldier bloodied. Imagine all the violent men you could change into lovely objects." The Capo's force, the power he had gathered over an entire life, hit me like one of the great waves at the Violetta Coast, spun me, stopped me from seeing anything clearly. "I have intelligence that promises the first of the Eterran invasions will begin in less than a month. Armies have been seen marching toward the Neviane."

The northern mountains had always been our first defense. The white peaks rose higher than the Uccelli. They slowed the progress of armies, but they couldn't hold one back forever.

"You have an army," I said. "Stop them."

"It's one thing to win a few battles against the vain, petty lords who tried to resist what true Vinalians want. This is a different matter entirely. Vinalia hasn't pushed back an invading force since the empire," the Capo reminded me. "You and I can change that."

He was taking away my power and trying to hand it back to me on his own terms. He wanted me to be grateful. I fought down panic and told myself to stay calm. To reason clearly.

To think like a di Sangro.

Eterra was trying to invade us. Why? I found myself back at the ball, taking in the show the Capo had put on. He'd given the Eterrans a picture of a newly unified and weakened nation, one rich enough to plunder and not yet strong enough to defend itself.

"You want the invasion," I said, barely shocked by the truth. "You've been courting it this whole time."

"I spent twenty years bringing Vinalia together. You think I want to see it trampled?" The Capo laughed, his rich voice blanketing the courtyard.

I could hear the truth crawling under that sound. "You speak of showing our might to the world, but if you run around Eterra starting wars, you lose the loyalty of your people. Tempt the Eterrans into an invasion, and you will bring Vinalians together. Unite them like nothing else could. If you win, you become the great defender of our homeland."

I finished breathless with understanding, certainty, and no small measure of pride.

"This," the Capo said, clapping as hard as a pistol shot. "*This* is why I need you. No one else has been able to riddle that out, not even my brother, and you did it in less than a minute. I've never met a strega with such a mind for strategy. I've seen it at work since the moment you arrived. Really, I shouldn't be surprised. You were raised by Niccolò di Sangro."

"Yes," I said, biting down on the word. "I was raised by a great man. And you nearly killed him."

The Capo's look had a sharp edge of victory. "Is that the only problem left between us?" He turned to the far end of the courtyard. "Come here, Delfina."

She walked over to him on unsteady feet, shielding her eyes against the mild sun. I wondered when she had last seen the sky. She had been locked up by a man who came to her village, torturing her until the best fate she could imagine was a cell where she was allowed to sit unbothered. Now she was being made to use a power she didn't even wish to have, one rooted so deep in her soul that she couldn't dig it out.

"I won't fight her," I said. "She saved my life once."

Delfina gave me a smile, gone as quickly as it had appeared.

"Very noble of you," the Capo said. "Noble, and unnecessary. There will be no fighting today."

He pulled out a dagger and drew a neat line across Delfina's throat. She grabbed her neck, but the pressure only made the blood pour faster. I wanted to hold her up, to help, but the Capo stood firmly in my way. He brought a small vial out of his pocket and held it up, collecting a rivulet of red.

When the glass was full, he let her slide to the ground. The grass Delfina breathed on turned black and withered.

And then she stopped breathing.

I fell to my knees.

Delfina's death retreated in the distance. The world squeezed down to the head of a pin. Magic stretched to take up the space, until I could feel nothing else. I was choking on magic. More and more, a sort of endless swallowing. I howled with pain and a savage kind of happiness.

"Delfina's power is entering your body," the Capo said. "It might be overwhelming at first, seeing how many streghe she has killed."

I stayed on my knees, full in a way that didn't seem natural, hands slicked with tears. Delfina's body lay a few feet away. Her green-gray eyes stared up at the sky. Her blood fed the grass below.

The Capo knelt in front of me and grabbed my hand, uncurling it before he set the vial in my palm. I couldn't feel his skin on mine, a small mercy. My body was overstuffed. My mind cracked in two.

I hated that Delfina had died.

I wouldn't have given her magic back for anything in the world.

"This is the antidote your father needs," the Capo said. "A gift to prove how serious I am. Take it home. Give it to Niccolò. Save his life and then come back to me. If you don't, things will become very difficult in the Uccelli."

I knew a poorly delivered threat when I heard one. I snatched the vial from the Capo's hand and left the courtyard without looking back.

I HAD ONLY MINUTES TO SLIDE MY THINGS INTO A PACK BEFORE I left for the Uccelli. My fingers grew careless as they stuffed dirty clothing in. I picked up one of Cielo's shirts and pressed it to my face. It smelled like nighttime in the garden. It smelled like magic.

I laughed, a sharp, broken sound, and shoved the shirt in my pack. I couldn't imagine leaving without saying good-bye to Cielo. I couldn't imagine coming back to honor the silent, needful agreement I had made.

I was the Capo's strega. I had unthinkable power, and a chance to use it without hiding behind a mask of manhood. The Capo must have thought he'd offered me everything I wanted. If I had never met Cielo, never shared the dream of his mother, the Capo's deal might have been enough. Now it sickened me, turning my thoughts as dark as the bloody grass beneath Delfina's body.

My fingers closed around the vial. I had to save Father. If that meant pledging my magic to the Capo, it was only in service to the wordless trade I had made as a di Sangro.

My life for my family's.

Always.

Besides, if I worked for the Capo, I might find ways to undermine him and keep the rest of the streghe safe. I thought of Cielo captured, forced to live the same bondage as Giovanna. I would never let that happen. And I vowed that I wouldn't take any more power, even though my magic might crave it.

I picked up my pack and strode past the guards in the doorway and almost directly into a group of people waiting outside. It was the boys, the full set. Ambrogio stood slightly off to the side. Vanni lingered by Mimì and Lorenzo, who stood pressed together. Favianne had her arm tightly linked through Pasquale's, imprisoning him. Pasquale looked uncomfortable, like he was still wedged between a bootheel and a vile foot.

"Are you here to boast to the others?" I asked. "To tell the tale of how you revealed the strega to the Capo?"

"He shouldn't have done it," Vanni said.

"You're a di Sangro," Lorenzo said in agreement. "Even if you are . . ."

"A girl? A strega? Better at plotting than anyone you've met?"

Lorenzo let out a surprised laugh.

"Is it true?" Favianne asked me, with the shine of amazement in her eyes. I'd thought she would hate that I'd tricked her, flirted with her, and turned Pasquale into a common household object. Instead she stared. For the first time in my life, I was the subject of wonderment and envy. "Do you really have magic?"

I brought out the ring I'd borrowed from her, the one stamped with the Malfara family crest. *Change it back to gold*, I told the magic, and watched as the wolf slid off like the last of the winter snowmelt, the somber gray giving way to a bright shimmer.

Favianne took the ring back, turning it around and around in the light. I could see her keen mind, picking the notion apart. She slid the ring back on her finger and smiled at me, not so unlike the smile she'd given the boy she'd believed to be Luca di Sangro.

"Don't look so impressed," Pasquale muttered.

"You were a girl this whole time." Vanni's smile was a nervous, flimsy thing. "I can't believe I said all of that in front of a girl." He looked as though a lump of polenta had gotten trapped in his throat and he had to work it down.

"It's not a bad habit," I assured him.

"I wish we had met in better times," Lorenzo said. "I would have liked to know this Teodora di Sangro."

"Why?" I asked. "So you could have asked me to fill out a round of dances?"

He stood a little taller and looked me straight in the eye, bringing his full presence into the room. "Women have ruled Salvi in the past. I would not have been as surprised as you like to think."

Mimì put her hands in mine and added, "You should come see our home, when you can." She leaned in and whispered, "It's nothing like this place."

I returned the press of her hands, but I couldn't give my word that I would visit. *This place* was more than likely where I would spend the rest of my days. Or on some battlefield, using my magic at the Capo's bidding.

Ambrogio tried to catch my eye, and it made my magic spark and flare in a dangerous way.

"Give my love to Mirella," he said.

I gave a small, stuck nod. Not for his sake, but for my sister's.

"Make sure the five families take care of each other until I get back," I said. "And keep your eyes on the Capo."

"I thought you worked for him now," Vanni said. "He announced it to the entire court. That's why we came to find you, to see if it was true. His strega, Teodora di Sangro, the daughter of the five families."

"Yes, well." A bitter smile pressed to my lips. "Keep an eye on me, too." I threw my pack over my shoulder and marched out of the Palazza.

19

The Capo wanted to see me off at the grand arch. I was made to wait, held in place by a small formation of soldiers. The heat of Amalia's summer refused to crack, leaving the city under a heartless gray sky.

The Capo marched out of the Palazza with another detachment of guards. A crowd gathered, choking the square. The Capo loved spectacles, making a show out of loyalty. I feared he would make me kiss his family's ring or recite a mindless oath. Instead he held out a uniform. Green and black. Unification colors.

I was a soldier now. *His.*

"Today a new strega has been dedicated to the service of Vinalia!" the Capo shouted. He looked at me but kept his voice pitched for the crowds. "Come home safely, Teodora di Sangro."

My heart went tight and blank, a room with no doors. The Capo could buy my loyalty with a vial of blood, he could redraw the lines of the world, but there were things he couldn't change. Home was a fireplace and Fiorenza telling strega stories. Mirella painting in her tower. Father in his study, Luca in his laboratory. Home was the bright face of the mountains.

Most of all, it was the castle. The song of the wind against the stones. The feeling of being tucked safely away from the rest of the world.

"I will come back," I said, "to Amalia." I wondered if the Capo noticed the rebellion folded into my words. I took the sickly green clothes and turned to leave. A voice rang from the great arch of the Palazza.

"Strega!"

I turned to find Oreste in his priest garb, rushing into the square, steps stilted by dragging along an old woman with a hooked back and a strong odor of flour, butter, and woody-sweet thyme.

Oreste hadn't called out to me.

He had the kitchen strega in his grip.

"Traces of recent magic were found in the kitchen of the Palazza," Oreste said, with a waver of pleasure. The Order of Prai must have given him the power to publicly hunt streghe, and it couldn't be a coincidence that he'd picked one who wouldn't cause an outright war with his brother. "This woman has been charged with plotting to harm members of the Vinalian court."

I pushed forward, making the vial of blood in my pocket slide and tip. "She was helping me."

The Capo held up his hand, and I stopped.

He looked down at the kitchen strega with a hard benevolence, a father doling out needed punishment. "This strega has not taken an oath of loyalty. If she chooses to tithe her magic to Vinalia, as Teodora di Sangro has done, she will be doing the work of God and country. Otherwise, I have to assume she is against us."

The kitchen strega looked up into the face of the Capo,

her wrinkles an unreadable language. She wrapped one root-like hand around my mother's necklace, and then spat on the Capo's fine boots.

That language was clear enough.

Oreste staggered forward through a haze of anger as thick as the day's heat. He grabbed the kitchen strega by the hair and motioned to a man who had clearly been staged to wait. He pushed forward a cart full of stones—not the precious marble stolen from the Uccelli but harsh limestone that could be found anywhere in Vinalia. The Capo nodded slightly to his brother, and in that look I read a deeper truth. He was doing more than allowing this death. The brothers had struck their own foul bargain. The Order of Prai would be allowed to kill any strega who did not fall into line with the Capo's great plan.

The stonemason went to work, blocking the woman into a small prison in the center of the square, as she screeched like a bird kept from the sky. The people all around us watched, sweating pale droplets.

"Higher," Oreste said. The mason and his men shifted great blocks. The whole thing was viciously slow. I remembered the history Cielo had taught me, how the Order of Prai had buried streghe in the dark earth without killing them first. The priests must have known about *the brilliant death*, and feared the magic of murdered streghe would slide into their waiting souls. I doubted it would work on them—their souls weren't rich enough soil for magic to grow in.

Stop this, my magic said.

I wouldn't let it touch this man, as pitiful and danger-ous as he might be. He was Cielo's father, and I would not take more from Cielo than the world already had. But that didn't mean I would let Oreste walk away unscathed.

I walked over to the priest, as if inspecting his work. "Odd," I whispered. "I'd always thought Giovanna's lover would be nicer to look at. And not wearing a robe, of course." His face took on the color of pages in an old prayer book, greased and grayed.

"Who told you . . . ?"

I nodded to the kitchen strega being encased in stone. "If you do not stop, I will tell everyone in the crowd."

"Giovanna tricked me," he said.

"You know that isn't true."

The priest's eyes marbled with softness, and I could sense the kitchen strega's magic working even now, a memory he'd lost wafting back to him. "Giovanna . . . she loved me once . . ." Revelation moved slowly over his face, waging a war against fear and disgust.

"Oh, look, another magical statue for the public square."

I knew that voice. I turned to the crowds to find Cielo in boyish form, striding from a side street into the square. His white shirt snapped, his black hair striking out against the sky. His green-and-purple cloak spun around his ankles in an unnatural wind. "Sorry to be so late," he said. "It looks like you've gotten started."

Cielo cut across the square, and wherever he passed, statues toppled. The masons ran off, leaving their work unfinished. The wind blew into the collection of stones, and as they crumbled, the kitchen strega climbed out of her broken prison.

She vanished into the crowd.

Oreste ran from the sight of his child—a coward, always. Cielo flickered in and out of form, a wind, then a boy, then a wind again. The book rushed through the air and landed in his hands.

I thought he would go after his father, but instead he drew a straight line toward the Capo. The guards bristled and closed ranks. A small number rushed to subdue Cielo, but I couldn't have that. I focused my attention on the guard who ran fastest, sword drawn.

Change him into something firm and blockish.

The magic blew me off my feet, and I fell, skinning a strip off my arm. When I looked up at the guard, his arms reached for the strega, grasping at the air, but his feet had turned into two lumps of rough stone.

So had the feet of all the guards.

How did you do that? I asked. The magic had never changed more than one person at a time.

Delfina's stolen power prickled through me.

Cielo stared at the Capo. I readied myself for some great pronouncement, but Cielo's voice came out half-broken. "You can't have her."

My heart knotted; I couldn't pick hope apart from pain. I should have known Cielo wouldn't leave me to the Capo's devices, especially not when his mother's fate rang so loudly in his ears.

"Who are you, that you would claim my strega?" the Capo asked, looking amused, even though half of the statues he'd commissioned had been dashed to the ground and his guards had been bolted in place. "No, don't tell me." The Capo studied the strega's face like a map, and it led him, step by step, to the inevitable place. "You're Giovanna's child."

The Capo's emotions were all carefully wrought to flatter, convince, or intimidate, but what rose to the surface now was real. A sharp sense of wonder. Truly bottomless greed. "I thought you were dead, *boy*." And with that word came the scrape of the Capo's fear.

Cielo was the Capo's blood.

Cielo was the Capo's heir.

"We should get to know one another," the Capo said carefully, each word a strike into unknown territory. "Shouldn't we, nephew? With the understanding that I would never harm the di Sangro girl. She and I have made an alliance. We can all work together."

"You suppose I do not know the truth about my mother," Cielo said. "You are hideously wrong, of course." The lines of his body blurred as the strega became air. He crashed into the front of the Palazza, and the arches cracked with mighty sounds.

Cielo landed in the center of the square, breathing like a hard wind. He riffled at the edges of his book, muttering, "What next?"

He tore a page out and went up in flames.

I staggered back from the heat as the fire built, a raging wall. The Capo clapped and clapped at Cielo's performance.

He stopped when fire took root in his clothing. His ring prevented the flame from burning his skin, but smoke rose into his mouth and nose. The Capo tore at his shirt, gagging. Fire spread beyond him, catching on the guards and the wooden carts in the street, consuming them like a living beast. Buildings around the square went up in smoke of all colors.

Amalia was burning.

"Setting the world on fire to save me?" I asked. "Funny, I thought you didn't believe in that sort of thing."

Cielo came back to her girlish form long enough to spin

around with dismay. The strega had started this destruction with magic she barely understood and didn't know how to control. The Palazza smoldered from the inside. People ran out of the gates and away from the square, spreading chaos.

Stripped down to his underclothes, the Capo looked less like a soldier of Vinalia and more like a madman. He stalked toward Cielo, his eyes raging as bright as the city around us. "That magic you are using is stolen."

Cielo looked exhausted, her muscles sagging and her hair raked with wind until it fell in lank sheets. But she had enough will to meet the Capo's eyes. "You're right, Uncle. *Stolen* is exactly the word I would use."

The Capo lunged and the strega became a wind in his grasp. Cielo whipped and screamed through the square.

Smoke attacked my eyes. I crouched low, coughing on ash that floated on the hard breeze, searching for breathable air. The Capo spun in a circle, yelling at nothing and everything. "You want me to stay and choke to death on magic that belongs to me. Clever. But I'll have it back, today or tomorrow. Whether you are alive or dead." The smoke doubled, and the Capo left on the heels of his people.

I stayed behind, breathing thick handfuls of darkness.

I longed for the moment when Cielo tumbled back into human form with a limp smile and a dramatic bow. The more I waited, the taller the fires grew, until they scratched at the sky. I would have to bring the strega back from the grips of magic.

I tried to take a deep breath, but there was not enough air left in Amalia. So I whispered, hoping the strega would hear me, "You are not my fate, Cielo Allegri. You are the choice I make for myself." I coughed, black bits of ash coming up in my palm. Heat crept closer, until I felt sure it was about to overtake me. "Do you truly need me to be this obvious?" I closed my eyes, and in that darkness, anything might be true. "You are my strega. I am yours."

I heard a cry, like a broken-winged bird.

My words had snatched Cielo out of the air.

She fell to the stones.

I DRAGGED THE STREGA OUT OF AMALIA, STEP BY GROANING step. By the time we crossed the bridge, Cielo could walk, dead-eyed and limping. One of her arms had twisted where she had landed on it, and she couldn't even hold the book in that hand. I wanted to let her rest, but we had to get as far away from the Capo as we could.

We passed through grape fields starred with purple fruit. The Uccelli was a flock of dark birds gathered on the horizon. When we reached the foothills, the strega tucked into the underbrush and flipped a page, turning back into a boy. "The bandits we meet on mountain passes might think you can't take care of yourself, and then I'll have far too many trinkets on my shelf," Cielo said, wilting on the final words. He collapsed against my side.

"We have to keep moving," I said, hauling him back onto the path.

"Remind me *why*," the strega whispered. His skin was gray, his voice scaled with smoke. "Sleep sounds better than all of the olives in Vinalia. Sleep sounds like a friend I haven't seen in a very long time. Sleep—"

"You're hurt," I interrupted. "And when you've taken a

great fall, say from the sky to the stones of a city square, you aren't supposed to sleep." I clapped him to my side and tried to shock him back into the moment, like casting a person into cold water. "Are we going to talk about the fact that you're the heir to the leader of Vinalia?"

"If you love me," he said with a slight cough, "we are not."

We kept up a rough, jagged pace all the way up Weeping Mountain. Soon Cielo could walk on his own, but I insisted on setting his arm with a branch and binding it with a few strips torn from the bottom of my shirt.

"No one looks good in this insipid green," Cielo said, scowling at the cloth from my soldier's uniform.

"It will have to do for now."

We rushed down the far side of Weeping Mountain, taking the steep path at a jolting pace. I wanted to stop at Luca's graveside, but I didn't trust myself ever to start up again.

"Do you hear that?" Cielo asked as we came down into the crown of the Uccelli.

"What?" I asked, but as soon as I'd said it, I heard a rattle in the underbrush.

We were being tracked.

"That's not the Capo," Cielo whispered, slipping into the dark coat of strategy. The strega might have given me magic lessons, but I had taught him a few things too. "The Capo would send a guard storming through the mountains and grab us in the showiest possible manner. A song and dance. A puppet show."

"You're right," I said. "This is someone who wants to savor chasing us down before he kills us." A rush of hot, sickly certainty came over me. "Beniamo."

"I thought your brother was . . ."

"An owl," I said. "Because I changed him into one. How powerful was that undoing magic?"

Cielo grimaced.

"Keep walking," I whispered, and then I doubled back. I thought that it would be better to see Beniamo now. To face the fact that he was here, instead of waiting to be hunted down.

I hid behind a tree as my older brother came into view. Lack of food had hardened the lines of his body. The bones of small animals adorned his shoulders and hips, their bones still attached to the pelts. Blood crusted his mouth and fingernails. His eyes were no longer orange, but they burned with a fire that didn't belong to any human.

I caught my breath and held it.

Change him, I told the magic. *Nothing with claws this time.*

The magic tore out of me, eager to act. The trees all around Beniamo turned into statues. White marble, each in the shape of our dead brother. Luca was everywhere, his face turned up to the skies to study them, his hands torn to bits, his eyes closed in death.

My magic had changed the entire grove. It hadn't touched Beniamo.

What are you doing? I asked. Delfina's power must have thrown me off-balance. If I couldn't control my magic, I had nothing to face my brother with—unless I wanted to dispatch him with Father's knife.

The vial of blood sat in my pocket. If Beniamo killed me, which he probably would, the antidote would never reach Father.

I couldn't make that trade.

There was some satisfaction, though, in watching

Beniamo look up at the statues of the brother he'd killed. Then he smiled, a great slice of bloodstained lips.

"Teodora?" Beniamo asked, his voice as round and empty as an owl's cry. "Sister, I know it's you. And your *magic*. You might as well come out."

Stop him, I thought again, and this time the magic sent great snakes of earth up from the ground, twisting over Beniamo's legs, binding him in place. His howl split the air into pieces and carried for miles.

"Teodora," he whispered, trying to draw me out. "You stole from me. I won't stop until I have what is mine. Won't rest until you are nothing. I will steal from you. Your body, your life." The sounds grated against his throat, harsh, a hunting cry. "It won't matter that I was your brother, once. You made me something else."

He fell upon his legs with another great shriek, and when his eyes broke from mine, I ran as if I'd been released from a trap. His screams followed me as I ran to catch up with Cielo, who walked down the path at a slow, steady pace.

"It's him," I said on a spent breath, grabbing Cielo's arm. "And he remembers. Everything." Clearly, being an owl had lingered with Beniamo, the way being a music box had clung to Pietro. Everything I knew about owls came secondhand, through Luca. "Beniamo's eyes will be able to pierce from miles away, and his hearing can be focused in any direction to catch the slightest rustling of prey." I let my gaze slip sideways, catching on Cielo's. "If we run now, he'll track us."

"And if we don't run, we'll be waiting politely for him to catch up and kill us."

My brother was still raving behind us. He called me

sister, and he told me that if I came out now, he would split me open fast.

If I hid, he would split me open slowly.

I pulled out the vial from my pocket and curled it into Cielo's palm, firm enough that he would have to take it, but not so hard that it would splinter the glass. "Change into a bird," I said. "Take this to my father."

"I'm afraid my wing is broken," Cielo said, holding out his sling. "Besides, I didn't leave you to the Capo, and I won't leave you to a murderous bird-boy."

"So we die together," I said. "That seems operatic."

"Together," Cielo mumbled, as if the word were a stone he could turn over, looking at it from every angle until he noticed a new fleck of crystal caught in the seams. "I have an idea."

His hand that wasn't bound went to feverish work, sliding beneath the fabric of my shirt, roughing out possibilities.

"I've had that idea too," I said, "but this is not the time."

"Trust me," Cielo said.

The strega's hand ran over me with a sort of loose, knowing calm. Cielo closed his eyes and breathed out. He lowered his face to my skin and breathed me in. It felt different from when we'd kissed. That was a matter of breaking apart and coming back together, two great forces, meeting and changing in the places where they overlapped.

This was something else.

Cielo pulled back and looked at me, not like I was some new subject to learn. He took me in with his stare as surely as he'd taken me in with his hands, his breath. I had only seen him look this way once before, when he had the book in his hands at the side of the pond. He had changed it by thinking of it as part of himself.

He was thinking of *me* as part of himself.

Or at least he was trying.

But he was touching me too lightly. I couldn't imagine that the strega was this delicate with his own body.

I took his hand and pressed down, giving his fingers permission to be bold, urging the strega to learn me in a way that I had learned myself slowly, over the course of years. Cielo had to catch up, but I knew he could.

The strega was a quick study.

I kissed his fingertips, then pulled them down past my collarbone and through the valley between my breasts, over the soft plains of my stomach, and farther, over softness and into the dark. I didn't gasp. There was no surprise, only bright pleasure.

No distance left between us now.

I barely had time to think about how strange this was, kneeling in the brush at the side of the road, when I began to shift. I folded and then I shrank down. My bones grew light. My feet fused and branched. I felt all of it, every last bit of the transformation.

I looked up at Cielo, who now towered over me. Was this how it felt every time the strega changed form?

I looked down to find red feathers along the stalks of my legs. I was a songbird. Not quite di Sangro red, but a brighter color, one that would draw the eye for miles. Cielo should have switched me into something drab and colorless, but maybe it wasn't entirely his choice. Maybe part of the form came from me, twined up with me like magic.

Cielo pulled a string free from the fraying end of his pants and secured the vial of Delfina's blood to my leg. "Hold tight to this body," he said. "When you're safe in the castle, you can let it go. Not before."

Obviously, I tried to say, but a loose thread of song slipped out instead. Cielo cupped his palm, picking me up from the ground, lifting me toward the sky. *The sky*. It was what I had been longing for.

It was the true path home.

As I FLEW, MY MIND DULLED IN SOME WAYS AND SHARPENED IN others. The wind sang to me in a chorus of wild voices. The earth spread beneath me like a rumpled green blanket laid for a picnic. A set of hidden lines beneath the earth tugged at me.

A stretch of mountains that would have taken me half a day to cover fell away quickly. I could not feel the hours, only how long it took to sew up the distance between two peaks. My mind went blank with freedom. Only the slight weight of the vial reminded me who I was.

When I crested the mountain I called home and saw the castle clinging to it, memories of being Teodora di Sangro filled me. If I wasn't careful, they would take over, and Cielo's magic would wear off before I reached the castle. No wonder he had warned me.

I sped toward the stones, thinking only of the ruffle of wind and the draining light. I landed on the perch of an arrow slit. The vial clinked hard against stone.

I hopped down into my bedroom, the string bursting free from my leg as I changed back into Teodora. I couldn't have been anyone else here, no matter how many years I lived or how much magic I used.

I unfolded into my human shape, feeling impossibly large. My hair spilled out like vines. My hands spanned as wide as my entire bird body had been. I had never felt how much of the world I took up. I had always been made to feel smaller than I was.

I stepped into a dress I'd left on the floor when I was packing for Amalia. Then I snatched the vial where it had fallen, and tucked it in my bodice.

"She's here!" said a voice in the dark.

As my eyes cut through the gloom of the castle, I saw that I wasn't alone. I cocked my head at the sight of men. Many, many men. They leapt from the places where they had been sitting. They stared at me with accusing eyes.

They stuffed the air with their cries of "Strega!" and "She'll change us again!"

I pushed myself up from the floor. Standing on legs proved an unsteady business. Feet were blunt and ridiculous after the sublime ease of flight. "You're not welcome in this castle," I announced in a tone borrowed from Father. "Leave, or I'll be forced to return you to your magical forms."

"All we want is to go," one man said. I remembered him. He'd been a thief for a while, and then a small knife, suitable for opening letters or stabbing people in the back.

"We've been locked in here for days," another man said, which was easy enough to believe by the strong bodily odors that needled at me.

"Why didn't you raise a din and make someone let you out?" I asked.

"Who knows how many of you are streghe?" the first man said. All of them, no matter how much hatred lived in their eyes, kept a sliver of distance between us.

They were afraid of me. Properly afraid.

I'd thrilled to that feeling before, longed for it even, but now that I'd gone to Amalia and collected a great number of enemies, I no longer valued them. Their cruelness added nothing to the world, and took a great deal out.

"I'll find you a rope and you can climb down," I said. "But if you tell anyone where you've been, *what* you've been, I will find you, and your wives and children, and their children's children." A showy and overdone threat, and one I would never follow through with, but the men didn't know that, and I had no time to be subtle.

Father was close now. The set of mountains that had separated us had become a mere set of doors.

I used my magic to turn my least favorite dress into a long rope, the men hissing as it changed. I handed it to one of them and waited impatiently as they poured out of the window.

I left my room and ran down the stairs.

"Teodora?" Carina cried. She knew the sound of my feet on the steps. "Mama, Teo is back!"

"That's impossible." Mirella stamped out the spark of hope in her voice.

But Carina and Adela were already running up the stairs. I caught one in each of my arms. Fiorenza came next, surging hard up the steps, her hands crimping her skirts. Mirella waited at the bottom of the stairs, more reserved, or perhaps too wary to give into the relief our younger sisters felt.

I couldn't speak another word until I told them all the truth.

"Luca is dead."

Fiorenza fell to her knees. Mirella ran up beside her, stroking her back. She looked at me without surprise. "Who did it?"

I didn't know how to explain about Beniamo. "We were attacked on the road to Amalia."

Fiorenza grabbed wildly at my legs. At first I thought she would tear me apart, take her revenge on me for not keeping Luca safe as I had promised. But she brought me close, folding me into her grief. She stroked her hands through my hopelessly tangled hair. She cupped my face in her long, trembling fingers. "You came back to us."

"How did the Capo let you stay at the Palazza without an heir?" Mirella asked.

"I can explain," I said, with a tight ball of dread in my throat. After everything that had happened, I was still afraid to show them my magic, to let them see who I truly was. "First, come." I pulled Fiorenza up by her arms.

I strode through the close, dark rooms until I reached the one where Father had been laid out. His eyes were closed, his hands neatly folded. He had fresh clothes on, and someone had trimmed the wild hedges of his beard. He looked more serene than I'd ever seen him.

All this time I had insisted on saving Father, but I had never thought about the life I was asking him to bear. I would bring him back to stand against a storm of troubles. Maybe it was best to leave the antidote with Fiorenza, tell her to wait until the winds died down.

But the five families needed a strong leader.

They needed Niccolò di Sangro.

I pulled out the vial that I had cradled all the way across the mountains. The vial a girl had died for. I held it up and let the crimson drip out, sliding along Father's cracked, dry lips and into his mouth.

He opened his eyes slowly. When he drew his first breath, it was so deep that it seemed to stir the entire room. "Teo," he said with a weary smile.

Fiorenza rushed to his side. If she'd been wild in her grief, she was more reserved in her joy, each movement tipped with fear. "Niccolò."

"The last thing I remember . . ." he started roughly. "That letter." He took in the room, his daughters and wife standing around him. "I can't believe I'm seeing you again."

My magic danced as if it had done something wonderful. It whirled and set itself on fire with delight. It had always been attached to Father in a way that it wasn't to anyone else. At least, not until I met Cielo.

Father strained to get out of the bed where he'd been confined for so long, but Mirella barred his way. She acted as a battlefield doctor, checking his wrists for a strong pulse, his forehead for fever. She kissed his cheek with a confused sigh. "Anyone who saw you would think you'd barely been ill."

"Odd," Father said, dismissing the matter.

And then it tumbled together. The way the magic felt about Father. How healthy he looked. The healing charm he had passed down to Fiorenza. The reason Father lived for so long when the rest of the family heads had died.

He had kept the same secret I had for all of these years.

My father was a strega.

20

Fiorenza stole Father and closed them both in his study. I needed to speak with him, but more than anything in this world or the next, I needed sleep. I let them have a moment alone to mourn Luca.

I climbed the stairs toward my bed.

Carina followed, tugging at my fingers. "Sleep in our room," she said, nodding at Adela at the bottom of the stairs.

"Not tonight," I said.

Carina's face went hard, and I knew her plan wouldn't easily be shoved aside.

"Tomorrow night. I'll tell you a story, too."

"*Stories*," Carina said. "More than one."

"As many as I can before my throat goes numb," I promised.

Carina dipped her chin to let me know we'd reached an agreement. My littlest sister was a di Sangro, through and through.

I dragged myself into my room and sighed as I hit the straw ticking of my mattress. It felt finer than any feather bed in Amalia. But the room was too empty. I had gotten used to Cielo sleeping near enough that I could always feel the strega's presence.

I looked out the window at a narrow slice of the evening. The mountains scrolled out, vast, and I had no way of knowing what had happened to Cielo when I had left him behind.

I slept wrapped in darkness. When I woke, I had no idea if it was night or near morning. I put on a dress, one that seemed to cling in uncomfortable new ways. I floated downstairs, toward the kitchens. I hadn't eaten since well before I left the Palazza, and I felt hollowed, scraped, raw. I needed a glass of milk to line my stomach.

I ran my hand along the stones, as I'd done when I was a little girl and I was still learning the shape of things.

Father was a strega. Both of my parents. I'd never so much as guessed. It would have been a miracle, if it didn't make me feel twice as lonely.

When I reached the kitchens, Fiorenza and Mirella were already there, my little sisters spinning around them like wooden tops. "She's awake!" Carina cried.

"You slept for two days," Adela told me with a solemn glaze over her voice and her wide, dark eyes.

"Mother thought you were dead," Carina informed me.

"I thought no such thing," Fiorenza said, although worry went hand in hand with her smile now, as if the two would never be parted. "Let's eat. Everyone must be hungry."

We sat down at the long table, and Father came out of his study to join us. Bowls clinked as Fiorenza ladled out beef and pepper stew. Adela handed us each a shining rosemary bun. She stepped in a wide circle around the chair where Luca should have been sitting, brushing over his spot with shadowed eyes.

Father said prayers, and then we sat in a simmering silence. I had so much to tell him, so much I needed to ask.

"Tell us about the city," Carina demanded as I tore into my bread, releasing the scent of butter and herbs. I ate with an endless hunger, and we spoke of small things, filling the castle with warm sound, raising our voices to blanket Luca's absence.

A loud, impatient knock came from the hall.

Fiorenza slid out of her seat. Everyone stared at me.

My stepmother reappeared a minute later, twisting her hands together. "There's a girl at the door who wants to speak with you, Teodora."

I rushed to the window, anticipating the sight of Cielo in girlish form.

I saw a dark-haired figure in a white dress like a nightgown. She had a creeping stain of dark hair, and dancing fingers. She pointed them up, and I looked just in time to see a stone dropping from the sky. And then another.

Azzurra was pulling stones out of the castle walls.

She skipped her fingers in a lilting way, making the stones waltz before she dropped them, shaking the ground beneath our feet.

Everyone at the table leapt up.

"It's an invasion," Carina said. She was barely old enough to know what that meant, but my littlest sister was right. Azzurra commanded the force of an entire magical army.

Fiorenza turned to me. "What's happening?"

"It's a strega," I said.

More stones dropped. Some must have fallen back on the castle, because the entire edifice shook, rudely awoken from a slumber that had lasted for hundreds of years. Carina grabbed the table with both hands. One of the candles rolled off, and Fiorenza stamped at the fire as Mirella blew out the rest of the shivering flames, leaving us in shadows.

Adela swayed. "A strega? You mean from the stories?"

"Yes," I said. "Something like that."

My little sisters looked eager to believe me. Fiorenza had the faintest dark slash of confusion between her eyebrows. Mirella said, "That's ridiculous," but her voice was so thin, I knew I'd broken a hole in her convictions.

Father didn't flinch. "Tell me about this girl. What does she want?"

"To take me back to Amalia," I said. The Capo must have sent her to retrieve me. This fight was mine to claim, not Father's.

"Stay here," I said, running. I passed through the torchlit halls, through the high gate, and onto the path. Night was coming, dragging purple skies over the mountains at a forced march.

The path was littered with stones.

I called on my magic.

"*Turn her into a flower*," I said. "*For Delfina*."

Magic cascaded from me, pushing me backward as it flowed. Instead of hitting Azzurra, it scattered, and flowers of all sizes and colors rose around us, a spectacle of blooms that made Azzurra laugh so hard, she clutched her stomach. "Is this how you fight? The Capo should have made you the royal gardener."

I'd faced the same problem in the woods, with Beniamo. Before Delfina and *the brilliant death*, my magic had never made a mistake. It had never *missed*. I'd also never been fed the power of dozens of dead streghe.

Azzurra held her fingers straight up in the air, then let them wilt. Stones crashed down, chipping away at the castle. I couldn't let this happen. My family couldn't die, not after everything I'd given up to save them.

I rushed down the path.

"I would stop there," Azzurra said. "But you never do listen."

I came to a halt ten paces from her. I asked the magic if we were close enough, but it was a buzzing nest of fury, not something I could speak and reason with. I thought of the guards back in Amalia, the ones whose feet I had encased in stone. I had been aiming for one man, and I'd changed twenty. If I didn't know how to direct my magic, it might work against my own family.

Azzurra frowned at the air above me, and another set of stones rose from the walls. The top of the castle had been stripped, and as the elements poured in, girlish screams rushed out. "Ah," Azzurra said. "I was hoping you'd have sisters."

Her fingers swirled. I had to stop her, even for a moment.

"What did the Capo offer if you caught me?" I asked. "Or do you do whatever he asks without even bothering to think?"

Azzurra looked at me and snorted roughly. "He *would* want me to capture you, to bring you back safely so we could work alongside each other. No matter that you killed my sister to claim her magic."

Dread crashed through me. The Capo hadn't sent Azzurra. She was here for plain, unvarnished revenge.

Another chorus of stones dropped.

My magic sprang to my fingertips.

"*Focus*," I told it, keeping my gaze on the gray-blue of Azzurra's eyes. That was what I had learned from Cielo. The more power I had, the more focus I required.

Screams tangled in the air.

"*Think of Azzurra*," I said. "*Not Delfina. Not my family.*"

"You know the old language?" Azzurra asked with a faintly curled lip, a close cousin to a sneer. "I'm almost impressed."

My magic dragged my attention away from the fight. Azzurra was the one who had brought the statues of the old gods to life in the square outside the Palazza. "What do the old gods have to do with this?"

"I'm done helping you figure out the ways of magic, mountain boy," Azzurra said. "Or should I call you mountain girl? No difference, really. You'll be part of your mountain soon, which is more happiness than you deserve." She plucked her fingers through the air, and stones ripped from the walls until I could see the pale curved lines inside, the bones of the di Sangro castle.

My family stood in the exposed dining hall. They huddled together as if that would save them.

Azzurra dropped stones, at least a dozen.

"*Flowers*," I ordered.

The stones broke apart and petals laced their way toward the ground.

Behind me, Azzurra shrieked. Another set of stones slid from the walls and plummeted.

"*Rain*," I said in a voice that was both mine and more than mine, spreading as large as the skies.

The stones split open and a hard rain rushed down.

I allowed a single second of relief before I gathered my

magic in a firm grip. The lack of precision that had hurt me before was helping now. When I tried to change Azzurra into a flower, I'd been using magic the same way I always had. But something about Delfina's power had changed it. Where before it had been a fine-tipped brush, now it was a broad stroke.

Another set of boulders tipped and tumbled.

"*Your turn*," I told the magic. "*Anything you like.*"

It broke the stones into a flock of blackbirds with red patches on their wings. When they flapped, the di Sangro color waved like a hundred small flags. The birds circled the castle, caught the rising draft of a wind, and flew away. A cry of unspeakable joy welled up from the same deep place the magic did. Azzurra might be able to take the world apart, but I could do better than that.

I could change it.

My magic churned, whitecapped and endless. It wasn't flagging or threatening to leave me like it had in the past.

I planted my feet and readied for the next strike. Then, without my permission, one of my hands crept up my body and fastened around my neck. My fingers dug into soft flesh, and my palm tightened against the cords of my throat. I tried to pry one hand away with the other, but at that moment, Azzurra sent her next attack. The stones rained down with new intensity, as if we'd only been playing at magic before.

"*Change them*," I said, my voice strangled by my own hand. "*Change them.*"

The stones hurtled down. Screams traveled up. More petals and rain and birds filled the air, a chaotic mess of transformations. A few stones hit the ground with a smack and a swelling of powdery dust.

A desperate sound climbed past the tightening hold of my fingers. I wanted nothing more than to end Azzurra's miserable life, but I knew that if I thought only of fighting her, she would redouble her efforts against my family. If I kept trying to save my family, I would choke.

A figure rushed through the high gate of the castle, which had survived the onslaught. At first I thought it was Father, come to help me, to use his magic to protect us all. But this person looked much too small against the maelstrom of wind and stones.

"Carina, go back in."

"You need help," she called down the path. "I want to fight."

"Go back!" I shouted, my voice thinned to nearly nothing. I almost yelled at her to send Father, but maybe he had good reasons for staying where he was. His magic healed people. Maybe someone had already been hurt. Or his magic had been drained to nothing by the Capo's poison.

A single massive stone slid out from above the gates with a scraped whisper. It hovered over Carina and turned, a vulture making a lazy circle. Azzurra laughed. I looked to find her spinning one finger. Toying with Carina's life.

"Don't do this," I said. "I'm sorry."

"I don't remember you using such nice words when you came storming out of there," Azzurra said. "And apologies don't work on the dead. Delfina is the one you hurt." Her face broke like a storm, the anger I had seen before splitting into streams of raw pain.

I tried to speak, but each word was becoming its own small battle. "He killed her."

Azzurra didn't look surprised, only twice as bitter as before. "I can't touch the Capo, can I?" So that was it. She was taking revenge on the only person within reach. And she wouldn't be satisfied until everyone I loved was buried.

Bury her, the magic said. I writhed at the uselessness of those words. I needed some way to change Azzurra. I couldn't bury her until she was dead. Besides, I had only buried someone once. That day on the mountain, after Luca had died.

The magic flared at the memory.

Bury her.

My vision blotted with darkness. It grew, a great nothingness. As empty as a grave.

Bury her, the magic said.

I could see what it wanted now. What part of *me* wanted. To send Azzurra down into the mountain, to carve a resting place. It would have to be bigger than Luca's, and deeper.

Like the Storyteller's Grave.

Carina leapt to the side of the path as Azzurra finally let the stone drop. The gates of the castle crumbled a bare moment after Carina ran through them. Screams came from every direction now, but the sounds broke over me like the soft slap of waves on a day at the seaside. I was farther from the shore than I'd ever been. I was going to lose myself to the cold, dark waves.

My heartbeat tugged at my chest. It throbbed an echo in my throat. This was the simple song of my life, and I wasn't ready for it to stop. I used the last of my breath to whisper, "*Hollow the ground beneath her feet. Open the earth to swallow her up.*"

A fierce tide knocked me down. I spent a moment curled on the ground with my eyes open, unseeing. My vision came back in patches as I struggled to my feet. The earth crumbled away from Azzurra. I ran as the slit in the ground opened and stretched. It was a smile, widening.

The mountain opened and took her.

21

I was already on my knees when *the brilliant death* came for me. I had dropped there to pray and found myself ripped apart with pain. I screamed into the dirt, my voice pulled down into the freshly made ravine. It wasn't my body that needed relief, but my soul. The magic of so many streghe burdened it.

I stood and walked back to the ruins of the castle. Carina met me in the collapsed doorway, her hands pulled tight across her small frame. We climbed over the catastrophe of wood and stone that had been the front gates.

I checked Carina for injuries, but she looked unharmed. I asked how she felt, and she said in a small but resolute voice, "I'm glad we won."

I smiled down at her, but it felt hollow.

We picked our way across halls strewn with petals and studded with stones. The castle looked so changed that I couldn't imagine it ever returning to its former severe glory.

Father, Fiorenza, and Adela were still where we had left them, in the remains of the dining hall. The table had been cracked in half by a great stone. Adela was pinned beneath another stone, her lower half caught. Fiorenza spoke to her in soothing tones. The sweeter she got, the surer I felt that I was about to watch my sister die.

I called on my magic. It brooded at the request. I could feel it brewing darkly, considering a violent overthrow. For all of its stubbornness, it had never refused me, not unless I had exhausted it.

"*Sand*," I ordered.

My magic overdid things, springing out of me like a fiery whirlwind. It left me singed inside, almost charred black.

The stone on top of Adela dissolved, a heap of white pouring over the floor. What was left of the walls dissolved too, sending cascades of sand to the floor. Adela coughed as Fiorenza's strong arms pulled her from the sliding grains.

Adela's eyes stared past Fiorenza, focused on a place far away that none of us could imagine, let alone see. Fiorenza pressed her gently but firmly, head to toe, and when she reached Adela's chest, Adela cried out, a slice of pure agony, her arms and legs curling. Fiorenza turned to Father and whispered, as if that could keep Adela safe from her own injuries: "Some of the ribs are cracked, and her lungs were pinned." Father rushed to Adela's side, smoothed her hair back, and spoke to her quickly.

The magic had always loved Father's voice. The fact that he was alive to tell Adela a story had the glimmering edges of a miracle about it. The one he'd picked sounded familiar. I wandered through the castle of my memories, following the words until I found their source.

This was one of the stories Father had scoffed at so many times when I was little. A strega story.

Adela's coloring shaded from gray to olive. Fiorenza

pressed at Adela's chest again, and she let out the slightest whimper, then took a deep, thirsty breath. Fiorenza looked at Father with a mystified scowl and a deep tilt to her head. Carina was too little to be amazed; she simply rushed over and embraced her sister.

Adela reached out her arms to Father. "Tell me the rest."

"So the little tyrant has returned." Father stumbled his way back into the story as Fiorenza kissed Adela's cheeks.

In a swell of worry and guilt, I remembered Mirella and the baby. I trudged through the sand as fast as my grit-filled boots would allow. I checked each of the doorways that led out of the dining hall until I found Mirella crying in a small compartment of stones that had once been the landing to the back staircase.

"Mirella," I said, rushing to her and kneeling at her side. I found her half gasping, half laughing with relief. Her long dark waves of hair stuck to her cheeks with the glue of tears. She looked up at me and laughed even harder.

"Teodora," she said. "I thought you were dead. More than once."

"I know I haven't made things easy for you," I said, grabbing her hands.

"No," she said, turning mine over as if they were pages of a book and she might read all of my secrets there. "But when have you ever done that?"

She cried and laughed, and I sat there, admiring her, as I always had. She sat there, loving me, as she always had. I couldn't believe that a few weeks ago one of my greatest wishes was to leave the mountains to see her married. Now I would pay any price in silver, gold, or magic if it meant I never had to look at Ambrogio again. And yet I sat down with her and held a hand out, fingers shyly hovering near her stomach.

"Go ahead," Mirella said. I touched the curve and found it slightly raised and hardened. It was barely anything. It was the beginning of everything. Mirella looked around at what used to be the castle. "It's so strange to be sitting here, our lives ripped to pieces, and I don't care about any of it as long as he's fine."

"A boy?" I asked. "How do you know?"

"Father. He says he's always been able to guess . . . except with you." She shrugged.

I felt that shrug as keenly as the cold night filling the castle. If I'd been born a boy, I could have gone to Amalia as myself. If I'd been a boy, none of this would have happened.

"Don't," Mirella said. "Whatever terrible thought you are having, kill it quickly. You have done everything you could."

I braided back my sister's hair with fingers that still shook from the fight outside, from *the brilliant death*. "So have you." Mirella had survived a world as harsh as the one at the Palazza, where all that mattered was finding a husband and giving herself away. She had done as much for the di Sangro family as I ever could. Ambrogio might not value her, but that didn't take away a centesimo of her worth.

I stood up and helped Mirella to her feet. We returned to the dining hall together, and she went to kiss Adela while I walked up to Father. "Should we go to your study?" I asked. "We have things to discuss."

Father looked at me as if I were speaking a language from halfway around the world. Then I remembered that I'd been spending my time as a boy. I had grown accustomed to trading words without question or apology, and expecting to be taken seriously.

I didn't apologize. I just waited.

Father looked around at the skeleton of the castle, picked clean by the winds. "I don't believe it matters where we go anymore," he said. "This all looks like the end of the world to me." But we still headed in the direction of the study. We were di Sangros, hardened by habit.

As soon as we had gained enough distance that no one could hear us, I turned to him. "You saved Adela."

"You saved us all." Father added no polish of awe or surprise to those words. He stated them as dull fact.

I took a breath and marveled at the sky. The castle walls framed it in a way that was both broken and beautiful, columns of stone jabbing up toward the stars. "There are things you should know."

Father clasped his hands behind his back. "Watching you made it clear enough." And still he made me wait before he added, "You're a strega."

Even after everything I'd been through, it was almost impossible to talk about certain things without my throat rebelling and my eyes being invaded by tears. "I believe . . . when Mother died . . . she handed her magic down to me."

Father looked at me strangely, blinking as moonlight and shadows flitted over his face. "Luciana wasn't a strega."

It was my turn to stare in confusion.

"No one knew that I had a . . . certain ability," Father said. "It didn't turn up until several years after I was made head of the family, and I worried that the other families would do worse than unseat me if they found out. The church had a firm hold on the five families the last time magic was in the world."

"So you hid it," I said, my voice still rough from choking myself with my own hand. "From everyone. Your whole life."

Father blinked harder, and I felt the flutter of a warning. "It was the right thing."

If my magic didn't come from Mother, where had I gotten it? The rules of *the brilliant death* were clear enough. Before this week, I had seen only two people die. Mother, and the stranger on the stairs.

That night was the first time I'd ever used magic.

And just like that, the story changed. It felt as if I had dropped the glass again and was waiting to hear it splinter. "That man who came for you, the one I saw when I was little. He was a soldier of Erras, wasn't he?" I asked, the truth forming words without any help from me. "He must have found out that you were a strega, and you wouldn't use your magic."

That was why my power was so strong, why Cielo had been able to feel it all the way from across the Uccelli. The soldiers of Erras claimed the fallow magic of streghe in the name of the old gods. And there was only one way to do that.

By killing them.

The man on the stairs had come for Father on that winter-slicked night. And when he failed, and Father killed him instead, the man's magic had passed to the person who wasn't even meant to be there. The one who had come downstairs to steal a glass of milk and lingered in the shadows.

"That's safely in the past," Father said. He took his place in the walnut chair that I used to believe was a throne. "Now tell me what happened in Amalia." Despite the ruins around us, despite how upset I was that Father wouldn't tell me more about my own magic, I thrilled to the question. I was in Father's study, reporting to him, Niccolò di Sangro's right-hand man.

"Ambrogio betrayed us, for a start," I said. "He sided with the Capo in a grab for our lands."

Father made a harsh noise in the back of his throat. "How did you discover this?"

"I overheard their conversation," I said. "Also, I was a boy."

"You mean, dressed up as one?" Father asked, his fingers drumming on the moon-polished table.

"No," I said. "I *was* a boy."

Father stared at me for a long moment.

I summoned the magic, stirring it up. I needed Father to understand. There were no mirrors in his study, so I walked forward, drawn in by the high shine of the table. When I looked down, moonlight silvered the wood. I could see myself in the reflection, pale and watery.

"Please," I said. *"One last time."*

The magic wanted to show Father as much as I did. It wanted him to know how much I was capable of.

When I shifted, my broad hands spread against the table. Father rose from his chair and moved quickly, his legs almost betraying him. I fought down memories like bile. The last time we'd been in this room together, he had fallen, shaking. The meaning had melted off his face until it was blank.

Father smiled now, a lively play of light and shadow. "It's so convincing. A perfectly wrought disguise. Those cogliones must have been fooled!" Father clapped his hands to my shoulders and kissed both of my cheeks, the way he would greet any other man. "Should I call you Teodoro? Or just Teo?"

I felt a wave of pride, chased to shore by a darker one.

Father had never acted this delighted when I was his daughter.

I kept a tremble out of my voice as I continued. "Teodora will be fine," I said. "And there's more to tell. The rest of the family heads were killed by the same poison the Capo used against you. The five families are weak, on the verge of losing their hold. The Capo will let the boys pretend at power, but he wants full loyalty."

"Which means they are in his hand, and he can squeeze them anytime he likes," Father said.

I nodded gravely.

"I'm glad I have no more sons to throw to that wolf," Father muttered. "My sons are dead."

"Not Beniamo," I said, and Father gave me a sharpened look. This part would not be easy to tell. Even if Father knew that Beniamo shouldn't lead the di Sangro family, he was the eldest son. There was honor in that, earned or not.

"I found him torturing Luca. My magic wanted to save my little brother. I wanted to save him. And, well . . ." There was no good way of saying this. "I changed Beniamo into an owl. But he's been changed back, and he's here in the Uccelli." I should have stopped, but a fire kindled in my gut, my words glowing like coals. "You can write him down in your ledger as dead, because if I ever see him again, I'm going to kill him."

Unless he kills me first, I thought.

Father took a slow breath, leaving plenty of time to shift the pieces of his strategy. I had seen him do it so many times, but I'd rarely been part of the plans. "We will mourn Luca in every way we know. But we don't need to find Beniamo." He drummed his fingers on the table again. "What I said before . . ." He tapped a single finger on the wood, the way he often did when he stood at the edge of an important conclusion. "That was wrong."

"What do you mean?" My voice sounded strident, even though I was confused.

"I do have another son," Father said, straightening to look at me. "You will take over the di Sangro family."

No, the magic said.

When I'd left the castle, this was all I'd wanted. The fate I thought I was meant for. But now I found myself arguing, "Why can't I be the heir to the di Sangro family as Teodora?" During my time in Amalia, I had found truth in knowing I was not one fixed thing, and now I couldn't imagine living *only* in a boy's form because it was easier to wield power as a man. Besides, if I had learned one thing from trying to keep my magic in the shadows for so long, it was that I couldn't spend a lifetime hiding part of myself. *Any* part. "Why can't I help you as a strega, instead of a son?"

"The five families don't use magic," Father said.

"That's how I saved us," I said. "That's how you brought Adela back from the brink of death. And the necklace you gave Fiorenza . . ."

"It didn't save your brother, did it?" Father asked.

"I was wearing it when he died," I said, guilt slicing me open all over again. Would I have been in danger of bleeding as much as Luca did if I hadn't worn Father's healing charm? Would I be dead on the mountain, alongside my brother? "That necklace kept me safe on the road to Amalia. It saved me, more than once." I thought of the kitchen strega who wore it now. Wherever she'd run off to after Cielo saved her in the square, she carried a shard of my father's magic.

"The di Sangro family has survived for centuries by following tradition." Father waved at the castle, from the missing walls to the new ravine that had opened itself outside. "Magic is a tempting path, but it doesn't lead anywhere good. Even healing magic seems like a blessing until the moment it's not enough to save someone you love." The windswept bitterness of his tone carried me to an inevitable place.

Mother.

He had tried to use his healing magic to save her, and it hadn't worked. *That* was when his magic splintered. He gave Fiorenza the necklace hoping it would never happen again. The iron charm hadn't belonged to Mother—it was a reminder of how Father had failed her. He lived with that every day, the same way I would live with Luca's death.

But I didn't see how that meant we should stop. If anything, it meant we needed to be stronger. "You never trained your magic," I said. "Things could have been different. They could *still* be—"

Father cut me off with a savagery I'd never seen in him before. "Magic is not your fate. This family is." He turned his back on me, circling to his right and proper side of the table. "And besides, the other families will never accept a girl. You know that."

"I know that you won't try to change it," I said.

The dreams that had seemed perfect to me as a little girl wilted and faded, the way dreams always did on the moment of waking. I could grab for their wispy comforts all I wanted. They were gone.

I slipped out of my boyish skin, and when I was back in the girlish body I knew so well, all I could do was stand in the moonlight and shiver—from cold, disappointment, the exhaustion of an endless ordeal.

Father's face shifted as I became his daughter again, the ends of his smile unraveling. He put both hands on the desk and leaned over them, his eyes sharp with starlight. "Give me one well-reasoned argument for denying your place at the head of this family."

You don't owe him reasons, the magic said. *Only love.*

As on so many occasions, my magic and I disagreed. "The Capo will be coming to the Uccelli soon, to claim me. I don't want to fight him without magic. Do you really prefer killing so much?" I hated that I had killed Azzurra to keep my family safe. I hated that Delfina and so many other streghe had died. We were all being used as pawns by powerful men. These were not the lives—and deaths—we deserved.

"It's not a question of what I want," Father said. "It never has been."

I asked myself what I wanted. For so long, the answer had been to help my family. But I'd done my best to save them. Now I could finally admit that I wanted to learn more about magic. I wanted to stop denying it at every turn. I wanted to see Cielo's stubborn, beautiful face again.

"I don't belong here," I said. My voice shook like a sapling in a fierce wind. I couldn't imagine walking away from my family. Never seeing Mirella again. Missing the birth of her son. Leaving them to rebuild the castle without me.

Saving Father only to turn my back on him.

Then I thought of Cielo, and possibilities came to life, a row of candles lit after Father had blown them all out.

I turned to leave.

"What are you doing?" Father asked.

Walking away from him could mean he would never speak to me again. He was the great Niccolò di Sangro. His pride was as legendary as his fairness. But I was Teodora di Sangro, and someday there might be stories about me, too. The strega girl who knew how to change anything, including Vinalia.

That has a fine ring to it, the magic said.

"I will always be your daughter," I said. "But I can't accept this." I dug in my sleeve and tossed Father's knife on the desk, where it sat patiently in the moonlight. I waited, but Father did not meet my eye, and I could not wait forever.

The Beginning

When I was no longer a little girl, I learned that my father was only a man, no more or less than any other in Vinalia.

Our family lived in a pile of stones that had once been a castle. It looked like someone had taken hold of the mountainside and crumbled it. If I squinted long enough, I could see the home I had always known.

The first time I killed someone, it made perfect sense. The girl was a strega, and I had to protect my family and my mountains. But her death stayed with me, clinging to each step as I walked away from the ruined castle. I would carry Azzurra's magic forever, a reminder that lived in my blood.

I stopped in Chieza and traded my ruined red dress for a plain gray one. By the time I finished lacing it, I looked like any other girl from the Uccelli. People in the village asked questions. They wanted to know what had happened to the castle. They wondered if it had anything to do with the sudden reappearance of forty-six missing men from Chieza.

I told them a storm had come through.

They looked at the suspiciously bright sky and muttered the same word they always did. *Odd.*

Some spoke of curses, others of God. Some said that streghe were returning to Vinalia. A few swore they had never left. I smiled at these people for the last time, and headed up the mountain.

The walk was a small eternity, giving me plenty of time to fear what came next. The Capo would hunt me. Eterran invasions could begin at any moment. I had no choice but to meet the future filled with a magic I didn't understand.

But when I saw Cielo coming down the path, a smile broke through my worries and scattered them like leaves before a strong wind.

"I felt you coming," the strega said as I strode closer. I opened my mouth to scold Cielo about keeping out of sight, but I didn't bother.

Neither of us was good at staying safe.

We did have other talents though.

Cielo turned one of them on me as he pulled me to him with his right arm, pressing us together. His left arm was still bound, but he held it more easily against his body. "You look better," I said.

"You look worse."

I would tell Cielo what had happened with Azzurra and Father, but not until we'd put a few miles between ourselves and the di Sangro castle. Not until the rough edges of the memory stopped cutting into me.

"Why did you wait in the Uccelli?" I asked. "Did you have some way of knowing I wouldn't stay at the castle?"

"A guess," Cielo said, shrugging one finely wrought shoulder.

Perhaps it wasn't, though. Perhaps Cielo knew me better than anyone.

"Are we going to find the other streghe?" he asked in a low voice he only used for one purpose: to parcel out hope in small amounts.

Everyone who had magic, everyone like us, needed to be warned about the Capo. Someone would have to help the streghe of Vinalia plot and scheme. I turned my face to the sharp blue sky and considered the notion. "Fine," I said. "But that twenty-seven-part favor I owe you? This is part two."

When Cielo walked away, I found I couldn't follow. "Let's get started, Teo," he said. "It's a long walk, and night will come on sooner than you think."

I closed my eyes. For the first time, I didn't give my magic an order. I asked it a question, and told myself that I would trust it, no matter how it answered.

What should I do?

At first, there was only the muttering of the wind. Nothing happened. Nothing changed.

I looked at Cielo, waiting for me.

Behind the strega, a milky cloud lifted over the rise—or it looked like a cloud, at first. When it came closer, I could see it was made not of misty white air, but wings. Moths with lace wings, rushing as fast as uncertain heartbeats.

They matched the moth I had summoned on that winter night, long ago.

The cloud paused at the top of the mountain and then turned back the way it had come. My magic was showing me how to leave.

I grabbed Cielo's hand and skimmed fast, to the top of the rise, my edges blurring into the wind. I pulled the strega over the mountain, on toward a life I could barely imagine. The earth was warm under our feet, the last of summer's sunlight brash on our shoulders. My fate had not been left behind in the castle. It did not belong to the di Sangro family. It came with me down the path, keeping pace with this new journey, changing with every step I took.

Acknowledgments

I feel like I've been writing this book since I finished read-ing my first fantasy novel. It's the story that has been in my heart the longest, gathering its pieces, waiting patiently (and sometimes not-so-patiently) for the moment when I had what I needed to tell it. Which means that there are hundreds of people who have influenced it over the years, more than I could ever thank at once. But here are a few:

My agent, Sara Crowe, whose faith in stories is astounding.

My editor, Kendra Levin, the most insightful traveling companion I could have asked for on a journey to Vinalia.

The team at Viking: editorial assistant Maggie Rosenthal; cover designer Dana Li; interior designer Kate Renner; copy-editors Janet Pascal, Abigail Powers, Krista Ahlberg, and Marinda Valenti; and everyone else who brought their bril-liance to this book and championed Teodora and Cielo.

Maya Chhabra for her insights on linguistic and cultural details.

Kelly Barson, Kristin Sandoval, Julia Blau, Adam Gac,

Emily Nummer, Ann Dávila Cardinal, Will Alexander, Alice Dodge, Kekla Magoon, Tirzah Price, and An Na, who saw me through this, inspired me with their own creative work, and helped me survive a cross-country move mid-novel.

The VCFA community, especially Martine Leavitt, who kept me coming back to the stories I love most, even when they tried to slip away from me like unhelpful fish.

Italo Calvino, whose *Italian Folktales* gave me the magical ground for my streghe to stand on.

My family, of course. Especially the ones who are gone—I remember your stories.

Maverick, for loving strega stories as much as I do (thank you, Tomie dePaola!), for slipping wonder in the pockets of my days, and giving me my favorite nickname—Princess Witch.

And

Cori, my very own sexy magic tutor.

INTRODUCING

The Seven Princesses and the Strega

—an original short story written

by AMY ROSE CAPETTA

Dear Readers,

Some of you have asked me about the magic in *The Brilliant Death*. Like everything in a novel, there are many strands that twist together to form a braid. Some of Teo's and Cielo's magic comes from my own head and heart. I've been inspired by the empowering wonders of modern YA fantasy. But magic is an alchemical combination of time and place, of belief and need. To substitute one magic for another simply won't do. To write an Italian-inspired fantasy, I needed Italian-inspired magic.

The oldest strand in this braid comes from folktales.

Not many people outside of Italian culture are familiar with our folktales. They are lovely and funny and wondrous, with titles like "Invisible Grandfather," "The Science of Laziness," "The Daughter of the Sun," "The Little Girl Sold with the Pears," and "Dear as Salt." There are often witches—streghe—but no wands and not much that resembles spells. Instead, there is a sense that the world is utterly and constantly changeable.

Transformation magic.

Cielo's book was inspired by one in "The Canary Prince." A witch gives a woman a special book. If she ruffles the pages, her lover at the foot of the tower becomes a bird who can fly up to see her. When she ruffles them back, he returns to human form. I started to imagine a magical book of my own. My imagination ruffled its feathers, took off, and hasn't really landed since.

There is so much to love in old folktales, but they can also reflect a way of seeing the world that wears at my heart. Women are sometimes the clever ones, but more often they are daughters to be married off, or prizes to be awarded to the cleverest man. In a landscape full of wild change, gender and the roles that come with it can feel so rigid.

When I set out to write my own folktale for Vinalia, I hoped to be true to the stories that shaped my fantasy world while making changes of my own. What happened next felt like magic. This is the kind of story that Teo would tell her little sisters right as the year turned warm again, when everything feels possible.

I hope you enjoy reading it as much as I loved writing it.

—Amy Rose

The Seven Princesses and the Strega

Several hundred years ago, every patch in the great quilt of Vinalia was its own kingdom. Every bit of sky-pricking mountains and swollen fields and seacoast had a name, a ruler, and its own set of laws. You could stand in one spot on a high hill and stare at a dozen kingdoms at once; a hundred if the sky was clear.

Of course, not every patch of Vinalia was worth ruling. There were swampy bits that never drained, where mists hung like angry sighs. No man would claim those lands, and so they belonged to the streghe.

And there were bits of Vinalia that every man wanted for his own. A source of particular lust were seven hills near the Oscurra River, each one green and lofty. These were no ordinary hills. Besides being beautiful, each yielded a beautiful bounty. The first grew black grapes that made the most luscious wine. The second was filled with a rare storm-colored marble. The third, fourth, and fifth were home to Vinalia's sheep that gave the warmest wool, the sheep that gave its creamiest milk, and the world-famous goats that bleated in harmony, like opera singers. The sixth had a walnut grove known throughout the land for superior walnuts, which gave bitter-dark oil when pressed and could tell the future in their folds. The seventh hill was simply the most beautiful in Vinalia. People came from all over to stare at it with hazy eyes and hearts.

Many skirmishes were fought over these hills. When hundreds had died and only seven men still stood, they decided that the best thing to do was to take a hill each. But the men weren't satisfied with having only hills, so they imported seven women to be their wives. These queens were happy enough, except for the wife of the walnut king. After ten years, she ran away with a commedia player whose leather mask, tooled into devil's horns, could not hide his beauty from her eyes, which had grown sharp from picking at walnut meat. She ran away with her lovely devil. The stories said that she died not long after.

The seven wives bore a profusion of sons, the princes of the hills. They anticipated becoming kings one day, all except the son of the wool king, whose soul was soft from so much carding. He ran away on a winter morning, too sick of wool to take his cloak along. The stories said that he died not long after.

As for daughters, each queen bore only one, all the same age—a crop of princesses as perfect as anything else that grew in the seven hills. After eleven years of shouting at each other from the hilltops, they conspired to meet in the swampy valley underfoot.

"Won't there be a strega down there?" the wool princess asked.

"I hope so," the walnut princess said. "Maybe she can read walnut fortunes because I definitely can't, and everyone expects me to tell them if they're going to have a strong harvest or a baby by next year."

They gathered when the moon was one sliver away from full: the wine princess, the walnut princess, the wool princess. The princess of marble graves and the princess of goats and the princess of soft cheese. And the princess of unmatchable beauty.

They shared the stories of the walnut queen and the wool prince. They whispered about their own futures. None of them would leave their homes and come to tragic ends. They made a promise that they would stay together, always.

To seal the promise, they decided to visit the strega.

FOR SEVEN YEARS, THE PRINCESSES MET EVERY MONTH BY THE light of the near-full moon and unspooled their dreams for each other like so much silver thread. It was meant to embroider their days, but they let themselves imagine lives woven from silver, shining and pure. They learned that the princess of graves dreamed of kissing the innkeeper's daughter, and the princess of soft cheese dreamed of never kissing at all, except perhaps touching her lips to the reflection of the moon on the sea. The princess of singing goats wished to travel the world, not to admire its sights or to taste its fine foods, but to gather new sounds. She could no longer stand the clattering hooves and bleating harmonies that had become both painful and normal to her ears. The princess of unmatchable beauty whispered that she wished to be a strega, so she could make a potion that showed the truth: each woman was beautiful in a way that had no exact compare.

Together they wove the steps of delicate dances and sang bawdy songs. They called one another's names—their true names. Even though they spent their days being called beautiful, this was when they *felt* beautiful.

It only added to their shine.

Young men began swarming the nearby kingdoms to get a glimpse of these glowing princesses. Of course, nearly every young man in Vinalia was a prince, and so hundreds of suitors believed they were owed a chance. They gathered in the nearby inns, starting fights with each other, eating the soft cheese and spilling the near-black wine.

The girls had a plan, though.

"There will be no fighting," announced the princess of goats when they had their fathers all assembled. "Instead, every man who wishes to woo us will spend seven days with the strega who lives in the valley. If she believes he is suited to a princess, she will use her magic to bring them together."

Everyone was quick to agree—especially the kings, who did not want men spilling blood on their grape arbors.

"You do remember that you won these hills by making men bleed all over them," the wool princess said. She was not as soft as her brother had been. Her ways had grown pointed from a lifetime of shearing.

"Yes, and now we would like to keep them nice," said the wool king.

When a man mounted the hills and begged for the hand of a princess—any princess—he was sent to the strega. The prince in question would enter a valley swollen with mist and hungry for visitors. He would find the only dwelling in the place, a hovel built of stone with a wooden door painted as white as the missing sliver of a near-full moon.

He would knock on that door.

The strega would answer.

What happened next, no one could say. The trial lasted seven days, and by the seventh each prince had been driven away in disgrace or died, his grave marked by a headstone of storm-colored marble.

So the princesses stayed on their hills, while word of a fearful strega in the valley leaked across the many little kingdoms of Vinalia.

The inns grew quiet, and the kings started to fear no one would stay long enough—or live long enough—to wed their daughters. They opened the challenge to men who had no kingdom to their names.

Soon enough, a not-prince arrived. In that time, the princesses had learned to sing in seven-part harmony and sharpen the halves of the wool princess's old shears into very pretty knives. The young man saw seven armed princesses standing like guards outside the halls of their fathers, and it made him smile. That was the first sign to the kings that he was the wrong sort. He also had a dark smudge of a mark on his neck, like charcoal that would never rub off—a mark that meant he had been touched by magic.

The kings of the hills tried to dismiss him right then and there. What if this man brought foul magic into their kingdoms? What if *he* was a strega? The princesses waved away their fathers' objections like so much smoke. "Don't listen to those old men," said the princess of graves. She was used to seeing dead men carted onto her hill, and very few living things inspired fear in her. "You know, they weren't born kings."

The kings glared at their daughters.

Their daughters glared back.

"First you will need to live through seven days with the strega in the valley," the princess of goats said.

"I would like nothing more than to visit your strega," the young man who wasn't a prince said. He scratched the mark on his neck. It looked faintly red, as if it had been bothering him for years.

"We will need something to call you, not-prince," the wine princess said.

"My name is Alessandro."

"That will do." The wine princess, who had started her day with a rather large goblet, was feeling generous.

The young man marched into the valley alone. He faced the strega in her hovel without flinching, though she was unspeakably old and had killed many men. Neither of those things seemed to bother Alessandro.

The strega took note.

She was old and skinny and bent like twigs. "My magic changes me each night," she said. "I am a strega with a face for each day of the week, and if you can impress me seven times, you have a heart to match a princess of the seven hills."

"What is your name?" Alessandro said.

The old woman clutched at her cloak, her knuckles shiny with the best bitter walnut oil. "No one has asked my name." They had asked about the princesses, the trials, the likelihood that they might survive. Not once had a suitor asked a question about the strega.

"What shall I call you?" Alessandro asked, pressing the matter, but not unkindly. His eyes were the same brown as the soil of the hills. His voice sounded like one the strega had heard all her life, murmuring so lowly she barely knew it was there.

"Sette," she said. "I am Sette."

"Very well, Sette." Alessandro had the smile of a young man who hoped for success. Sette had seen that smile on other young men and it had made her stomach boil. But there was something different in the lines of Alessandro's lips. As if they'd known disappointment. As if he'd failed before.

"For the first trial, you must sleep the night outside with neither bedroll nor pillow. My magic will remove your bravery. If you can spend the night stripped of confidence and come back tomorrow, you will be allowed to stay."

He left the hovel at dusk. The ground was a stew of mud, the air grew cold, and in the dark Alessandro heard whipping cries. Many princes had run off at that point, not craving the kiss of a princess enough to risk the snap of a wolf.

Alessandro touched the mark at his neck and reminded himself why he was there. Perhaps the wolves had their reasons for howling. His heart had sounded that desolate on certain nights. He walked toward the sound—and found a brace of goats, their voices twisted to resemble wolves. "Clever things," he said, letting them eat from his hand.

In the morning he found Sette looking shorter and plumper beneath her cloak. She had, indeed, changed in the night. She held out a dark glass bottle. "Now you must drink this wine and attempt to fly from the hovel's roof."

Many princes had called this challenge foolish and refused; others jumped and broke their legs.

Alessandro simply said, "May I borrow a pair of wings?"

"What makes you think I have wings?" Sette asked. Her voice that day was darker, richer.

"You're a strega," he said with a shrug. "If you can change your face each day, you can surely fashion wings."

"Which one of us is being tested here?" Sette huffed. Still, she left and came back an hour later with a pair of beautifully wrought wings, all twisted grapevine and fluttering leaf. Alessandro admired them greatly, tied them to his shoulders, and jumped. The wings slowed and smoothed his descent. He didn't even turn an ankle. When he turned to smile at the strega, the face she wore that day was undoubtedly blushing. It was a good thing no one could see it beneath the hood of her cloak.

On the third day, Alessandro was tasked with spinning the wool of a sheep into pure silver. An impossible chore, and one that had baffled many princes. But Alessandro started in with gusto, the whole time asking Sette questions about her dreams. When the wool was finished, her eyes glimmered with tears, and the wool looked silver.

Everything did.

On the fourth day, Alessandro was given a leather devil's mask. "This will bring the worst in you leaping to the surface," Sette said, sure that she would finally see Alessandro stumble. The mask had made a dozen princes go cold and peevish, while another dozen heated with rage. But the worst that Alessandro did was make a scrunching face all afternoon, because the smell of leather tickled his nose.

The strega found herself laughing.

She had never laughed before.

On the fifth day, Alessandro was told to milk a sheep. "Do I drink this, too?" he asked, bringing a full, frothing pail back to Sette, who looked exceptionally tall that day. She spilled the milk over the floor of the hovel. Alessandro leapt back, and Sette watched the patterns as they spread. "You are suited to the wine princess," she mumbled, surprised to find the words coming out of her mouth. But they were true, or she wouldn't have spoken them.

Alessandro did not respond with a cry of victory, or even a chuckle of joy.

On the sixth day, he was given a block of marble and told to carve his own gravestone.

"Where's the magic in that?" he asked.

"You'll see tomorrow."

The seventh day, the strega removed her cloak to reveal that she was young and beautiful, her body a harmony of soft and firm. She was now an unmatchable beauty. "You must sit with me in this room, and not approach unless I ask, and not touch me under any circumstance. My magic will strike you dead if you do. It's a good thing you have that gravestone ready."

The few princes who had made it this far always failed. They started to inch toward the beautiful young Sette, reaching for her with impatient hands. Alessandro turned slightly away from her to be polite, asking questions about the largest thing she had ever changed with her magic.

"Thank God," Sette said as the church bells of the seven tiny kingdoms tangled together, marking midnight of the seventh day. "You've passed the test." She spun around the hovel and said, "Girls, you can come out."

Six princesses crawled and tumbled and crept out of their hiding places.

"Have you been spying on the trials?" Alessandro asked, amused.

"We *are* the trials," the princess of soft cheese said.

Now that he was looking, he could see the seven different forms of the strega echoed in the seven girls around him.

"Each one of us has given you a test, and you passed them all," the princess of unmatchable beauty said.

"I am happy to say that you are suited to one of us," the wine princess added, bursting with happiness that had been green all week, now come ripe.

Alessandro looked confused, then devastated. "I didn't come to win the hand of a princess," he admitted. "I came to see a strega of great renown, whose magic is the strongest of any in Vinalia."

"That's going to be a problem, since she doesn't exist," the wool princess said.

"What do you need the help of a strega for?" the princess of graves asked.

Alessandro sighed and set down his story, a great burden he'd been carrying. "I am the only brother of seven sisters. When they came of age, a riot of men started demanding them as brides. I tried to fight off the worst of them, but it was never enough. Seven of the men banded together and with bribery and threats got my father to agree to the matches. I argued, but he would hear no reason. The next day, my sisters were gone, and the hills you know so well appeared. My clever sisters had found a strega to change them.

"I vowed to change them back as soon as it was safe. I asked the same strega to stop my life from moving forward, just as theirs had, until I could help them." Everyone's eyes went to the charcoal smudge on his neck, its meaning suddenly clear. "The men who would have taken my sisters are all dead now. But so is the strega who helped us. I have wandered up and down Vinalia for years seeking another whose magic is strong enough to change them back."

"You mean the hills we've lived on our whole lives are your sisters?" the wool princess asked.

"I'm afraid so."

"That's why they're so beautiful," mumbled the princess of graves.

"And so sad," the princess of soft cheeses added.

"There is no strega in these valleys at all?" Alessandro asked, the hopelessness of his voice breaking seven hearts.

"I'm afraid there is not," the wine princess said, her happiness rotted on the vine. "There is only us."

"Only us," the princess of unmatchable beauty echoed.

Which gave her an idea.

She ran home to her father, the king of the most beautiful hill, and begged for his help. She lied about Sette (who was already a lie) and said that the strega had driven another perfectly good husband away. It was the only kind of reason her father would listen to.

"Another strega should be able to stop Sette," she said. "A *very powerful* strega."

"Very well," the king said. "I will send for the best one in all of Vinalia. But then you must settle into a good match right away."

The princess of unmatchable beauty took a deep breath, nodded, and sealed her own fate.

THE REAL STREGA ARRIVED A WEEK LATER. HER NAME WAS Beatrice. She was only a breath older than the princesses, with brown hair that stretched to the backs of her knees, and feet that touched the earth like a lover caressing the skin of her beloved. The princess of graves couldn't stop staring.

"Are you the ones I've been summoned to help?" Beatrice asked.

The seven princesses pulled her into the fog of the swamp, where they could talk without being seen or heard.

The princess of graves came back carrying seven small rocks that looked like old women, one for each of Sette's faces. "Beatrice made short work of her," she said, hiding the tools she'd used to make the carvings in deep pockets.

"Good, good," the king of graves said.

Alessandro strode out of the fog next. The smudge on his neck seemed to have washed off. Perhaps it was never magic at all, the kings thought. Perhaps he was just the thing they needed to settle these wild girls down.

Then the sound of Beatrice's voice rang out in the fog, as clear and copper-bright as church bells. Alessandro smiled as, above them, the hills shook and shrank, twisting and changing. The kings could have sworn they looked like the bodies of seven beautiful women.

And then, that's exactly what they were.

Seven sisters took a single look at the kings who had lived on their backs for so many years. Their words had not yet emerged from a long, deep silence. Instead of saying anything, they spat at the kings' feet.

"This is an outrage," the kings said.

But at least they still had their daughters.

"Remember your promise," the king of the most beautiful mountain said.

"What promise is that?" Beatrice asked, getting between the girl and her father, a hard look in her eye.

"I said that I would settle into a good match if you came," the princess mumbled.

The strega sized her up, pinching the girl's chin between two fingers. For the first time in years, the princess felt like someone wasn't just looking at her beauty but was actually looking at *her*.

"I can find you a match, if you'll trust me," Beatrice said.

The girl nodded. She knew a clever woman when she saw one.

"Your daughter is meant to settle down with magic. I will take her on as my new apprentice. Unless you have a problem with that?"

After seeing what had happened to Sette, her father didn't say a thing against it.

The wool princess had run off to get cloaks for seven young women, greens and yellows and browns to match the hills they had once been. Alessandro embraced his sisters, and they touched the spot on his neck. They knew his sadness; now he shared their joy.

The girls joined arms and ran toward the river which had turned to pure silver in the afternoon light. They laughed as they walked straight into the water, splashing toward their destinies on the other side.

The seven princesses watched them go.

But they did not follow.

"We made a vow never to leave the place where we grew up," the princess of goats said. "But the place left *us*."

"Our promise wasn't to the hills," the princess of unmatchable beauty said. "It was to each other."

So, while their fathers packed up and went in search of something new and beautiful to conquer, they stayed right where they were and made a home of the swamp. Alessandro packed his bags the next morning, yet he couldn't seem to leave.

The wine princess approached him, afraid that if he refused her again she would shrivel and die. "I know you didn't come to find a princess. But would it be a terrible thing if you did?"

"I suppose, if that is what the spilled milk told you . . ."

"That wasn't me," the girl said, blushing down to the roots of her dark hair. "I'm the one who gave you wings."

"What is your name?"

"Argenta. And since the hills are gone, I suppose I'm not the princess of anything."

"Then we might be a match," Alessandro said, taking her hand. He didn't look at it like it was a treasure. He looked at it like it was skin and bone. And that was exactly what Argenta spent the rest of her life thinking of as *beautiful*.

The princess of walnuts never read another fortune, but only lived to see what the next day would bring. The princess of goats went off to hear the world, though she promised to come back with stories tucked in all of her pockets. The long-lost brother of the wool princess arrived only a week later, eyes picking over the horizon until he found his younger sister, who had barely known him when he left the hills.

She threw her arms around his threadbare traveling cloak. "The stories said you were dead."

"Of course they did. If they said I lived happily, every prince would leave home."

"Have you heard anything of the walnut queen?" her daughter asked, shaking with fear and hope.

"Still in love with her devil."

The walnut princess smiled, finding the bitterness that had lingered at the back of her throat so long was gone.

Seven months went by, and the princess of graves didn't

see a single dead man. Their stone faces slipped away, and now all she knew when she closed her eyes was the long, tangled hair of Beatrice. Instead of harvesting marble, she gathered herbs that grew in the swamp and brought them to Beatrice in the hovel, because so many wild and growing things were needed to do magic. One morning she held out a bouquet of lemon thyme, and Beatrice kissed her until she dropped the herbs on both of their feet. In the precise way they scattered, a great love story could be read.

The princess of soft cheese was friends with everyone, including the moon. No matter how much time passed and how their lives changed, she let them know when the silver light in the sky was a sliver away from full.

And seven women met in the valley, running wild, dreaming of seven hills who never settled down.

Turn the page for a sneak peek at
The Storm of Life,
the sumptuous and powerful conclusion
to this gender-fluid duet

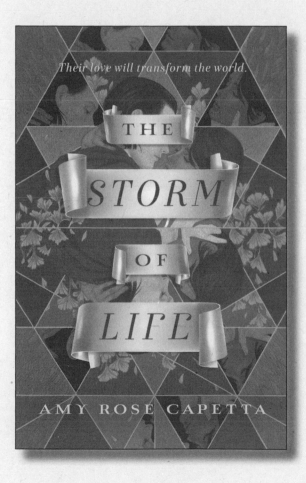

The End

When I was a little girl, my father's tours of Vinalia carried him far from home. While he conducted di Sangro business in the darkest corners of the finest palazzos, I sat on his black walnut chair, a crown of violets in the bramble of my curls, and made decrees.

I told my brother Luca that he was the bravest young man in my kingdom, which was true—my kingdom was no wider than Father's study, though it ran as deep as my stepmother's old stories.

I told my little sister Carina, barely born, that she must be a great strega. With her pickled face, solemn eyes, and perfectly timed wails, she seemed both young and old, wise and wicked.

I told my older sister, Mirella, that she'd been declared the queen of a neighboring kingdom, and I would trade with her if she had my favorite almond paste sweets.

I did not tell my brother Beniamo anything.

One day at the turn of winter, as the cold made its first advances into the castle, I sat alone at Father's desk, working on a scrap of Mirella's drawing paper with a stick of charcoal from the kitchen fire. I wrote out rules for my subjects, my hands smudged black, my mind burning with the bright frenzy of creating a kingdom. The magic inside me liked this business as much as I did.

It had been with me for nearly a year, since the night I went downstairs for a glass of milk and saw a man murdered on the stairs. The magic I'd inherited from this stranger ached to be used, but I couldn't transform objects openly. My family might be frightened or jealous; they might scoff at me or stubbornly choose not to believe. So instead of showing them the whole of who I was, I snuck to the fields on the mountainside, changing ice to white linen sheets. As summer breathed hot down our necks, I turned white poppies to snow that melted in my hands and trickled it down the back of my stuffy red di Sangro dresses.

The scrape of a foot against stone pulled my attention up from the papers on Father's desk. I'd been so deep inside of my schemes that I hadn't heard the door as it opened. Beniamo stood on the threshold, watching me. Honeyed light from the hallway clung to his dark curls, and if I did not know him a bit, I would have thought he looked like a saint.

"What are you playing, Teodora?" he asked.

I wasn't playing a game. I was perfectly serious.

"Nothing."

He'll hurt us, the magic whispered. *Stop him.*

I'd never changed a person before, and my magic was suddenly hungry to try it. But if I changed Beniamo, Father would disown me: strip me of my di Sangro name, send me away from the home and family that I loved.

"*Not now*," I whispered hotly to the magic.

"Are you talking in church words?" Beniamo asked. I

hadn't known I was doing that until he pointed it out. "You wish to be a priest *and* a king? Isn't one stupid dream enough to fill your day?"

I shoved the magic down. Shame and anger rose to fill its place, a natural spring pushing up to my cheeks. I vowed that I would never speak aloud to my magic.

"You know you can't rule anything, don't you?" Beniamo asked, his voice burning low and steady. He waited for me to give an answer that he could transform into the proper punishment. I wondered what a queen would do.

"This is my kingdom," I said in an ironclad whisper.

"Yours? What if it's invaded?" Beniamo crossed the room swiftly. Things were moving now, and I could not slow them, could not stop them. I locked my legs around the posts of the chair, edges biting through my stockings and into my skin.

Beniamo pushed me, toppling the black walnut throne.

I rolled free, and Beniamo kicked me in the chest. Once, twice. I curled around the broken feeling, gathering the pieces. It wasn't safe to cry out. Beniamo would enjoy it too much. He would kick me harder, to hear me shout again.

I watched from my place on the floor as his boots strode toward the crown of violets that had fallen from my hair. Beniamo smashed the deeply blue flowers beneath his heel. I had spent hours on the mountainside picking the ones with perfect cups of black in the center.

"You have been unseated, sister," Beniamo said, laughing as he dropped the ruined crown back on my head. He stepped back and studied me with a flat expression. "I'm only preparing you for the rest of your life. You should kneel and thank me."

I must not have acted quickly enough, because he kicked me once more, a sharp toe to the shins.

I whimpered, stuffing a louder cry back down my throat.

"Go on," he said.

I pushed the heels of my hands against the floor. My knees scraped the stone as I shifted, and because I could not look at his face without giving away the force of my hatred, I stared at my brother's stomach, thinking about how soft and unprotected it looked. "Thank you," I spat, the words as bitter as blood in my mouth.

And I started counting the days until I would never have to kneel again.

One

Defiance Doesn't Come for Free

Cielo and I left at dawn, before the black crepe sky shed its mourning colors. We'd barely stayed long enough for me to learn the name of the town we now fled. Pavetta, or maybe Paletta. By day, each new place Cielo and I passed through offered memorable features—a jewel-colored piazza, a fortress that stubbornly carried the weight of a dead empire, a church whose stone walls wept grime that the villagers called God's Tears.

This was no grand tour of Vinalia, though.

We were warning every strega we could find of the Capo's plan to use their magic in the war he'd stirred up. Wherever we went, a growing number of doorways bore the green-and-black flag of the Capo's unified nation. I spotted one over the door of a palazzo and resisted the urge to turn my magic on that flag, frying it crisp as a sage leaf.

Now that I'd taken on more than my share of magic, things were different. I had to be careful in a new way, tiptoeing around my own power. It worked on a much grander and more unruly scale, and it didn't always wait for my command.

The town ended abruptly, and we left Pavetta and its half dozen streghe behind. Cielo had helped me pick them out on market day, her eyes sharp as hooks, fishing through the crowd for others with magic. She'd mostly stayed in girlish form since leaving Chieza, which meant we were easier prey for bandits on the road, but also that strangers were more likely to speak with us, delighted and defenseless, when Cielo offered them even the smallest fraction of a smile.

All smiles died a swift death when we told them of the Capo's plan to use their magic as a sacrifice, feeding the might of a small number of streghe. *His* streghe.

That was the magic I carried now: the death inheritance of two sisters who had given themselves over to the Capo's schemes and taken the lives of our own kind. One had her throat slit by the Capo himself. One fell into the earth after I tore it open beneath her. As Cielo and I chased rumors of streghe, and I hunted down the worst of the criminals I had let escape from the di Sangro castle, I kept thinking of Azzurra's wild attacks on my home, her unshakable love for her sister, the guilt I felt at killing a fellow strega instead of finding some way to save her.

My magic had always craved greater strength, but now that I bore the death-passed magic of dozens of streghe, it didn't feel like I held a single, seamless power inside of me. It was a collection of splintered pieces.

"Do you think the streghe we met in the market yesterday will heed our warning?" I asked.

Cielo pulled her cloak, one of our few possessions, tighter against the newborn cold. We'd left summer behind in Amalia. "Who knows with the northern streghe? They are ferociously independent."

If Cielo thought that, I felt little hope.

We kept moving—north as far as I could tell. Cielo tested

the winds by becoming one, flicking the pages of the book she used to control her changes. Not that the strega's magic was obeying the rules now, either. Only an act of unchecked power had been able to break me away from servitude to the Capo. I was the reason Cielo had lost control of the magic she'd worked for years to bring to heel.

We had lost so much to gain each other.

The wind that was Cielo swirled around me, raking through my hair, toying with the hem of my dress, sliding under my collar and working its warm, sure way down the valley between my breasts.

A blush started in my cheeks and then went on a rampage. "Not now," I said roughly.

I ran my hands down my dress, pretending to smooth it from the ruffling of the wind but really savoring memories of Cielo's hands, Cielo's mouth, Cielo's skin.

The wind breathed over the book, flipping it to a well-worn page that turned Cielo back into the boyish version I had first met on the mountain those months ago. He stood up, naked and grinning, and I tossed a pack directly at his stomach.

"We need to lay a course," I said as he removed a shirt from the pack and shook out the wrinkles.

He hopped into his pants and then removed the green-and-purple traveling cloak that had snared my attention the first time we met. As it turned out, the web of stitching on the back was not just a rich design—it formed a map of Vinalia, including the locations of all streghe known to Cielo.

"We're here," Cielo said, jabbing a finger at the silk.

Pavetta—or Paletta—sat in the western foothills, as far as we could walk before the Uccelli dwindled to nothing, soon to be replaced by the sharp angles and snowy creases of the Neviane. My mind filled with those peaks and the war the Capo waged there.

"Let's see if we can make it to the hazelnut fields of Alieto by midday," Cielo said. "From there, it's only a short hike to—"

"No," I said, stabbing through the heart of Cielo's plans. "We should be doing more than skulking from village to village, warning a few streghe at a time, always afraid we're about to be caught. Unless we find some way to unite the people, *our* people, the Capo will be able to pick them off."

My hands slid into knots, and Cielo eased them back open. "Don't think of him."

"He's *your* uncle," I muttered.

"I take no responsibility for that," Cielo said. "I didn't choose my uncle any more than you picked Beniamo from a batch of possible brothers." Even the mention of Beniamo felt like an attack, and I cringed away from it. When I blinked, light alternated with fractured bits of memory—turning my brother into an owl, watching him come back more vicious than before. The last time I'd seen him, he'd vowed to make my life an endless parade of pain and loss.

"You're shaking," Cielo said, taking me by the shoulders.

"I'm not." I forced myself to stillness and then realized I hadn't been the only thing shuddering. The ground shivered subtly beneath our feet.

I hoped this was one of the earthquakes that seized the Uccelli on a monthly basis, gave the mountains a quick shake, and then died. But the feeling grew steadily, and so did the dread in my chest. Cielo dropped to one knee and spread the cloak over the ground. It jolted and danced.

"Someone's coming." Without so much as touching the book, Cielo split into a flock of birds. Dark wings rose into a sky as pale as a fevered brow.

I called on my own magic and found it restless. It hissed, angry that I had been holding back for so long. When I pulled, there was no smooth and ready response. Instead, I grasped for sharp edges. There were so many of them, so many different ways to hurt.

I turned to the mountain and focused on its smooth hide. *I need a place where I won't be seen.*

A dozen spots on the mountain burst as if they'd been hit by cannon fire. Above me, the flock of Cielo-birds crowed.

Not very inconspicuous, I told the magic.

It buzzed a rude, angry response. It had become a chorus of discontent, always pressing me to do more. I rushed to a pockmark in the mountain's newly pitted face and settled behind a great stone that gave me a perch to spy from. Just as I rounded the corner, the road came alive with dust.

Men marched across the foothills of the Uccelli, wearing green and black. They were moving north from the Capo's beloved capital of Amalia to the brutish cold of the Neviane, their necks slung with scarves, their sweat evident under winter coats, even from here. The Eterrans had chosen to swarm over the northern mountains: the least forgiving approach, but their navy was tied up in constant skirmishes with the Sfidese. Keeping their army alive meant trusting the known passes through the Neviane, and only one was large enough to allow a great number of troops through its harsh, rocky embrace. It sat just north of the town of Zarisi. These Vinalians were marching toward the pass, pouring over the fields, a river of bodies. There had to be at least two thousand trampling crops and fallow fields alike. They kept their eyes ahead on the glory of coming battles.

I thought about changing them now, to spare them the pain and death of this ridiculous war. The Capo shouldn't have so many lives at his disposal. I could save them all in one great sweep.

Turn them into a field of toy soldiers, the magic said.

Would that be mercy? What would I do when the Capo, bereft of soldiers, lost the war? When the Eterrans broke into the country and took whatever they pleased? It was no secret that the northern invaders had their eyes on our rich fields. They wished to claim our glories in science, art—possibly even magic. Eterrans were empire builders. For a few centuries they had been focused on spreading over the seas to the virgin continent, but they'd lost most of their colonies there to war. Now they had their eyes on Vinalia, and they were well practiced in taking what was not theirs.

I remembered that moment of being forced into the Capo's army—my body, my magic, belonging to him.

Would Eterra try to claim the streghe? Would our magic be the first thing they stole?

The Capo had exposed us to the world and then brought on a war in the name of his own glory. My rage took flight, but I kept still. These troops might not have been sent to scout for the two streghe who had set magical fire to Amalia, but if they caught us along the way, it would certainly earn them the Capo's gratitude.

One of Cielo's flock landed at my feet.

"He's sending more troops," I whispered. "You know what that means."

The bird tapped its beak on the rock, with the impatience

that Cielo possessed in all forms. Above, several of the Cielo-birds flew ahead to note the path the soldiers took toward the Neviane.

Pavetta had been dripping with whispers of the war. The Capo was losing battle after battle, even though our men fought bravely. Everyone knew the Eterrans came from a cold, drizzly land where they spent all their time indoors plotting conquests. Soon they would take the pass at Zarisi.

Vinalia was on the verge of losing its first war.

❧❀☙

HOURS LATER, WHEN THE SOLDIERS WERE ONLY A SMUDGE IN the distance, Cielo's flock came together, wings blurring and molding into a tall, black-haired, distinctly human sil-houette. Cielo's skin had finally taken on a hint of color by the end of summer, but my strega was still startlingly pale. I wondered what Cielo would look like in winter—if we ever lived to see one together.

"We have to stop them," I said.

Maybe I should have waited until Cielo was clothed for such a grand statement, but it couldn't wait.

"You escaped the Capo's service only months ago," Cielo said, crossing his arms over his chest, as if that covered anything—notable. "I thought you didn't want to be any-where near the front." I worked hard to keep my focus on Cielo's eyes, which had gone mostly gray, a color that came out of hiding when the strega was in a heightened state. Anger, sadness, passion of any sort.

Cielo took a step toward me, capturing my chin between

two fingers. My breath changed, as pitched and short as if I were climbing a mountain.

"I refuse to win wars for the Capo, but I can't allow . . . *this*." I shook my fingers at the troops marching toward the Neviane.

"Those men are allowed to do whatever they please, including join armies, Teodora," Cielo said.

"What about streghe, then? Now that magic is no longer a secret, who knows how we will be treated by an invading power? They might want to rid the world of our magic or claim it as their own. The Eterrans could break through the pass and march on Amalia at any time. We have to act quickly."

Cielo's fingers worked at my buttons, slipping me out of the tired, dirty shell of my traveling clothes. "I was thinking that, too."

Cielo took a single step closer, and full contact came with a sigh that my throat released gratefully. The feeling of Cielo's skin would have been enough to distract anyone except a di Sangro. I pressed down harder on my point. "If we had more streghe on our side, we could win the war ourselves. It would show Vinalians that we're to be trusted. And the Capo is not."

"A strega army," Cielo said, trailing a finger where he had just undone my buttons, tracing and retracing. "Is that what you dream about at night? You make such triumphant little noises."

My dreams had *not* been warlike, but I got the sense Cielo already knew that.

"It wouldn't be an army," I insisted, my voice thick in my throat as Cielo's hands settled over my hips. "More of a campaign."

"Ah, yes," Cielo said. "Should I salute you now or later, General di Sangro?"

I leaned over and bit his shoulder, an attempt at punishment that he seemed to take as a reward. His eyes flared delightedly, and his fingers doubled the strength of their grip.

"There's the slightest hint of a problem," Cielo said. "Streghe usually turn down social invitations, especially ones that might end in their death."

My mind stormed through possibilities, but my usual di Sangro ways wouldn't help in this matter. "If I threaten or bribe streghe into joining me, I'm no better than the Capo."

"You are better in every way that can be named or numbered," Cielo said, stepping back to look at me. "If they ever paint your portrait, and I have no doubt they will, it should look exactly like this." He nodded at how my hands capped my hips. "Goddess, naked and arguing. Now please stop talking about the Capo. It's ruining the moment."

"What moment?" I asked, pretending at innocence.

Shyness moved over Cielo's face, changing it as surely as clouds cast their spell over the sky. "I believe it's time to put the magic we've purchased in town to good use. I'll . . . ah . . . just need a moment." The strega reached for his cloak and the hidden pockets of the inner lining.

"Don't you have it?" My body was in a charmed state, but my voice sounded far away. Teodora di Sangro couldn't be here, in a cave formed by magic, a lifetime's expectations of marriage to a noble young man shed as simply as my clothing.

Not that Cielo and I had been anything close to virtuous in the past months. But there was a bridge we hadn't crossed yet, mostly because of the looming toll neither of us wished to pay.

"Of course I have it," Cielo said, thrusting his hand in each pocket, more frantic as each turned up empty. "I wouldn't come all this way and then lose such a necessary thing. This is *not* the time or place to have children." He looked around with a scornful air. "I know I'm not an expert in families, but I believe a nursery should have walls. And fewer nightmarish shadows."

In Pavetta, we had visited a strega Cielo knew of, with knuckles as large and shiny as walnuts. She kept a shop of herbs and poultices—or at least, that was what she sold to most people who knocked.

When Cielo and I asked for her help, she looked back and forth between us, no doubt trying to figure out which one the magic was for. Her eyes settled on Cielo, whose girlish form was carved of confidence.

I missed my boyish form, even more now that I didn't need it simply to command the respect of the five families. If I shifted into another variation of myself now, it would be for me alone, a tempting notion. But with the unwieldy new power in my body, I was afraid to work the reversal of magic needed to shift. And the truth that I'd found in Amalia, the warm glowing knowledge that I held close to me now, was that my body could bring me comfort or frustration, distance or delight, but it didn't dictate who I was. That boyish side was with me, no matter how I looked to the world. No matter what rested between my legs.

Yet people like the strega in Pavetta saw only one side of things—and what she saw were girls, at least one of whom wanted to avoid bearing children.

"If you tell certain people about this, I'll be arrested. Or worse."

"Don't worry," Cielo said. "*Certain people* can leap off a cliff."

"Use it before, not after, you hear me? The effects should last for six moons. You'll bleed less, too."

Now Cielo unwrapped the package the old woman had given us, his hands gentle and slow. It contained six vials of milk, each a slightly different color, ranging from an icy bluish white to the near tan of an eggshell.

"What now?" I asked.

"You're supposed to drink one," Cielo said.

I nodded as I inched the first vial out from its small loop of cloth.

I sent thoughts of my sister Mirella, who must have given birth to her first child by now, scurrying away.

"What if it's stronger the more you take?" I ask. "Won't milk spoil if we leave it for so long? Should I drink two?"

Cielo shook his head, and his certainty felt like the solid rock beneath my feet. "You might sicken if you take too much. The milk won't curdle—it's magic. And we want these to last. Who knows how long it will be until we pass through Pavella again?"

"*Pavella*," I said, hammering the town's name into place in my head. We had been wandering Vinalia in such a frantic haze that I did not know where my feet took me anymore. But when Cielo's hands settled on my thighs, softly stroking as I downed the tangy-sweet milk, I knew precisely where I was.

I could draw the shape of what I wanted.

I pushed Cielo down onto the stones, on top of his silky

cloak. I slid myself onto him, and he lifted his hips slowly, eyes half-closed, a catlike rumble of warmth in his throat. I kissed him on a rush of pure delight, and then I kissed him with a great wildfire need, and then I couldn't hold back a second longer. I hovered over him, aligning our bodies. When I stared down at Cielo's nervous smile, I felt too small to hold the sum of every feeling that had been building as we waited for this moment—anticipation and wild joy and a single prick of fear.

It overwhelmed my blood.

It called out to my magic.

Power came crashing out of me. The mountain above us had been weakened by the holes I'd blown in it, and now it ground its stones together, a great gnashing of teeth.

"I believe our rocky friend is displeased," Cielo said. His voice was delicate and not particularly urgent, but I knew we needed to move. The more danger we faced, the politer the strega grew.

Cielo grabbed his book and cloak, while I took hold of whatever clothes I could. Stones began to fall from the cave's ceiling, and I was almost crushed to powder as I doubled back to grab the precious vials of milk.

I left the cave, following Cielo, his bare ass showing under the shirt he'd hastily tugged on. We pelted for the safety of the fields as rocks roared down behind us. Only when I felt certain we wouldn't be caught in an avalanche did I grab Cielo's hand and pull him to a panting stop.

We turned and found that the mountain was now a crater, puffing granite dust.

As if that wasn't enough, my body announced that it was

not delighted at being cut off from the pleasure I had been so intent on. By the depths of Cielo's frown, I gathered that he felt the same.

"Well," Cielo said, surveying the wreckage. "At the very least, we have made our mark on Vinalia."